THE
TESTAMENT

THE
TESTAMENT

ERIC VAN LUSTBADER

A TOM DOHERTY ASSOCIATES BOOK

NEW YORK

This is a work of fiction. All the characters and events portrayed in this novel are either fictitious or are used fictitiously.

A Forge Book
Published by Tom Doherty Associates, LLC
175 Fifth Avenue
New York, NY 10010

www.tor.com

Forge® is a registered trademark of Tom Doherty Associates, LLC.

Library of Congress Cataloging-in-Publication Data

Lustbader, Eric.
    The testament / Eric Van Lustbader.—1st ed.
        p.   cm.
    ISBN-13: 978-0-765-31463-5
    ISBN-10: 0-765-31463-0
    1. Cryptographers—Fiction. 2. Medievalists—Fiction. 3. Secret societies—Fiction. 4. Christianity in literature.   I. Title.
    PS3562.U752B73   2006
    813'.54—dc22

                                                        2006003297

First Edition: September 2006

Printed in the United States of America

0   9   8   7   6   5   4   3   2   1

For Victoria
and
My Poonies

INSPIRATION COMES IN MANY GUISES.

MY THANKS TO:

Dorothy Dunnett's *Niccolò* series
for introducing me to the history of Trebizond

The city of Venice

A Dictionary of Medieval Terms and Phrases
by Christopher Corèdon and Ann Williams

and Keith

PROLOGUE

AUGUST, 1442—
SUMELA MONASTERY,
TREBIZOND

ON A BLAZINGLY HOT LATE AFTERNOON IN HIGH SUMMER, three Franciscan Gnostic Observatine monks foraged in the midst of their daily perimeter patrol. They were grateful for the dappled shade and the heavy emerald light as they stepped carefully through the dense woods surrounding the Sumela Monastery, where they currently hid. The monastery was an altogether fitting place for their forced and rather desperate retreat—it had been founded during the reign of Theodosius I by the Greek Orthodox, with whom the Order had a special bond.

Though the men wore the plain, undyed muslin robes of their ascetic order, they patrolled heavily armed with swords, daggers and longbows. They were Guardians, trained in weaponry and hand-to-hand combat as well as the words of Christ and St. Francis. It was their sacred duty to guard the other members of the Order, especially those of the inner circle who ruled the Order, the Haute Cour.

The brutal sun, on its slow journey to the horizon, had by this time heated even the normally cool mountain air, so that the Guardians' robes were shot through with sweat stains, spreading from their armpits and down the center of their broad, muscular backs. They moved in the same way they said their prayers three times a day—the way they held themselves, the wariness of eye and foot as they quartered the western wedge of tangled land under their jurisdiction, could only be described as ritualistic.

Nearing the seventh and final hour of their shift, their muscles ached, their vertebrae cracking now and again as they bent to examine some track or spoor to make certain that it was made by an animal and not by their fellow man. Their training demanded they be careful, as did the history of the Order, for so long under threat from the Pope and his strong mailed fist, the Knights of St. Clement of the Holy Blood. Since the time of the first crusade, which had been launched in 1095, the Knights had made the island of Rhodes their base. Danger arose in the Order's having secreted itself so close to the Holy Land, where its enemies teemed, but they well knew the wisdom in hiding in plain sight. Over the year and a half that the Order had been at Sumela, no Knight of St. Clement had ventured to the monastery, which was not and never had been in their domain. It belonged to the Emperor Justinian, and then to the Comnenos, the emperor-dynasty of Trebizond, on the southwestern shore of the Black Sea, with Anatolia and the highly lucrative camel route to Isfahan and Tabriz at its back, an eight-day journey by ship from Byzantium.

At the edge of a clearing, the three Guardians paused to take water and a bite of unleavened bread. Yet even in this moment of relative ease, their iron discipline forbade any talk, and their eyes in faces lined with tension were never at rest. As they chewed and swallowed, they scanned the glade into which the lowering hulk of the sun spilled ruddy light. Hands at their foreheads, they squinted into the glare.

Birds twittered and swooped, insects droned sullenly, butterflies and bees crisscrossed the glade. The air sat exhausted and sweating, beaten down by the sun glare. The Guardians' attention momentarily shifted as a brief rustling came from the underbrush perhaps fifty yards distant. They waited, immobile and staring, their hearts pounding as the sweat formed in the hollows of their necks and crept down their spines. The rustling came again, closer this time, and one of them went into a crouch, put fletched shaft to bowstring, pulling it back taut, the forged iron arrowhead aimed and ready.

A small form appeared, and the archer grinned in relief. Only a small mammal foraging through the underbrush. Another of the Guardians laughed under his breath, raised his hand to his companion's tautly arced bow, as if to lower it.

He never got the chance. A brief evil humming made itself heard above the drowsing chitter of the insects as a crossbow bolt flashed through the air. The Guardian, impaled through the chest, flew into shadow, his arms flung wide. His archer compatriot, crouched still, drew back his bow, frantically trying to draw a bead on the hidden enemy, but before he could loose his arrow, another bolt flew out of the sun's glare and pierced his neck. Flung onto his back by the force of the arrow, he lost his grip on the bowstring, and his arrow shot skyward in a crazy arc.

Fra Martin, spattered with his brothers' blood, dove for cover, drew his broadsword and gathered his wits about him. His brothers were dead, both killed in a matter of seconds by a hidden assassin. But from the way they fell, he knew where the archer had secreted himself.

He now had a crucial decision to make. He could either circle his way forward, keeping to the shadows while he skirted the glare of the forest glade, engage the Knights and avenge the murders of his brothers, or he could discreetly withdraw, making all haste back to the monastery to warn the *Magister Regens* and to gain reinforcements with which to hunt the enemy. The sun glare within which the archer had so cleverly cloaked himself mitigated against immediate engagement.

However, if the archer was, indeed, a Knight of St. Clement, he had surely identified his prey as members of the Gnostic Observatine Order. If he escaped and returned to Rhodes with news of the Order's whereabouts, a veritable army would be sent against the monks. Then they would be facing an all-out assault, against which they surely could not stand. No, there was no time to seek reinforcements from within the monastery—he had to find the enemy now, identify him and kill him before he could inform the Knights of the Order's hiding place.

Fra Martin knew the forest well, remembered that just beyond the glade a sheer drop-off into the deep ravine, guarded on either side by naked cliffs and jagged boulders, snaked its way back to the treasure-laden city of Trebizond on the southern coast of the Black Sea. Picking his way to the left, he described a rough semicircle. All the while, he kept the glade in view, through which ripples of wind caused a succession of rustlings. Muscles bunched, ready with his sword, he kept moving crabwise to his left, always keeping the sun-dazzle of the glade in the periphery of his vision.

A swift sat on a branch above and just ahead of him, its head cocked as it warily eyed him. All at once, it took off in a flutter, and with a prickle at the nape of his neck, he whirled to his left. As he did so, he flipped his sword to his left hand, swept it around in a flat, vicious arc.

As forged steel bit into bone and flesh, he heard the scream even before he identified his foe as a Knight of St. Clement. The Knight staggered under his blow, began to bring his own sword down toward Fra Martin's head in a skull-cleaving blow. Fra Martin, slipping inside the other's guard, stayed his opponent's arm with one hand while he drove his own sword hilt-deep into the Knight. The Knight watched him malevolently out of bloodshot eyes. Then his lips curled back from bared teeth and a laugh spilled out from deep inside him just before the death-rattle overtook him.

Fra Martin kicked the corpse aside. The imminent danger dealt with, he moved with greater confidence along the edge of the ridge. He could not discount the possibility that there might be other Knights stalking through the forest. No matter, he would become the stalker now. All his senses rose to their most heightened level.

Quite soon he came to an area that had eroded in the last rainstorm. A large tree had been uprooted and others partially so, leaving great clots of red earth exposed like wounds. This afforded him a hitherto impossible view into the deep ravine, the only way to and from Sumela.

The sight below turned his blood cold. Lines of the Knights of St. Clement marched in concert, heading toward the monastery, the last bastion of his Order. He had made a fatal mistake. The Knight who had attacked him and his compatriots had not been alone but was an advance raider sent to destroy the Order's sentinels. He had to assume that other such assassins had been dispatched to deal with the other Guardians on patrol. There could be no doubt, the Knights had launched a full-scale attack.

As he turned, on his way back to the monastery, a crossbow bolt sliced through the flesh of his arm. He staggered sideways, his booted right foot sliding on the bare earth, and he went over the edge.

He slammed into a tangle of tree roots jutting out from the side of the earthfall and almost had his breath taken away. Still, he had the presence of mind to reach out and grab on. Panting, he swung in midair, dizzy and nauseated, a thousand-meter drop yawning at his feet. Far below him, the line of Knights continued their march. Blood leaked from his wound, and pain lanced through his arm all the way up into his shoulder. He tried to pull himself up, succeeded only in tearing open the wound. It was only a matter of time before his blood, running more freely now, would drip down, giving him away to the enemy below.

He began to pray, gathering himself into the essential core of his being. But though his soul spoke to God, at some point he could not help but notice that the huge uprooted tree above him rolled as if of its own accord, slowly at first, then more quickly, until it shot out and down, amid cries of dismay and pain, onto the marching enemy.

Dumbfounded, he swallowed thickly as he watched the chaos spreading through the ranks of Knights.

"It's a divine intervention," he whispered.

"In a way."

He looked up, sweat and the red silt of Sumela in his eyes, for the source of the voice. He was at first certain that St. Francis himself had come to his aid. Then the striking face resolved itself.

"Fra Leoni," Fra Martin whispered. "Thank God."

Fra Leoni was well named, for he had a leonine face atop a mass of curling hair black as pitch. From this unruly surround the startling blue of his eyes broke like sun through storm clouds. "Hurry, while they are still in disarray. There's no time to lose." Fra Leoni's powerful hand, covered in flakes of moss and tree bark, grasped him, tugging him up.

SUMELA Monastery appeared to be carved out of the bedrock on which it sat, a jagged tooth in the Karadaglar, the Black Mountains that lay between Trebizond and Armenia.

"The Venetian fleet has been turned back by Sultan Murat II and his Ottoman navy," Fra Prospero said as he addressed the somber-faced priests ranged around the dark wooden trestle table in the refectory of the monastery. "Any day now Trebizond will come under attack. No matter how well situated, this time the Golden City will fall, and afterward, the Ottoman filth will be breaking down Sumela's door."

"We have a more immediate disaster staring us in the face."

The priests of the Order of Gnostic Observatines turned as one to face the bloody-robed figure who filled the doorway. Above their tonsured heads, the vaulted ceiling arched like the heavily muscled shoulders of a giant warrior.

Fra Prospero, *Magister Regens* of the Order, lifted a hand, palm up, in the traditional gesture of welcome, but his large black eyes held a different message. He did not like being interrupted, let alone being contradicted.

"Enter, Fra Leoni, and pray enlighten us." The *Magister Regens* bared his teeth. "What could be more of a disaster than the heathen Turk overrunning our toehold island, the bastion of Christ on the shore of the Levant?"

Fra Leoni reached into the darkness of the hallway, bringing in the wounded Fra Martin. Two of the priests rose and rushed over to take him to the infirmary.

"What is this?" Fra Prospero said. "What has happened?"

"We are under attack," Fra Leoni told them. "The Knights of St. Clement have found us. They landed in secret at Sinope five nights ago. Their main force is but an hour away."

At this remark, a meaningful glance passed between Fra Leoni and the *Magister Regens,* but neither of them said what was on their minds.

Instead, Fra Prospero sighed. "Indeed, our worst fears have been realized. This Pope's thirst for temporal power led him to create the Knights of St. Clement—his own private army, used to crush those who went against the will of the Holy See. Three weeks ago, the Knights received by courier a communique from the Pope, charging them to destroy our Order." He was a massive man, with a round, florid face like a sunflower and the clever black eyes of an inquisitor. He was possessed of a deep, rich baritone that reached with uncommon ease to the farthest corner of the refectory. "Our teachings have already put us at odds with the Pope. But now a Vatican council has judged what we preach as heretical blasphemy and has condemned us as dangerous to the rule of the Pope. We have been marked for eradication—and who better to perform this task than the Pope's so-called soldiers of Christ, the Knights of St. Clement of the Holy Blood?"

The priests looked at each other with fear and consternation plainly visible on their faces.

Fra Sento's narrow brow furrowed. "Why weren't we informed sooner of this despicable edict?"

"What good would it have done," the *Magister Regens* said, "save sow the seeds of panic?"

Fra Sento stood, leaning forward, body tense, clenched fists on the table. "We could release the Testament to the world," he said, "and so reveal the falseness of this power-mad Pope."

At the mention of the Testament an awful blanket of silence swept down upon them. Deepening shadows crawling through the west-facing windows slowly smothered the fire of the sunset.

Sizing up the situation in an instant, Fra Leoni took a step into the room and before Fra Sento's contagion had a chance to spread, said, "Haven't we put this question to its death yet? Who but Church and clergy and a handful of scholars can even read? The Church's power and influence is far too vast for our discovery to be readily believed, let alone accepted as gospel. No, we'd be reviled, cast out, stoned to death by the faithful, like as not—and the Testament itself would fall into the hands of our enemies within the Church, who would destroy it rather than know its truth. Besides, it is neither our duty nor our desire to topple the very institution to which we have pledged our minds, bodies and souls."

Fra Sento, scowling still, crossed his arms over his chest. He knew Fra Leoni was right, but he couldn't see past his burgeoning fear to acknowledge it.

The *Magister Regens* now rose. "Well said, Fra Leoni, thank you. The enemy is almost upon us. We must now turn to the practical matter of our defense. The fact is, we have been practicing for this every day since our arrival at Sumela. Do you believe that we could be better prepared for the inevitable?" His piercing gaze on Fra Sento, he said, "Would anyone here gainsay my decision?"

Fra Sento looked down at his lap and, slowly, his arms unwound. With another covert glance at Fra Prospero, Fra Leoni respectfully took his place at the table.

"We all suspected the Pope would find a way to rule against us," Fra Kent said. He was a jowly priest, tallest of them all, with a quick wit and a helping hand for others. "Now, the hour of our greatest trial is upon us, and it is more imperative than ever that we act as one mind, one strong heart."

The *Magister Regens* nodded ever so slightly as he looked around the table with his sternest expression. "I trust I can count on each and every one of you to perform your duties and defend the principles of our Order."

There came an explosion of assent from every priest in the room, Fra Sento's voice joining Fra Kent's and the others'. Then the *Magister Regens* spread his arms wide and, as they stood as one, addressed his charges formally:

"There is courage in all our hearts, faith fires our souls. We, who have been charged by St. Francis to be his everlasting voice on earth, to carry out his will for generations to come, now gather our strong arms. Though the storm clouds of war gather, though our enemy has sought us out, now we gird ourselves for the battle. Man the battlements south and east, the staircases and the courtyards that have come to be our home. Rain down upon our enemies the retribution for their unwarranted aggression. It is a red day, an evil day, a day of sorrow and of pain! Blood will flow and lives will be lost! Both heaven and hell will receive its share of souls before its end!"

A great, massed cheer rocked the huge room, after which the refectory emptied quickly. As Fra Prospero had said, his priests had been well trained and exhaustively drilled. However, no sooner was he alone with Fra Leoni than he said in a voice filled with an anguish he had not allowed the other priests to hear, "They know."

"I'm afraid so." Fra Leoni nodded. "Somehow the Knights of St. Clement have managed to penetrate the Order."

The *Magister Regens* looked stricken. "Not just the Order. The Haute Cour—the inner circle—of which you and I are a part."

The enormous fireplace, into which even Fra Kent could step without bowing his head, loomed black and desolate. The stone floor was hard and unforgiving beneath their sandaled feet. They looked at the refectory table, now nearly deserted, as if it were a compatriot who had been struck down by sudden illness, who they would likely never see again. So filled with sudden emotion was Fra Prospero that he was obliged to put his fists on the table to steady his bulk as he rose. He walked to Fra Leoni's side, and together the two left the room, closing the massive door to the refectory behind them.

AT that time the Sumela Monastery was divided into three parts. The lower section was built around a central courtyard and, below, an enormous cistern into which the aqueduct emptied. The middle section, the western half of which the Order inhabited, contained the kitchen, library, chapels, and guest rooms. Overlooking these layers was the Rock Church with its sacred icon of the Virgin Mary.

Together, the two members of the Haute Cour went down the corridor, ascended a steep flight of stone stairs and, by means of a narrow wooden door with a great iron lock, passed onto the ramparts. They breathed in the sharp scents of the mountain air, scented with the coming of night and steel—and, therefore, war. They soon reached their goal, and, peering through a gap in the mountainside, swaddled in thick evergreens, they could make out the deep gorge at the highest point of which Sumela rose on its steep and jagged mountain eyrie. On the horizon, farther than they could see, lay the full bounty of Trebizond, which had so irresistibly drawn the Greeks, the Genoese, the Florentines, the Venetians, the trading nexus between East and West, where camel trains from the Armenian hinterlands, from far-off Tabriz unloaded their wares to be transshipped to the warehouses of Europe. The defile was as yet empty, but it was only a matter of time before it was choked with the Knights of St. Clement of the Holy Blood.

"So even here we are not safe from them," Fra Leoni said. "You see the greed of mankind, Fra Prospero. We guard too many secrets, they are too valuable. Man is venal, corruptible, and therefore contemptible, for he falls too easily into sin."

"This is hardly the teaching of St. Francis."

"Our founder lived in a different time," Fra Leoni said bitterly. "Or else he was blind."

"I will not countenance blasphemy!" the *Magister Regens* snapped.

"If the truth be blasphemous, then so be it." Fra Leoni engaged the other with his eyes. "The pope believes we preach blasphemy, so what is the truth but what we observe with our eyes? Religion, like philosophy, is a living thing. If it isn't allowed to change with the times, if it is left to calcify, it will surely become irrelevant."

Fra Prospero's eyes slid away, and he bit his lip in order not to say something he would doubtless regret later.

"To return to the subject," Fra Leoni said, "you know as well as I that our secrets must not be allowed to fall into the hands of our enemies." He opened his palm. "I will have your key."

A brief flicker of some dark emotion—fear or perhaps doubt— marred for a moment the face of the *Magister Regens*. "Is this what you think of our chances?"

Fra Leoni's eyes locked with those of Fra Prospero. "Would you have me regurgitate the rules of our Order? In times of crisis, there is ordained only one Keeper." A brief but unpleasant silence engulfed them. A chill wind stirred, rising from the ashes of the lowered sun, raced up the defile as if itself afraid of what was behind it in the quickening darkness. Fra Leoni knew that he had not answered the other's question. "They outnumber us, and, since the pope has access to everything, it is safe to assume that they are better equipped than we could ever hope to be. These are simple exigencies of war, and can be overcome, with the right amount of cleverness and the correct strategy. And, of course, we have this stone fortress to act as our stout bulwark." He broke off abruptly and his head turned and, like a canny animal, he put out the tip of his tongue, absorbing the news brought to him on the wind.

"But?" Fra Prospero said, not a little irritably.

Fra Leoni turned back. He possessed the sometimes unnerving ability to direct his full scrutiny on whomever was with him, and that had often proved more than some could tolerate. "But the enemy is clever— far more clever than we gave him credit for. Fra Prospero, there can be no doubt that there is a traitor in our midst. Unless we discover his identity and stop him, tonight Sumela may become our grave rather than our sanctuary."

Fra Prospero's eyes sparked as he shook his head. "You know that I have never been an advocate of the single Keeper."

"And yet now you see its strength," Fra Leoni said. "We have been betrayed from inside the Haute Cour. Seven priests including you and I know of our cache of secrets, but only two know its location and have the key. Otherwise, the secrets would undoubtedly already be in the hands of the Knights of St. Clement. Come now, time grows fearfully short."

Still Fra Prospero hesitated, but then from the highest rampart of Sumela the lookout's cry took up Fra Leoni's intent and drained the blood from his heart.

"They come! The Knights are upon us!"

And, indeed, as they turned and looked, they saw the Knights of St. Clement, their emblematic banner with its seven-pointed purple cross flying along with that of the Pope, charging on horseback, armor glimmering in the twilight, toward the gates of the monastery.

The *Magister Regens* leaned over, gripping the parapet with tense fingers. "A frontal assault," he snorted. "They will be days at it, and meanwhile we can get word to Lorenzo Fornarini, who so bravely aided us in Trebizond and now will—"

Fra Leoni rudely and urgently stopped him in midsentence with an iron grip on his arm. He had been counting the Knights and had found their number wanting. The only explanation . . .

"It is too late for Sir Fornarini or anyone else, for that matter, to come to our aid." He pulled Fra Prospero away from the wall as the first arrows whirred past them. "The main force has circled around from behind. That's why it took them days to reach us." They ran down the steps into the interior. "They're already inside, otherwise this group would not have shown themselves."

"Impossible! I refuse to believe—"

"Quickly!" Fra Leoni snapped his fingers. "Your key!"

The *Magister Regens* dug in his robes, but Fra Leoni grabbed it from his fist, tore it off the chain to which it had been attached to a wooden crucifix. It lay in his palm, a key like no other, save its twin, which he possessed. It had a strange burred end and along its length seven star-like notches of different depths and widths.

The *Magister Regens* dug his clawed fingers into Fra Leoni's robes. "Your insolence will be your downfall one day."

"Mayhap," Fra Leoni said. "But not today."

Without taking his gaze from the obsidian eyes, he lifted one hand up and slowly, finger by finger, freed himself the other's grip. "Today your heartfelt prayers go with me, *Magister Regens*, for I am the sole Keeper of our secrets now. If I die, the Order dies with me."

All at once, shouts rose from below, the sound of steel whistled through the air, cries and terrible groaning.

"Now you have your proof," Fra Leoni said tersely. "We have been betrayed again. Our citadel has been breached."

Fra Prospero's eyes flickered with a tiny stirring of fear. His bearded face glistening, he drew himself back to the urgent conversation. In a lowered voice, he said, "And what of the one secret—the one that dwarfs all others, the one even those who come, even he who sent them, is unaware of? Will it be safe with you?"

"It is why I was ordained Keeper. The trust is sacred; it can never be broken. I guard them all with my life, the one secret especially."

Fra Prospero nodded. If he was not pleased, then he was at least satisfied. He had to be; he had no other choice. "Then God go with you, my son. In Christ's name, be safe."

"And if we both survive, you know where to meet me."

"Within a year," Fra Prospero said. "Yes."

"Then we will see each other again, and resume our debate."

"God willing," Fra Prospero said.

Tucking the hem of his robe into his belt, Fra Leoni went down the western spiral staircase. Where the blood had dried, the fabric had become stiff and uncomfortable. Passing the first in a line of windows, he could see the darkening stain of night climbing upward into the cobalt vault of the sky. Closer to hand was the brief sloped ridge of the kitchen's tile roof and, beyond, the pillared terraces of the royal wing. An evil flicker of light caught his eye. Someone had started a fire close to the walls.

Just below, he encountered fighting, already at a fierce pitch. Seeing two of his brothers under attack by four Knights, he drew his weapon and threw himself into the fray, beating back a Knight who had come close to cleaving Fra Benedetto's skull in two. This was not what he should be doing. His first and only duty was to save himself and, in so doing, keep the cache of secrets safe. The trouble was, he could not help himself. His brethren were in dire straits; how could he leave them?

He parried a blow weakly, giving his opponent a false sense of his prowess, then as the Knight recklessly stabbed at him, he neatly knocked aside the strike, drove the point of his sword through the other's midsection. Another Knight attacked on his right, and he sliced through the enemy's wrist. But now six more Knights leapt up from below, and he was forced to leave the defense to the others, retreating back up the stairs to the level of the trefoil window. He beat back the broadsword thrust of a Knight who had broken away from the pack to bring him down, struck what seemed a rather awkward blow with the flat of his sword. It had the desired effect, throwing off the Knight's balance. And while he was thus at a disadvantage, Fra Leoni kicked him hard in the shoulder. The Knight spun, his booted foot missed the edge of the step, and he tumbled heavily backward into two of his compatriots.

Fra Leoni took this moment and, gaining the stone sill of the window, leapt out onto the tiles of the kitchen roof. From here, he could see into the lower courtyard, swarming now with Knights of St. Clement. He could see the wall that had been permanently smoke-blackened by

Saracen siege fires. *Betrayed,* he thought bitterly, *from within our most sacred inner sanctum.*

Then a crossbow bolt passed not a foot from his head, and he dove to his left, stretched fully on the tiles. As soon as he raised himself on one elbow, another bolt was loosed at him, though he could not make out the bowman. Not that it mattered; his antagonist was far outside his reach.

Flattening himself again, he contrived to pull himself across the tiles. His intention had been to gain the kitchen below, and thence out a passage beneath the stone flooring. But one glance at the bloody chaos that had overtaken the courtyard told him he would never make it to that section of the lower floors, let alone to the kitchen. That being the case, he needed to gain the library. He changed direction, scuttling back up to the crest of the kitchen roof. This had the disadvantage of making of him an excellent target for the three or four seconds it would take him to heave his body across the crest and down the other side to the eastern wing of the monastery's belly.

There was no help for it; no other way presented itself for him to get to the library. But he needed to lengthen his odds, he needed a diversion. Just below the crest, he waited, gathering himself, slowing his breathing. He searched with his free hand until he found a loose tile. Ripping it from its moorings, he launched it into the air in the opposite direction from which he intended to go. He heard it shatter onto the cobbles of the courtyard below, heard the shouts of the Knights raised in warning. Immediately, he rolled over the top, onto the eastern side of the roof. No crossbow bolts followed him and, without pausing to catch his breath, he made his way as quickly and unobtrusively as he could, at length swinging down onto the library terrace. On his way down, he had disturbed a bird's nest and, knowing he might not get another chance at sustenance for some time, he ate the three eggs, for once his scent was on them the mother would no longer sit on them but would cast them out, just as his Order was being expelled from the bosom of the Church.

He went quickly through the room, filled with shelves of precious volumes. Even now he was terrified that the Knights would set fire to the monastery and all this knowledge would be lost forever.

Fra Leoni cautiously stepped from room to room, moving ever eastward. He needed to gain the eastern wall. From time to time, like the tide rushing recklessly onto hard shingle, he heard an upsurge in the terrible sounds of war that set his teeth on edge—the clash of steel on steel, the animal grunts of warriors straining one against the other, coarse oaths and the deep groans and cries of those wounded or near death.

In the semidarkness, he at last reached his goal, the eastern wall, which was entirely tiled in a bewildering Greek pattern. He felt with callused fingers for the mechanism that would allow him entry to the hidden stairs—a tile, fifth from the floor, third from the left—and was about to press it when a sound came to him, both low and sharp. He froze and allowed his senses to quest outward. At first nothing, then it came again, the scrape of steel against stone. Someone was in the chamber with him. But instead of attacking, he was watching and waiting.

Fra Leoni quelled his instinct to open the door and flee. He could not let the enemy know of this escape route, for if he did, the Knights would come after him with everything they had.

As casually as he could, he moved his hand down the tiled wall, walked away. And then he did the last thing his enemy expected him to do: he moved directly toward him—or more accurately, because he couldn't see his enemy, toward the origin point of the noise. He had been right, and there was a small, tight smile of triumph on his face when the brief flash of rising steel crossed his vision. But in that moment, he saw that the Knight was aiming a hackbut point-blank at him. Fra Leoni sprang forward as the Knight squeezed the trigger of the firearm rather more quickly than he had intended. The loud report stung the monk's ear like a swarm of bees, and for a moment he felt as if his head was filled with lead shot.

Then he had barreled into the Knight and the hackbut was spinning away. He used his fist, then drew his weapon. He and the Knight of St. Clement crossed swords.

Now that they were on equal footing he felt better, but almost immediately the other drove him backward beneath a series of vicious blows. Fra Leoni fought back in a peculiar way—he defended himself. In this way, he was able to gauge the ability of the Knight without giving the level of his own ability away. The Knight was larger and more powerful than he was—and was also skilled and confident. Fra Leoni, driven ever backward beneath the hail of blows, allowed the Knight's confidence to blossom. A penultimate two-handed blow sent him to his knees. The Knight, grinning in triumph, raised his sword for the killing blow. Fra Leoni, withdrawing a dagger, slashed the entire length of its blade through his assailant's Achilles tendon. At once, the Knight fell, his sword swinging wildly. Fra Leoni knocked it away. Then he was on top of the Knight, assured that he hadn't been hit, and drove his dagger through a gap in the other's armor.

Panting, he levered himself off the corpse, half-staggered to the Moroccan tile wall, pressed the mechanism, and before anyone else could appear, he vanished through the doorway, closing the hidden door behind him.

In absolute darkness, he made his way down a steep spiral staircase. Both he and Fra Prospero had made this journey numerous times, first with crackling reed torches when they had explored, and afterward, in pitch black, to immunize themselves against just such a situation.

He reached the bottom of the stairs without incident and thence made his way to the base of the eastern wall. From the corner he paced off fifteen feet, then he felt for the locking mechanism set flush with the wall. Here was another secret doorway leading to a steep iron staircase that wound down through the thick walls of Sumela—through the hewn stone itself—to emerge some half mile from the monastery grounds. At once, he hurried down the underground passageway, which reeked of mold and the sharp mineral odor of water seeping through stone. He made as little noise as possible, but under the circumstances it was impossible to be absolutely silent. Nevertheless, he was impelled to hurry, and at last, he reached the end of the tunnel. Like a blind man, he reached out, found the rope ladder that led up to the old well, which had never been a well at all but an escape portal should the monastery ever be breached.

He climbed, and kept climbing until he could smell all the myriad scents of the forest. There was another scent, however, overlaying the others, an acrid scent that was altogether familiar. . . .

A powerful hand gripped his shoulder as he climbed out of the well.

"Keep still and absolutely silent," Fra Kent whispered in his ear.

"How did—?"

"This way," Fra Kent said urgently, overriding his question. "We've been betrayed. Our enemies are lying in wait for you."

And, indeed, he could see the bobbing flares of light that spoke of torch-lit search parties.

Fra Leoni followed his guide, who led him away from the lights, deeper into the forest, until the torch flares were no longer visible. A moon, huge and lambent, rose in the sky. By its monochromatic light, Fra Leoni saw the tall priest's visage, which was tense and terribly drawn. And yet, there was a flicker of elation, for they had eluded their enemies.

Fra Leoni turned to him, grasped his forearm in fervent thanks.

"Don't despair," Fra Leoni said. "We've found a way out, the Order will live another day."

For an instant, he thought the blue moonlight was playing tricks on him, for it seemed to him as if the look of elation on Fra Kent's face had turned it demonic. Then Fra Kent had driven the point of a dagger into the meat of his shoulder. As he lurched backward, pain like a fire inside him, Fra Kent came after him.

"What . . . what are you doing?"

Fra Kent grabbed him, shaking him like a leaf. The look of obsessive concentration on his face was terrifying. He had no interest in Fra Leoni's momentarily confusion. In fact, he no longer had an interest in holding onto the dagger. He was clawing his way through Fra Leoni's robes, frantically trying to find the keys.

In that moment, Fra Leoni shook off his pain and shock. Against all odds, Fra Kent was the traitor. He understood, as well, that Fra Kent had betrayed everyone, even his new masters, the Knights of St. Clement. It was obvious by the look of naked greed on his face that he was determined to steal the cache of secrets for himself.

Fra Leoni twisted away from the fumbling hands and, with a cry of anguish, pulled the dagger from his flesh. Immediately, blood began to run from the wound and he grew dizzy. Fra Kent was on him in a flash, knocking the dagger away. Fra Leoni put his hands up an instant too late. Fra Kent's fist slammed into the point of his chin, knocking him off his feet.

Flashes of light filled his brain, and there was a gathering darkness pressing in on him that was altogether separate from the moonlit night. He could hear birds calling, and the hoot of an owl, far off, or was it the shouts of the enemy as they methodically ground through his brethren?

With a major force of will, he shook off the cobwebs, got his arms inside those of Fra Kent, dug white knuckles into the other's windpipe. A stutter of horrible sounds emanated from Fra Kent as he reared back, his huge torso towering over Fra Leoni.

Fra Leoni threw him off, gained his knees, his hand scrabbling for the dagger. Moonlight gave him a glint, all he needed, and he grasped the hilt, made to stab at Fra Kent.

But the other, coughing still, gripped his shoulder, as he had done when Fra Leoni had first emerged from the wellhead. But this time the spatulate thumb plunged into the open wound. Fra Leoni howled in pain, and his palsied hand released its grip on the dagger.

A grin washed over Fra Kent's face. With an almost languid movement, he snatched the dagger, turned its point toward his foe. His grip tightened and he turned the blade just so, about to run it across Fra Leoni's throat, when a shadow appeared from out of the forest and fell over them both.

PART ONE

PRESENT DAY—
NEW YORK CITY,
WASHINGTON, D.C.

1

ON AN EXCEPTIONALLY HOT AND HUMID JULY FOURTH, Dexter Shaw turned a corner and all at once found himself back in the tense days and edgy nights of his youth. Perhaps it was the sight of the nubile young woman in her sleeveless halter top or the drugged-out young man sitting in the hot shade of a white-brick building, a somnolent dog at his side, a cardboard sign between his knobby, scabbed knees, scrawled with the message, "Please Help. Lost Everything."

On the other hand, perhaps it was something else altogether. Confronting the crowds milling through Union Square Park, he felt as if he were a swimmer, far from the teeming shore, guided and controlled by winds and currents seen only by him. He experienced this separation even more keenly as he edged his way into the human surf. Secrets had a way of making you feel alone even in the midst of a jostling throng. It was true. The deeper the secrets went, the more profound the isolation. The murmuring of lovers, the chatter of friends, the morse-code conversations of businessmen on cell phones, mundane all, and yet to him they seemed exotic, so far were they from his own life. Of course, this had been his reality for decades, but today his own anxiety had transformed these differences into knife blades whose edges he felt against his ruddy skin like an immediate threat.

He became aware of a tall, emaciated man with an unkempt beard hiding most of his face moving toward him.

"I am he that liveth, and was dead; and, behold, I am alive for evermore, amen; and have the keys of hell and of death!" the man shouted at Shaw, quoting Revelations. His hollowed-out eyes drilled into Shaw's, as if commanding his attention. "Write the things which thou hast seen, and the things which are, and the things which shall be hereafter!"

Shaw moved away, but the voice, shrill and hard as cement, followed him: "The mystery of the seven stars which thou sawest in my right hand, and the seven golden candlesticks. The seven stars are the angels of the seven churches: and the seven candlesticks which thou sawest are the seven churches!"

It was the voice of war, the herald of doom. Ever since he had gotten word of the pope's illness, he'd known with a chill creeping through his bones, even before the murders began. Unless he could find a way to stop it, the countdown to Armageddon had begun.

The nauseating stench of death filled his nostrils, the sight of spilled blood filled his eyes. Shaking off the visions, he made his way through the crowds at the Greenmarket where, moments later, he spotted the Eastern European. He was a Knight of the Field, an operative involved in wet work—that is to say, killing enemies of his organization, of which Shaw was definitely one. A moment later, he had melted into the throng.

At once, Shaw left the market, went into one of the department stores on the south side of 14th Street. There, he spent the better part of twenty minutes, moving slowly from section to section. The Knight of the Field picked him up in housewares, where Shaw perused a display of kitchen utensils. His tail was patient and, if Shaw's skills hadn't been honed to razor-sharpness, he might not have noticed him at all. The Knight looked different—he had rid himself of his sports jacket, wore instead a neutral-colored Polo shirt. He seemed fascinated by a set of fine china, then once again vanished, only to reappear in men's sportswear at the extreme periphery of Shaw's vision. He never looked at Shaw, not even in his direction. He was very good.

Shaw selected several dress shirts, moved toward the rear of the store where the dressing rooms were located. The Knight of the Field drifted after him, interested because of the emergency exit at the end of the corridor.

The first three dressing rooms were occupied, which suited Shaw's objective. Keeping his eye on the emergency exit, he kept going. The Knight moved behind him, silently closing the gap. Shaw could feel the man's approach, and he lengthened his stride. His pursuer, overcompensating, came at him too quickly.

Shaw spun around, threw the dress shirts into the Knight's face. As he did so, he drew a potato peeler he'd palmed off the display in housewares across the Knight's cheek. Shaw grabbed the Knight's shirtfront, slammed him into the empty dressing room on the right, kicking the door closed behind him. No Knight would follow him to where he met with his son, this he vowed.

"What good is this?" the Knight said, wiping his cheek. "Do you think you can stop us?" He laughed. "It's already too late. Nothing will stop us."

Shaw hit him in the side, just at the end of his rib cage. The Knight bent but did not break. He half turned, drove his cocked elbow into Shaw's chin. He'd aimed for Shaw's throat, but Shaw had just enough room to shift away. Still, the blow made pain explode in his head. The Knight followed up his advantage with a kidney punch. Shaw landed a blow on his sternum.

Beneath the harsh light, their reflections blurred, they fought in silent, intense fashion, striking and blocking like martial artists, feinting and parrying like fencers, using short, sharp, vicious blows dictated by the tiny room.

Until they stood locked together as if in a lover's embrace.

"You're finished," the Knight said. "It's the end."

Freeing one hand, Shaw buried his thumb into the soft spot beneath the Knight's left ear where the carotid artery pulsed. The Knight, seeing his end, fought like a maddened beast, but no matter what he did, Shaw held on, tenacious as a bulldog. At last, the Knight lost consciousness, slipping to the floor.

Shaw took a moment to calm himself while he rearranged his clothes. He thought about what the Knight had said: *"It's already too late. Nothing will stop us."* Could it be true? he wondered. Could the Knights be further along than even he knew? The possibility chilled him to the marrow. It was now more imperative than ever that he talk seriously with Bravo. Whatever ill feeling stood between them, they must put it aside.

He stepped briskly back into the corridor. Quickly, with a keen and wary eye toward more possible Knights, he exited the store through the employees' entrance on 13th Street.

From there, he plunged into the heart of the Village, turning south onto University Place, then west onto 11th Street. Alone again, he might have slowed down, but instead he hurried on at the same alarmed pace. What breeze had existed in the park had died. A midsummer haze bleached all color from the sky, and the air was freighted which, combined with the stillness, clung to him with an unwanted intimacy.

So, despite all his precautions, they knew his location. Perhaps not so surprising, considering the meticulous planning behind the concerted attacks of the past two weeks, culminating with Molko's capture. Molko had been tortured and, when that proved fruitless, killed—an hour, perhaps even less, before Shaw had mounted a rescue mission.

Terrible luck. He and Molko had discussed the issue more than six months before the first killing. Molko, to his credit, had accepted Shaw's plan without protest. But within hours of the meeting, Molko had been taken, tortured and killed. Shaw had to assume that the enemy had the second key.

The keys of hell and of death.

He found French Roast, the café Bravo had suggested, and went inside. His son hadn't arrived as yet so he asked the pale question mark of a woman at the podium for an outdoor table. At the tiny metal table, he sat in the sun, ordered a café au lait and thought of the Knight of the Field, and of the prophesies of Revelations. He knew a lot about prophesies, far more than most people. *"The things which thou hast seen, and the things which are, and the things which shall be hereafter. . . ."* He imagined that the words spewed out by the religious zealot referred to the war footing on which he found himself.

The café au lait arrived, and he tore open three packets of sugar. Taking the oversized cup in his two hands, he sipped and immediately thought, *Goddamn French coffee. It's strong enough to strip the lining off my stomach. Where's some good old Maxwell House when you need it?* Typical of Bravo to suggest this place, he mused. But then Bravo had spent the last three years in Paris, much to Shaw's dismay. Perhaps some of his colleagues' virulent anti-French sentiment had rubbed off on him, but that was not the reason for his displeasure.

Pushing the offending coffee away, he glanced at his watch. Where was Bravo, anyway? Twenty minutes late. Well, he was flying in from Brussels. Thank God he had consented to come to the family reunion after all. Jordan Muhlmann, the president of Lusignan et Cie, had sent him to Brussels for an important conference on risk management, but no sooner had he arrived than Shaw had talked him into coming.

"I'm best off not telling Jordan," Bravo had said from far-off Brussels. "He doesn't like change."

"I'm not surprised," Shaw had murmured.

"What? Dad, speak up. I can't hear you."

"I said you're doing the right thing, Bravo. Emma would have been devastated. Just get on the next plane to JFK and be done with it."

Truth to tell, Bravo must have wanted to come, because ever since he had informed Shaw that he had accepted the job at the multinational financial consulting firm of Lusignan et Cie, there had been a subtle rift between the two. Not that you could call it a war, exactly, but a certain chill had sprung up between them, their phone conversations shortened, their meetings less frequent. This was not what Shaw had desired—far from it. But experience had shown him that his son was as hardheaded as he himself was. Even though he had made it adamantly clear that he had wanted Bravo to continue his research work in medieval religions, his son instead had taken Muhlmann's highly lucrative offer. At least Bravo had continued the rigorous program of physical training he had insisted on.

Nevertheless, from the moment Bravo had met Muhlmann, the air had stunk of betrayal, but only to Shaw. While he never stopped loving Bravo, he had blamed his son, and, what's more, Bravo was smart enough to know it. But then again, Bravo didn't know the real reason Shaw had been so intent on him continuing his studies. How could he?

Tensely, Shaw watched the waiter navigating with a charming swing of her slim hips the narrow aisles between the round tables. She asked him if he wanted to order and he said not yet.

More than anything else Shaw wanted to mend the rift, more painful to him than he had ever allowed Bravo to know. Today had seemed to him to be the right time to start. The tradition of reuniting every July fourth that had been started by Dexter's late wife, Stefana, had been continued by their daughter, Bravo's older sister Emma, at the family townhouse in which she lived. Still, knowing his son as he did, he had been leery of rushing the rapprochement. But now, suddenly, he had run out of time. Circumstances not of his making had determined that he have the conversation he'd always imagined he'd have with Bravo, though not at this time and certainly not in this hurried manner.

Not that Shaw hadn't done his best to prepare Bravo for this moment. But then Jordan Muhlmann had stepped in and altered everything. Now he was not only Bravo's boss, he was his best friend. Never mind. Bravo was coming, and in a few moments both their lives would change forever. If Shaw had any doubts about his son, he had pushed them into the recesses of his exceptionally ordered mind.

He had faith that Bravo would be up to the task, no matter how daunting. He had to be. As the waiter moved out of his field of vision he saw a man crossing the street toward him. As he approached, Shaw felt his own muscles tense. The man picked up his pace and raised an arm. Then he was striding past Shaw, smiling, into the arms of a waiting woman, who embraced him with uncompromising passion. Just as Steffi had once embraced him.

Don't go there, he admonished himself. But there she was in his mind's eye in the hospital bed, little more than a skeleton, wasting away while he looked on helpless and enraged. What was life when you waited for death? Could it ever be more than that?

"I am he that liveth, and was dead; and, behold, I am alive for evermore, amen . . ."

The words came back at him with the force of a boomerang. If only Steffi hadn't died, if only. . . . But it wasn't meant to be. As his wife lay dying, his heart had broken.

"The keys of hell and of death. . . ."

Then he saw Bravo coming toward him and his heart leapt. He was sure that what he had done, what he was about to do, was the right thing—the *only* answer to the only question that mattered to him.

"Write the things which thou hast seen, and the things which are, and the things which shall be hereafter!"

He had already done that in the way he and Bravo knew best.

FROM the moment he saw his father sitting in sunlight at French Roast, Braverman Shaw was filled with conflicting emotions. The small boy in him wanted to run down the block, his arms open wide; the teenager wanted to thank him for the designated path he'd insisted on for his son, for Bravo had forgotten nothing of his studies in medieval religion, had lost little of the excitement he'd felt from the first day his father had cracked open the thick, illustrated book he kept by his bedside, introducing the child to the mysteries that would consume him for years to come. But the adult, who felt that he had been manipulated, took on the very attributes he hated most in his father, so that they came together not as father and son but as unstoppable force and immovable object. That term—*immovable object*—was appropriate, Bravo thought, for the man whose life and motives he found ever more puzzling and opaque.

"Dad."

Dexter Shaw stood. "It's good to see you again, Bravo."

They shook hands, formally and rather awkwardly, and sat down.

Braverman Shaw was thirty, taller than his father by a head, slimmer, but with the wide shoulders and long, powerful legs of a swimmer. In his own way, he was just as handsome. His hair was dark and curling, his eyes a blazing blue. He had the singular look of a seeker after knowledge, not of a risk management consultant. Emma had nicknamed him Bravo when she was six and Braverman was four. The name had stuck.

Bravo, eyeing the virtually untouched cup of café au lait, said, "Too much flavor for you, Dad?" He said it in a bantering tone—whether to break the stony silence or as a form of self-defense he couldn't say.

Either way, it rankled Shaw, ruffling feathers he'd prefer remained sleek and undisturbed, especially now. "Why must you do that?"

Bravo called a waiter over. "Do what?"

"Provoke me."

Bravo ordered a double espresso. When the waiter had gone, he said, "I was under the impression we provoked each other." He engaged his father's eyes with his. "Don't you enjoy it?"

"As a matter of fact, I don't."

The espresso came. It had been six months since the two had seen each other. An undercurrent of loss and a certain sorrow was passing between them, amplified by the prickly exchange. It was the particular friction that arises between two people who are too much alike. Without the buffer of his mother, who had died ten years ago, sparks often flew between them. This was true even before Jordan Muhlmann, whose mere presence seemed to have aggravated the problem, possibly because he was French and Dexter's dislike of the French was all too well-known to Bravo. *We're both headstrong,* Bravo thought. *Not to mention opinionated, forceful and determined.*

Dexter shifted in his seat. "I want to talk to you about your future."

No, Bravo thought at once, *I simply can't do this again.* "Dad, you're always wanting to talk to me about my future. I'm too old for lectures—"

"First of all, you're never too old to learn something new. Second of all, this isn't a lecture. I want to make you an offer."

"Does the State Department have you recruiting now?"

"This has nothing to do with State." Dexter Shaw leaned forward, his voice low, urgent. "Remember your old training?"

Again out of self-defense, Bravo glanced at his watch. "We're late, Dad. Emma must be wondering what's happened to us. Besides, I rushed in from the airport without any time to get her a present."

Dexter sat back and gave him a basilisk stare. "You know what I think? I think Muhlmann sent you to Brussels deliberately."

Bravo's head came up. He was like a dog on point. "Now don't start—"

"Muhlmann knows perfectly well about your annual family reunion."

Bravo laughed. "You're not implying that he set up an international conference just so—"

"Don't be absurd, but he could have sent someone else."

"Jordan trusts me, Dad."

A silence descended over them, thick with the implied accusation. Horns blared as a car lurched out into traffic, and with a metal clang the rear doors of a delivery truck opened.

Dexter Shaw sighed. "Bravo, can we call a truce? It is urgent that we talk. In the space of a week, the world has changed—"

"After dinner."

"I told you this was urgent."

"I heard you, Dad."

"I don't want Emma—"

"To overhear. Of course not. We'll go for a walk, just the two of us, and you can make your pitch."

Dexter shook his head. "Bravo, it's not a pitch. You have to understand—"

"It's late and getting later." Bravo stood, putting money on the table. "You go on to Emma's while I forage for a present."

"I'd like to go with you."

"So she'll be pissed at both of us?" Bravo shook his head. "You go on, Dad."

As Bravo turned away, Dexter Shaw took his son's arm. There was so much to say, so much that needed to be communicated and now, at the eleventh hour, with bells tolling in his head, he knew that he should feel closer to Bravo than he ever had. Instead, there was between them a kind of chilly chasm he recognized as being of his own manufacture. He had tried to shield his son from the terrible responsibility of what was to come for as long as he could, but what, in the end, had he accomplished except to make him feel as if he wasn't trusted, as if he'd been manipulated for an unknown reason. Secrets, lies and the truth, he thought now, sometimes there wasn't much to choose from between them.

In any case, he had chosen, but it wasn't until this moment that he understood the depth of his failure. Steffi had warned him that it would come to this, Steffi who had known him—and their son—better than anyone. She had begged him not to involve Bravo in his shadow life—she'd ranted, wept, she'd flown at him like a hellion—and still he'd held fast to his convictions. *My darling Steffi, wherever you are, please don't hate me.* But of course she had, just as he knew completely and irrevocably that she had loved him with all her heart and soul. She could not have helped but fear him—that other Dexter Shaw who was rigid, rule-formed, intractable, who disappeared for days or weeks at a time into a world she of necessity only dimly knew. At last, spent and defeated, she had said to him, *"You're like a rock, all of you —no blood, no feeling, no hope at all of change or movement. This is the life you will condemn Bravo to."*

Tears welled in his eyes, the sudden onrush of unfamiliar emotions rendering him inarticulate. There was a chance now to change all that, but, no, it was too late. The die had been cast, what choice he'd ever had had been stolen from him. That was the essence he saw now in a moment of blinding revelation, the heart of the matter that Steffi never understood and he could never explain. In his world, choice was nothing but a dangerous illusion, offered up by a cunning devil.

"Dammit, son."

For a moment, Bravo was shaken—his father never cursed. Whatever was on his mind was important, he knew that much. But now, really and truly, they had no time. Carefully he disengaged himself. His voice, when he spoke, was warm and conciliatory. "I'll be along soon enough, and then we'll have our talk. I promise."

Dexter Shaw hesitated, gave his son a resigned nod, turned and headed to the curb. Bravo watched him crossing the avenue, then turned and headed south. But where was he going? He suddenly realized that he had no idea what to get Emma. His father was the one who always knew what his children would like best. Reluctant as he was to feel once again the pressure of his father's judgment, he nevertheless swallowed his pride and, dodging traffic, jaywalked at a run across Sixth Avenue. By the time he'd gained the west side, Dexter was trotting up the stairs to the brownstone. Bravo called after him as Dexter went through the outer door.

Bravo ran all the faster, hoping to get his father's attention before Emma buzzed him through the inner door. He was mounting the front steps when the explosion blew out the front windows. The heavy front door, torn from its hinges, slammed into him, lifted him bodily, throwing him into the street.

Immediately, there came like ravens' cries the harsh screech of brakes, alarmed voices raised in anxious shouts, but Bravo, unconscious, was already oblivious to the growing chaos.

"NO," his father said to him once again.

Bravo lifted his nine-year-old head with its inquisitive blue eyes and tousled hair. "Where did I make my mistake?"

"It's not a matter of making a mistake." Dexter Shaw knelt down. "Listen to me, Bravo. What I want you to do is use your mind *and* your soul. Intellectual pursuits will only get you so far in life because *all* of life's great lessons involve loss." He glanced down at the puzzle he had set before his son. "A 'mistake' is something mechanical—a wrong way of acting, maneuvering, thinking. A mistake is a surface thing. But *beneath* the surface—where loss manifests itself—that's where you must begin."

Even if Bravo hadn't understood every word his father used he couldn't mistake the meaning or the intent. *Manifest,* he thought, turning over the word in his mind. It was strange and beautiful, like a gem he'd once seen in a store window, gleaming, faceted, deeply colored and, somehow, mysterious. He could feel his father's intent, a living thing, as palpable and intimate as a heartbeat. He knew what his father wanted for him and, naturally enough, he wanted it, too.

I want to manifest myself one day, he thought, as he threw himself mind and soul into solving the puzzle his brilliant father had devised for him.

A sharp pain racked him, threatening to draw him far away, and he fought against it, fought as hard as he could. More than anything, he wanted to stay by his father's side, to complete the puzzle because puzzles linked son to father in a very private and mysterious manner. But another spasm of pain clouded his vision and his father's face flickered like quicksilver, swimming away into a mist of voices that all at once had gathered around him like a murder of crows. . . .

"At last. He's coming around."

"It's about time."

Bravo heard these voices as if through a wall of cotton. He smelled a masculine cologne cutting through a peculiar sickly-sweet scent. He began to retch, felt strong hands on him, wanted to shake them off but lacked the strength. He had trouble stringing two thoughts together, as if he no longer wanted to think.

On opening his eyes, he was presented with two hazy shapes. As his vision slowly cleared these shapes resolved themselves into two men standing over him. The older one was slight. He had very dark skin and Indian features; he was in a white coat—a doctor. The other, perhaps a decade younger, had a face as rumpled as his suit. Bravo noticed his jacket had one frayed cuff. The strong cologne was coming off him in waves.

"How are you feeling?" the doctor said in a slight singsong accent. He had cocked his head, like one of those crows Bravo had imagined. His coffee-black eyes scanned the electronic readouts flickering above Bravo's head. "Mr. Shaw, please say something if you can hear me."

The invocation of his family name came like a splash of cold water. "Where am I?" Bravo's voice sounded thick and peculiar to his ears.

"In hospital. St. Vincent's," the doctor said. "You've got some deep bruises, contusions, burns here and there and, of course, a concussion. But most fortunately nothing broken or burst."

"How long have I been here?"

The doctor checked his watch. "It's just about two days since they brought you in."

"Two days!" Bravo put a hand up to one ear, but the doctor's slim brown hand stopped him. "Everything sounds muffled—and there's a ringing. . . ."

"Your proximity to the explosion caused a degree of temporary hearing loss," the doctor said. "Perfectly normal reaction, I assure you. I'm relieved that you've regained consciousness. I don't mind telling you that you had us all a bit on edge."

"That damn heavy door saved you, Mr. Shaw, that's a fact," the younger man said in a heavy New York accent.

And then it all came rushing back—the sprint up the block, mounting the worn limestone steps, a fury of sound and then . . . nothing. All at once everything looked flat. He felt hollow inside, as if while he was unconscious some great hand had passed through skin and tissue to scoop out his insides.

The doctor's brow wrinkled. "Mr. Shaw, did you hear me? I said that within a matter of days your hearing will be unimpaired."

"I heard you." In truth, Bravo had received this news with an equanimity bordering on stoicism. "My father?"

"He didn't make it," the suit said. "I'm sorry for your loss."

Bravo closed his eyes. The room began to swim around, and he seemed to be having trouble breathing.

"I told you. It's too soon," the doctor said from somewhere over Bravo's head. Then he felt a warmth, a sense of calm enter his system.

"Relax, Mr. Shaw," the doctor said. "I'm just giving you a bit of Valium."

Still, he struggled against it—the Valium and the tears that burned his lids, tears that leaked out onto his cheeks, humiliating him in front of strangers. "I don't want to be calm." He had to know. . . . "My sister. Is Emma alive?"

"She's in the room down the hall." The suit had taken out a pad and pencil. No PDA for him.

"Don't worry about her. Don't worry about anything," the doctor added soothingly.

"I need some time with him," the suit said gruffly. There followed a minor altercation, played out on the edge of Bravo's consciousness, which the suit ultimately won.

When Bravo next opened his eyes, the suit was looking at him out of liquid brown eyes, slightly red around their edges. Dandruff lay on the shoulders of his jacket like ash from a fire. Or an explosion. "My name's Detective Splayne, Mr. Shaw." He held up an ID tag. "NYPD."

Beyond the door, a conversation had started up, one voice old and querulous. The squeak of rubber wheels took them away. Bravo endured the deathly silence as long as he was able. "You're sure. There isn't any mistake?"

The detective produced two photos, handed them to Bravo.

"I'm afraid he took the brunt of the blast," he said softly.

Bravo looked at his father, or rather what was left of him, laid out on a slab. The second photo, unspeakably stark and therefore vile, was a close-up of his face. The pictures looked unreal, something from a gruesome Halloween prank. Bravo felt almost dizzy with sorrow and despair. His vision swam and, unbidden, the tears came again.

"Sorry, but I gotta ask. That your father? Dexter Shaw?"

"Yes." It took him a very long time to say it, and when he did his throat felt raw, as if he'd been screaming for hours.

Splayne nodded, pocketed the photos and went and stood by the window, silent as a sentinel.

Bravo wiped his eyes with the back of his hand. "How . . . how is Emma?" He found that he was almost afraid to ask.

"The doctor says she's out of the woods."

Splayne's words momentarily reassured him, before the full force of his father's death came rushing back to him, blotting out everything. Dimly, he became aware of the scrape of a chair's legs, and when he next opened his eyes, Splayne was sitting beside the bed, watching him, patient as a cat.

The detective said, "I know this is difficult for you, Mr. Shaw, but you're an eyewitness."

"What about my sister?"

"I already said."

" 'Out of the woods.' What does that mean?"

Splayne sighed as he ran a huge hand across the worn facade of his face. "Please tell me what you remember." He sat still, hunch-shouldered, directing all his attention at the man lying on the hospital bed.

"When you tell me Emma's condition."

"Christ, you're a piece of work." Splayne took a breath. "Okay, she's blind."

Bravo felt his heart jolt. *"Blind?"*

"They've gone in and done whatever they could. The doc says that either she regains her sight in a week or two, or the blindness will be permanent."

"Oh, God."

"See, this is what I wanted to avoid." Splayne leaned forward. "You aren't gonna pass out on me, are you?"

With fingers like steel pincers, he steered Bravo's face in his direction, stared hard into his eyes. There was a slight cast to the left eye, as if something terrible had happened to that side of his face. Bravo caught the other's intensity, allowed it to bring himself back from the edge of panic and despair. His father dead, Emma blinded, all in the space of a single breath. It was too much, he couldn't accept it as the truth. There must be another reality out there—one in which his father had survived, where Emma hadn't lost her sight—if only he could find it.

"Mr. Shaw, I need you to tell me what happened. It's important, okay?"

"Yes," Bravo said in a reedy whisper. "I understand." He recounted as best he could what he remembered of the brief chain of events just before the explosion.

When he had finished, the detective looked at him. "To be honest, I didn't expect much more than that."

"Then why was it important to talk to me?"

"Hey, I gotta close this thing out, otherwise the paperwork will hound me like a bitch in heat."

Bravo felt a renewed surge of anger. "Do you know what caused the blast?"

"Gas leak in the basement. It was an old brownstone, maybe the heating system was in need of repair. The fire department's going over the place now." Detective Splayne's pen was suspended over the notebook. "One other thing, who's Jordan"—a quick glance down to his notes—"Muhlmann? He's been calling twice a day to check on your condition."

"He's my employer and my friend."

"That's what he told me. So. Anything else?"

Bravo shook his head.

"Then my work here is finished." With a sense of finality, Splayne closed his notebook. "I wish you well, Mr. Shaw."

"That's it? That's where the investigation ends?"

Splayne shrugged. "To tell you the truth, Mr. Shaw, it's where most investigations end. This is a big city, millions of people in it walking in shadows, running away from the light, crawling in the sewers like maggots. It's the maggots I get to spend time with, day in, day out. This here's clean and clear-cut compared with the shit I get most days. I swear, it's enough to hollow you out inside, turn even a hard-case optimist into a cynic." He rose. "Like I said, I'm sorry for your loss, but it's time I was getting to where I'm really needed."

Bravo, still fighting the effects of the Valium, twisted in bed. There was a question he'd wanted to ask. What was it?

"Wait a minute, did you talk to my sister?"

But Splayne had already gone.

BRAVO lay back for a moment, his head swimming. The moment he closed his eyes his father reappeared. "All *of life's great lessons involve loss*," Dexter Shaw said and laid his hand on his son's damp brow. *"Don't forget what I've taught you now."*

With a growl, Bravo pulled the Valium drip from his arm, ripped off all the monitoring devices. He sat up, swung his legs off the high bed. The floor felt cold as ice to his bare feet, and when he put his full weight on them he was obliged to clutch the bed linens lest he fall. His heart pumped hard in his chest, and his legs felt as if their bones and muscles had dissolved during the forty-eight terrible hours he'd been unconscious.

He had to shuffle across the room to the door, and when he opened it he was confronted by an angry-looking nurse, clucking away like an offended nun.

"What have you done, Mr. Shaw?" She had a wide nose, a firm jaw and café-au-lait skin. "Get back in bed this minute."

She had reached out to turn him around, but Bravo checked her, "I want to see my sister."

"I'm afraid that's im—"

"Now."

He held her eyes for so long she knew he wasn't going to back down.

"Look at you, weak as a newborn, you can't even walk." Still, his eyes would not let her go. At length, capitulating, she fetched a wheelchair, brought it around behind him. He sat down, and she pushed him forward.

Outside Emma's room he held up a hand. "I don't want to go in there like this. Let me walk."

The nurse sighed. "In her current condition she won't know the difference, Mr. Shaw."

"Maybe not," he said, "but I will." Hands on the armrests, he levered himself up. The nurse stood, watching him, arms crossed over her bosom, as he grasped the door frame and moved slowly into the room.

Emma, reclining on the bed, looked a mess. Not only her eyes but the upper half of her face was heavily bandaged. He sat on the edge of the bed, sweating alarmingly inside his gown. His heart was pounding so hard it threatened to squeeze through his rib cage.

"Bravo." Emma's voice, rich and musical, varied as an artist's palette, rose to him, the one word like a song.

"I'm here, Emma."

"Thank God you're alive." Her hand fumbled for his, found it and squeezed. "How badly are you hurt?"

"It's nothing compared—" He barely had time to choke off the rest of the sentence.

"Compared to me, you mean."

"Emma."

"Don't do that, don't you pity me."

"It isn't pity."

"Isn't it?" she said sharply.

"Emma, you have every right—"

"Don't be such a good sport!" She turned back. "Who should I be angry at, Bravo? Who did this to me?" Then she shook her head. "It's disgusting. I've had enough of terror and anger and self-pity."

With an enormous effort of will she smiled, and like sunlight flooding the room he saw her as she had been, carriage erect, her mouth open wide, honey-colored hair flying in the wind created by the stage fans, her huge emerald eyes, wide cheeks and generous mouth so much like their mother's, one hand uplifted as the aria emerged from her, glorious and full-born, as he always imagined Puccini had heard it when he'd first composed it.

"I've waited two long horrible days to feel you, to hear your voice." She took his hand again. "This makes me happy, Bravo, this cuts through my endless night. Even in my worst, blackest moments, I was able to rise above it long enough to pray for your recovery, and God heard my prayers and kept you safe." Her smile widened. "So now I want you to do the same—to rise above your anger and your self-pity. I want you to have faith, Bravo, if not for yourself, then for me."

Faith? Faith in what? he asked himself. His father had wanted desperately to tell him something, and because he had hardened his heart, because he hadn't been able to forgive him for his manipulations, he'd never know what was so important. His jaw clenched. Wasn't forgiveness a major component of faith?

"Emma, Dad is dead and you're—" His throat was filled with bitter bile.

She placed her soft hands on either side of his face, as she had done when, as a child, he had become agitated and frustrated. She pressed her forehead to his. "I want you to stop and listen," she breathed in a musical murmur, "because I'm sure that God has a plan for us, and if you're filled with anger and self-pity you'll never be able to hear it."

His throat was clogged again with all the emotions boiling up from inside. "Emma, what happened that day?"

"I don't know. Honestly, I can't remember." She shrugged. "Maybe it's a blessing."

"I wish I could remember something—*anything*—about what happened."

"A gas leak, that detective said. An accident. Put it behind you, Bravo."

But he couldn't, and he couldn't tell her why.

"Now I need you to help me get to the bathroom," she said, breaking into his thoughts.

When Bravo stood up his legs felt stronger. They reached the bathroom without incident. She seemed strong to him, despite what had happened to her. Was that her faith he felt, deep and rippling like a stream at spring's first thaw?

"Come inside with me," she said, drawing him in before he had a chance to protest. She locked the door behind them, then opened her hand, revealing a pack of cigarettes and a small lighter. "I bribed Martha." Martha was her personal assistant.

She sat on the toilet and with surprisingly little difficulty lit up, drawing the smoke deep into her lungs and holding it there. On the exhale, she said with a laugh, "Now you know my secret, Bravo. The smoke gives my voice that depth the critics so rave over." She shook her head. "God works in mysterious ways."

"What does God have to do with it?"

At once, she stood up. "Oh, Bravo, I hear the anger, you can't keep it out of your voice. I wonder if you know how ugly it is, how it distorts the beautiful tenor of your voice."

"It's you who has the beautiful voice, Emma."

She stroked his cheek with her fingertips. "We both have Mama in us, only maybe—just maybe—I have a bit more."

"I know you thought Dad loved me more," he blurted out, because it had been on his mind.

"No, Bravo. He loved me, too, but you and he had some—I don't know—some special connection. It hurt me so to see the two of you at odds." Her face turned up to his. "Have you cried yet, Bravo? I know you have." Her fingertips traced the bandages over her eyes. "I envy you that luxury."

"Oh, Emma."

"The first few hours afterward when I was first hit with what I had lost I fell into a black pit. But faith is a tree, growing new branches even in the face of a storm. And when the time is right, those new branches bear fruit. It's faith that sustains me, faith that makes sense out of chaos, faith that holds the world together in the face of crisis." She took another, smaller drag from the cigarette. "I wish I could make you understand. When you have faith, despair is not an option. I grieve for Dad. Inside I'm crushed because a part of me has been ripped away and I'll never get it back. That, at least, I know you understand. But I also know that his death, the loss of my sight, either temporary or permanent, is for a reason. There *is* a plan for us, Bravo. My faith shows it to me, even without the use of my eyes."

"Was it God's plan to have Dad blown up, for Mom to waste away?"

"Yes," she said firmly and deliberately. "Whether you can accept it or not."

"I don't understand how you can be so sure. This is a part of you I never got, Emma. What if your faith is an illusion, what if there is no plan? That would mean that there *was* no purpose."

"No purpose we can yet see."

"Faith. Blind faith is as false as everything you rail against." Bravo thought of what Detective Splayne had said, and his hands curled into fists. "How can you live in such a world and not be cynical?"

"I know your cynicism is a facade, because *cynicism* is just another word for frustration," Emma said softly. "We spend so much time trying to maintain control over everything that governs our lives, but it's futile— and terribly frustrating—because, really, what can we control? Almost nothing. And yet we still seek the impossible, even knowing that it's a hollow pursuit. What can fill the void, can you tell me? No. But, listen, listen, when I let go of everything, when I sing, I *know*." Her cigarette had burned down, unsmoked. She must have felt the heat on her fingers because she groped behind her, flicked it into the toilet. With a brief angry hiss, its lit end winked out. "Bravo, the explosion may have taken my sight, but miraculously it left me my most precious possession—my voice is unharmed."

He held her tight then, feeling her substance, as he always had, ever since he could remember. "I wish I had your faith."

"Faith is a lesson to be learned, just like everything else in life," she whispered in his ear. "I pray that one day you'll find yours."

And in his other ear his dead father whispered: "Beneath *the surface—where loss manifests itself—that's where you must begin.*"

2

"BRAVO, I AM SO RELIEVED TO HEAR FROM YOU," JORDAN
Muhlmann said when Bravo finally returned his call. "I haven't heard
from you in days. I was going out of my mind with worry."

"I'm sorry, the concussion has made things a little fuzzy," Bravo said
into the cell phone.

"Yes, of course. As long as I know you're all right."

"I'm fine." He was walking down the street toward his bank. He had
recovered enough to be discharged from the hospital and he was ready
to leave New York; there was only one thing to consider—besides, of
course, Emma.

"You can't be fine, Bravo," Jordan said. "It's altogether understand-
able that you're not."

"You're right, of course."

"It's not simply what I say, *mon ami*. It's what I feel. You are family,
Bravo, you know that."

Of course Jordan would understand. Though he was six years
younger than Bravo, they had bonded almost immediately. During one
long drunken evening in Rome, when they had freely exchanged confidences, he'd told Bravo that he'd lost his father at an early age, and
mourned him still. He knew about family and loss. All at once, Bravo
missed Jordan, his life in Paris. They spent so much time together, had
gotten so close in the space of just over four years, they *were* like family.
"On that score, I have no doubt."

There was a cop on one corner, leaning against his car, drinking coffee out of a paper cup. Across the street a little girl skipped along with
her dog, her mother by her side. Just behind the girl and her dog, a man

and woman held hands. They were young, both blond and blue-eyed. He wore black slacks and shirt, she a short skirt and sleeveless top.

"Listen," Bravo went on, "I'll be home in a couple of days. I want to get back to work."

"*Non,* you have more important matters to deal with."

A dam burst, and Bravo's eyes abruptly filled with tears. "My father dead, my sister blinded—this is a nightmare, Jordan."

"I know, *mon ami.* My heart goes out to you—Camille's, as well." Camille Muhlmann, Jordan's mother, was his advisor, and an integral part of Lusignan et Cie. "She wishes me to tell you that she's sick with grief."

"As always, she's exceptionally kind. Thank her for me," Bravo said.

"Take your time. Do whatever you have to do. In all things you have my support, whatever you need you have only to ask."

The woman laughed at something her lover said and glanced at Bravo. She had the face of a hungry cat.

"Thank you, Jordan. I appreciate . . . everything."

"Ah, no. I just wish I could do more."

The couple had stopped to chat with the cop, but the woman's eyes remained on Bravo. She smiled a secret catlike smile behind her lover's back.

"You scared the hell out of me, you know. You could've been killed, and then where would I be?"

The lovers had moved on, but the woman's smile lingered in his mind.

"Now listen to me, *mon ami,* you must take your time winding up your father's affairs. We will manage without you. And, Bravo, remember, you must call on me if there's anything I can do. Here in Paris, so far away, I feel helpless. It will be better for both of us if I can help in some way."

He was outside the bank. "*Merci,* Jordan. Just talking to you . . . this connection. You know, I feel a whole lot better."

"Then I am happy. *Bon, a bientôt, mon ami.*"

Putting away his cell phone, Bravo went through a glass door into the bank. As he crossed the marble floor he remembered his father taking him in here when he was eight, recalled with a startling vividness the confidence he felt with his hand clutching his father's. Dexter had opened up the account for him. When he'd turned eighteen, at his father's behest, he'd gotten the safety deposit box. Though he now lived a continent away, he'd never gotten rid of them. Their importance to him was immeasurable. Wherever he might be in the world, part of him always would remain here in New York.

At the rear of the bank, he asked to see the manager. Within moments, a middle-aged woman in a conservative business suit was escorting him downstairs to the vast vault where the safety deposit boxes rose in gleaming reinforced steel banks. The vault had about it the oppressive look and air of a mausoleum.

Inside, he sat in a curtained booth while she went to fetch the box. He knew he was lucky to have a friend like Jordan. They had met in Rome five years ago when Muhlmann had come to the university where Bravo was then working. Bravo had had a unique position in the department of medieval religions. He was not expected to teach but to research the ages-old mysteries that dogged his field. Though Bravo was then still in his twenties, he had already gained something of a reputation not only as a scholar but also as cryptanalyst. As it happened, that very field of knowledge fascinated Jordan, and he was eager to observe firsthand Bravo's facility in decoding medieval texts and solving seemingly unsolvable puzzles.

Jordan had stayed in Rome six weeks. During that time, he and Bravo had struck up a close friendship based on common interests and outlooks. They had studied together, run track and hit the heavy bag together, had even squared off in fencing matches—remarkably, their skills matched each other in the épée and the saber. They went out to dinners and got drunk on good food, excellent wine and fascinating talk. Finally, Jordan had made Bravo an offer to join Lusignan et Cie. Bravo at first declined, but Jordan had persisted and, eventually, after some further back and forth, he had managed to persuade Bravo to come work for him.

The manager returned with a long flat gray metal box and, setting it down on the table in front of him, left him. He took out the key and opened it. Inside, he discovered stacks of money, neatly wrapped and bound, his secret fuck-you money. Yet another thing Dexter Shaw had taught him. There were two layers, each double bundle bound together. He untied the lower left-hand corner bundle, pulled from between them the key his father had given him six months ago.

The meeting had been brief but unprecedented inasmuch as Dexter had flown into Paris, something Bravo couldn't recall him having done before. They hadn't even sat down but instead at Dexter's suggestion had crossed the Seine on the Pont d'Iena, walking briskly along the rather unlovely Quai de Grenelle. The morning was unnaturally warm for a normally raw and forbidding February, and people could be seen strolling happily with their winter coats open or slung over their arms. Once they passed the Hotel Nikko the tourists vanished and the natives dwindled, which was apparently the whole point of the exercise. That was when Dexter had handed him the key, an old-fashioned item, odd in both shape and design.

"If something happens to me," Dexter had said, "you'll need this."

"If what happens? Dad, what are you talking about?" Another dark and unfathomable secret, another bit of shrapnel lodged in his chest so close to his heart he could feel it flutter.

The sky was the color of peat. The overheated weather was causing mist to rise off the river, smudging the outlines of the buildings on the Right Bank. Halos throbbed around the moving lights. A horn hooted mournfully as a barge slid slowly past them. Down on the lower quai a dog was running loose, its tongue out and lolling. The leaves of the horse chestnut trees rustled, as if anxious.

"Just listen, Bravo. Put the key somewhere safe, will you promise me that? And if something happens, take the spare key I gave you and go to my apartment." Dexter Shaw had smiled, gripping his son's shoulder. "Don't look so stricken. Chances are it'll never come to that."

But now it had. Detective Splayne believed that the explosion had been caused by a gas leak, and that conclusion had been confirmed by the FDNY. Sitting here, staring at the key with the globular burr on the end, the seven incisions along its length, each in the shape of a star, Bravo couldn't help but ponder what had been on his mind from the first—what if both Splayne and the FDNY were wrong? Six months ago Dexter Shaw had traveled all the way to Paris, a place he despised, in order to deliver to his son the presentiment of his impending death. Steeped in the real and true mysteries of medieval religions, Bravo was not a believer in the occult. His father wasn't psychic—he'd known something, or at the very least had had a strong suspicion that his death was coming.

Shaking himself from the ominous web of his thoughts, Bravo pocketed the key, along with two packs of bills. Then he closed and locked the box and, emerging from the booth, handed it back to the patiently waiting manager.

Not for the first time, he considered the possibility that Dexter Shaw's job at the State Department was only a cover and that he was, in fact, a spy.

"I think he's yummy," said the young woman with the face of a hungry cat.

Rossi shook out a cigarette and lit up. "Donatella, you surprise me. You need to be more discriminating."

"Don't be jealous, darling." She ran her long fingers over his biceps. "I have no intention of leaving you for Braverman Shaw."

"But a one-night stand wouldn't be out of the question, hmm?"

When she reached his black silk shirt, she used her nails so that he could feel her through the tissue-thin fabric as she drew them across his chest. "How nostalgic!" she murmured. "You remember our first meeting."

"How could I forget?" Rossi glanced past her to the bank's entrance.

They sat at a café diagonally across from the bank into which Bravo had vanished some ten minutes before. They had chosen a table situated slightly back from the window so that they could surveil the street without themselves being seen. Rossi and Donatella spoke perfect, unaccented English, but when no one else could hear they had fallen into the habit of communicating in the precise, almost formal version of the language used by all Romans.

All at once, he grasped Donatella's porcelain wrist.

"You're hurting me!" she gasped, but he did not relinquish his iron grip.

Slowly, he manipulated her wrist until her hand revealed what it held: the pendant at the end of the gold chain around his neck. "I told you, didn't I? What did I say?"

Donatella pouted, her fingertips caressing the seven-pointed purple cross. "But it's so beautiful."

Rossi knew that she meant powerful. She always said beautiful when she meant powerful.

"All the more reason to keep it hidden." Without taking his eyes off her face, he unwound her fingers so that the pendant disappeared beneath the opening of his shirt. "What do you think the consequences would be if our Mr. Shaw should catch a glimpse of it?"

Donatella swung around, her cat's eyes raking the baking street. "He'd know," she said in an unmistakable finality. "He'd know everything."

OUTSIDE, a fist of heat greeted Bravo rudely. After the chilly, metallic semidark of the vault, the light was blinding, but already he was wondering if he'd seen the man across the street before. He looked vaguely familiar, but Bravo couldn't quite place him.

Bravo moved off, and the man went into motion. Turning the corner, Bravo saw him reflected in a store's plate glass window, against a background of earthy Moroccan pottery and bright Turkish plates. It was his gait that gave him away, that brought back the woman's feline smile while her lover spoke to the lounging cop. Her eye contact had been deliberate—she was attempting to keep him from remembering her lover, who had now taken up the surveillance.

Or was he imagining it all? He wasn't paranoid, and he was no spy. Perhaps, neither was his father. But he didn't believe that, not really. The evidence was mounting, and now with this strange key in his possession he had become part of the game. If only he had a clue what the game was.

EMMA had taken a suite in an exclusive boutique hotel not far from St. Vincent's while the brownstone was being repaired. Her bandages were smaller, and he could see that her hair had started to grow in. Martha, who had opened the door for him, was busy fixing lunch in the galley kitchen.

Bravo had spent fifteen minutes walking away from the hotel and then back again, ducking into a convenience store and suddenly out again, until he'd satisfied himself that neither the man nor his female partner was shadowing him. Only then had he entered the hotel.

He came in and kissed his sister on the cheek. "How are you?"

"Better." She smiled. "And you?"

"Ready to roll."

Keeping the smile on her face, she said, "You know, I get the feeling that you've been wanting to tell me something for days. Now that you're about to leave I really think you ought to tell me."

He looked around, but Martha, humming to herself, was oblivious. "It's about Dad. I. . . ."

She cocked her head. "Bravo, this is me." She patted the sofa and sighed when she felt him sit down beside her. Feeling his warmth beside her, she said softly, "It's all right. Whatever it is, surely saying it will help. Have faith."

Bravo pressed his thumbs against his eyelids as if he could relieve the pressure building inside his head. "That day, Dad had something to tell me. It was important, at least it was to him. And I kept putting it off. I told him that we'd talk after dinner." Like a sprinter always gaining on him, that terrible day overtook him again, rendering him mute.

"Maybe what he had to say to you was important," Emma said. "But that's not the issue. You've got to go on, and you won't be able to do that unless you can forgive yourself." Emma put her arm around his shoulders. "Do you think you can do that?"

Bravo kept silent, knowing that she neither wanted nor required an answer. He simply listened, gave himself over completely to what she was saying. The truth was, despite whatever sibling-type fights they'd had when they were young, he'd always admired her, not just for her talents but for her innate intelligence.

"Before you turned your talents to risk management you were a scholar. The fact is, you're still a scholar, just as I'm still a singer. We're who we are, Bravo, whether or not we choose to believe it, because it's imprinted onto us at birth. By God? Yes, by God, through genetics. A risk manager is what you do, but that's not the same thing, is it? Dad understood that, even when you yourself lost sight of the fact."

Well, that was something, he thought as he walked out of the hotel. More than something. Right now, it was all he had.

3

BRAVO TRAVELED TO WASHINGTON ON THE SHUTTLE, CHECK-
ing the faces and demeanor of his fellow passengers both in the terminal and on the plane. He took with him the two keys—the seven-star
key, as he'd come to call it, and the more pedestrian Medeco key to his
father's apartment—and nothing more, except for the money he'd
taken from his safety deposit box. He didn't know why he'd brought
the money—a hunch, or a presentiment similar, perhaps, to the one that
had brought his father to the Quai de Grenelle six months ago. One other
thing: he also carried in his head a growing constellation of facts in
search of a pattern.

The dense southern humidity rolling up the edge of the Chesapeake
attempted to smother him the moment he strode out of the terminal.
Halfway toward the rank of taxis, he stopped, as if abruptly unsure of
himself. The sky was a uniform white, tinged with the palest blue lower
down, away from the burning sun. Small eddies of a spendthrift wind
stirred fistfuls of soot and candy wrappers into brief trembling spirals.
Without warning, he turned and purposefully retraced his steps. Back
inside the terminal, he walked past the huge plate-glass panels, watching
the crowds coming and going. What he was looking for he could not at
that moment have said, but like an animal with its snout to the wind he
had responded to a peculiar prickling in the hollow between his shoulder blades. He went and got himself a cup of coffee, stood sipping it
while he covertly watched the faces of passersby. Part of him felt ridicu-
lous, but another, growing part of him, would not allow him to relax.

At length, satisfying some deeply buried instinct, he threw his paper
cup into the trash and headed back out to hail a taxi.

DEXTER Shaw had lived in a modest one-bedroom apartment in Foggy Bottom, that curious section of Washington between the White House and Georgetown. A century ago, the low-lying area was damp and swampy, owing to its proximity to the Potomac. Fog swirling in off the river often combined with a thick, greasy airborne mass, an industrial London-like smog emanating from the nearby Washington Gas and Light Company, Godey's lime kilns and Cranford's Paving Company. Nowadays, it was home to many legislators and a good place to network, which was, after all, the currency that greased the wheels of DC's curiously old-fashioned engine.

The apartment complex was in a huge redbrick building that took up most of the block on H Street. It was a modern, completely anonymous structure without ornament or interesting angle, form following function, typical of an unfortunate school of postmodern architecture.

Identifying himself to the uniformed doorman, Bravo took the elevator up to the twelfth floor, went down the blue-carpeted hallway. He slipped the Medeco key into the front door to his father's apartment. It didn't work. He tried again, wriggling it back and forth as if perhaps it needed only some small encouragement to fulfill its function.

He was about to try for a third fruitless time when he heard a voice behind him and, turning, found a small, dark-faced man coming toward him.

"I'm Manny—the super. Johnny—the doorman—phoned down to tell me." He offered his hand. "You're Mr. Shaw's son, ain't you?"

"That's right," Bravo said.

"We were all tore up when we heard of Mr. Shaw's untimely passing. Everybody in the building liked him. He was quiet, you know, kept to himself—but friendly all the time."

My father, the politician, always honing his image, Bravo thought as he thanked the man. "I thought he'd given me the key to the apartment, but it doesn't work."

"No worries." The super took out a ring of keys and, searching through them, inserted one in the lock, opened it. He stood back for Bravo to enter.

"I gotta stay here while you have a look around," he said. "Building rules. You understand."

Bravo said that he did. But when he entered the apartment, he realized that he understood nothing at all. The apartment was empty. As he moved through it, looking in all the rooms and closets, he could find not a stick of furniture, not an item of clothing, nothing that would indicate that the apartment had ever been occupied.

Stunned, Bravo turned to the super. "I don't understand. Where are all my father's belongings?"

The super pursed his lips. He smelled of tobacco and sweat. "I thought you'd have known. They removed the contents of the apartment days ago."

"They?" Bravo shook his head. "Who are 'they'?"

The super shrugged his shoulders, "State Department, government men. Showed me their ID and everything. Was there something in particular you was looking for?"

Bravo shook his head, unable to speak. His father's entire life, where had it gone?

The super gave him an almost furtive look of pity and said that, after all, he thought in this one instance it would be okay to leave Bravo alone in the apartment. Bravo thanked him, and he left.

Bravo closed his eyes, breathing deeply as if trying to find a lingering trace of his father. His eyes snapped open and he went again from room to room, checking drawers, closets and cupboards in the kitchen and bath. Not only had the contents been removed, but the apartment had been thoroughly cleaned from top to bottom. Sanitized. He'd once heard his father use the term when they'd had to abandon the embassy in Nairobi several years ago.

He took out his cell phone and called his father's office at State. After several minutes, he was connected with Ted Coffey, a senior analyst his father had introduced him to several times.

"Hey, Braverman, I'm so sorry. How are you doing?"

"As well as can be expected, I suppose," Bravo said.

"And Emma?"

"Also."

"We all miss him, you know, but no one more than me. He was a goddamned fixture around here. Twenty-plus years, I can hardly believe it myself. Frankly, I don't know what I'm going to do without his expertise. That goddamned analytical brain of his simply can't be replaced, and everyone here knows it."

"Thanks, Ted. That means a lot to me." Bravo walked into the center of the bedroom, turning slowly in a full circle. "Listen, Ted, what did you guys do with my father's belongings?"

There was a moment's pause. "I don't understand."

"Well, I'm standing in his apartment in Foggy Bottom and there isn't a stick of furniture or an item of clothing here. Everything's been cleaned out."

"It wasn't us, Braverman."

"The super said some government men came. He saw their IDs."

"I don't care what the super said," Ted Coffey said. "No one authorized the removal of the contents of Dex's apartment, and that's a fact. Strictly against departmental policy."

Bravo stood for a moment in the silent, bare apartment. Vainly, he tried to imagine his father in this place. Thanking Coffey for his time and heartfelt condolences, Bravo closed the connection.

He looked down at the Medeco key, using his remarkable memory to once again recreate the conversation on the misty Parisian quai. What was it exactly his father had said? Ah, yes. *If something happens take the spare key I gave you and go to my apartment.* He'd never said that this was the key *to* the apartment. Bravo turned the key over and over, light glinting off its machined facets. What had he meant, then?

Assuming he'd wanted Bravo to go to his apartment if something happened to him, why was there nothing here? Again, he felt the peculiar pricking between his shoulder blades. Was this a warning of some kind? Bravo remembered the couple outside the bank, shadowing him. What did they want?

As these thoughts rolled around in his head, he was staring at the key, and now he thought he saw something glittering that he hadn't noticed before. Taking it over to the window, he saw etched into it a string of sixteen tiny letters. They seemed to have no rhyme or reason—certainly they formed no known word. Bravo wondered what they signified.

All at once, a familiar thrill raced through him. He was thinking of the grand games he and his father would play—the messages his father would leave for him in code—which would drive his mother crazy because only he and his father could read them.

It was a basic number substitution code that needed to be worked out because some of the letters were used to tell you which letters to substitute for the ones written. Taking out a pad and pen, Bravo wrote down the letter string, then sitting with his back against the radiator, set to work. What would have baffled a cryptographer was laid out for him like a blueprint. Within five minutes he'd broken the code and what appeared before him was a single word: *gangplank*.

He knew, of course, what a gangplank was, but he had no idea what his father meant or why he had bothered to encrypt the word. Sunlight, filtered through dirty panes of glass, shot repeating patterns across the parquet floor and barren walls, sadly emphasizing the utter emptiness of the space, which had been scrubbed clean of every last vestige of Dexter Shaw's presence.

As Bravo took one last circuit around the apartment, he searched his memory for an instance of the word *gangplank*, but he couldn't recall his father ever using it. Leaving the apartment was more difficult than he had imagined. He recalled with a painful vividness his mother's illness and felt now as he had each time he'd left her dying in the hospital: heartsick that she was held prisoner by her illness, by the betrayal of her body, when he was fit and free to walk into the cool neon-lit evening air.

At the elevator, he paused and turned back toward the apartment door. If only he could reach inside and extract whatever was left of his father.

On the way through the lobby, he asked the doorman for directions to an Internet café, the closest of which, it turned out, was on West 17th Street, more or less midway between Dupont Circle and Scott Circle. He called a cab and waited in the cool of the lobby until it pulled up to the curb.

TEN minutes later, he was sitting at a computer terminal, an iced coffee and a roast beef sandwich at his right elbow. He searched *gangplank*, but so many results came up that he knew he'd have to narrow his search criteria.

As he munched through half his sandwich, he considered the possibilities. Going on his father's principle of hiding in plain sight didn't work with this particular problem, because Dexter Shaw had gone to a lot of trouble to encrypt the word. Why would he do that? Bravo frowned, concentrating. He no longer tasted the sandwich, no longer heard the soft murmur of voices of those around him; he'd entered into that extraordinary private world his father had observed in him even at an early age. His entire being was directed at unraveling the puzzle at hand. And in the silence of his concentration something came to him. If his father had hidden the word, then gangplank was something well known—something in plain sight. Bravo's head came up. He knew he was right—his father had simply applied his "hidden in plain sight" dictum in a different way.

Putting what was left of his sandwich aside, Bravo returned to the computer terminal, his fingers flying over the keyboard. On one of the many Washington, DC sites, he typed in the word *gangplank*. What he came up with surprised him. Gangplank was the name of a marina within walking distance of the Washington Monument and the Capitol Building.

AT the marina office, a grizzled old-timer with a cigarette between his bloodless lips told him that there was no boat registered in the name of Dexter Shaw or anyone named Shaw for that matter.

Thanking the old-timer, Bravo walked down to the water and out onto the slips. The day was overspread with a glare of haze that reduced the visible spectrum of light, leveled everything to the dull colors of old laundry. He inhaled the sharp, almost rotten mineral smell of the water as he passed one boat after another. He didn't yet know what he was looking for, but there must be something here—his father's message told him so. Then, on the third slip over, he saw a dark blue and white thirty-seven-foot Cobalt 343. *Steffi* was stenciled across its stern plate in gold. Steffi, his father's pet name for Bravo's mother. He stood very still, his aspect tense and watchful. It could be a coincidence, but he didn't think so. He didn't believe in coincidence.

He glanced down at the mysterious Medeco key. The more he thought of it, the more it seemed likely that his father would not have kept a boat registered under his own name, especially in light of what had happened to the contents of his apartment after his death. The boat meant something, he suspected, something vitally important, otherwise Dexter wouldn't have named it *Steffi*, then hidden it so that only his son would find it.

All at once, the marina appeared bleached out, the skyline of DC receding to some other reality. He was alone on the wooden slip, feeling the last remnant of his father he'd been searching vainly for in the apartment. A connection had been established through the boat, a kind of umbilical that drew him ever closer.

It was with this profoundly altered sensibility that Bravo went aboard. He was looking for clues now, the part of his father that remained after his death: an elaborate set of clues and codes that would guide him—and *only* him—to what his father wanted him to know. He paused, considering this notion for a moment. What if there were others after whatever it was Dexter wanted his son to find, others he was wary of, even afraid of? Bravo thought of the blond couple, the man's incongruous shoes, the woman's feline smile that now seemed to him sinister, a sign not of a flirtation but of a secret she knew and he didn't.

Once again, he felt that peculiar prickling between his shoulder blades, and with an eerie sense of foreboding, he looked around, abruptly fearful that his inattention would lead to sudden disaster. What if they were here, what if he was being watched as he had been in New York? But no, he saw no one suspicious in the general vicinity. The marina was quiet, virtually deserted. Anyone trying to spy on him would have been revealed in an instant. And yet, as he looked farther afield, he saw high-rises whose dizzying banks of windows faced him. Behind any one of them someone could be standing with high-powered binoculars or a telescope, recording his every movement.

With an acute and uncomfortable sense of his own helplessness, he turned and, with equal parts resignation and determination, concentrated on what had to be done now. He began his search in the crescent high-tech cabin with its cream-colored seating-area storage compartment and head, but found nothing there. Returning deckside, he spotted a compartment door just to the left of the wheel, below the array of dials. In its center was set a Medeco lock. With his heart beating fast, he fitted the key into the lock, turned it. The door popped open.

Inside, he discovered a rat-eared address book, a pair of cubic gold cuff links, an enamel American flag lapel pin, a pair of eyeglasses, two packs of cigarettes, a gunmetal Zippo lighter. That was it. Taking this assortment of everyday items, he returned to the cabin, where he slit both packs of cigarettes down the sides, spilled out the contents. To his disappointment, he found only cigarettes. These he slit, too, pawing carefully and vainly through the tobacco.

He held the cuff links in the palm of his hand, as if he could feel in their considerable weight the lingering presence of his father. Flipping open the Zippo, he lit the flame and almost immediately extinguished it. His vision went blurry as he peered through the glasses. They weren't magnifying lenses that could be picked up at any drug or convenience store, they were prescription lenses.

He held the glasses at arm's length, wondering, because so far as he knew Dexter Shaw had perfect vision, he'd never needed glasses.

But perhaps he was wrong, perhaps this was one other thing his father had kept from him. There was only one way to find out. He leafed through the address book, found the number of his father's opthamologist and called him. He was busy with a patient, but when Bravo told his receptionist who he was, she retrieved Dexter Shaw's file.

"Glasses?" she said when she came back on the line. "Why would Dr. Miller prescribe glasses for Mr. Shaw? His vision was exceptional. He had no need for glasses, even reading glasses."

And yet, here he was holding glasses with prescription lenses. Another clue? What other hypothesis was there? He decided that he'd have to go with that one until it proved incorrect.

Now he examined the glasses more closely. On the inside of the right temple was the manufacturer and the model. On the inside of the left was stamped the name and address of an optician. He phoned a taxi service, then carefully gathered up everything he'd found and left the boat.

Walking briskly back down the slip and out of the marina, he kept an eye out for anyone loitering or seeming to work when he actually wasn't. Two teens on bikes sped past him, and a middle-aged man carrying a six-pack of beer and a too-large gut strode by. Bravo turned and watched him walk out onto the slip, climb aboard a boat named *TimeGoesBy*. Then he resumed walking, hurrying up the street to where the red and white taxi was waiting, engine idling. He got in, gave the driver an address in Georgetown.

TWELVE minutes later, he got out in front of the Four Seasons Hotel, an elegant low-rise brick building at 2800 Pennsylvania Avenue. Without looking around, he strode into the lobby, then turned right and stood, shoulder against a column, peering through one of the huge windows at the avenue. The atmosphere was cool, hushed, serene, a perfect sanctuary to gaze out upon the world and once again wonder whether he was being vigilant or paranoid. For a time, he watched taxis and Town Cars pulling up, disgorging fashionable women in stiletto heels and expensive coifs, festooned with shopping bags. Two businessmen stood smoking and chatting, then moved off. He saw no one suspicious, yet he had to wonder whether he knew what to look for.

Exiting via the side entrance, he walked a dozen blocks, turning at length onto P Street where, a block further on, he came upon Trefoil Opticians. The owner's name—Terrence Markand—was stenciled in discreet gold letters on the window. It was a clean, well-lighted store in an old brown stone Federalist building. While the man behind the counter adjusted a pair of sunglasses on a woman, Bravo perused the displays of high-tech, fashionable frames with heart-stopping prices. Behind him, the woman walked out of the store. The man at the counter was tall and gaunt, with sunken cheeks and the complexion of an avocado. He gave Bravo a narrow smile along with his attention.

"How can I help you, sir?"

"Are you Mr. Markand?"

"I am, indeed." The smile stretched a bit.

"My name is Braverman Shaw," Bravo said, holding out the glasses. "I found these among my late father's effects. Your name is on them so I assume you made them for him."

"You're Dexter Shaw's son?" Markand said with an odd brittleness. "I read about his untimely death. I'm so sorry for your loss." He seemed on the verge of saying something more, then thought better of it, biting his lip.

Bravo nodded his thanks. "I wonder if you could tell me anything about the glasses."

"What would you like to know?"

"The prescription, for instance."

Markand didn't bother to examine the lenses. "I can't, because I didn't grind them. Mr. Shaw's arrangement was with the technician who did grind them."

Bravo took back the glasses. "I'd like to speak to him."

"Her," he corrected. "I'm afraid she no longer works here."

"I see. And why is that? An altercation of some kind?"

"Not at all." Markand peered at Bravo for a moment, his lips pursed. "She just up and quit, without any notice, mind you. Young people, no manners at all, wouldn't you say?" He shook his head ruefully. "Damn shame, too, she was the best tech I'd ever had, and I've been in business almost thirty years. Take those glasses, for instance, the lenses are ground using a technique I couldn't even begin to guess at."

"When did she leave?" Bravo asked.

"Ten days ago, precisely. She walked out of here and didn't even bother to collect her back pay, either."

Ten days ago, Bravo thought. *The day after my father died.*

Markand frowned. "But she did leave me an envelope, said it was for you." His rather delicate hands rested on the glass countertop. "No offense, but would you mind showing me a picture ID? Just so I can be absolutely sure, you understand."

Bravo dug out his US driver's license. The optician nodded, then reached under the counter, unlocked a drawer and extracted a heavy vellum envelope, archaically sealed with red wax.

Opening the envelope, Bravo discovered a slip of paper on which was written an address in a clean feminine hand. He looked up to see the cadaverous optician regarding him with a tense smile.

"Good news, I trust?"

"That has yet to be determined," Bravo said as he folded away the paper.

The optician nodded. "Then there is nothing left, Mr. Shaw, but to wish you a good day."

THE moment Bravo left his shop, Markand turned, and with a sinking feeling in the pit of his stomach, went back into his office. It was opposite the grinding lab and smelled of heated sand and plastic, and now something more. Donatella lounged in the swivel chair behind his desk, her wide lips forming a half smile that spoke of the kind of mystery that put dread into Markand's painfully thudding heart.

"You did well," she said. "He came just as you said he would."

"My granddaughter," the optometrist said. "I want her back."

"In time." Donatella sat up.

"If you've harmed her—"

"What?" Donatella's eyes grew flinty as she pushed the chair back and came around the side of the desk. "What will you do, Markand?" She laughed unkindly as she patted his cheek.

He couldn't help himself, but involuntarily tried to recoil. In a terrifyingly quick movement, she grabbed the back of his head.

"I would tell you not to worry, but, actually, you have a great deal to worry about, Markand. We haven't finished with you."

He closed his eyes and whimpered like a child.

Donatella, her face very close to his, shook him like a rag doll until his eyes popped open, wide and staring. She could see the whites all the way around, and this pleased her enormously. "You understand, don't you, that Angela's life is in your hands."

He shuddered, almost overwhelmed with nausea. There was something unspeakably offensive—evil, even—hearing his only granddaughter's name spoken by this creature. For that was how Markand had come to think of her—considerably less than human—a nightmare beast who, with her male counterpart, had stolen into his life and now held it hostage. His training meant nothing now; only Angela mattered. He would endure any humiliation or deprivation, he would sell the soul of everyone around him in order to ensure her safety.

"What do you want me to do now?" he said hoarsely.

Donatella placed a clamshell cell phone into his trembling hand and said, "Call him."

Markand opened the phone and dialed a local number. "He just left," he said when he heard Rossi's voice. "Of course I know where he's going, I already told you. Yes, I'm sure." He could feel the creature's eyes on him like the breath of a fanged beast, jaws gaping, and his bowels loosened.

PLUNGED in contemplation, Bravo walked back to the Four Seasons where he picked up a taxi. He told the driver to take him across the Potomac to Falls Church, Virginia. The address on the slip of paper was an old stone house with a steep slate-gray shingled roof on a quiet, tree-lined street. A surf of pink climbing roses decorated the white picket fence that enclosed the front yard, which was shaded by a Bradford pear tree on one side and a cut-leaf Japanese maple on the other. A thick four-foot privet hedge was planted up against the foundation. Between neat rows of sheared azalea, a moss-edged flagstone path led to a door lacquered blood-red.

The door opened even before he had a chance to ring the bell, revealing a slim, lovely young woman with cinnamon hair pulled back in a ponytail from her wide forehead and large gray eyes, slightly upturned at their outer corners. "Yes?" she said in a tense voice.

"I'm Bravo Shaw."

"What took you so long?" she said, making room for him to step inside.

The expected welcome draft of cool air did not come. In fact, despite the stone walls the interior of the house was quite warm, seemingly without any air stirring at all. He saw a polished wood floor, devoid of any carpets, a sofa of a nubbly umber fabric and two matching chairs, a glass coffee table with curved bronze legs, an oversized stone fireplace one might expect to find in a hunting lodge. Against one wall was an antique walnut breakfront, displaying plates and bowls behind diamond panes of glass, and on the other a large painting—a portrait in dark, brooding hues of a seated woman, young and arresting, her hands held loosely in her lap, her head thrown back almost in defiance, pale eyes regarding the viewer with a peculiar intensity; there was about her the intent of motion, as if she were an arrow in a drawn bow, about to catapult across the room.

"Are you—?"

"Jenny Logan. I made those glasses to your father's specifications." Her gleaming oyster-gray sleeveless blouse and hip-hugging jeans revealed her fitness as well as showed off her shapely legs. Her shoulders were square, her arms sun-browned and firmly muscled, her neck long and elegant. She gave the impression of scrutinizing everyone and everything she came upon.

"Why?" Bravo said. "And why did my father want me to meet you?"

She was about to answer, when her head swiveled. Her entire body tensed. Bravo, concentrating, heard it, too, and he was already moving toward the front door. But she stopped him, pointing to a pair of men emerging from a dark sedan, running full-tilt toward the house. At that moment, a thunderous crash reverberated through the house as the back door yielded to a hand-held battering ram.

4

JENNY GRABBED BRAVO'S HAND, PULLING HIM THROUGH
the living room, seemingly toward the back of the house. But in the hallway, she flipped up a patterned runner, revealing a trapdoor. As they
heard voices shouting, the panting of determined men, she lifted the door.

Voices came to them, harsh and urgent; curt orders were given, and
then they heard the pounding of heavy feet. The house was completely
surrounded. By whom? Bravo had no idea, and now was definitely not
a good time to ask Jenny.

Down he went, missing the first three rungs of a vertical iron ladder,
wrenching his right shoulder. With a soft grunt he balanced himself as
she came down after him. Glancing up, he saw her pause to pull the
runner back over the trapdoor as she silently lowered it and threw a
thick steel bolt, locking them in.

ROSSI, loaded Glock at the ready, followed the two men into Jenny Logan's house. At once, he signed to them and they dropped the battering
ram, drawing their weapons and sprinting down the hall. For his own
part, Rossi leapt up the stairs, taking them three at a time. He went methodically through the second story, checking the two bedrooms and
closets. He was a master of precision, not someone who fired a gun
wildly, spraying the vicinity in the vain hope of hitting his target.

He hated this assignment and, in particular, he hated being in America. He longed to be back in Rome with its sun-drenched streets, the excited jabber of friends and neighbors, the grit of centuries long past under
his fingernails. Here, everything was bright and shiny, gobbled down fast-
food style in insatiable amounts, ugly in its aggressive newness. As he

went through closet after closet, he reflected sourly that for America nothing was ever enough, no matter how much it had or would ever have. He saw with Old World sensibilities a kind of hysteria that lived beneath the skin of every American, that brooked no recourse, no negotiation, no . . . what was it the Americans liked to say? *It's my way or the highway.* Oh, to be back on Via dell' Orso with the earthy smells of brick and fresh-baked bread, slyly eyeing the young women with wide hips, thrusting breasts and flashing eyes!

By the time he reached the bathrooms, he was joined by the two men who'd used the battering ram. They shook their heads in the negative. He ripped down the shower curtains, stomped on the tile floors, hammered against the walls in search of hidden trapdoors to hidey-holes. He had no illusions about this being a normal house. The occupant was no normal female; she would have spent months in the preparation for just such an invasion.

"Well, they're here somewhere, either in the attic or the basement," Rossi said as he led them out of the second bathroom. "You two find the attic and get in. I'll take the others into the basement."

FOR a few moments, they were in utter darkness. Bravo could hear her breathing, smell his scent and hers mingling as she stepped off the ladder in close quarters. All at once, louder sounds—muffled through the floorboards—came to them as the house was fully occupied. How many men? Bravo asked himself. Two in the front, the same number in back? More?

He very badly wanted to talk to Jenny, but now she was taking his hand again, leading him across the basement, which smelled of stone, old wood and paint. She had no trouble negotiating the space in the darkness, which led him to believe she'd performed this drill many times before. Why? Had she been expecting this attack? It was becoming clear to Bravo that his father had been involved in something secret, something deeply hidden, even from his family. Why had he kept his secret life from them? Why had he deceived them for so many years? What kind of person could do that?

Thoughts stuck in his mind like thorns he couldn't reach. They had stopped in front of what seemed to be a solid stone wall. He reached out, confirmed his supposition. All at once, he heard an explosion, and he winced, sweating freely, memories of the other, larger explosion that had caught him vivid in his memory and now the heart-stopping moment of impact brought immediately and terrifyingly into the present. The basement door had been shattered by a gunshot and now came the quick and ominous scrape of shoe soles against concrete.

Then he felt her hand on his shoulder, pressing firmly, and he crouched down beside her. He heard her scramble forward and followed her into what at first appeared to be a recess in the wall. But once inside, he felt a draft of sodden heat and, glancing up, saw the gauze of pale sky contained in a black frame, an abstract image of the world outside. This was the chimney or, since no flue was visible, a space hidden behind the chimney. In the dim light, he could see Jenny pushing down on a square section of the stone wall—a door, he saw now, set on rollers, that fit precisely and securely into the space through which they had entered the chimney. When the door was in place, the wall appeared seamless.

Jenny turned in the cramped space and, picking up a paint can she must have grabbed in the basement, began to climb up a series of metal rungs set at regular intervals into the brickwork. Without hesitation, he followed her.

WITH a soft grunt, Rossi blew apart the lock on the door to the basement. As he raced down the stairs, his two men close behind him, he felt the familiar swirl of venom in the pit of his stomach. There was something about blood, the rising of it in his own body, the heat it produced rushing into his palms, fingers and toes, the copper taste of it as if he had bitten clear through a metal bar, that made him feel elemental, larger than life, immortal.

His nostrils flared like a wolf on the hunt. They were down here, their scents like a fading vapor trail in the sky. He lifted his left arm and the two men switched on battery-powered floodlights. At once everything was thrown into stark relief. There was no place to hide, no nooks or crannies, no shadows save their own, trailing obediently after them.

He directed them to the walls first. They pounded on the concrete with the butts of their semiautomatic rifles, pulled cartons and boxes away to peer behind them. Rossi knew that there must be a way out of the basement. The woman would not have taken Shaw down here without one. It was simply a matter of finding it.

While the men systematically stabbed at the walls and floor, he checked everything else. There wasn't much that could be of use to them: a boiler, a hot water heater, the solid brick rectangle of the chimney, no central air or vacuum. The boiler and heater stood away from the wall. Nothing there for him, so he turned his back and went over to the brick chimney. He walked all the way around it, then stood staring at it, wondering why it went all the way down to the basement. There was no opening that he could see, no reason for it to be here.

He put the flat of his hand on the brick, closed his eyes. One of his men said something to him.

"Shut up!" he snapped.

Dead air silence. And then . . .

He felt—or thought he felt—a trickle of vibration transmitted through the brick, coming to him from inside the chimney.

What if there was an opening in it that led upward?

Rossi called softly and his men began to move.

THE occupation of the basement came to them through sound and vibration. Bravo tried not to think of the pursuit as he continued after Jenny, climbing until surely they were past the first floor. He saw no opening to the fireplace and realized that the shaft they were ascending was built behind the bricked-off real chimney.

Just above him, Jenny kept up a steady pace. He estimated that they were now above the second floor, the attic, the roofline. All the while, the air inside the chimney grew hotter and wetter, the patch of sky expanding until momentarily it grew dark as Jenny's body eclipsed the sunlight. Then she was out and he could see her face peering down at him.

"Come on," she mouthed urgently. "Come on!"

He emerged into the blazing sunshine. He squinted as he joined Jenny, who was sprawled on her belly across the slate roof tiles. The roof pitched downward so that as he crawled forward to lie shoulder to shoulder with her he could see the street at the front of the house. A black Lincoln Aviator was parked at an angle, blocking the street, its curb-side doors open. A man sat smoking in the driver's seat. One hand was draped across the wheel, gripping a gun. Another man leaned against the Aviator's front fender. He was staring fixedly at the front door. If he was armed, he was hiding it well.

Bravo felt Jenny touch his arm. Her scent came to him, lavender and lime. Her hair shone copper in the hazy sunlight. She was pointing to herself, making a gesture. He was about to ask her what she meant when she began to slither away. He moved after her, but she frowned, holding him in place.

"Stay here," she mouthed. "Wait for me."

He nodded, watched her crawl to the side of the roof. There, she pried open the lid of the paint can, set it at the edge of the tiles. Then, turning briefly onto one hip, she took out a lighter, flicked it on. In one practiced motion, she lit the contents of the paint can and shoved it over the side. As she came back toward him, there came a crash, then, an instant later, a shout and a chorus of raised voices as a plume of oily smoke rose up, followed by the first ruddy lick of flame.

By this time, Jenny was at his side, and together they moved to the edge of the roof. Below them, the Aviator stood deserted, its driver and companion having run toward the commotion at the side of the house. Jenny went over the edge, landing in the thick privet hedge. Bravo dropped down after her. Branches cracked beneath his weight and he felt his shirt tear in several places, bright pinpricks of pain across his shoulders and back.

Then she was hauling him out of the hedge, and they ran across the sidewalk to the Aviator. Pushing him in, she climbed behind the wheel. The keys were in the ignition, no doubt to better facilitate a quick getaway should the need arise.

The engine growled to life and she threw the SUV in gear. As they shot away from the curb, Bravo watched the rearview mirror fill with running figures. He squinted, then turned around. Was that the man who had been outside the bank in New York, following him? A figure beside him raised a gun in the Aviator's direction and Bravo shouted a warning to Jenny, but just before they swerved around a corner, he thought he saw the man push the gunman's arm down toward the pavement.

As Jenny took another turn, she said, "Why did you turn around?"

They were racing down Little Falls Street.

"I thought I recognized someone."

"Well, did you or didn't you?" she said shortly. Amid an outraged bray of horns and squeals of tires she turned left onto Route 7.

"Hey, take it easy!"

"You were the one who warned me they were going to shoot," Jenny said without taking her eyes off the road. "Do you think they won't try to follow us?"

She maneuvered the Aviator around a lumbering delivery truck and accelerated. By the angle of the sun, Bravo could tell that they were heading roughly southeast.

"You didn't answer my question," she continued. "Did you recognize one of the house invaders?"

"I did," Bravo said after a moment. The sharpness of her tone angered him, but beneath that he realized that the urgency she projected had the effect of focusing him. This annoyed him even more. "I saw him before in New York City."

"You're sure?"

Bravo nodded emphatically. "Yes. He was following me."

"Was he with a woman?"

"What?"

"Young, striking in an aggressive sort of way."

Bravo turned his head so sharply his vertebrae cracked. "How did you know?"

"It was an educated guess." She gave him a tight smile as she made a hard right through a light turning red, onto Lee Highway. Horns shouted again, and a voice cursed briefly. "The man's name is Rossi. Ivo Rossi. Usually, he works in tandem with a woman named Donatella Orsoni."

"They looked like lovers when I saw them together."

"Animal magnetism," she said dryly. "But I wouldn't want to be made love to by either of them."

She headed right onto Jackson Street and then by way of small residential streets toward a growing swath of green.

"Just who are these two?" he asked.

"Members of an ancient sub rosa group known as the Knights of St. Clement."

She said this so nonchalantly that he almost missed her trailing phrase: "You've studied them, I imagine."

Indeed he had. He'd read all there was to read about them. "The Knights were instrumental in bringing the papal word of God to the Holy Land before, during and after the Crusades."

Jenny nodded, frowning. "In doing Rome's bidding, they were the pope's thinly veiled fist against both the Islamic infidel and those religious sects the pope or his puppet council deemed heretical to current teaching. Rossi and Donatella are Knights of the Field, named after the warrior-priests of their order sent to the Holy Land to fight the Ottomans during the Crusades. These people are expressly trained to kill."

It was impossible to hear about the Knights without also thinking of the Order. "How do you know so much about them?"

She glanced at him for a moment. "I'm their mortal enemy. I'm a member of the Order of Gnostic Observatines."

"This can't be. History records that the Knights of St. Clement wiped out what remained of the Order in the late eighteenth century."

"There's history," she said, "and then there is the secret history of the world."

"Meaning?"

"It's true that the Knights tried to annihilate us, but they failed. Every time they attacked, we went deeper underground."

"The Order still exists, the Knights of St. Clement still exist."

"You yourself have seen two of them. What else fits the pattern of the last several days? What else fits the pattern of your whole life, for that matter?"

"Again, I—"

"Your training in medieval religions, your physical training, your father's unexplained absences."

Bravo felt a ball of ice forming in the pit of his stomach. Much to his horror, incidents and thoughts, suspicions and seemingly disparate long-held notions started fitting together.

Glancing over at him, she saw all this on his face. "You know it now, don't you, Bravo? Perhaps, somewhere deeply hidden inside you, you always knew it. Your father was a Gnostic Observatine."

Bravo felt like a vise had been put to his temples. He had trouble breathing. He looked out the windshield, hoping for a kind of solace in nature, but now that they were closer, he could see amid the trees monuments of carved white stone and granite as speckled as a bird's egg: National Memorial Park. She was taking him to a cemetery.

Superimposed over this scene was the specter of his father's face, and then the familiar voice: *"No matter how hard you try, you can't outrun the past."*

IVO Rossi, Knight of the Field, astride a powerful black and yellow K 1200 S BMW motorcycle, rendezvoused with the delivery truck Jenny had passed on Route 7. Donatella was behind the wheel, handling the three-ton vehicle as if it were a Honda Accord. They spoke to each other by cell phone in the stripped down, almost codelike sentences of people intimate with each other.

"According to the electronic tracker in the Aviator, they're on Timber Lane, heading due west," Rossi said.

"The cemetery." Donatella was always one step ahead of everyone. That was what made her so valuable to Rossi and so scary to everyone else. They had known each other since they were preadolescents, finding each other in the crawling filth of Rome's back alleys, exploring a sexual landscape both new and dangerous. Opportunistic to the core, they survived by feeding off the misfortune of others, which more often than not they themselves manufactured.

The moment of their first encounter was forever tattooed on his memory. Lithe and impossibly thin, she had been running down the narrow street where he had been looking to break into the back of a store for money or food. She was lit up from behind by the headlamps of a battered Fiat jouncing after her. Her eyes were wide and staring, her mouth was open as she sucked in air. She had been running a long time; he did not need to see the desperation on her face to know this was clearly the end of the chase. He had hefted the crowbar in his hand and, as the Fiat approached, had slammed it into the driver's-side windshield. The Fiat bucked and swerved like a wounded beast. It slid along an ancient brick wall in a shower of sparks. Even before it came to a stop, the driver had leapt out. He was dressed in a long black leather coat. There was a gun in his hand. Rossi, at a dead run, had swung the crowbar again, cracking the man's wrist. The gun went flying and the man turned, drove a balled fist into the pit of Rossi's stomach. Rossi bent double, gasping and helpless, and the man yanked the crowbar out of his nerveless fingers. Rearing back, he drove it point first toward the top of Rossi's head, but Donatella had scooped up the man's gun and, walking purposefully toward him, had emptied the clip into him.

Since then, they had been like twins, recruited into the Knights of St. Clement together, training together as Knights of the Field, whose bloody purpose they quite naturally understood. Often, they began and finished each other's sentences, thought the same thoughts, for the same reasons. They had been set loose together, stalking prey, infiltrating organizations and institutions as their orders dictated. Always, they had done what had been asked of them, willingly, happily, with a devout—almost holy—sense of purpose, for the Knights of St. Clement had become the orphans' mother and father.

"It's not logical, of course," Rossi said as they sped west. The highway was filled with cars, trucks, SUVs, limitless possibilities. With a familiar burst of exhilaration, he was aware of what his life in the Voire Dei had given him. It had legitimized his natural instincts; instead of running from the law, he and Donatella were beyond it, immune. Only another member of the Voire Dei could understand what he was and oppose him, but with the death of Dexter Shaw there was no one left for him to fear, certainly not this Guardian and her hapless charge.

"But what would you expect of her," he said, "once you take into consideration what's on her mind every day and every night?"

"A weakness that will prove their downfall." Donatella smoothly up-shifted and accelerated. On a mission, she felt the world open to her like a flower, and she was happy. In the dead spaces between, she starved herself sexually, suffered from insomnia and bit her nails until the quicks bled. At those times, there was no emotion in her but pain, and none other that she could imagine. Now, however, purpose hummed inside her like a hive of bees, and she felt that there was no pain, no deterrent capable of stopping her or even giving her pause.

THE cemetery spread out all around Jenny and Bravo, a vast, hushed, peaceful city of the dead—lush and green, smelling of new-mown grass, loosestrife and wild onion. There was a respite of sorts in the deep shade of the old oaks, hawthorns and Virginia pines. Birds flittered among the heavily laden branches and the drone of insects was everywhere. Directly behind them were the gates to Miamonides Cemetery, and on their left, to the south, was the larger, more imposing National Memorial Cemetery.

Jenny led them at a fast clip down a paved walkway between two rows of squat stone mausoleums—a necropolis gleaming dully in dappled sunlight.

As if at last making up her mind, she stopped abruptly and turned to him, engaging his eyes with her own. "Listen to me, Bravo, I need to tell you something. Your father was killed by an explosive charge."

Bravo felt something clench painfully in his belly. "But the police said that it was a gas leak." All at once he felt dizzy. "They assured me it was an accident."

"That's just what they—and you—were meant to believe." Jenny stared at him for a moment, unblinking. "But his death was no accident. Dexter Shaw was murdered."

"How do you know that?" He was aware that his voice was harsh, almost antagonistic. He didn't want to believe her. Of course he didn't want to believe her.

"Dexter Shaw was a member of the Haute Cour—the inner circle, the leaders of the Order. Over the past fifteen days, five members of the Haute Cour have been killed—one choked to death on a fish bone, another was a victim of a hit-and-run incident. The third fell—or rather was pushed—from the balcony of his twentieth-floor apartment, and the fourth drowned while he was boating. Your father was the fifth."

Bravo followed her account with a sense of mounting horror, and all at once a memory flooded through him. *"I want to make you an offer,"* Dexter Shaw had said in characteristically cryptic fashion. *"Remember your old training?"* This bit of the last conversation he'd had with his father stuck in his mind like a moth pinned to a lepidopterist's table. She was right, and he knew it. Of course. He'd known it, he realized with a start, from the instant she had said it. It was as if the multiple shocks of his father's death, his sister's maiming, his own concussion had caused a latent instinct to arise in him—a long-held sense of danger, conspiracy, secrets, a sense of a hidden world he'd inherited from his father.

They had begun to walk again, urged by Jenny, as if she knew that movement—even of the most pedestrian sort—was what he needed most now.

"Breathe, Bravo," she said to him softly, kindly, as she observed him. "You'll feel better the more deeply you breathe."

He did as she said and in the process felt keenly a sensation of being in her hands. It was not altogether unpleasant, for he was in the midst of a dawning realization that ever since he'd awoken in the hospital his world was changed forever. Sometime during his state of utter unconsciousness he'd entered an unknown territory. Suddenly alone, he was grappling to come to terms with a new world order of which he had no knowledge.

"I need some answers," he said. "From my studies, I know that the Gnostic Observatines were a supposedly heretical suborder of the Franciscan Observatines, who broke with both the traditionalists and the mainliners. Is it still a religious order? And what about you? I was under the impression that the Order was strictly male."

"Once it was," Jenny said. "And believe me, there are those in the Order who wish it was still, who bear me nothing but ill will. We will get to them in time, but for the moment, to answer your first question, the Order is now apostate, we've moved out of the strictly religious sphere."

"Why?"

"Once, religion was the law, the supreme power in the world, but gradually that power eroded, ceded to kings, warlords, parliaments and presidents. As religion's power waned, the Order moved with the times, into the power centers of the secular world. We became businessmen and politicians.

"And all the while, we followed the Knights, whose mission it was to keep power concentrated in as few hands as possible: the Kaiser, Hitler, Mussolini, you get the picture."

"Are you telling me that the Knights of St. Clement were behind—"

"They certainly played their part, they greased the wheels, and we— the Order—did our part to stop them, to ensure the democratization of power. This is the essence of the clandestine world—we still call it by its ancient name, the Voire Dei, the Truth of God—in which we operate, Bravo."

"But if the Order is no longer religious in nature, what has it become?"

"Through the 1940s, we kept Hitler mesmerized with a blizzard of astrological charts from which he made every wrong decision he could make, overextending his army in Russia and Western Europe. We kept the Nazis from learning about the Manhattan Project, despite Werner Heisenberg's work as Director of the Kaiser Wilhelm Institute for Physics in Berlin. In 1945, members of the Order spoke to Harry Truman to ensure the atomic bombing stopped at Hiroshima and Nagasaki. Since then, we have strived to limit the proliferation of nuclear weapons. In 1962, one of us met with Nikita Khrushchev in a dacha outside Moscow and persuaded him to back off his stand on Cuba.

"Through economic means, we spent a decade ensuring the fall of Communism and the breakup of the USSR. Today, we work continuously in Africa to stop the spread of disease, in Eastern Europe to keep governments stable, in Western Europe and Asia to educate Islamics, to try to protect them from the desperate measures of terrorism. Extremism catches hold when all hope is gone, when a human being has been stripped of everything except hatred. We do all this behind the scenes, otherwise we'd continuously be under attack by the Knights. Sometimes we're not successful or only partially successful—the onrush of world events is sometimes overwhelming. But with the original mission St. Francis gave us to travel the world to do good, to keep nothing for ourselves, we have persevered. Until now, when the entire world is threatened, when at any moment it might come under the thumb of the Knights of St. Clement."

She turned, and together they hurried down the path, a narrow aisle between the granite gravestones and polished marble mausoleum walls.

"The secrets in the cache are our power," she continued. "At first, they were the schemes of kings, merchant-princes, cardinals to murder their rivals, to corner the Dutch commodities markets that we ourselves created in the seventeenth century. Later on, plots by governments to back this dictator, assassinate that one, to wage war and then, afterward, award the plum contracts for infrastructure rebuilding to companies who contributed to their election; backdoor politics that distributed aid sent to poor countries into the hands of political leaders who needed it least. Embezzlement, coercion, treason, shall I keep going? The under-the-table deals between businesses to wipe out rivals, the embezzlement of funds, the breaches of fiduciary trusts, the venality of those at the top of the ladder of power. All the injustices man commits against his fellow man.

"Used judiciously, our knowledge of all these and more gives us a unique wedge, opening doors otherwise closed to all outsiders. It allows us to influence leaders, politicians, businessmen into making decisions beneficial to the world, and to the prospect of peace."

"And the Knights want war?"

"The Knights want our secrets—our power. I assure you they would not use them so judiciously. They seek to consolidate their power, to at long last break free of the Vatican's yoke. They want to influence governments and business to their own ends."

It seemed odd to him now, but he had always suspected there was more to history than could be read in any library book or doctoral thesis. And why not? His father had trained him to intuitively understand the nature of secrets, to not only accept their existence but learn to unearth and unravel them.

"The secret history of the world," he said, repeating the phrase she had used.

She nodded. "And up until now we've managed to thwart all their efforts. Just so you understand the stakes: what happens in the next week will be crucial not only to the survival of the Order but to the world itself."

"But why now?" Bravo said. "The Knights have been trying to steal the cache for centuries."

"The pope is gravely ill."

"There's been no news—"

"Of course there hasn't—not yet, anyway. The Vatican has seen to that. But his illness has thrown the Vatican into chaos—especially the cabal of cardinals who back the Knights. The Knights have used the panic to galvanize the cardinals' full power behind them once and for all—lengths to which even these cardinals had been afraid to go until the pope was incapacitated. The Knights have come after us as never before. This is the Order's last stand, Bravo. Here we survive, or die."

"How many of you are there?"

"Five hundred, give or take."

"Not so many."

"We're strewn around the globe, in every major country and a smattering of minor ones, but of members like myself there are less than fifty. I'm a Guardian. Have you come across word of us in your studies?"

Bravo shook his head.

"I'm not surprised. The Guardians were deliberately undocumented, a closely held secret. It was—and is—our job to keep the others, especially members of the Haute Cour, safe from harm."

He felt suddenly angry. "And yet you and your fellow Guardians allowed five of the Haute Cour to die. Where were you when my father was killed?"

"Remember I told you that one of the Haute Cour drowned while boating? He was my father. I was in the middle of the Chesapeake Bay when your father was killed. I was in a wet suit, searching for my own father's body."

Her words momentarily took the edge off his rage. "Did you find him?"

"No. The tides were strong and a two-day storm offshore had churned the water to murk. It was impossible to see anything clearly, let alone find a body."

"I'm sorry," Bravo said.

"So am I."

His anger fought to reassert itself. "If it wasn't you, then who was assigned to protect my father?"

The knifepoint of his voice pricked her. "Are you out for revenge, Bravo?" she said shortly. "If so, I suggest you save it for those who murdered him."

Racked by his own tragedies, he hardened his heart against hers. "You didn't answer my question."

They had come to the end of the necropolis, though there was a scattering of other mausoleums in the near distance. They stood facing one another, glaring.

"Your father ditched his Guardian some time before he met you. He also disabled a Knight of the Field who was shadowing him. He was an expert at losing himself whether he was in a crowd or not, and, in retrospect, it's clear he wanted to be alone with you—completely alone."

Bravo took some moments to digest this as they continued down the path she had chosen, then he slowly let out his breath. "You seem to have all the answers, and you're resourceful. Is that why my father led me to you?"

"I wish I did have all the answers." She cocked her head. "Why did your father ditch his Guardian, why did he want to be alone with you?"

I want to make you an offer. Remember your old training?

"I don't know," he said, but there was another clutch in his stomach and he had to fight the urge to hit something. He knew what his father had meant for him, all right. The only question was whether he'd accept it. "No," he said after a moment's thought. "He asked if I remembered my old training. Of course he knew I did, he was simply preparing me. I'm certain he was going to ask me to join the Order."

For a moment she was silent, checking the immediate vicinity as she had done at random intervals ever since they had stolen the SUV. Judging by the dates on the gravestones—all in the eighteenth century—they had entered the oldest section of the cemetery.

"I'm hardly surprised."

"You're not?"

"Your father was someone different, special. He was far more than simply a member of the Haute Cour," she said slowly and deliberately. "But to understand this, I have to start from the beginning. As you know, the Gnostic Observatines were once Franciscans."

Bravo nodded. "The original Order was founded in the thirteenth century by followers of Francis of Assisi, and almost immediately upon his death there were those friars who believed that they should be living in apostolic poverty. This angered the pope no end because it was the Church that owned the riches accrued to its Orders. But it wasn't until 1517, almost three hundred years after the death of St. Francis, that the Order formally split into two separate factions, the Conventuals, who wanted to stay put, and the Observatines, who were convinced that St. Francis wanted them to remain itinerant—wanderers exploring far-flung territories so as to bring the word of Christ to those most in need of His gospel.

"Some Observatines knuckled under and even became the pope's envoys on forays to the Levant in order to gain troops and money for a crusade against the increasingly aggressive Ottoman empire. At the time, the Ottoman's powerful navy was taking the islands of the eastern Mediterranean and had begun to threaten even the Republic of Venice.

"But the Gnostic Observatines resisted the pope's edicts for them to renounce their apostolic poverty. They refused and, at length, they had no choice but to flee, going underground. The pope, angered, sent one of his military orders—the Knights of St. Clement, based in Rhodes— in an effort to once and for all bring them to heel."

"For those few of us academics who remember anything about the Gnostic Observatines at all, that is what passes for common historical knowledge. It is correct in the general, but false in its particulars," Jenny said. "Long before the official schism was recorded in history, an internal battle arose, leading to a horribly acrimonious secret rift in the Order. This was scarcely surprising. From the first, the Dominicans and Benedictines, the older and more established orders, aligned themselves against us."

"Why, exactly?"

"For the same reason I was drawn to the Order," she said. The trees left only small ovals of sunlight winking through the rich green of the leaves, through which they picked their way, side by side, like lovers on their way to a trysting place. "We had an advantage in being formed later than the other orders. We had the benefit of William of Ockham."

"Ockham's razor."

"A theory that followed an Aristotelian path different from Thomas Aquinas's faith-based doctrine. Aquinas had moved beyond Aristotle in saying that when we understand the laws of nature we begin to perceive God's plan. 'Ockham's razor' argued that Aquinas was dead wrong: by insisting that reason was the path to unlocking God's intentions, he had demystified God. So a split was formed that would exist forever more.

"The Order followed Ockham in believing in the basic separation of faith and reason, religious doctrine and scientific investigation. How can an astronomer deduce from the orbits of the planets God's design? How can man, using concepts created by the mind of man, possibly come to know God's will?"

Nearing its end, the path pitched gently down toward a low-lying field that bordered a placid-looking pond, drowsing in the heavy sunlight. A high stone wall, the farthest limit of the cemetery, was in sight. The gravestones were thin and flinty, with the bony shoulders of extreme age. Some were so obscured by lichen and moss that it was virtually impossible to decipher the inscriptions. Just beyond, where the path ended not far from the stone wall, hunkered a final mausoleum, quite plain. A jagged crack ran up the left side, as if at some time in the distant past it had been dealt a violent blow by vandals. The ancient stone was as rough as a carpenter's palm. The elbow of a tenacious weeping willow root had inveigled its way into the foundation, as if nature itself was making a bid to reclaim what man had sought to preserve.

A small dark bronze door presented itself to them, above which was a stone pediment, wide and low-pitched, blackened by the elements and acid rain, a triangle of sorts in the center of which, thrust into shadow, was etched a name: MARCUS.

As they stood looking up at the name, Jenny said, "What you may not know is that the rift had been predicted—some have said prophesied—by the twelfth century abbot Joachim of Fiore. Fiore had written a number of compelling apocalyptic tracts which trumpeted a coming age of the Holy Spirit, when the Church would be reformed by two religious Orders, one living in apostolic poverty. Between 1247 and 1257, Giovanni Burelli of Parma was the Minister General of the uneasy Franciscans. He was summarily deposed because he was close to the Spirituals, a sect of Franciscans from whose ranks the founders of the Order would eventually come. The Spirituals were followers of Joachim of Fiore, whose writings echoed precisely their main doctrine and complaint against the rest of the Franciscans. In 1257, the pope ordered Giovanni of Parma to resign, exiling him to Greccio."

Bravo nodded. "I'm familiar with these facts. He was sent to La Cerceri, the Franciscan hermitage on Monte Subasio near Assisi. He was incarcerated there for the rest of his natural life."

"Or so it was reported to the pope." She took out a key, placed it into the lock on the bronze door. "This is where your knowledge ends, this is where the secret history begins."

She opened the door, and they stepped inside. They were greeted by the smell of must and air seeming as old as the mausoleum itself. At first, he thought the inside was clad in sheets of marble, but on closer inspection, he discovered that walls were in fact plaster, painted in a faux marble pattern as beautiful as it was cunning. A pair of bronze crypt doors were set flush with the wall. They were long and narrow to accommodate the caskets within which rested the remains of the dead. At intervals, just above eye level, there were old-fashioned wrought-iron sconces along the walls, some with lights, others obviously receptacles for flowers, for there hung from two of these the glass-encased withered remains of poppies and irises like skeletons in a haunted house.

"In fact, Giovanni was never a prisoner," Jenny continued as she lit the lamps. "As it happened, a number of the friars in charge of La Cerceri were Spirituals. They were not only sympathetic to Giovanni but were instrumental in installing him as the *Magister Regens* of the Order, which was even then gathering to it secret followers."

Bravo gestured. "But this is a Jewish cemetery, the family name on this mausoleum is Marcus."

Jenny gave him the ghost of a smile, her strong white teeth showing. "Giovanni of Parma had a sister, Marcella. She fell in love with a painter by the name Paolo di Cione, but it wasn't until after they were married that he told her that he was an Italian Jew, that his family name was Marcus."

She put the flat of her hand against one wall. "You see, Bravo, it wasn't simply our insistence on apostolic poverty that so angered the pope that he sent his private army to hunt us down. The Order has a secret—one so important, so potentially dangerous, that only the members of the Haute Cour knew of its existence.

"Consider the logic of it. The Order had taken a vow of poverty and therefore couldn't own anything, as the other orders did. How, then, were we to survive? It was Marcella, Giovanni of Parma's sister, who came up with the solution. It happened that before he was deposed, the pope allowed Giovanni to pick his successor. He chose Bonaventura Fidanza. It was widely believed that Giovanni chose this master at the university of Paris because they were friends, but in reality it was because Marcella knew that Bonaventura had violated his vow of chastity and fathered a child by Marcella's cousin. This secret she confided to her brother, and thereafter the acquisition of certain select secrets became the currency by which the Order continued their work.

"Eventually, as I told you, the cache became a litany of the evil in the world. The important thing to keep in mind now is that with the power of these secrets we were often able, as I said, to influence kings, merchant-princes, generals—at times, if we were very clever and very lucky the course of history was altered by our intervention. We protected those with knowledge, scientists and writers, independent thinkers born ahead of their time who otherwise would have been persecuted, burned at the stake, publicly flogged or hanged. We hid firebrands, muckrakers and whistleblowers so that they could continue exposing the workings of dirty politics, revealing difficult truths. Of course, we didn't always succeed, but we always did our best to work for the greater good of mankind. Still, our work made us anathema to the Vatican, which is a storehouse of secrets, lies and repression."

Jenny's face was half in shadow. Her gray eyes were very large and in them floated motes the same color as the freckles that dusted the bridge of her nose.

"And then, there came into our possession an artifact so valuable that the Haute Cour was compelled to move the entire cache, to protect it with multiple measures. By tradition, two men possessed the key to the cache and the knowledge of where the cache was buried: the *Magister Regens* and one from among the Haute Cour whom they called the Keeper."

Several strands of hair, glowing like live copper, had come loose from her ponytail, riding against the surge of her cheek, and she pushed them behind her ear. "The Keeper is special, Bravo, never more so than now. There has been no *Magister Regens* for decades. The Haute Cour governs the Order now. The Keeper is the official key-bearer, but there was one other from the Haute Cour used as a backup, should anything happen to the Keeper."

"You said *was*."

"The backup was a man named Jon Molko. He was the first taken and tortured by the Knights. When they discovered he wouldn't talk, they killed him, just moments before your father found him."

"What happened to Molko's key?"

"We don't know."

Bravo put his hand in his pocket, fingered the strange key his father had given him six months ago in Paris. His father's key. But what about Molko's key? Did the Knights of St. Clement have it?

"Our cache of secrets," Jenny was saying. "All that keeps us strong, all that will keep us strong is in the Keeper's hands. This awesome responsibility, this terrible burden was handed down from one Keeper to the next through a process of meticulous and painstaking selection." She moved her head back and forth in an intimation of wariness, and the ruddy lights glimmered on her skin, burnished her in a glow that seemed centuries old. Her lips, bright crimson, were half-parted, and her voice, when she continued, was breathless. "Bravo, your father was the Keeper of all the Order's secrets."

IT was a curious thing, but the only time Donatella felt at peace was when she was in a graveyard. For this reason she had made herself familiar with the cemeteries in every city to which she had traveled. DC was no exception, and though the area had an inordinate number of cemeteries, at one time or another she had explored them all, in sunlight and moonlight, in rain, snow and fog. And, in truth, there was none she knew better than Miamonides. It had been a long-held belief of hers that an important secret held by the Gnostic Observatines resided in the Marcus mausoleum—the tomb of the sainted Fra Leoni, a personal touchstone for every member of the Order—but not even the last two members of the Order's Haute Cour she and Rossi had dispatched had been able to provide confirmation. A pity, because raiding that tomb would be a psychological blow from which, she was certain, the Order would not recover.

Now, as she realized where the Guardian was taking Braverman Shaw, she felt a slight tremor ripple down her spine, making her tingle. She and Rossi were moving between the mausoleums, on a line more or less parallel with the path down which their quarry walked. They had to be extremely careful, for the Guardian was being exceptionally watchful and, though Rossi might unconsciously underestimate her, Donatella was determined that she would not.

Rossi had no tolerance for anything he perceived as weakness. His faith in Donatella was absolute—a curious anomaly in his feelings about women—and she had no intention of giving him the slightest cause to doubt that faith.

When she saw the Guardian take Braverman Shaw into the Marcus mausoleum she could hardly contain herself. As if sensing her extreme excitement, Rossi approached her and, curling his fingers around her forearm, said softly in Italian, "You won't forget yourself, will you?" His eyes sought hers, engaged them. In his gaze were all the terrible incidents of their shared past, all the pain and despair, all the blood taken and spilled. To him, her vulpine eyes were like a looking glass in which he saw the best of himself and at the same time recognized the worst. "We have our orders, we cannot deviate from them, yes?"

She nodded, but her mouth was dry and her pulse was heavy in the side of her neck. His fingertips on her carotid picked up the throb as if it were a seismic shift. "This is how you are when we're about to have sex," he said softly. "Your eyes change color, your pores exude an intimate odor, and I know that you're ready." He leaned toward her, his nostrils dilating as he inhaled. "You see? But still I must wonder what complex changes take place inside you."

Mutely, she dug in her pocket, produced a small matte-black canister, which she held like a conjurer between thumb and forefinger. Rossi smiled, releasing her.

Weapon drawn, ready, she headed toward her heart's desire.

"FAITH is a tree, growing new branches even in the face of a storm," Emma had said. *"There is a plan for us."* Was she right, Bravo asked himself now, or was this nothing more than a mirage?

But no. At long last, it seemed that he was beginning to understand his father—why Dexter had encouraged the study of medieval religions, why he was bitterly disappointed when Bravo abandoned those studies, his antipathy toward Jordan Muhlmann, who, Bravo could see now, he blamed for leading his son astray. In the case of Jordan, it was a monumental misunderstanding, and Bravo wished more than anything that his father were standing beside him so that he could explain the nature of his deep and abiding friendship with Jordan.

"You said there was one secret greater than all the rest," he said now. "What is it?"

"I don't know," Jenny said in that perfectly sincere voice of hers.

He did not believe her, but perhaps there was a good reason for her lie. The wariness between them likely flowed both ways.

"You still haven't told me why you brought me here." His carefully neutral tone was an attempt to draw her out. "You could have told me the history of the Order anywhere."

"True enough." Her fingertips moved over the veining of the faux marble walls with the questing delicacy of a safecracker's. The rest of her, however, was utterly still. "But there is the question of initiation."

"Initiation?"

"Congratulations. You've just become the most important human being on earth."

He stared at her, for the moment unable to speak or even to think clearly.

Jenny turned toward him, her pale, slightly upturned eyes glimmering through the semidarkness of the antique masonry. He recognized in her glance, in the way she stood, a certain complicity. Entombed together in the intimate blood-temperature warmth, they seemed to be moving in concert, returning in ritual fashion not only to the Order's storied history but to Dexter Shaw's lifelong conspiracy. And all at once tears sprang into his eyes because in a sense gloriously real to him, his father was being resurrected before his very eyes.

Her head dipped and the strands of hair came free again, fiery in the lamplight, curled against the ripe duskiness of her cheek. She took his hand to transmit to him, he assumed, her utter stillness. But instead he felt a vibration of intensity so extreme it quickened his blood; he became aware of her intent, as if, like the young woman in the portrait in her house, she was an arrow in a tautly drawn bow, about to be released.

"There is much to do and I doubt that we have much time."

As if to underscore her words, there came a hollow sound, ugly and thoroughly unmusical, as a small, matte-black canister hit the stone floor and began rolling toward them. Then the door to the mausoleum slammed shut.

Bravo ran to the door, but it was shut tight; they were trapped. A soft hiss made him turn, and he saw the tear gas foaming out of the canister, a venomous wave that surged toward them.

5

DONATELLA AND ROSSI, THEIR FACES MADE BESTIAL BY black and silver snouts, burst through the bronze mausoleum door. They had waited for precisely three minutes before they had donned the gas masks. Then they had heaved open the heavy door. Weapons at the ready, they rushed inside, taking up first positions, Rossi just inside the door, Donatella into the western corner.

The atmosphere was that of a building after a fire. The gas, having dispersed, now hung in gauzy tiers like industrial smog, obscuring the ceiling. Nevertheless, there was no doubt that they were the only two living people occupying the mausoleum. They glanced at each other. Even through the lenses of the eye pieces, they could read the consternation and anger in each other's eyes.

"They're here," Rossi said, his voice slightly muffled.

Donatella walked along the western wall, eyeing the plaster with its constellations of faux striations. "The Order is fond of secret escape routes." Her head swung around. "You know what to do now."

Rossi, near the doorway, stood in the last of the afternoon's ruddy light. "Now that the time has come, I find I don't want to leave you."

She lifted the gun into his line of vision, deliberately tapped the butt against the rear wall. "You're wasting time."

He grunted and disappeared through the open doorway.

"Now," Donatella said softly, as she returned to the problem at hand, "where are you, my little cockroaches?"

WHEN the canister hit the floor, Jenny and Bravo had at once held their breath. Nevertheless, their eyes had begun to sting and tear, and the delicate flesh of their nostrils swelled painfully. Jenny had turned to the lower of the two crypt doors and with arms spread wide, depressed a pair of hidden studs, all but invisible in the complex pattern of faux veining.

The bronze door had opened, revealing not the mahogany side of a coffin but a swath of mysterious darkness. Already an ache had begun deep in his lungs as his body called out for oxygen. He did not think that they could hold their breath much longer. Apparently, Jenny had come to the same conclusion because she gestured toward the opening. He climbed in, making sure not to hit his head. He was reaching his hand up to feel the surface of the low ceiling—and fighting claustrophobia—when he felt her climb in beside him, and he inched himself further into the recess. In a brief aureole of light, he saw her fingers work something, then the heavy crypt door swung shut. This was accompanied by a peculiar sound, as of air hissing from a damaged tire, and with a renewed surge of claustrophobia, he realized that an air-tight seal had been activated, the better to preserve the mortal remains of the entombed loved ones. Then, as panic was about to set in, he saw Jenny's face as she switched on her pencil flashlight. A sly smile crossed her oval face. And then he understood—the air seal was what would save them from the tear gas. No matter how saturated the inside of the mausoleum got, the gas could not affect them in here.

They started as the sharp report came to them from the other side of the casket door. Bravo felt sweat break out on his skin, but his mouth was abnormally dry. He remembered his father telling him of the terror-filled moments just before the desperate retreat from the Nairobi embassy. *"I was sweating all over, but curiously, my mouth was dry. Fear does that to you, Bravo. And I was relieved, which you might find even more curious, but the truth is, those who aren't afraid wind up dead."*

AT close range Donatella examined the two casket doors, tapping here and there, softly, softly in a rhythmic pattern, her head cocked all the while, her ear close enough to evaluate the sounds returning from her gentle probing.

All at once her eyes widened and she drew out of her pocket a length of a puttylike material. Without haste, she worked the pliable material into the hinges of the lower casket door. She flipped open a lighter and held the flame against one end of the material until with a bright flash it began to burn with a devastating heat. She smiled and, with grim satisfaction, said, "Yes, indeed, I have you now."

ANOTHER noise came to them, an evil sound as of the hollow rattle of a poisonous serpent, and then a blast of heat like the livid flame of a blowtorch was transmitted by the metal.

He heard her voice, soft but filled with urgency, "They're melting the hinges off the door. Quickly, now! Go!"

In the brief flare of the penlight he saw her point across his chest to his right, and in an awkward sort of wriggle he began to move, but to where? he wondered.

As if divining his question, she used the narrow beam of her penlight in lieu of words. Turning his head, he saw a passageway that sloped steeply downward, presumably below the mausoleum's foundation. As he wriggled his way toward it he marveled at the ingenuity, for the escape route must have been devised at the time of the mausoleum's construction.

Bravo crawled through the darkness, hemmed in on every side, with the unseen but very much heard enemy howling at his heels. The mineral scent of wet limestone mingled with the odors of decomposition that conjured up images of freshly turned earth, leaf mold, corkscrewed worms and ash. With Jenny close against his spine, he experienced a sense of the space ahead narrowing even further until it was no larger than his own body, and he discovered a fear inside himself, irrational and therefore overwhelming, that he was going to become stuck in this tunnel, unable either to move forward or back.

"What is it?" Jenny whispered in his ear. "Why have you stopped?"

Bravo said nothing. At the same time, he felt incapable of moving.

The heat seemed to follow them, growing in intensity. And with it he thought he could discern the first crack of light as the hinges on the casket door gave out.

Sensing his paralysis, Jenny said, "Lie flat on your back." She slithered atop him. "Press your shoulder blades against the floor." She stared down at him, her breasts flattened against his chest, her breath quick on his cheek. Her heat began to seep into him. There was nowhere left for him to move. Terror crept through him, primitive and compelling, and he fought to keep it at bay lest it lock him in its vise.

"Bravo!"

Light now, definitely, a sliver like the blade of a knife. And then, startlingly, a female voice—undoubtedly Donatella's—sang in a lilting alto, "Come out, come out wherever you are. . . ."

Jenny was gripping his jaw, her eyes boring into him, willing him to comply. As if in a dream he did as she asked, exhaling deeply, and after a moment of slow and torturous maneuvering, he felt her sliding, hips first, then midriff and shoulders, onto the far side.

She took his hand in hers, squeezed it briefly. "It gets wider from here."

Belatedly, he understood. She was ahead of him, in a position to lead them on and, hopefully, out.

The tunnel's ceiling did get higher, but not by much. At the same time the downward slope grew steeper, so that they half slid, half tumbled in a blur of sickening motion, scraped elbows and bruised hips. Bravo recognized a certain grimness to their flight. Like an animal being brought to bay, he felt the pressure of pursuit, as well as the terrible consequences should they be caught.

At length, there was enough room for them to crawl on hands and knees, though every so often the rough ceiling scraped across his back, further abrading his clothes. He felt a growing desire to look back, to judge the progress of their pursuit, but that would have meant stopping. In any case, there was no room to simply look over his shoulder.

They came at last to the end of the tunnel, were faced by a cement wall seeping water. Directly in front of it was an iron ladder that rose vertically and disappeared into what, in the limited light from the pencil flash, seemed to be misty infinity.

Without hesitation, Jenny grasped the rungs and hauled herself upward. Bravo scrambled after her. Just before he rose off the floor of the tunnel, he saw a piercing flash of light coming from behind them.

Jenny, climbing quickly and surely, soon reached the upper reaches of the escape route, which was a circular section of stones—a well, Bravo soon saw. In seconds, they emerged from the wellhead into a small clearing surrounded by dense underbrush and just beyond a pair of massive weeping willows, which provided natural cover and a kind of bower that, rising up and falling in a profusion of cascades, blocked out sun and sky.

The ground was uneven here. To their left, it sloped away steeply; to their right, it rose toward a flat plateau above which the oldest of the headstones could be made out through the trees.

Jenny gave him a small, tight smile of encouragement and began to lead them up toward the graves. At that moment, there was a small rustling off to their left, and Rossi appeared from behind the bole of one of the willows. He was holding a handgun at arm's length, aiming it with his left hand cupped beneath the butt to hold the weapon steady.

Bravo called out, his voice sharp in warning. Jenny was in the process of turning when Rossi fired. She spun toward Bravo, her eyes wide and staring blankly. Then her knees buckled and she toppled over into the grass.

At once, Rossi swiveled toward Bravo, who turned on his heel and took off in a ragged zigzag down the slope toward the sanctuary of the other willow. Something flew by his ear, and he flung himself sideways, tripped over a root and went sprawling head over heels down the slope.

There came a furious crashing behind him, as of a beast run amok. It was Rossi tearing full tilt after him, his head and torso pitched backward to keep himself upright. But at that pace there was no chance to get off a second shot.

Bravo, his attention divided between front and rear, stumbled as his shoe sole skidded off a rock slick with damp moss. Instinctively, he extended an arm, and a jolt of pain shot up from his hand as he went down hard. He was on the bank of the lake by this time, the ground steeply pitched, but his fall had slowed his forward momentum considerably, so that Rossi overtook him with heart-stopping suddenness.

Partly out of instinct, partly out of self-defense, Bravo extended his upper leg. Rossi, in the process of trying to forestall his headlong momentum, was unable to avoid tripping over it. At once Bravo was on him. Caught up in the other's momentum, Bravo found himself rolling over and over as he struggled to keep his grip on Rossi's gun wrist. Faster and faster they spun, locked in a death grip. Weeds whipped by them and mud flew off them as they kicked and clawed at each other, teeth bared, hearts hammering in their chests. They might have been two beasts fighting over territory, over a female, a breeding ground. Fists hammered against muscle and bone—they fought for the advantage of position as well as for the killing blow. Intellect was swept away in the dark undertow of primitive instinct. Preoccupied with survival, they plunged into the lake and immediately disappeared beneath the water. The water became an enemy to them both, slowing them down, entangling them, drawing them down into its airless embrace.

Spray flew as they rose up out of the lake, gasping, locked together. They slipped and slid on the gluey bottom. As they were toppling over, Rossi slammed his forehead into the bridge of Bravo's nose. Bravo felt as if he had been struck by lightning. He must have blacked out for an instant because the next thing he knew, he was under the water again. He gasped, taking in water, choked.

There was a restriction around his throat: Rossi's hands clamped against his windpipe. Rossi was pressing down, knees drawn up as weapons, all his weight centered on Bravo's chest. Bravo struggled, could see nothing through the churned-up water. Desperately he tried to pry Rossi's hands from his throat, but the fingers were like iron, and in his position he lacked leverage.

He began to see spots in front of his eyes, first white, then black; consciousness flickered in and out and he felt a growing lassitude in his extremities. And from this painless place a thought curled like a serpent: Why not let it all go? Why not close his eyes and just drift away?

Arms splayed out, Bravo knew that he was dying. And still, as if working of their own volition, his hands moved crabwise, the half-curled fingers scrabbling through the silt into which Rossi was in the process of burying him. It took him a moment to recognize the feeling transmitted through the fingertips of his left hand to his half-numbed brain. Then he curled his fingers, grasping the hard object, swinging his arm up and around, slamming the object as hard as he could into the orbital bone just above Rossi's left eye.

Rossi, thrashing in pain, relinquished his grip on his throat. Gathering all that remained of his strength, Bravo rose off the lake bed, gasping in a great lungful of air as he swung again. He saw what he held—Rossi's own gun, abandoned in the heat of the hand-to-hand combat—and he brought it down against the vulnerable spot just above Rossi's ear.

Rossi went down, thrashing, but one claw-fingered hand grabbed the front of Bravo's sodden shirt, took him off his feet, back under the water. Rossi struck out blindly, his fist catching Bravo on the cheek and side of the neck. Bravo staggered, felt a wave of dizziness threaten to overwhelm him. Rossi was turning, trying to reverse their positions so that he was once again on top. If he managed that, Bravo knew that he was finished. As blind as Rossi, he reached out. His nails scratched for purchase on the skull, caught at the thick hair and held on as he struck Rossi again and again with the butt of the gun. Finally, there was no more movement left.

More than anything now Bravo needed air. He rose up, but even in death Rossi kept his grip on the front of his shirt. He tried to pry the fingers loose, failed, began to frantically tear off his shirt, but the oxygen in his lungs was giving out, the silty floor of the lake was sucking him down, and he knew he wouldn't make it.

Then, at the last possible instant, hands reached down from above, plunging through the murk, grasping him, hauling with relentless strength. Bubbles streaming from between clenched teeth, he grasped the hairless forearms, female forearms, capable and powerful, and he knew that Donatella had found him and that now that he had killed her lover nothing could save him.

6

HE HAD THE PRESENCE OF MIND TO USE THE ONLY WEAPON at his disposal. But in his depleted condition Rossi's gun seemed as heavy and unwieldy as a refrigerator, and even as he lifted it, a blow to the inside of his wrist defeated his wavering aim. It was not a hard blow, and he wondered at that even as he heard a voice.

"Bravo . . . where is Rossi?"

A female voice, Donatella. Of course she wanted to know where her lover was. If he told her . . . He began to fight and was restrained. A familiar voice—had he heard Donatella speak before? He could not remember, but he must have because she was shaking him now. He wanted to see her face, to look into the eyes of the woman who was going to kill him, but there was water streaming across his face, and bits of mud and debris from the lake. Still he fought, though pinned, because it was the only thing he could think of to do.

"Rossi, Bravo . . . Bravo!"

A hand wiped across his face, clearing his vision, and that voice—of course it was familiar. He found himself staring up into a face as familiar as the voice.

"Jenny," he said. She was straddling him, fingers curled around each of his wrists, pinioning him to the ground. "I saw Rossi shoot you. You fell and . . ."

She leaned over, her eyes fever-bright. "Bravo, where is Rossi?"

"Dead. Rossi's dead. But you . . ."

"That's right, I'm bruised but unhurt."

He stared, wide-eyed, as she opened her blouse partway so that he could see the puffy bruise, already turning livid, around her collarbone.

"I . . . I don't understand. The bullet should have torn you apart."

She took Rossi's gun from his hand, ejected the ammo from the chamber, and held it out to him. "Not if it was a rubber bullet."

He sat up then, coughed as she scrambled off him, gave him a hand up. Taking one of the bullets from her palm, he rolled it between his fingers, as if the tactile sensation would help him to understand. "But why would Rossi use rubber bullets?"

"I don't know," Jenny said, "but let's not debate the issue here. We're too exposed and Donatella can't be far away."

Donatella! He looked around. Splashes of light drifted through the leaves of the weeping willow. He looked back up the slope toward the mausoleum, hidden by the trees and underbrush. At any moment Donatella could appear. It was a miracle that she hadn't already. He nodded, then allowed Jenny to lead him around the northern edge of the lake, through a thick copse of beech trees to a low stone wall over which they clambered. His head felt as if at any moment it was going to explode, and he could feel every blow Rossi had delivered like electric shocks running through him with each step he took.

Once on the other side of the wall, they were confronted by a narrow line of river maples beyond which was a road. They could hear the whirr and hiss of two-way traffic, reminding them of the normal world that existed all around them. For a moment, Bravo leaned back against the rough stones of the wall. He felt their age seeping into him, and he listened, as if they had a tale to tell him.

"Bravo, we have to keep moving," Jenny said with some urgency.

He knew that, of course, but he remained where he was. It was imperative that he regain his inner equilibrium, but he was gripped by despair. He had just killed a man. Whether or not that man was also trying to kill him was, in a way, beside the point. It came to him that he had crossed some profound moral boundary, and now, belatedly, he wondered whether his father had had to kill a Knight of St. Clement to protect himself or the Order's cache of secrets. Now, an idea that would once have struck him as unthinkable did not seem in the least shocking. In fact, it seemed probable, and somehow this notion was like a beacon piercing the black despair. In his mind, this connection to the other, secret world that his father had inhabited was like a lifeline, and the moment he grabbed it he felt himself stand up straight. Seconds later, he was following Jenny through the grass and hedges, through the thin line of the flaky-barked maples to the verge of the road.

AT last, Donatella emerged from the wellhead. Because of the mechanism that hermetically sealed the interior of the crypt, it had taken her far longer to get through the bronze casket door than she had estimated. Precious time when her quarry was moving farther away from her. She consoled herself with the thought that every step they took brought them closer to Rossi, but, truth be told, she didn't want Rossi to get to them first. She wanted that pleasure all to herself. She'd known it as soon as she had flirted with Braverman Shaw on the street. Drawing attention to herself had been a stupid thing to do, she'd known when she'd smiled at him, but she couldn't help herself. There had been something in him, some deeply suppressed animal part she had recognized instantly and responded to. There had been something profoundly intimate—primal—in that moment, two animals scenting each other in the forest, that she now carried around with her like a photo in a locket.

Just as she carried Ivo's essence with her wherever she went. Her isolation was what made him so vital to her existence. Nothing else mattered but Ivo—and, of course, their prey. She and Ivo had sacrificed for one another, tended one another when they were ill. They had killed together, and when they came together it was with the incandescence of the sun.

The way ahead of her sloped downward toward a veil of weeping willows beyond which was the lake. There were three sets of footprints, prey followed by hunter. She followed them down the slope until she saw something that gave her pause. Squatting, she ran her hand over the muddy surface where, she was certain, there had been a struggle. Immediately, her head snapped up and with narrowed eyes looked all around her. Then, her body tense, her gun cocked and ready, she rose, following the rolling trail down to the edge of the lake.

There she stood, the water lapping at her boots, while she stared out at the placid vista. A pair of ducks quartering in from the southwest landed with a small flurry, began to paddle across the water toward a group of nesting mallards. There came across the lake a brief quacking, and then all was still. The last of the afternoon light was reflected in the water, giving it a ruddy hue.

Suddenly, her attention was directed toward a disturbance just where the water was reddest, a stirring as of fish nearing the surface, preparing to feast on water spiders and gnats. A moment later, a curved shape broke the surface, wheat-colored and slick-looking. Then it rolled; a Roman nose appeared, then lips and cheeks.

Donatella stood absolutely still, but it seemed to her that the thunder of her heart must shatter her into pieces. No, she told herself, it couldn't be. But then the face turned its blank eyes toward her and she ran, unmindful, into the water. The muck of the bottom pulled at her, slowed her down, making her powerful thighs work all the harder. At length, she reached him, cradled his battered head in her hands. When she kissed his cold and rubbery lips an ice pick pierced her heart.

She opened her mouth and threw back her head. Air filled her lungs and his name was ripped out of her.

"Ivo!"

A void yawned inside her that could only be filled by blood vengeance.

BRAVO and Jenny, on their way toward the cemetery's maintenance building, heard the animal howl, and their blood turned cold. They looked at one another but could not bring themselves to utter Donatella's name.

Hurrying along, they arrived without incident at the low brooding building. While Bravo stayed out of sight, Jenny went to reconnoiter. Bravo leaned against a huge chestnut tree and, despite the heat, shivered. Now that the shock was wearing off, the pain rushed through him like a tide, pulsing stronger with each beat of his heart. It was difficult to get Rossi's rage-filled face out of his head. He had never before encountered someone with the will and desire to kill another human being. A chilling memory he would take with him to the grave.

At the sudden throaty roar of a large engine his head snapped up. He saw a hearse moving slowly toward him, and he shrank back. Then the driver's side window rolled down—it was Jenny who was behind the wheel. The hearse slowed, and he loped out from behind the chestnut tree, opened the heavy door and slid in beside her on the bench seat. The moment he slammed the door, she took off in a spray of gravel.

She maneuvered the unwieldy vehicle out of the cemetery precincts. He did not ask her how she had managed to steal the hearse; he didn't want to know and, oddly, didn't much care. She had once again found them a means of escape, that was all that mattered.

"You said that Rossi was dead. What happened after he shot me?"

"I ran," he said. "I ran and like an idiot I fell. He came after me and I tripped him. We went into the lake. He was going to kill me, I could see it in his eyes, I could feel it with every blow."

Jenny let air out of her pursed lips. "Rossi's a trained killer. And yet you survived. . . ."

"Maybe I was lucky, I don't know. I killed him, that's the bottom line."

"You did what you had to do. Your father trained you well."

He was sickened by the look of admiration she gave him, so he turned away, gazed out the smoked window. What was he doing here? He had been pursued, beaten up—he had killed a man. For what? This was his father's battle, but was it his? He realized that he could walk out of here now, buy some new clothes and fly back to Paris, resume his job as if nothing had happened. Everything appeared dark, behind a veil, part of another country through which he seemed to be shooting like a meteor. He wondered whether this feeling of separation was something his father had ever experienced. That was when he understood that something had happened, not only to his father but to him, as well. Strange as it might seem, he was no longer the person who had met his father in the Village for coffee.

"I told you this was urgent."

"I heard you, Dad."

But he hadn't heard his father, not really. And now, even from the grave, his father was again talking to him.

"The first time is always the hardest," Jenny said, misinterpreting his deep silence.

He stiffened. "I don't intend for it to happen again."

"An admirable sentiment, but did Rossi give you a choice?"

"Those were extraordinary circumstances. I don't foresee—"

"No one in his right mind foresees the taking of a life." Her eyes were focused on the road ahead. "But consider this. In the outside world there would be no reason to even have this conversation. You're no longer in society—the world everyone else inhabits, Bravo. You're in the Voire Dei, for good or ill, and believe me the sooner you come to terms with that, the better your chance of surviving will be."

He stared blankly out at the ribbon of landscape whizzing by. He did not want to think about that now—he simply couldn't process it yet, despite Jenny's warning. Instead, as was his habit when he was upset, he set his mind a specific task—that is, to understand why Rossi's gun had been loaded with rubber bullets. And almost immediately a memory popped into his head: Rossi pushing down the gunman's arm as they sped away from Jenny's house. He had not wanted them shot then, and he hadn't wanted to kill Jenny, either. And yet there was no mistaking the set grimace on his face as he'd grappled with Bravo in the lake—had Bravo pushed him over the brink?

He licked his lips, said to Jenny, "I don't think Rossi and Donatella had orders to kill us."

This comment caught Jenny's attention. "What makes you say that?"

"The rubber bullets for one," he said. Then he told her what he had seen as they had sped away from her house.

"Of course!" Jenny said. "They think you know everything your father knew. They want to capture you and get the information out of you."

"But I don't have any information."

"You know that and so do I," she said, "but it's clear they don't."

"Then we have to find a way to tell them."

Jenny laughed harshly and shook her head. "You heard Donatella back there. Do you really think she'd believe you?"

"But it's the truth!"

Jenny glanced over at him, her eyes hard. "In the Voire Dei, there *is* no truth, Bravo. There's only perception. Donatella and those who control her will believe what they want to believe, what best fits their perception of reality."

Was there another way out for him? he wondered. Or was he fated to continue on with this nightmare?

You're no longer in the world everyone else inhabits.

With the words echoing in his head, he rolled down the window and stared out at the passing landscape. Over the white noise of their passage, he said, "How do you bear such a terrible burden?"

She knew precisely what he meant. "Some like it, you know. The Voire Dei is the only place they feel safe. Others revel in it. In fact, they know of no other way to live. For them, society is pale, indistinct, of minimal interest. They feel privileged to be part of the Voire Dei."

"What do you feel?"

They had left the Falls Church area far behind. Jenny took a turning to the left, went perhaps a half mile into an area of increasingly large and luxurious houses. The hearse navigated a long, snaking road that rose toward the crest of a hill. A half mile on she made a right into one of a number of sweeping streets of large Colonial houses with slate roofs, formal English gardens and impeccably manicured lawns. She pulled into the driveway of a cream-colored two-story house with front columns and an imposing porte cochere. Past that, on the side of the house, was a three-car garage, on the other side of which was a small windowless gardener's shed. She stopped on the concrete apron directly in front of the garage doors and got out. To one side of the leftmost door was a small plastic box. Swinging up the protective panel, she punched in a number and one of the garage doors opened. She got back behind the wheel, drove the hearse into the garage and shut the door. Next to them was a Mercedes convertible.

"My father's house," she said, leading him inside.

"Isn't this the first place Donatella is likely to look for us?"

"The neighborhood is patrolled by members of a private security firm. All the men are ex-cops and they know every face in the neighborhood."

Bravo was astonished. "You can't seriously believe that will stop Donatella."

She heard the edge to his voice. "I don't think you're in any position to make that decision."

"After what we've just been through I sure as hell wouldn't put us in more danger, if I were you. I say let's get out of here."

She put a key into a lock and opened a door. "As a Guardian it's my duty to protect the Order and the members of the Haute Cour." Stepping into the darkened room, she turned to face him. "I promised your father I would protect you, but if you renounce the Order, renounce the role your father trained you for, then my obligation to him is done."

A swath of harsh light banded her face, turning her features hawklike, almost predatory. Her eyes were steady, her expression determined. If she was bluffing, Bravo couldn't detect it. He made to turn; it was important to see how far she would go.

"Have you forgotten your father's glasses? If you leave now, how will you find out what he left for you?"

He turned back. "Where is the Order now that we need them, where are its resources? The Order must have any number of safe houses we can use to hide out in."

"I think you should concentrate on the business at hand," she said coolly. "Leave the rest to me."

"If I left Rossi to you," he said unkindly, "I'd be dead."

"Then surely you don't need me." She turned, but not before he saw the hurt in her eyes. He waited as she disappeared into the darkness.

"Why won't you tell me what I want to know?" he called out.

"Why do you think?"

He could turn now and walk away, but would that put Rossi's death behind him? What's done is done, he told himself. I go back to Paris now, back to my old life. It would be so easy.

But it wasn't easy. He felt rooted to the spot, unable to turn around, let alone walk away. He thought of his father, thought of the way in which he had misjudged everything about him. He'd allowed his own selfish emotions to blind him to the truth. His father was involved in something so important Bravo felt himself enveloped by it. But he also knew that the biggest mistake he could make now was to fight his father's fight out of guilt. He'd end up dead, like as not. No, he had to do this because he wanted to.

Without even consciously realizing what he was doing, he crossed over the threshold and entered the gloom. In darkness, he passed through a small mudroom whose walls were ribboned with wooden pegs on which hung various caps and hats, windbreakers and golf sweaters, before reaching a large country-style kitchen with its center island of blond beechwood and pale granite. There were acres of cupboards and an old-fashioned bay window, beneath which was a padded window seat. They stood in shadows, listening to the small creaks and hums inside the pipes and ducts of the house.

Outside the multipaned window twilight had descended, cobalt shadows clinging to the flagstone steps, weaving themselves into the shrubbery of the garden. Lights had come on, lemony, haloed in a grainy mist that rose from the ground like a specter. Not far away a dog barked; headlights flashed as a car turned a corner. Cicadas shrilled.

He watched her as she observed the immediate environment with a professional's eye. After a time, he could see that she was analyzing the pattern of the vehicular traffic, her mind working much like that of a bridge or poker player, who is not only aware of what cards are on the table but also weighing probabilities, what might be held close to the chest.

"Are you hungry?" she said, after a time.

"Yes, but I'd like a shower more." He said it harshly, but the moment the words were out of his mouth he knew it was proof of his capitulation.

Wordlessly, she led him to a door beyond which was a standard wooden staircase down to the cellar. She pulled the door shut behind them, turned on a light. Below him was visible a swath of sea-green carpet, the rolled arm of a leather sofa, a section of bare pale-green wall. Reaching the bottom of the stairs, he could see that the place was immaculate—the furniture he'd seen, some more stacked against a wall, a refrigerator and separate freezer, a four-burner stove, a large soapstone sink and counter with a row of drawers beneath—but it was also Spartan and deliberately impersonal, like a hospital waiting room. There were no windows, only metal air grilles. The light, indirect and coolly fluorescent, drained all the colors of warmth.

Jenny showed him to a small, metal-walled bathroom. Inside, he stripped off his filthy, half-shredded clothes. As he was reaching to turn on the shower, he caught sight of his reflection in the mirror. He halted in mid stretch, appalled. His face was cut, bruised and unnaturally reddened, his body swollen, abraded and discolored in innumerable places. He hardly recognized himself, but it wasn't because of the abuse his body had taken. It was the look in his eyes, the particular depthless expression he recognized only too well—it was the look he would see in his father's eyes when the elder Shaw was about to leave home on one of his mysterious trips abroad. As a child, the expression had seemed mysterious, but now he understood what it signified: his father had tuned his gaze away from society—he was returning to the Voire Dei.

Wincing in pain, Bravo stepped into the shower, but the hot water felt unutterably delicious as it sluiced over his naked body. When he emerged, he found fresh clothes folded neatly on the toilet seat, waiting for him. Part of her dead father's wardrobe, he deduced. Opening the medicine cabinet, he found antibiotic ointment and bandages, but he was unable to apply them to the cuts and abrasions on his back. He pulled on underwear and a pair of khaki trousers, then opened the bathroom door.

Jenny had obviously taken a shower in another part of the house because like him she was dressed in fresh clothes—black jeans, black sleeveless top, thin-soled boots of a leather as supple as a ballet dancer's toe shoe. Her face was scrubbed clean and her hair, combed straight back and unbound, fell down to the hollow between her shoulder blades. It was still damp, gleamed with the bronze luster of a helmet. The solid line of her jaw gave her a diligent, almost studious aspect that lent depth and dimension to her beauty. It was the extremely rare kind of confluence that attracted Bravo. The truth was that had he spotted her across the room at a crowded party, he would have found it impossible to leave without talking to her. He had to remind himself that he hardly knew her, had no idea how much he could trust her, save for the fact that his father had trusted her—he'd deliberately steered Bravo to her. That wasn't quite enough.

She had made sandwiches, and there was a carafe of ice water and two red plastic tumblers on an old-fashioned folding bridge table to which she had pulled up a pair of metal folding chairs.

A part of him didn't want to talk to her at all. She was so willful and hardheaded. Then, astonished, he realized that it had been those two words his father had often used to describe him. He waited a moment, unsure how to proceed. In the unkind light, the duskiness of her skin turned sallow, her gray eyes receded into pools of dark shadow. Her wide mouth held no promise for him. How long could he be angry with her for the situation he was in? He felt suddenly spent, as if his anger was a candle that, having burned low, was now guttering.

Turning to reveal his lacerated back, he said, "I need your help."

She hesitated only a moment. Wordlessly, she took the ointment from him. He sat straddling the toilet, bent slightly forward while she applied the antibiotic cream. He was acutely aware of her fingertips as they moved across his shoulder blades.

"Relax," she said shortly. "It will hurt less."

At length, he said, "You never told me how *you* feel about being part of the Voire Dei."

He heard her let out a breath and wondered if part of her also wished to remain silent.

"I don't think about it at all," she said, "at least not in the way I think you mean; it's my home, just as it was my father's—and yours."

"If it means more killing, I don't know whether it's a world I can commit to."

"That's the billion-dollar question, isn't it?" The stiffness had returned to her voice, but her fingertips never stopped their motion. "I have to tell you that there are those in the Order who don't believe you will, they don't believe you don't have it in you."

"Really?"

"Don't move," she said sternly. She had begun to apply the bandages. "They don't like me and they don't trust you."

"You don't trust me, either."

"Let's say we don't yet trust each other."

He thought about the truth of her words, as well as the promise they held out. Then his mind made an abrupt leap. "Is that why the Order won't help us?"

"He was the Keeper. Part of his responsibility was to identify and train his successor." It was not an answer to his question, but for the moment at least it was all he was going to get from her.

For some time Bravo thought about what she'd just said. He had been four when his father started him on his course of physical training, six when his father began to read to him from treatises on medieval religion.

"He chose me."

"That's right." Jenny put away the ointment and bandages, washed her hands. "You can finish dressing now." She walked out of the bathroom before he could say anything more.

They sat at the rickety table, eating their sandwiches as an awkward silence settled around them. At length, Bravo wiped his hands on a paper towel and placed on the table the pair of glasses he'd found aboard the *Steffi*.

It lay between them, a symbol both of what drew them together and what had set them against one another.

"Tell me—"

"We can't go on, unless you commit." She shook her head. "It's no good, you know, blaming me or the other Guardians for mistakes we've made. Now—this moment—is all that matters, whether we go on or leave it here. If we leave, then all is lost. To you, I may sound terribly melodramatic, but the truth is I'm being as forthright as I can. The continuation of the Order, the safeguarding of the secrets that have been entrusted to us for centuries, is on your shoulders. Only you can find the cache, your father made sure of that." She took a breath. "It all boils down to whether he was right about you, or whether he made a fatal mistake."

In that moment, Bravo heard again his father's voice as if he was sitting beside him. *"A 'mistake' is something mechanical—a wrong way of acting, maneuvering, thinking. A mistake is a surface thing. But* beneath *the surface—where loss manifests itself—that's where you must begin."*

He gazed down at the glasses, trying to sort out the welter of feeling swirling inside him. As if from a distance, he saw his hand reach out, pick up the glasses and feel the weight of them in his palm.

"Jenny, I want to know something," he said slowly. "Why did you choose to join the Order? Was it because of your father?"

"My father?" A small, bruised sound escaped her lips. "My father did everything he could to stop me, because I was his delicate daughter. He even had someone picked out for me to marry, a nice, dull guy from a prominent family inside the Beltway. It sounds positively medieval, doesn't it? But there you go." She swept a wisp of hair off her face. "When he saw he couldn't dissuade me, he made things so difficult— my training would have broken a lot of men. I fractured my left ulna twice and my right tibula once, and so many bruises. . . . It was torture."

"Why did you persevere? Was it out of spite?"

She laughed. "It so easily could have been, but, no, it was something else."

"What?"

"My faith in what the Order represents: a group of sane men working in an insane world for the betterment of mankind." Her eyes flashed. "I suppose that sounds insipid to you."

"No, but it does sound idealistic."

"Maybe it is." She shook her head. "I don't know about you, Bravo, but I have to have something good to believe in. I have to believe that what I do in the world is going to make it better."

So it all boiled down to faith.

Glancing up, he saw Jenny's pale eyes regarding him steadily, curiously. There was a fervor in her voice—a tiny tremor—he recognized as coming straight from her heart. She believed every word she said to him; now it was up to him to have faith that what she had told him was the truth. It made sense to him. He knew that more than anything his father had wanted to make the world better, despite the odds—or per-haps, knowing Dexter, because of the odds. He knew it because it had been instilled in him.

It seemed to him now that he faced a looking glass that showed him how the world really worked, that shone a different light onto his life up until now. Everything he had experienced, everything that had come before was prelude, had led him to this moment.

He put the glasses gently down. "You said something before about an initiation. I think we'd better get on with it, don't you?"

"YOU know what 'cupping' is, I imagine."

"Of course," Bravo said. "Medieval physicians believed that illness—what they called 'humors'—resided deep inside the body, that they need to be brought to the surface to be expelled."

Jenny nodded. They were sitting on the folding chairs, which they had brought over to the stove, along with the card table. Apparently, she had turned on the stove some time ago, possibly when he was in the shower, for there was a pot on it, filled with water at the boil.

"Put your right arm on the table," she said, "so the inside of your forearm is exposed."

When he had done as she asked, she took up a pair of long metal tongs. Dipping them into the boiling water, she withdrew three glass items that looked like nothing more than diminutive egg cups. These she set one by one on a paper towel to dry.

"Wouldn't an autoclave be better?" he said.

Jenny gave him a dry smile. "Sometimes the ancient ways are the best ways." She brought the three cupping devices over to the table and sat down beside him.

"Ready?"

Bravo nodded.

She put one of the cupping devices onto the inside of his arm, struck a long wooden match and held the flame to the bottom of the glass. The heat from the air inside began to draw, and the skin inside the ring of glass gradually turned red.

"It isn't 'humors' we wish to draw out of you in the initiation, but obligation. Once you are a part of us there is no changing your mind, no going back. You're a part of the Order for life."

She snuffed out the match just as the cupping was beginning to burn him, he watched as she rose and, opening a drawer beneath the sink, returned with a pewter phial. Unstoppering it, she turned it over. Three seeds fell out into the center of her palm.

"These are the seeds of three trees—cypress, cedar and pine, all evergreens and in their way symbols of eternal life." She placed them one by one in his mouth. "When Adam lay dying, his son Seth placed beneath his tongue seeds from the cypress, cedar and pine that had been a gift to him by an angel. Chew them and swallow," she instructed. As he did so, she said, "It is said—and members of the Order have seen the proof of it—that the cross on which Christ died was made of wood from these three trees. This, the first of the three rites, is a symbol of your death—the severing of yourself from society, the world that you knew. Do you swear that once you enter the Voire Dei you will never seek to leave?"

"I swear," Bravo said as a wave of dizziness rushed through him.

With a deft corkscrew motion, Jenny plucked the cupping glass from his aching arm and, in almost the same gesture, placed the second one in a spot three inches from the first. She lit its bottom as she had the one before.

As his skin again grew angry and red, she said, "In the Book of Revelation, it is written: 'Satan shall be loosed out of his prison, and shall go out to deceive the nations which are in the four corners of the earth, Gog, and Magog, to gather them together to battle, the number of whom is as the sand of the sea.' The medieval map of the world found in Hereford Cathedral shows the world as a perfect circle with Jerusalem in its center, like a navel. Near one edge is depicted a legend that tells us that Alexander the Great, in his conquest of the world, encountered the forces of Gog and Magog. He defeated them but could not exterminate them. Instead, he locked them away in the Caspian Mountains, defying what the prophets wrote in Revelations."

She kept the flame against the bottom of the cupping glass even though Bravo's flesh was raised and puckered. The length of the cupping was three times that of the first one. "This, the second part of the rite, symbolizes resurrection, for our most sacred vow is to be standing between Satan's hordes and mankind when the day of Revelation arrives. Do you swear this?"

"I swear." The dizziness returned, more insistent this time. He was beginning to feel like a Sanguinati, the twelfth-century cathedral monks subject to *tempora minutionis,* periodic bloodletting.

Again, Jenny switched the glasses, removing the second, replacing it with the third, three inches from where the second had been. She opened another drawer beneath the sink, snapped on a pair of latex gloves. This time she returned with a stone mortar and pestle and three tiny glass containers, the contents of which—white, yellow and gunmetal-gray—she deposited into the bottom of the mortar where she began to grind them together.

"Salt, sulphur and mercury," she said, "the three basic elements of alchemy and, therefore, of transformation into a new life." The elements mixed, she carefully transferred them into a peculiar locket half as long as her forefinger, fashioned in the shape of a knight's broadsword.

She looked into Bravo's eyes and said, "Are you prepared to sacrifice your work, your friends, your family for the greater good of your fellow man?"

"I am."

She tapped him on the left shoulder with the alchemical sword.

"Do you swear to safeguard the secrets of the Order, with your life, if need be?"

"I do."

She tapped him on the right shoulder.

"Do you swear to oppose our enemies *à outrance*?"

À outrance. It had been some time since Bravo had heard the phrase, which in medieval terms meant jousting to the death. Now, uttered in this unsettling tomblike chamber, with all the implications that went with it, including the prospect of his own death, the words were was alive and full of meaning as they had been in centuries past.

"I do."

She tapped him on the crown of his head, removed the last cupping device, which had been on three times again as long as the second.

"It is done, heart, body and spirit, you are part of us now."

7

DONATELLA DID NOT KNOW HOW LONG SHE KNELT IN THE water. Ivo's head grew cold and heavy between her hands, as if it had turned to lead. At some point a profound sense of unreality set in, so that it seemed to her that she was cradling an effigy instead of a human being. Dimly, she was aware of the fading light, of the world moving around her, but it was as if at the moment she saw Ivo's head breaking the surface of the lake, his fixed and staring eyes blindly upon her, the entire Voire Dei ground to a halt and was now suspended between them. She wanted to vomit, but she could not; she wanted to die, but she did not. Her body, betraying her, continued to draw ragged breath, sobs pulled from deep in her belly, burning her throat like acid. She began to shiver, the trembling far beyond her control. And though her cheeks were flaming, the rest of her was as cold and heavy as Ivo.

Gradually, she became aware that two long-fingered hands were gripping her shoulders, quieting her tremors. Someone was standing behind her. She felt his warmth seeping into her, and slowly she allowed herself to relax back against his knees and shins.

"I did not believe that this day would come. I did not believe that it would happen this way." The deep male voice reverberated through her like distant thunder. "I remember the day the two of you came to us. You were hollow-cheeked, emaciated, stinking and crusted in grime, and yet in your eyes I saw something." The fingers dug into the flesh of her shoulders, lending her strength as well as warmth. "They were going to throw you out, you never knew that. I stopped them. They were not happy, they said you were my responsibility. I was to train you, and after thirty days you would be tested. If you didn't measure up, you would be thrown back into the street and I would face dire punishment. I smiled at them and accepted. As you know, I love challenges."

Donatella, listening with every fiber of her being, was cast back to the first days with the Knights of St. Clement.

"I worked you hard—mercilessly—and never once did you or Ivo complain. Instead, you worked all the harder, slept standing, ate in quick, ravenous mouthfuls, and returned to your training as eagerly as pups."

"You gave us something to live for," Donatella said thickly. "It was the only gift anyone ever gave us."

One hand released her shoulder, the long fingers tangling in her hair until she groaned.

"One day Ivo came to me. He was sick of training, he said, tired of—how did he put it? oh, yes—tired of performing like a circus animal. 'I am like an arrow,' he told me, 'whose point has been sharpened to a razor edge, but has never been nocked into a bow.' And, you know, Donatella, he was right. That was the genesis of your first mission. Do you remember it?"

"Yes," she whispered.

He caressed her. "How could you not? You were almost killed and I—I was almost undone by an enemy from inside the Knights. Ivo saved us both, didn't he, yes." The fingers pulled lightly, lovingly on her hair. "I never forgot the service he did me that day, now it is time to repay him."

Gently but powerfully he pulled her to her feet, turned her around to face him. "Leave Ivo to me, Donatella. I will bury him with the honor he deserves. No, no." He shook her a little as she fought him. "Listen to me, you have your quarry to think of, you have Ivo's murder to avenge."

She looked into the eyes she knew so well. "But our orders were to capture Braverman Shaw, not kill him. You were quite clear about the matter."

"That was before Shaw murdered Ivo." His thin lips curled into a chilly smile. "Go now. You are loosed upon our enemy *à outrance.*"

"I'VE waited a long time for this," Dexter Shaw said. *"I never for a moment doubted it would come."*

He looked older to Bravo, his beard whitened, longer, the lines on his faced etched more deeply, but then again Bravo himself was a child of eight or nine. Father and son sat on the porch of a shingled house—a place, it seemed to Bravo, that only existed in his dreams. It was late autumn, because the light, vivid and clear, filtered through a mare's nest of bare branches on the perfectly symmetrical beeches. But curiously, he felt no chill. They might have been inside for all the air that stirred. And beyond the trees there was a haze that obscured everything, so that it was impossible for him to tell if there might be houses or fields, brooks or mountains, or even if there were clouds in the sky.

"I killed a man, Dad. I had no other choice."

"*Then why blame yourself?*" Dexter Shaw said.

"A life is still a life."

"*Do you think that, or do you think you should be thinking it?*"

"Does it matter?"

"*Very much. Haven't I taught you not to fool yourself? You're in a war, Bravo, that's what the Voire Dei is all about—it has been from the beginning. In war there are casualties and there are victors, there's no room for doubt, and believe me when I tell you that semantics breeds doubt. In order to prevail you must cast out all doubt.*"

Bravo looked bleakly at the figure next to him. *My father is dead*, he told himself. *What am I doing here in this strange place having a conversation with him?* He was about to ask his father this question when Dexter Shaw spoke.

"*You're one of us now, Bravo, as it was meant to be from the moment of your conception. Your mother knew this, of course, and it terrified her. To be honest, it drove a wedge between us that I was never able to dislodge. She never wanted you to be a part of the Order. 'It's only your belief, Dex,' she'd say, 'only your stupid, stubborn belief. If you love me, you'll promise to keep our baby safe.' No matter what I said, I couldn't make her understand that it wasn't a matter of what she wanted or even of what I wanted. She never forgave me for that, not even at the end.*"

"You were only doing what you needed to do, Dad," Bravo said. "She had to have known that. And, in your own way, you were doing what you could to keep me safe. I need every bit of the training you forced on me. I wish I'd understood that sooner."

Dexter Shaw sighed. "*So do I, Bravo, but there was no way to tell you before now. I don't mean to say that I haven't made mistakes in my life—I have regrets, plenty of them, but I have faith. In you I know I'll find my redemption. . . .*"

Head bowed, hunched over, Bravo shivered with the last echo of his father's voice. It was just as well that he was sitting, because he might otherwise have collapsed onto the floor.

"The weakness and vertigo will pass quickly," Jenny said, speaking of the cupping.

As she was putting away her paraphernalia, he said, "Will you tell me now why my father had you make the glasses?" Already, he was feeling better now, his head remarkably clear, as if he had fallen deeply asleep for a half hour.

She returned to her seat beside him. "The glasses are important for one thing only: what is etched into the right lens." She plucked them off the table as if they were crown jewels. "It's also why we had to risk coming here."

Without another word, she rose, and he followed her across the basement to a plywood door he hadn't noticed before. She pulled it open and he found himself in a small, cramped laboratory filled with equipment he could only guess at.

"This is where you ground the lenses?"

She nodded, seating herself at a backless stool. "No optician's office would have the machinery needed." She pulled over a goosenecked lamp, turned it on. Brilliant light flooded the worktable. She put her hand on a squat metal machine that looked to him like nothing more than a deli meat slicer. "This is a very special grinder; I designed it myself."

"What I don't understand," Bravo said, "is that if you ground the lenses why can't you simply tell me what's on them?"

Jenny gave him a sly smile. "I may have ground the lenses, but I didn't etch them. Your father did."

"He was here? *He* did it himself?"

"After a little practice, yes. He was an astonishingly quick learner."

"Yes, that was one of his extraordinary abilities." Bravo thought of the porch behind the shingled house in a never-never dreamland.

"After he etched the lenses, I sealed them with a specially formulated coating."

"So the etching would appear only under certain conditions."

"That's right."

Jenny turned off the gooseneck lamp, twisted it so that it was pointed at a bare wall, then snapped on another switch. An oval of eerie greenish illumination was cast on the wall.

"Here goes," she said, taking the glasses and placing the right lens between the light and the wall.

Nothing.

She moved the glasses slightly so that the right lens was in the greenish glow. Immediately, a set of numbers appeared within the oval of illumination.

"Magic!" Jenny said with a small laugh. She turned to look at Bravo, who was scrutinizing the numbers.

"Do you know what they represent?" she said.

He frowned in concentration. "To be honest, the groupings look vaguely familiar, though I can't say why."

"A mathematical formula, maybe."

"Yes, that would make sense." He grabbed a pad and pen from Jenny's workspace, jotted down the series of numbers and spaces precisely as it was projected. "The fact is, though, mathematical formulae are difficult to decipher. Right now I think you'll agree that we don't have time to work on it. Unless there's another reason for us to remain here, I think we should leave as quickly as possible."

"I agree." Switching off the lamp, Jenny handed the glasses to Bravo and stood up.

They went back up into the dark house. Light from the winding street and the neighboring houses came through the window in a haloed glow.

Careful to stand well back, Jenny peered out at the street. She was so still he could barely see the rise and fall of her breast.

"What are we waiting for?" he said, but she immediately raised a warning hand to silence him.

After a moment, she moved further back into the shadows of the room, taking him with her.

"We can't leave," she whispered, "at least not as we are."

"Donatella?"

"The delivery truck across the street."

"What about it?" he said.

"If it was here on legitimate business its lights would be on, wouldn't they?"

He stared out at the darkened van. Was someone—Donatella—in there, clandestinely watching them? The thought sent an unpleasant chill down his spine.

"That's a hell of an assumption to make."

"I saw that same truck when we were on our way to the cemetery."

Bravo let out a long breath. "What do we do?" he said. "We can't stay here."

"No we can't. And as you've pointed out, the quicker we make our exit, the better. Our only chance is to change our appearance." She turned her back to him, as he had done with her, and said, "I need your help."

She instructed him on how to braid her hair and pin it up onto her head. The hair cascading down her back was thick, heavy and lustrous. When he first took hold of it, the sensation was new to him, clear and direct without prior associations. What she was asking him to do was basic, so simple she could have done it herself. But for him it was intimate and erotic, so that when he was done, he was reluctant to let go. He wondered, fleetingly, whether her request had been a deliberate attempt at reconciliation—or a stab at binding him to her.

They went back to the door to the garage. In the mudroom, she grabbed one of the baseball caps, set it firmly on her head, pulled on one of her father's windbreakers, gave Bravo an argyle cardigan to wear.

THEY crossed the garage, hurried past the vintage Mercedes and passed through a door on the far side, entering the gardener's shed. Jenny immediately went to one wall against which sat a collapsed wheelchair. She unfolded it and gestured.

"Take a seat."

Bravo stared at her for a moment, then he gave a low laugh. Shaking his head in wonderment, he settled himself into the wheelchair's leather seat.

"Hunch over, try to pull your shoulders up around your ears." Jenny pulled on a pair of fingerless driving gloves. "That's right. Think like an old man."

Bravo's hands on the armrests began to tremble.

"Nice touch," Jenny said as she wrapped him in a shawl. Then she pulled open a side door and wheeled him through. "Here we go."

DONATELLA, sitting behind the wheel of the delivery truck, did not expect a light to go on in the house; she was looking for movement. With the ATN PVS7-XR5 Night Vision goggles strapped to her head, she looked strange, like some sort of giant nocturnal sloth. While the infrared function couldn't penetrate walls or glass, it was providing an accurate reading. Apart from a single ghost reading as she was setting up the equipment—and that might have been a cat or a racoon—there had been no human movement around the house. That did not mean Braverman Shaw and his Guardian weren't inside—just the opposite, to her way of thinking. After all, how many places did they have to go?

Why this Guardian had been assigned to Shaw remained a mystery to Donatella, one that nagged at her. She did not like mysteries, especially when they applied to Dexter Shaw, who had been legendary for the mysteries with which he surrounded himself. His demise had been attempted three times since she had joined the Knights of St. Clement, all without success. The successful attack had been in the making for months, maybe even years—long before the crisis had come upon them and the timetable had been moved up. The desperate rush had necessitated that less competent people be utilized, and this had inevitably led to some mistakes. She was certain that Braverman Shaw's Guardian knew that the recent deaths of the five members of the Haute Cour was a concerted attack by the Knights, a push to finally gain the cache of secrets the heretical Order had been hoarding for centuries.

She shifted her head, so that another vector of the property was visible. Despite the fact that she was an enemy, Donatella felt a certain secret kinship with Braverman Shaw's Guardian that had nothing to do with philosophy and everything to do with gender. Ivo, like the male Guardians of the Order, hated Jenny's status, hiding that hatred behind a cruel and unjust derision. As a result, Ivo had consistently underestimated Jenny's abilities, and Donatella would not put it past Dexter Shaw to have assigned Jenny to guard his son for just this reason.

The infrared was picking up movement to her right, and she swiveled her head like a dog on point. The configuration was odd, and she switched to conventional night vision. An old man in a wheelchair was being pushed by a slim young man—possibly his son—in a baseball cap and windbreaker. But then again maybe not. Flicking open her cell phone, she pressed the first speed-dial numeral. When the voice answered, she asked for a list of all the residents on the street. Research was everything, and the resources of the Knights of St. Clement were vast.

"I'm looking for an invalid, seventy years of age or above."

Ninety seconds later, she had her answer and, her suspicions confirmed, fired the truck's ignition and drew her gun.

"SEE that black Lexus sedan on the next block?" Jenny said as she pushed Bravo along the sidewalk. "It belongs to my father, he kept it there for emergencies. That's our ticket out of here."

The rain came down in sheets, turning the walls of the houses black and menacing. A car engine coughed to life, and Bravo started. They were perhaps a hundred yards from the Lexus when he heard the deep, phlegmy cough of a truck's engine, saw movement out of the corner of his eye.

Apparently, Jenny had heard it, too, because she gave the wheelchair a huge push, sending it barreling at the Lexus. As she ran, she unlocked the doors electronically. Bravo had wrenched the door open even before the wheelchair smacked into the car's side.

The truck was roaring at them as Jenny launched herself in beside him. He scrambled over as she slammed home the key, fired up the Lexus. Putting it in gear, she stepped on the gas. Tires squealing, the Lexus sped down the street, the truck thrumming ominously behind it.

A single shot rang out, and then they were racing around the first curve, wind whistling, rain thick as sleet against the windshield, picking up speed with every second.

BENDING low over the wheel, Jenny steered the Lexus through the road's sweeping curve. Ahead lay the first of the switchbacks as the road followed the steep contours of the hill. They flew past large houses, swaths of lawn and flower-bedecked side gardens. Here and there was the lush, heavily treed open space of a vacant lot, brief glimpses of the area's pristine beauty before the developers had unleashed their bulldozers.

A rising sound caused her to shout, "Take a look behind us!"

But Bravo had already swiveled around as far as he could. "The truck!" he shouted back. "I think it means to ram us!"

Jenny had more immediate things to worry about. Along this middle stretch, the road was pitched much more steeply, and with the slick

asphalt and terrible visibility it was taking every ounce of her concentration to keep the Lexus from careening into a curb and overturning.
Several times she came perilously close, and Bravo's heart rose up into
his throat for fear that they would crash. Then, by some clever trick,
she would right their course, and they'd be back on the middle of the
deserted road again.

The deep roar of the pursuing truck echoed off the house facades.
Bravo could see that it was gaining on them. It was so close now that a
passing streetlight momentarily flared along the driver's face. Donatella!
She didn't fire again; in this upscale residential neighborhood she wouldn't
make the same mistake twice. Instead, she concentrated on devouring the
space between them, until the engine became a roar in his ears and he
thought he could feel its heat like the breath of a demon hound.

He wasn't far wrong. An instant later, he felt a tooth-rattling jar as the
corner of the truck's front bumper struck them. The Lexus went skidding
toward the curb, and he saw Jenny whip the wheel over, jerking the car to
the left. For a heart-stopping moment, the car skidded, kept to its deadly
course. Then it seemed to hesitate, as if unsure what had been asked of it.
Just as they were about to hit the curb, the tires caught, the Lexus moved
sharply to the left and the crisis was averted. But now the truck's throaty
roar seemed to redouble as Donatella drove in for the kill.

Up ahead, a BMW sedan with a teenager behind the wheel was
coming toward them with only its parking lights on. Hard-core rap
poured out of the open windows. The kid, drunk on beers and music,
was going too fast for the road, even if it had been dry and the car had
been less powerful. The BMW slewed slightly this way and that as its
inexperienced driver tried to deal with the effects of wet leaves and
slick patches on the tarmac. His lips were pulled back in a manic grin,
but his eyes were wide and staring—it seemed clear that he had not yet
seen them.

Jenny checked either side of the road, then taking advantage of his
near-panic, maneuvered the Lexus directly toward him. In a flash, the
kid saw them, and immediately the BMW changed course. The kid
stepped hard on the brakes, sending the car into an uncontrollable skid.
In a heartbeat, it had flashed by the Lexus and glanced off the high
fender of the oncoming truck.

But instead of braking herself, Donatella pushed the accelerator to the floor. Like an elephant brushes off a fly, the truck swept the dented BMW out of its way. The kid leaned out the window and screamed obscenities.

"She's still coming!" Bravo shouted, and he heard Jenny curse in reply. The roaring was immense, filling the night with its ominous sound. "She's right behind us!"

At the last possible instant, Jenny directed the Lexus into a driveway, across a swath of newly mown grass and onto the neighboring vacant lot, which, judging by the heavy equipment parked on it, was in the process of being cleared. They shot forward as the truck jumped the curb and drove onto the lot. They bumped along for perhaps five hundred feet.

"Oh God," Jenny said in his ear.

They were at the edge of a precipice, hidden until now by trees and the equipment. There was no time to maneuver, no time even to think. In an instant, they went over, plummeting down. They struck the bare earth with bone-jarring suddenness. The Lexus bounced once, catapulted over on its side so that Bravo and Jenny were thrown together.

"Jenny," he said, "are you all right?"

She nodded. "You?"

"Just shaken up."

He reached up, tried to open the window, but the electronics were shot. Lifting his leg, he smashed the sole of his shoe hard against the glass once. The safety glass shattered, but held together. He kicked again and a hole appeared. Using his heel to smash out what shards were left, he levered himself out, then turned and helped Jenny out.

For a moment, they lay on the ground. Regaining his breath was easier than regaining his composure. Above them, the twin beams of the truck's headlights struck out into the night, seeking to capture them in their glare. Then, as Bravo groaned and rolled up onto one elbow, he saw another beam flash out and down, probing the tangled darkness in which they lay. Donatella had switched on a portable searchlight.

Jenny reached out, wordlessly pulling at him so that he followed, both of them crawling into the densest swath of undergrowth. The rain continued unabated, a natural shield against detection.

"Are you all right?" she whispered.

He nodded. "You?"

"Nothing a good night's sleep wouldn't cure." Her face was close beside him. She gave him one of her thin smiles. "Let's go."

They moved cautiously through the underbrush until they reached the road. Keeping to the lush verge, they headed away from the crash site. But they hadn't gone more than a hundred yards when a late-model Lincoln came racing around a curve toward them. Jenny grabbed Bravo, dragged him back into the foliage.

They could hear the purr of the engine as the car slowed and stopped, and they crept further into the jungle of undergrowth. They crouched, listening to the sound of their own breath.

Jenny whispered, "Don't worry. She'll never find us."

At that moment, they heard a rustle terrifyingly close by and, turning, saw the outline of a figure looming over them.

A metallic glimmering brought to them the image of a gun, and a English-accented male voice said in a self-satisfied tone, "I wouldn't count on that."

8

"I KNEW IT. I KNEW YOU'D RUN INTO TROUBLE YOU COULDN'T handle."

"Kavanaugh!" Jenny said. "What the hell are you doing here?"

"What do you think?" the figure said. "Watching your sorry ass."

Bravo looked from the man to Jenny. "You know him?" he said to her.

"Braverman Shaw," she said by way of introduction, "meet Ronnie Kavanaugh."

"You poor bastard." Kavanaugh didn't offer his hand. "But all's well now that Uncle Ronnie's ridden to the rescue."

Reaching up and behind her, she undid the braid Bravo had made of her hair. "Kavanaugh is a Guardian, like me."

"Oh, not like you, princess," Kavanaugh said deadpan. "I know what I'm about."

"Is this the sonuvabitch who failed to protect my father?"

"I know you aren't referring to me." Kavanaugh had the cold, hard, domineering sneer down pat. "Surely you can't be that ignorant."

"He was never assigned to your father," Jenny said tightly. "Dexter Shaw would never put up with his attitude."

Bravo glanced upward through the rain to the top of the precipice. All was dark and still. Where had Donatella gone? He scrambled to his feet, held out his hand to help Jenny up. She ignored it, quickly stood beside him.

Kavanaugh gestured like a lord to guests newly arrived at his manor house. "Shall we?"

Under his guidance, they moved off into the thick, black underbrush.

As they pushed back bullbriers and squelched through earth churned to mud, Jenny told him about Rossi and Donatella.

"I caught a glimpse of her," Kavanaugh said, "but where's Rossi?"

"Bravo killed him," Jenny said.

Kavanaugh raised his black eyebrows. "Did he now?"

"Drowned him in the cemetery lake."

"A novel manner of murder, to be sure. Well, that's one less bastard to deal with, but now his bitch is out for blood, isn't she." He was a handsome man and, despite the inherent cruelty of his smile, at once rugged and refined. Bravo could picture him in a made-to-measure Saville Row tuxedo, a single-malt Scotch in his hand, playing chemin de fer at a fashionable London casino.

"There's only one road down this way." Kavanaugh pointed toward the hazy globe of a streetlight. "I parked in the shadows just there to the right."

Perhaps a hundred yards from the car he stopped and handed the keys to Jenny. "Here's what you're going to do, princess. You and Shaw will get into the car and drive through the pool of light."

"Are you crazy?" Jenny said. "That's just what she'll be looking for."

Kavanaugh grinned. "Isn't that right. She's so maddened, she'll come after you without a second thought."

"You bet she will," Bravo said, as unhappy with Kavanaugh's plan as Jenny obviously was.

"And when she does," Kavanaugh said slowly, as if reciting the alphabet to a slightly dim child, "I will be waiting to gun her down."

Jenny shook her head. "You're using Bravo as bait. It's too dangerous."

"Strong emotion of any sort—most especially rage—makes one commit stupid acts. I'm using Donatella's rage against her," Kavanaugh said. "D'you have a better notion?"

In the ensuing silence, he drew his gun. "I thought not. Let's get to it."

THE car—a large Lincoln—was precisely where Kavanaugh said it would be. Jenny circled the vehicle, her fingertips running lightly over the painted metal.

"Okay," she nodded, "get in."

"You gave in too easily," Bravo said as he strapped himself into the passenger's seat.

"What would you know about it?" she said tartly.

"So you really think this will work?"

Jenny inserted the key into the ignition. "It's a good plan, but I'll deny I said it if you ever tell him. I couldn't stand the smug look on his face."

Bravo regarded her a moment, weighing something in his mind. "You have a thing for him, don't you?"

She snorted. "What? Are you kidding?"

"Your cheeks are pink . . . princess."

She turned on him. "Don't be an ass."

Turning on the ignition, she put the Lincoln in gear, drove it onto the road, which ran in a more or less north-south direction. On their right was the rock face of the precipice, on their left was underbrush, glades and thick stands of leafy ash, beech and alder. They headed north, and the halo of illumination grew as they neared the closest streetlight.

"See anything?" Bravo said.

"More than you do," she snapped.

The rain had lessened, but a pearly mist had sprung up, blurring distant objects, dimming house lights to a soft, indistinct glow. They drove into the pool of illumination, which lay on the mist like a silver pond. The tarmac was altogether invisible.

They were just passing the streetlight when all at once they saw a large, blocky vehicle coming very fast toward them from out of the mist.

"It's a truck!" Bravo said. "Donatella's truck!"

"Kavanaugh, you bastard, where are you?" Jenny said as she turned the wheel hard to her right and simultaneously took her foot off the accelerator.

The truck came on at the same trajectory. Bravo, risking a look behind them, saw the tall broad-shouldered figure of Kavanaugh step out into the light from behind them. His feet were planted wide and his arms were held rigid as he began to fire into the driver's side of the truck's windshield. Calmly, with a kind of serene confidence, he squeezed off three-four-five shots. They all struck the windshield within six inches of one another.

It was at that moment, as Bravo was marveling at the man's marksmanship, that he heard Jenny say, "Dear God, there's no one behind the wheel!"

"She's dead," Bravo said. "Look at where he shot. She's already dead."

Jenny swerved again, and the truck passed by them, slammed into the streetlight. In a shower of sparks, the pole came down and with it, the utility junction box. When the box struck the tarmac, it smashed open and the line was pulled from its connectors, the live end sending sparks eerily through the low-lying mist.

Kavanaugh had turned to watch the final outcome of his neat handi-work when a bullet slammed into his chest. He spun around, his mouth open in shock, and a second bullet took off one side of his face.

"Someone's firing from that copse of ash across the road," Bravo said. "I saw the flashes."

"Oh, that evil bitch, she deadmanned the truck," Jenny said. "She taped down the accelerator and threw it in gear. That's why the truck never changed course even when I did."

Jamming on the brakes, she drove off the side of the road into dense blackness. Before Bravo had a chance to say a word, she had bolted out of the Lincoln and had vanished into the misty gloom.

DONATELLA, bent on one knee in the copse of ash trees, watched with an inexpressible bliss the second bullet she had sent flying take off the side of her enemy's head. The resulting spray cut through the mist, col-oring it, and she let out a tiny sigh. But her work was hardly done, and she slung the 7.62 SVD Dragunov sniper's rifle across her back.

There was a certain poetic justice in how the situation had changed, she thought as she faded back deeper into the copse. And, yes, a form of beauty that perhaps only she and Ivo could understand. She moved swiftly and silently to her right. Ivo had warned her that the Order would not leave the safeguarding of Braverman Shaw to their lone fe-male Guardian. This argument she had attributed to his inveterate chauvinism, but he had been right. The Order had assigned another Guardian as a backup. Not that it mattered to her now. She knew how to handle Guardians, male or female.

As she moved through the slippery darkness, she smiled grimly to herself. Retribution was laid out in the palm of her hand. She had left the truck several hundred yards north of here along the lower road, to which she had driven in low gear and with all her lights off. It had taken her six minutes to wire the accelerator—longer than she would have liked, but the light was very bad and she could not afford to switch on her searchlight even for an instant. It was essential that her quarry be given no advance warning of her whereabouts.

She reached the battered PT Cruiser without incident. It was precisely where she had been told it would be. Climbing in, she placed the rifle at her feet and her handgun on the seat beside her. Then she drove slowly and without lights toward the nearest of the road's turnouts.

She was south of her quarry. Her intention was to drive north, come at them from behind while they were looking for her up ahead or, if they had been observant, within the area around the copse of ash. But just as she was approaching the turnout, she felt a weight on the off-side of the car and without a moment's hesitation she whipped up the gun and shot three times through the passenger's side window. A moment later, there was a shattering of the window's safety glass and something had her by the throat.

IT was a combination of good luck and instinct that caused Jenny to head due south as she left the Lincoln. She knew that it would be a mistake to look for Donatella in the copse of trees. She had fired from there, according to Bravo, which meant the moment she knew Kavanaugh was dead, she'd have left the trees. She was now a moving target, and it was imperative that Jenny find her immediately because it was in the first few minutes after a shoot that the sniper was most vulnerable. To do that, Jenny knew, she had to put herself in Donatella's head. Where would the Knight go now, what would she do? Her job was incomplete; she'd be coming after Jenny and Bravo, but now she would have to substitute speed for the element of surprise. To Jenny, that meant she would not approach them on foot.

Jenny was looking for a vehicle when she heard the sound of an engine coming toward her. The instant she saw the PT Cruiser swing into view she leapt onto the running board. Through the window she saw Donatella reaching for her gun and she ducked down. The shots passed over her head and she came up, slamming her elbow into what was left of the window. Then, gripping the door handle and using it as a fulcrum, she launched herself feet first through the opening, slamming her shoes into Donatella's face.

Donatella's torso arched up in reflex, and her right arm swept around, her forefinger itching to pull the gun's trigger. But, prepared for this, Jenny took hold of her wrist and twisted. Donatella grunted and the gun dropped from her nerveless fingers onto the seat. Jenny locked her ankles around Donatella's neck, squeezed her legs together, creating a vise. Donatella screamed, tried to reach for her weapon, but Jenny tightened the lock on her neck and, gasping, she abandoned the intent.

Jenny's head and shoulders were still outside the car, and as Donatella stepped on the accelerator, the PT Cruiser leapt forward, slewed on the loose gravel of the turnout and gained the road. Jenny was slammed against the window frame but maintained her choke hold on her foe.

On her side of the road there was a narrow verge and then the almost sheer rock face above, which was the precipice over which she and Bravo had tumbled. Donatella turned the wheel to the right and the car crossed the verge toward the rock face. Sparks shot off the front fender of the PT Cruiser as the metalwork made contact with a stone outcropping, so that Jenny was obliged to grip the top of the open window in order to lever herself the rest of the way inside. In so doing, her ankle grip loosened and, with a violent wrench, Donatella extricated herself. At the same time, she leaned over, her outstretched fingers reaching for the gun.

Jenny kicked out, her heel striking Donatella's rib cage with such force that Donatella lost her grip on the wheel. The car slammed into the rock face, bounced off, shot wildly forward, then struck an outcropping and spun around in two complete circles before its rear end struck the rock wall for the final time. With a harsh grinding of gears and screaming of rent metal, it rode up on two wheels. Skidding back onto the road, it traveled another five hundred feet on its side until it struck the fallen utility pole and then the high square grill of the truck Donatella had rigged.

The two passengers, shaken up and bruised by the short but heart-stopping flight of the careening car, fought groggily for the upper hand, but during the final jarring few feet, Jenny's head struck the dashboard. Even before the car had come to rest, Donatella had grabbed her by the front of her shirt and slammed her back against the door. She struck Jenny once, twice, three times.

A burst of white stars clouded Jenny's vision and searing pain filled her head. She tried to retaliate, but she didn't seem to have the strength.

Like a hammer blow about to fall on her, she could feel a manic energy coming off Donatella and was terrified. Groping desperately behind her, she pushed down on the door handle even as Donatella drew back her arm to throw another punch. The door opened, and she fell backward out of the PT Cruiser.

For a moment she lay sprawled on the road, dazed and despairing. Then she felt the rain on her face and, as if taking strength from it, managed to stagger to her feet. Her legs were rubbery, her knees weak; she was dizzy, and when she put her hand to the back of her head it came away smeared with blood.

In the car, Donatella had scooped up the gun.

BRAVO waited until the PT Cruiser came to rest. By the dim glow cast by the streetlights north and south of their position, he saw that Jenny was in trouble. But it wasn't until he saw that Donatella was concentrated solely on her that he knew how best to help her. He ran through the swirling mist toward the car, mindful of the downed power cable. He periodically lost sight of his goal and, once, he felt certain that he was running in a circle and had missed it entirely. He stopped then and tried to gain his bearings, but it was like being adrift on a raft in the middle of the ocean. All landmarks were obscured and the light that fell on him seemed perfectly even, sourceless, so that he had no clear idea of which way was north or south. Then a small gap opened, and he caught a brief glimpse of painted metalwork and set off in that direction as fast as his legs would take him.

By the time he reached the car, both women had abandoned it, Donatella with the handgun. But almost at once he saw the sniper's rifle lying on the floor, and reaching in, he grabbed it.

JENNY, in a position that was rapidly becoming untenable, glimpsed Bravo through the oyster-gray mist and knew what she had to do to give herself the ghost of a chance. She ran, fell, picked herself up and on uncertain legs ran again.

Donatella, stalking her, saw the logic of her flight. If Jenny could get far enough away, she would be able to slip away into the mist. The thought of losing her now was intolerable, and Donatella sprinted headlong after her. There was a dim sparking toward which Jenny had headed, and this was the way she went.

Through the thick mist she saw movement, and then a figure, lithe and slim, became briefly visible. She aimed and fired even as she continued inexorably forward. The mist swirled as if stirred by a giant hand, and once again Jenny became visible. Donatella trained her gun on her foe and was about to squeeze the trigger when she heard a voice behind her.

"Drop your gun!"

She turned back, glimpsed Braverman Shaw behind the open car door pointing the Dragunov at her. She laughed to see how amateurishly he held the weapon. He wouldn't be able to hit her, even without the fog. She could kill him with one shot to the head. This she wanted to do more than anything else, and turning fully to face him, brought the muzzle of the gun to bear on him. She could sense Ivo near her, and she spoke to him under her breath so that he would know that his revenge was at hand.

"You heard me! Drop it now or—"

She squeezed the trigger.

MOMENTS before, Jenny had reached her destination, but not in time. Donatella had already shot once, barely missing her. Now, as the mist parted, they could see each other. Jenny had only needed a moment longer, but it was not to be given to her. She held her breath as if that would better prepare her for the onrush of death.

Then Bravo called out and Donatella turned toward him. At once, Jenny crouched down, picked up the broken power cable. There was a buzzing like distant dry lightning or bees swarming and a light that seemed unnatural. As she stood up, she almost pitched over, so dizzy had she become. Her head hurt terribly and her heart was pounding painfully against her rib cage. Staggering forward, she thrust the live end of the cable out in front of her. It touched Donatella just as she pulled the trigger. Her body jerked and spasmed as she leapt a foot in the air. The stench of burned flesh and hair was palpable, making Jenny's gorge rise.

Bravo, who had seen the bullet go wide but did not see the cause, lost Donatella as the mist swirled in again, obscuring the scene. Without a second thought, he quit his position behind the open driver's door and ran, leaping over the utility pole, tearing past the battered truck.

He found Jenny, bloody and breathing hard, standing over Donatella's corpse. He was about to ask about the stench when he saw the power cable still in her left hand.

"Jenny, put it down," he said gently. "Put it down and move away."

For a long moment she did not move, then slowly she looked up at him.

"Jenny. . . ." He slung the rifle and went over to her. Very carefully, he took hold of the cable with one hand and pried her fingers off it with the other. "It's over now," he said, pulling her back and away with him into the thickening mist.

9

BUT IT WASN'T OVER.

"I've got to go back," Jenny said.

"Back? Back where?"

"To see Kavanaugh."

"Jenny, we've got to get out of here. There isn't time."

"There's always time," she said, "to say good-bye."

She turned and Bravo went after her, through the underbrush.

He struggled to understand what she was feeling as she stared down the mess the bullets had made of Ronnie Kavanaugh's head and torso. He didn't look all that tough now.

After a moment, he stirred. "Jenny, please come away now. The police could show up at any moment, and if not the police, then motorists who can become potential witnesses to our involvement in two violent deaths."

She lingered for a moment longer, her lips moving silently. Then she nodded. "Let's get out of here."

They hurried back to Kavanaugh's Lincoln. On instinct, he told her he'd drive. She didn't put up a fight. Making a broken U-turn, he headed south, careful to keep to the posted speed limits. The two-lane road quickly became a four-lane thoroughfare and, not long after that, he was able to turn onto the highway. The Lincoln was comfortable and, more importantly, drove well. Kavanaugh had had the foresight to have it completely tricked out with satellite radio, rear object sensors and a global positioning system.

Within five miles, Bravo saw the lighted sign of a gas station. They used the grimy restrooms to clean themselves up as best they could and met back at the Lincoln. Jenny had managed to get all the blood off her, and her hair was glistening with water. When he bade her turn around, he held her hair away, moving her gently into the sodium lights. He could see that the wound was a scrape and that it had stopped bleeding.

"Okay?" he said.

Her eyes flashed and her tone was sharp. "Once and for all, let's get this straight: I'm protecting you."

A gentle breeze fully exposed the nape of her neck, the caramel skin glimmering, the bones beneath gently curved like sea glass. On impulse, he embraced her, holding her fast for a long moment. The instant he let go of her she climbed back into the car without saying a word or meeting his eyes.

Nearing the outskirts of Washington proper, he pulled into an all-night roadside diner, the only eatery open at this late hour. He chose a booth in back where he had a good view of the door and plate-glass window out onto the highway. Instinct had taken over without his being fully aware of it. Jenny sat staring out the window streaked with light and the ghostly reflections of faces. He waited, then ordered for both of them: coffee, eggs over easy, bacon, home fries for him, wheat toast.

When the food arrived, her eyes came back into focus. "I don't like bacon," she said.

Bravo reached over, put her bacon onto his plate. "You like eggs, I hope?"

She stared at him.

"Do you want something else with them?"

"I like potatoes."

Without a word, he used a spoon to transfer his home fries to her plate. He smiled at her as he began to eat.

An old couple paid their bill and left, a middle-aged man with a giant wobbly gut entered, made his way to the counter, his buttocks overflowing the stool, and ordered steak and fries. A young heavily made-up woman with a lot of hair stood outside smoking. One hip was canted out; her leather skirt barely covered her upper thighs. A car pulled up and Bravo tensed. The heavily made-up woman stubbed out her cigarette and walked on stiletto heels toward the car. The door opened and with a practiced liquid move she slid in. The car drove off and Bravo exhaled softly and went back to his food. Inside the diner, there were perhaps a half dozen other characters. No one seemed to pay anyone else the slightest attention.

"Jenny, talk to me," Bravo said, after a time.

She continued to eat with an eerie kind of mechanical precision, as if she knew she was required to fuel the system but was tasting nothing. Her gaze was neither on him nor on her food but was focused on something—or someone—he would never be able to see.

He had just mopped up the last of his eggs when she suddenly spoke: "It's just that, you know, we didn't bury him."

"Do you really think that would've been wise?"

"Now you're an expert?" As if she had just noticed the food, she dropped her fork with a clatter, pushed the plate away in a gesture of disgust. "This tastes like week-old grease."

"Jenny, do we have to be at odds?"

She stared at him, mute.

"I'm sorry he's dead. I can't begin to imagine what he meant to you, but—"

"You're an idiot, you know that?" she said vehemently. "You think you have it all figured out, but you don't. You don't know anything at all."

A familiar silence rose between them, bristling with the defensive thorns they brought out in each other. At length, he held out a hand, palm up. "Why don't we make a pact to put aside our personal anger and grief, whatever their causes?"

For a long moment she did nothing. The way her eyes searched his face made him think that she was trying to get a sense of whether his offer was genuine.

She drew herself up and her expression became defiant. "You can forget about screwing me."

He laughed, somewhat surprised and, quite possibly, disappointed.

"I'm serious."

"Okay," he said, sobering.

At length, she extended her hand until it rested lightly in his. She looked at him, her eyes glittery, magnified by her tears. "A pact would be good."

BACK in the Lincoln, he pulled out the paper on which he'd copied the number-and-space sequence his father had etched onto the lens of the glasses. "I've been thinking about this," he said, "and I think I know what it might be."

"You've had time to work out the math formula?" she said.

"It's the wrong configuration for a formula." He held the paper up so that they could both see its reflection in the rearview mirror. "This is a trick my father taught me when I was a kid. Reverse the *entire sequence* even though each letter—or in this case, number—isn't reversed. That way, to anyone who doesn't understand the cipher, the sequence will look wrong even if viewed in a mirror." Rummaging through the glove compartment, he found a pad and pen, and while Jenny held up the paper, he copied the sequence down in reverse. What he was looking at were three sets of six numbers, followed by one set of four numbers.

Jenny looked from the sequence to Bravo's face, trying to read his expression. "Well?"

Leaning forward, he took the GPS out of its cradle and punched in the numbers.

Jenny was dumbfounded. "It's a location?"

"The three sets of six numbers are longitude and latitude, down to the minute."

"But what about the last four-digit set?"

"I don't know." He showed her the glowing GPS screen.

"St. Malo," she said. "France, right?"

He nodded. "Brittany, to be exact."

"That's where we're going now?"

"Right." Bravo reached for his cell phone. "But not on our own."

IT was already midmorning in Paris and Jordan Muhlmann was in his office at Lusignan et Cie. He was a tall slender man with dark hair, dark, deep-set eyes and a long jaw. His was a powerful face but somehow haunted. He was speaking with a woman in her late forties, her beauty undimmed by time. She was dressed in a chic black Lagerfeld suit, under which she wore a buttery silk blouse. A single strand of matched pearls glowed at her neck, and a gold band with the head of a woman incised into it circled one finger. She sat, wrists crossed over her knee, with a Zenlike serenity.

Outside could be seen rising the sterile white stonework of the Grande Arche de la Défense, which was not an arch at all but a cube with the center carved out of it. Fitting, in a way, Jordan thought, for Paris's modern-day monument to business. Farther away was the solid, magnificently carved Arc de Triomphe, monument to the military triumphs of France's last great military hero, Charles de Gaulle.

The day was bright and clear with only a hint of clouds low on the northern horizon. The new sidewalks were filled with suits. Though they were from all over the world, you could not tell them apart. They spoke a common language, prayed to a common god, wished upon a common star, and that was commerce. After the cultureless euro, faceless electronic transfers, corporate takeovers that involved two, three or four countries, did any variations remain of the beauty that had flowered here for centuries?

Like everything else in this self-consciously postmodern sector of Paris, the facade of the building Lusignan et Cie owned was in keeping with its surroundings: contemporary, sleek, stark, entirely without character. The office complex was, however, the opposite, filled with Old World garnishments and charm, especially Jordan's office suite, which stretched away in Art Nouveau majesty. There were virtually no hard edges: everything, curved and sculpted in high relief, had an organic shape to it. On the shelves were artifacts from an earlier age—French and German sculpture from the 1920s, pottery from the nineteenth century, fragments of ancient religious scrolls, the guard of a sword purported to be from the Crusades—remnants of civilizations long past. This fascination with history, culture and religion was one of the things that had drawn Jordan and Bravo so closely together.

The intercom buzzed. Muhlmann's secretary said, "It's Monsieur Shaw. He says it's urgent."

Jordan hit the speakerphone switch and picked up the receiver. "Bravo, I have been trying to reach you—as usual." The anxiety in his voice was palpable. "Is everything all right?"

"It is now," Bravo said.

"Ah, *bon,* that's a relief!"

"But I'm coming to Paris immediately. I'll be arriving early tomorrow morning with a friend of mine, Jenny Logan, and I'll need transportation."

"Of course. You shall have it. *Alors,* you must tell me more of this Jenny Logan. This is good news, indeed. In the midst of your grief you have found a companion—what is the American word?—a girlfriend."

Bravo laughed. "Girlfriend? Not exactly." He cleared his throat. "Listen, Jordan, I think I ought to tell you that things have taken a very nasty turn here."

"*Mon ami,* what do you mean?"

"Not over the phone," Bravo said. "But whoever you send must be absolutely trustworthy, do you understand me?"

At that moment, the woman stood up, walked over to Jordan's desk. Her movements were flawless. She held in her magnificent, fierce face the full knowledge of who she was and what powers she possessed. She exuded an innate authority that made it clear it would be foolish either to deceive her or to oppose her.

"Bravo, *un moment, s'il te plaît.*" Jordan jabbed the hold button, looked up at her expectantly.

The woman parted her lips and said very softly, "Let me do it, my love."

Jordan shook his head. "It's too dangerous. After what happened with Dexter—"

"Don't fret, I'll be careful," she whispered. Then she smiled.

"Jordan, do you understand me?" Bravo repeated.

He hit the hold button again and said into the phone, "*Mon ami,* I hear the urgency in your voice and my concern for you grows deeper."

"Then you *do* understand."

"But of course," he said. "I will come myself."

"Isn't the quarterly companywide directors' meeting this week?"

"Tomorrow, in fact. Not to mention the Dutch, who have come in to finalize the deal you and I have been working on for almost a year."

"What about the Wassersturms?"

"That deal is dead, Bravo, you made certain of that."

"They've proved to be remarkably insistent."

"I'll take care of the Wassersturms, *mon ami.*"

"Then there's no question, Jordan. As you have just confirmed, you have a company to run."

"But you're my friend—*more* than a friend."

"I know that and I appreciate it," Bravo said. "But send someone else. Please."

Jordan pondered his response to this request for a moment, then he nodded to the woman. "*Bon,* not to worry," he said into the phone, "I will send someone you know and trust."

"Thank you, Jordan," Bravo said with relief. "I won't forget this."

IT was dark on the plane. Late at night, in the jumbo jet thirty-three thousand feet over the black, restless Atlantic, most of the passengers in business class were either asleep or watching the tiny glowing screens of the portable DVD players provided by the airline. But exhausted as Bravo and Jenny were, they could not find it within themselves to surrender to sleep.

Instead, theatrically spotlighted by the lights above their seats, they talked in low tones. There was an unconscious need in them both to get to know each other better. They had survived pitched battles, saved one another from almost certain death. Soldiers fighting side by side in the strange invisible war that defined the Voire Dei, they had forged a link more intimate than sex, and yet they were still strangers to one another.

"The only ones who had faith in me were my father and yours—and of course Paolo Zorzi, my instructor," Jenny was saying. "The others opposed my being allowed into the Order, let alone my becoming a Guardian." The full duskiness of her skin had returned, and in the vertical shaft of illumination it was possible to overlook the bruises and small cuts to which her skin had been lately subject. "But your father was very powerful; many in the Haute Cour were afraid of opposing him to his face."

A flight attendant came by with water, coffee, tea and juice, but they declined. Several individual lights were turned out, and it was even darker now inside the plane. By his calculation they were closer to Paris than they were to Washington.

"Was your initiation like mine?" he asked.

An ironic smile escaped her generous lips. "I'm a woman. It was nothing like yours."

"But you said my father and yours and this Paolo Zorzi believed in you."

Jenny nodded. "Yes, but there are some traditions that even they found impossible to ignore. I was given a simple black robe to dress in, then I was led to a small darkened windowless chamber. Save for four long candles in heavy brass sticks the room was bare, more like a prison cell or an executioner's chamber. It was very cold. The floor was made of ancient stone blocks. I was instructed to lie on my stomach and told to kiss the stone. A black shroud was draped over me. It was gauzy enough so that I could see the candles being placed at my head and feet. While I swore to give myself heart, mind and spirit to the Order, your father and Paolo Zorzi intoned an ancient prayer in a language I couldn't recognize."

"Do you remember any of the words?"

Jenny closed her eyes and her brow wrinkled. She spoke three words, badly, as it turned out. Nevertheless, Bravo recognized the language.

"It's Seljuk," he said, adding, "The Seljuk were the dominant tribe in Turkey in the thirteenth century, and twice successfully invaded the important trading city of Trebizond that the Greeks had founded along the south coast of the Black Sea to supply Europe with silks, spices and, perhaps most importantly, alum—the substance used to bind dyes to cloth."

Jenny asked him to repeat the words until she could speak them correctly.

"Thank you," she said.

"Anytime. Now tell me about the rest of your initiation."

Jenny let out a breath. "Zorzi dug his knuckles into the small of my back until the pain was so great that I gasped and tears came to my eyes.

" 'Thus, like your sisters,' your father chanted in Latin, 'do you come in suffering and in pain to the Order.' "

"That sounds suspiciously like part of the medieval vow for taking the veil," Bravo said.

"Bingo." Jenny nodded. "The initiation was taken directly from the one administered to Venetian women in the sixteen hundreds when they became nuns. They were, in effect, made to witness their own funeral."

"So it seems that throughout its history the Order did accept women," Bravo said.

"It would seem so, though you and I know that history records it otherwise."

He thought about the injustice of this for some time. At length, he leaned closer to her and said, "There's something bothering me." He liked her scent; it made him pleasantly woozy, and he was only too happy to surrender himself to this voluptuous feeling. "You haven't once tried to contact anyone in the Order, and when I asked you about its resources you were evasive. Why?"

She was silent for some time, but her eyes were busy, as if she was trying to work out a particularly knotty problem. At length, she turned to him and said very softly, "It was your father's contention—and my own father's as well, I believe—that there is a traitor within the Haute Cour, someone who has been on the inside for some time, someone trusted, a sleeper, if you will."

"Obviously, you believe it as well."

"I had believed our people to be absolutely safe, untouchable. A traitor is the logical explanation for why the Knights suddenly have been so successful in assassinating five members of the Haute Cour, including your father."

"So, bottom line, we're cut off from our best resources."

"That's what it comes down to." Her eyes were hooded.

"There's something else, isn't there?"

"Yes. Dexter was so certain the traitor existed that he moved the cache of secrets without telling the other members of the Haute Cour."

"That would be just like my father." Bravo put his head back against the seat, and for a moment his eyes lost their focus. "I miss him." He shook his head. "But it's a strange thing—looking back on it, we had what you might call a . . . difficult relationship."

"Why?"

"He demanded so much from me and I didn't understand his motivations."

But he'd hesitated a fraction too long. Was there was something more he wasn't telling her? Jenny would hardly have been surprised. There were whole sections of her own personal history that she couldn't tell him.

"I know a little of your father," Bravo said, "but what about your mother? I didn't see any sign of her in the house."

Jenny looked away for a moment, as she was wont to do when he'd posed a particularly thorny question. She took a deep breath, let it out slowly and deliberately. "My mother left some time ago. She lives in Taos now. She's a potter, she has a Navajo teacher who I think is also her lover, though she hasn't said as much. Not that she would, that wouldn't be like her at all." She paused, then, almost as an afterthought, she said, "She's learning to speak the language, so she tells me."

"She wants to speak to her lover in his own tongue."

"What a romantic you're turning out to be," Jenny said with a bleak smile. "Sadly, no. More likely it's simply because the language is exceptionally difficult to learn. My mother tends to define herself by challenges."

"Did your father take her leaving badly?"

"Yes, but to tell you the truth I'm not sure of the reason. Did he love her or simply rely on her? You know men. They can accomplish anything in business, but they're helpless as lambs in the house. My father couldn't make himself a cup of tea, and as for using the dishwasher . . . well, a week after she moved out I had to clean up a ton of suds when he used Dawn instead of Cascade." She shifted in her seat, settling herself more comfortably. She had her shoes off and was curled up with her knees bent and her feet beneath her. "Of course, shortly after that he found someone else, as he was bound to do. He couldn't live alone and I couldn't keep taking care of him, even he knew that much."

"Did they like each other—your parents?" he said.

"Who can say? My father was in his own world, and my mother—I'll tell you a story about my mother. When I was sixteen I fell in love with this guy. We were living in San Diego then. He was a freshman in college, two years older than I was, sweet and kind, and Hispanic. My mother found out about the relationship and stopped it cold."

"How did she do that?"

"She shipped me across country to a boarding school in New Hampshire, where I stayed for two years. I learned to ski and hate boys. I came home after that, but it was too late, he was gone."

"You didn't write to him or—?"

She gave him a wry, bitter smile. "You don't know my mother."

With a soft chime the seat belt light came on, and the same flight attendant came around and asked Jenny to buckle up.

"You trust this man you called?" Jenny said when they were alone again.

"Jordan? With my life. He and I are as close as brothers—closer, even, since we don't have all that sibling-rivalry baggage."

Jenny nodded. "I know what you mean. My sister Rebecca and I were always at it with each other. We're fraternal twins but look very much alike. I can't tell you how many times we stole each other's boyfriends, but when it came to standing up for each other against our parents—especially my mother, who was always trying to play one of us against the other—there was never any question of where our loyalty lay." She sighed. "I miss her. I missed her when I was in New Hampshire. Separating us was another side of my mother's cruelty. She hated us ganging up on her." She sighed. "Becca lives in Seattle now with her partner and two kids. We don't get to see each other as much as we'd like." She turned to him. "How is Emma? She was hurt in the explosion that killed your father, wasn't she?"

"Emma is blind," Bravo said shortly. "She seems fine, but who really knows?"

"DEAD? Both of them?" Jordan grunted. "*Surprised* isn't the right word. I already suspected as much." Phone to his ear, he stared at a small medieval painting of the Madonna and Child. It was wrought with an obvious fervor, which in his opinion lent it an unearthly power. "What I can't fathom is why you waited so long to inform me."

A discreet electronic beep accompanied a light that had begun flashing on Jordan's console. He turned back immediately, saw that the call was coming in on the encrypted line. Only one person was authorized to call him on that line, and right now it was the last person he wanted to speak with. Nevertheless, he knew he had no choice.

"The cleanup?" he said, acutely aware that he had to cut the current conversation short. "Yes, yes, of course. As always, it's understood that police involvement is to be avoided at all costs. But I want you out of Washington immediately. Back here, yes." He was staring at the blinking light. Mustn't keep the caller waiting, he thought. "There will be more work for you, I suspect. I have another call, contact me when you arrive."

He hung up without another word, changed to the encrypted-line receiver. "Cardinal Canesi, forgive me." Felix Canesi was the pope's right-hand man. "A business call from Beijing. You know the Chinese, their formalities are endless."

"I'm a man of the world, Jordan, I understand the intricacies of diplomacy," Cardinal Canesi said in his deep, stentorian tones. "Though I despise being kept waiting, let us speak no more of the matter."

Jordan absorbed this back-handed rebuke with his usual stoicism. "I haven't heard from you in three days. How is his holiness's condition?"

"We come now to the purpose of this interview." Whether it was because he had spent too many decades inside the cloistered walls of the Vatican or because he had a pompous streak, Cardinal Canesi's speech was unnaturally formal, as if he were channeling a religious lord of the nineteenth century. "As you have been informed, his eminence has been in guarded status over the last ten days, but that is about to change."

"Good news, I pray."

"Hardly," Cardinal Canesi said in funereal tones. "His health has deteriorated alarmingly. Frankly—and I must stress that this information is between the two of us—the pontiff is dying. Neither prayer nor medical knowledge seems of any use." With the canny stagecraft of a veteran actor, he paused, the better to give his next words added significance. "Without the—"

"Please," Jordan said sharply.

"Yes, yes, quite," Cardinal Canesi said with a hint of huffiness. He did not care to be reminded of security considerations. "In any event, without what you have promised us there is no hope for him. We simply *must* have it within the week."

"Don't worry, Felix," Jordan replied serenely. "You'll have it; the pope will not die."

"You have given your word, Jordan. This is a matter of the gravest import. Over the centuries, the Vatican has been anxious to have this most precious of artifacts returned to the bosom of the Church from whence it sprang. Over the centuries, many popes have made it their life's work to retrieve it from the apostate Gnostics who stole it, to no avail. And so it has passed from fact into legend. I must caution you that there are those on the pontiff's council who doubt the . . . the substance exists."

"It exists, your excellency, of this you may have no fear."

"It is not I who will experience fear should you fail us," Cardinal Canesi said ominously. "We are at a perilous crossroads, nothing could be more clear. This is why we have exercised all our might and influence to help you in your sacred mission. But hear me: we have put ourselves at risk for you.

"His eminence has never declared his wishes for his successor. The college of Cardinals is contentious, filled with overeager and overambitious individuals, each with his own idea of which direction to lead the Church.

"Again I tell you this in the strictest confidence: either his holiness recovers, or the Church hierarchy will be plunged into an anarchy from which even I cannot say with any degree of certainty it will emerge unchanged."

Jordan knew what that meant: the probability of no more Canesi, no more cabal, no more backing for him.

"Do not fail us, Jordan. Remember: a week, not one moment more."

As he replaced the receiver, Jordan's mind was working furiously, parsing every word, every intonation he had used. He knew the cardinal better than Canesi suspected. His grace was the head of a clandestine cabal of high Vatican officials who attended the pope and depended on his favor in order to put through their policies. Canesi had as much to fear from this pope's passing as did Jordan, possibly more. The cabal needed this pope to continue to support them because over the decades they had gathered to them a veil of secret power the pope knew nothing about; backing Jordan had been only one of their activities. Jordan's plan, years in the making, had been triggered by Canesi's panic.

Jordan rubbed his chin, his face grave. He picked up his cell phone, dialed a number, spoke softly into it. "His grace called. I'm afraid we've run out of time far sooner than we anticipated. A week, not a moment more, he told me. Luckily, Bravo holds the key, which is just how we planned it. But now we will be forced to take further risks."

"Risk is part of the game, my love," the voice said on the other end of the line.

"Risk is what Ivo and Donatella took," he said gloomily, "and look where they ended up."

"But I have a plan. Herd Braverman Shaw and his Guardian angel like cattle, separate them, make them desperate."

Jordan sat up straight, his throat tight. "And then?"

"She is of no consequence," the voice said, "but when he has led us to the secret, he will die."

Jordan faced the window, but his gaze had turned inward. "Just as we planned," he said, "from the beginning."

PART TWO

10

CAMILLE MUHLMANN, AS BEAUTIFUL AND INTIMIDATING AS she had ever been in her life, was waiting for Bravo and Jenny at Charles de Gaulle Airport as they emerged from security. She was wearing one of her signature Lagerfeld suits, but in deference to the midsummer heat it was of a lightweight fabric, as was her blouse, through which the lace of her bra glimmered enticingly. She waved when she saw Bravo and embraced him, kissing him warmly on both cheeks.

"*Mon Dieu, quel choc!*" she said softly as she clung to him. "My poor Bravo, to have your father taken from you so prematurely."

Bravo kissed her tenderly, then pulled away, too slowly by Jenny's estimation. But before he could extricate himself entirely, she cradled his jaw in her hands.

"What happened to you? What terrible trouble did you run into?" The concern in her voice was palpable, grating on Jenny's nerves.

"Not here, not now," Bravo said with an abruptness that appeared to disturb Camille.

Instead, he made the introductions. "Jenny Logan, this is Camille Muhlmann, Jordan's mother."

"So you're Bravo's new girlfriend," Camille said.

Bravo frowned. "Camille, I told Jordan—"

Camille held up a hand and as she studied Jenny's face. "You're so lovely. We must find the ways to heal your wounds as quickly as possible, *n'est-ce pas?*" She squeezed Jenny's hand with an intimacy Jenny's found startling. Then she turned to Bravo. "I quite approve of her, my dear."

She laughed, linking her arm through Bravo's. "I hope you don't think me too forward, Jenny, but when it comes to Bravo I'm inordinately protective. I can't help it, you see, he's my son's best friend and is dear to my heart. He is family, you understand."

"Of course I understand, Madame Muhlmann."

"On such a journey we must dispense with formalities, Jenny. *Alors,* you must call me Camille."

Jenny smiled through clenched teeth. It appeared as if Camille had deliberately matched her stride to Bravo's, and with every step they took her hip brushed against his. What annoyed Jenny most of all, however, was how much Bravo seemed to enjoy being the center of Camille Muhlmann's attention.

"Luggage, *non?*" Camille ran the tip of her forefinger along Bravo's jaw. "Ah, you left Washington in such a rush it's a wonder you had your passports."

"Neither of us is ever without them," Jenny said.

Camille swung around, smiling easily. "Yes, and what is it you do, Jenny?"

"I'm a consultant to companies in developing nations," Jenny said without missing a beat. "I help them conform to the standards laid down by the World Bank and the World Trade Organization for international commerce."

"And yet you're here with my Bravo."

"Friendship is as important to me as it is to you, Madame Muhlmann."

Again she took Jenny's hand in that curiously intimate gesture. "Camille, please."

By this time they had reached the car park. The Parisian sky was full of slate-gray clouds, and the morning was already hot and sticky. A low rumble of thunder cut through the traffic noise.

"Now, Bravo," Camille said, "you must tell me what it was you couldn't tell Jordan over the phone. What happened to you in America that caused you both such violence?"

She stopped beside her car, a new dove-gray Citroën C5 sedan.

"You haven't rented us a car?" Bravo said.

"I'm driving you myself." When Bravo began to protest, she held up a hand. "These are Jordan's orders, my love. You must see the logic of it. Wherever you need to go, I can get you there faster and more securely. A rental car is identifiable by its license plates—*n'est-ce pas?*—and will therefore draw attention to you. It is not secure, yes?"

Bravo glanced at Jenny and, ignoring the brief negative shake of her head, said with a smile, "Jenny and I thank you, Camille. You're most kind."

"*Bon*, that's settled." She opened the car door. "You must be famished, and then we must get you some clothes, the two of you look positively bedraggled." She gestured for Bravo to get in. "While I drive you'll tell me everything."

Bravo opened the back door.

"No, my love, I want you beside me." She turned. "Unless this is not acceptable to you, Jenny."

"Of course." Jenny put a smile on her face, though she feared it was so brittle it would crack at any moment. She hated the way Camille had put it to her, as if it would be her failing if she refused.

Camille slid her hand over Bravo's and her wide-apart eyes held his. They were standing very close. Were their hips pressed together? Jenny sensed Camille Muhlmann's smoldering sexual energy. As she looked at the older woman with the green eyes of jealousy, it seemed to her that Camille's musk swirled around Bravo like Medusa's locks.

As she clambered into the Citroën's back, Jenny glared at Bravo, but he had been struck by a sudden melancholy, and his gaze was lost to her. He looked around and realized that his father would never again visit him here, that the haloed lights along the Seine would never again fall on Dexter Shaw as the two of them strolled its banks amid bursts of strained and now longed-for conversation.

AS Camille exited the airport, Bravo gave her a short, heavily edited version of what had happened after he had been released from the hospital. Camille made no comment as he described their escape from Jenny's house and the ensuing chase, allowing him to have center stage without interruption.

Bravo did not identify Ivo Rossi or Donatella by name. As for Jenny, he said she was a childhood friend of his from New York. "My sister had invited her to the July fourth dinner," he concluded. "She was detained and arrived after the explosion. When I woke up in the hospital hers was the first face I saw."

"How lucky for you," Camille said as her eyes met Jenny's in the rearview mirror.

"What can I say?" Jenny smiled what she imagined was the ghastly half-frozen smile she'd had plastered on her face ever since she'd met Camille Muhlmann. "I was born under a lucky sign."

Camille swung the Citroën onto the A11, heading north to Rouen.

"But, my love, who were these people following you and why?" Camille accelerated into the far left lane. "I must tell you that Jordan has a theory—he's convinced the Wassersturms are behind it."

"Wassersturms?" Jenny said.

"A business deal I was working on for six months." Bravo half turned his head toward her. "We wanted to buy a company in Budapest. Trouble was, there was already a deal on the table with a company from Cologne owned by the Wassersturm brothers. I did some research and found out that through a labyrinth of shell companies the Wassersturms were supplying the Russian mafia with illegal arms. I went to the board of the Budapest company with the evidence and within a week we had the deal."

"Revenge." With an angry shriek of the Citroën's horn, Camille raced past a vehicle moving too slowly for her. When she returned to the left lane, she accelerated even more. "The Wassersturms were in a rage when their deal was terminated. Jordan's worried that they're out to take their revenge on you. What's gotten him so upset is that he spent three days in Munich working on another deal with them simply to calm them down."

Bravo frowned. "He shouldn't have done that; there's no reason to trust them."

Camille laughed. "You know Jordan," she said lightly. "If he can get his terms, he'll make a deal with the devil."

"Well, he's wrong about this particular theory. The brothers may scream but I seriously doubt they have it in them to authorize a violent act."

"I take it, then, you have your own theory," Camille said.

"I suspect these attacks have something to do with my father's death," Bravo said after some hesitation.

Camille ventured a glance his way. "*Je ne comprends pas.* What do these people want with you?"

"I have no idea," Bravo said deliberately. "At my father's insistence, he and I met just before going to my sister's house. The fact is, he wanted to talk to me about something he said was important, but my anger got in the way and I put him off."

"Oh, Bravo." Camille signaled, moving right across the lanes of the A11. "And in this state your father was taken from you. *Quel domage!*"

The large gray modern office buildings of the northern outskirts of Paris had given grudging way to green fields interspersed with clusters of residential housing no less ugly, unfortunately, than their industrial brethren.

She exited and took the turn for Magny-en-Vexin. They passed between two magnificent allées of black-leafed hornbeam trees, a darkened bower with the sky lowered and the air heavy as sea water, arriving at length in the city proper. In the old city, they exited the car to the rumble of thunder and a livid flash of lightning somewhere in the turbulent gloom of the northern sky.

Bistro du Nord was on the rue de la Halle, a small, cozy restaurant three steps down from street level. It was long and narrow, filled with dark wood beams and the simple whitewashed walls of a *mas,* a French farmhouse. Framed paintings of the countryside, colorful and pleasingly primitive, were hung as if at random.

A young woman showed them to a table at the back, near the blackened mouth of a massive unlit fireplace. Bravo could not help but be reminded of the hearth in Jenny's house behind which was the vertical passageway that had saved them from Ivo Rossi's initial attack.

When Camille went to freshen up, Jenny leaned across the table and said in a hushed voice, "What do you think you're doing?"

"What are you talking about?" Bravo said.

"We shouldn't be taking her—or anyone else—with us to St. Malo."

"You heard her, Jenny. She had a good point. Renting a car might call attention to ourselves."

"There are a million rental cars on the road in France at any given time," Jenny said hotly. "Besides, I very much doubt your father would approve of involving this woman in your hunt for the truth."

"Why would you say that?"

"I simply mean—"

"Do you know your cheeks are flushed?"

"I simply mean," she persevered, "that knowing your father I think he'd feel that it's far more insecure to have her with us than for us to have rented a car, that's all."

"You're sure that's all?"

She picked up the menu, held it in front of her face and muttered, "Bastard."

Bravo took hold of the top of the menu, bringing her face out of hiding. He smiled winningly, but she wasn't about to be charmed.

"Why are you so determined to make fun of me?"

"I like you," he said.

She snorted and was about to make a nasty reply when Camille returned.

"Am I interrupting something? A lover's quarrel, perhaps?"

"Not at all," Jenny said, her eyes lowered to her menu.

Camille sighed. "Lovers are allowed to quarrel as long as it doesn't last long. *Alors,* you must now kiss and make it up with each other."

"I don't *think* so," Jenny blurted out, while at the same instant, Bravo said, "We're not lovers."

"No, of course not." Her tone of voice as well as her expression revealed that Camille did not believe him. She took both their hands. "My dears, life is too short to stay angry. Now listen to me, I won't be satisfied until you've kissed and I know all is well between you." She squeezed their hands. "Come on now, there has been too much sadness in your lives lately."

Jenny's eyes were clouded by anxiety, all the worse because she could tell nothing of how Bravo felt. Nevertheless, both understood that there was no getting around this profoundly awkward moment. With Camille looking on, her lips curved in a mysterious Mona Lisa half smile, they both rose and moved tentatively toward one another. Bravo pushed a chair away but even so they halted with a handsbreadth between them.

All at once, he took her in his arms and pressed his mouth to hers. Much to her astonishment, she felt her lips opening under his, felt his tongue enter her mouth, felt her own twine for a moment with his. The breath whooshed out of her and her heart seemed to stop. Then they were apart, standing close but no longer touching, and Jenny's heart rate slowly returned to normal.

"There now, isn't that better?" Camille said with an enigmatic smile.

As they sat Camille discreetly signaled the waiter, and they ordered.

Bravo was again engaged in conversation with Camille, telling her where they needed to go, but not why. Jenny saw this withholding of information as a small victory for her side, as she'd come to think of it.

Instead, they discussed the best route to take to St. Malo and where Bravo wanted Camille to drop them once they had arrived. Camille wanted to wait for them, but Bravo refused, telling her that he had no way of knowing how long he and Jenny would need to be in St. Malo and where they might be going after that. In the meantime, the food arrived.

"You're being terribly mysterious," Camille said between dainty bites of raw shellfish.

Jenny, who had an aversion to mussels, clams and oysters in any form, struggled to keep her gorge down while slicing into her steak frites.

"Not that I mind," Camille continued, "but I worry that you're in more danger than you're willing to admit. That is why you don't want me to stay in St. Malo with you, isn't it?"

"Frankly, yes." Bravo put down his fork. "You've already done more than could be expected. I won't put you in harm's way."

"But, my love, it's my decision—"

"No, Camille, it's not. In this instance I'm afraid I must insist. You're taking us to St. Malo, which is more than you ought to be doing. But that's the end of it. Understood?"

Camille regarded him neutrally for a moment. Then she sighed and turned to Jenny. "Dessert, my dear? The *tarte Tatin* here is not to be missed."

AFTER lunch, Camille took them to the pharmacy she had spoken of, where she bought them various creams and unguents for their bruises, cuts and abrasions. Then they went clothes shopping, changing into the new outfits as they went and consigning their old torn shirts and pants to the trash bin.

Back in the car, Camille drove at high speed, circumventing Rouen. They turned onto the E1, heading west, where the road became the EB1. Paralleling the coastline, they passed just south of Honfleur, where in the early nineteenth century the Impressionists reigned, and the posh seaside resorts of Deauville and Trouville. Twelve miles past Caen, the sky that had grown dark just before lunch now lowered enough to touch the tops of the bristling hawthorn trees. The buildings on either side of the highway grew black and menacing. In the distance, the horizon had disappeared in a muddy haze of rain, and then the downpour hit them, drumming against the roof of the Citroën, sluiced off to either side of the windshield by the wipers. The car's headlights cut through the hissing gloom like gas lamps on a coal-dark night.

Within an hour they had made the A11. The rain had lessened to a heavy drizzle, but the world outside appeared to consist of colors smeared with an Impressionist's brush. They were approaching Avranches when Jenny began to complain of severe stomach cramps. Glancing over his shoulder, Bravo noticed that her face was pasty, beaded with sweat. Several moments later, he spotted one of those peculiarly European travel restaurants whose setting was a bridge over the highway. In the same rest area were bathrooms and several thousand yards further on, a gas station.

Camille pulled over, Bravo helped Jenny out. Camille grabbed a raincoat and, holding it over Jenny, insisted on going with her. Jenny did not have the strength to argue, and together the two women hurried into the low, squat building. Bravo went around to the driver's side of the Citroën, the better to keep an eye on the traffic. The light rain was cool, and he enjoyed the feel of it on his face as he pulled out his cell phone and dialed an overseas number.

It would already be night in New York, the blaze of man-made lights dimming the stars, the great energy of the city flowing unabated through the streets while the tops of high-rises disappeared into the clouds.

Emma answered on the first ring, as if she had been waiting for his call.

"Bravo, where are you?"

"In France," he said. "On my way to Brittany."

"What are you doing there?"

"I'm on an errand for Dad. He spoke to me about it just before the . . . just before the end." There was an uncomfortable silence for a moment. "How are you, Emma?"

"I'm fine. I'm singing again, my voice coach was just here."

"That's wonderful—and your eyes? Any change?"

"Not yet. Never mind, it's you I'm worried about."

"Me?"

"I can hear it in your voice," she said.

"Hear what?"

"Trouble. Whatever Dad wanted you to do, it's trouble, isn't it?"

"Why would you say—"

"Because I'm not an idiot, Bravo, and I resent you treating me like one. The president of the engineering firm I hired read the report to me. The gas line wasn't faulty; it was tampered with."

He looked around to see if the women had returned from the bathroom, but they weren't in view. "You seem to have taken the news in stride."

"Dad was in a dangerous business, Bravo. D'you think I hadn't guessed? And once I had, he confided in me."

"What?"

"In fact, from time to time I helped him. He knew—and so did I—that there was a high degree of risk in his business with the Gnostic Observatines."

There was a short pause, during which Bravo could hear her take a sip—of tea, perhaps. He was trying hard to adjust to this new reality.

"Now that you're launched on this mission," Emma continued, "I want you to know that I can be of use to you."

"Emma—"

"I suppose you think it's different now that I'm blind, but you're wrong. I'm quite capable of taking care of myself—and I can take care of you. I always have."

"I don't think I understand."

"Who d'you think kept tabs on you and reported back to Dad when you and he weren't talking? The estrangement certainly wasn't his idea."

"You mean you spied on me?"

"Come off it, Bravo. I did what was best for all of us—you included. Do you think even now that Dad had any evil designs on you? He was worried, and frankly I don't blame him. You acted like an adolescent, as if he were the enemy, when all he was trying to do—"

Bravo took the phone from his ear and severed the connection. He sat down heavily on the driver's seat. His mind seemed numb, the traffic on the A11 a distant buzz. A car pulled in and a couple of tourists with skittish teenagers tumbled out, loped through the drizzle into the low building. A large truck rumbled away from the gas station back onto the slick highway. His eyes registered these small comings and goings without comment from his mind, as if he were in a theater, watching a film.

His cell phone buzzed.

"Don't you dare treat me the way you treated Dad." Emma's voice sounded sharp in his ear. "And don't hang up on me again."

"Okay, okay, sorry." Bravo felt sheepish and a bit as if he were hung over. "But you rattled the hell out of me. I mean, here I was wondering how you were getting from room to room, and you tell me that you can provide me with help the way you did Dad."

"I suppose that was a lot to dump on you at once, but really, Bravo, sometimes you're so clueless. If you knew me at all you'd have realized that I've been struggling all my life to live up to you and Dad's expectations. I dealt with that, so I sure as hell can deal with this."

Bravo thought about how poorly Jenny had been treated by the Order. But when he considered this it didn't seem much different from how women were treated in corporate life or most anywhere else for that matter. "Listen, Emma, I . . . well, you know, when you told me, I thought, there it is again—everybody knew about Dad except me."

"There was a good reason for that, Bravo. You must know what it is by now. Dad was grooming you to take over for him. That's why he trained you, why he was always so hard on you. He wanted you prepared when the time came, but until that day he didn't want you involved in the Gnostic Observatines. It was vital that his enemies believed that you had nothing to do with the Order, that your life had been set on another path entirely. If the Knights of St. Clement had suspected for a moment what he had in mind for you, you would've been in terrible danger."

"There's a woman with me—Jenny—"

"Right, the Guardian. Dad was very high on her."

"I know. He sent me to her. She says Dad believed there's a traitor inside the Haute Cour. Do you have any idea who it might be?"

"No. I think in the final days Dad had narrowed it down to a couple of suspects, but he never got a chance to tell me who they were."

"Right." Bravo turned, saw Jenny and Camille exiting the building. "Maybe you could do some digging."

"Sure, no problem." The tension had drained out of her voice. "I'd love to get back to work."

"How will you . . . ?"

She laughed. "Oh, Bravo, before there was e-mail, there was the telephone. I have a facility with voices: if I hear a tape I can be whoever I want to be. Don't worry, I did this all the time for Dad. It worked quite well—people nowadays are paranoid about e-mails and electronic files."

Jenny had on the raincoat, and Camille was gripping her with one arm around her shoulders.

"Listen, Emma, about what happened before—"

"Forget it. Now that we understand one another—"

He never heard the end of her comment because at that moment he saw a black four-door Mercedes sedan with German plates heading for the two women. As it closed on them, Jenny pulled Camille out of the way. The Mercedes swerved to come between them and the building. At the last instant, it slowed. A blacked-out window slid down, the offside rear door opened, and he saw the dark glint of metal as a hand gripping a gun appeared.

Before Bravo could make a move, Jenny planted her left foot and with her right kicked the door closed. Then she lunged forward with her upper body, chopped down on the hand, wrested the gun away and fired three bullets into the interior of the Mercedes.

The car shuddered on its heavy shocks as if it had been shot, and it lurched forward. Jenny was whipped off her feet. Bravo could see that the hem of her raincoat had been caught in the closed door.

Emma was screaming through his cell phone as he threw it onto the seat, turned the ignition and put the Citroën in gear. He shouted to Camille, who was running after the Mercedes as it dragged Jenny along the rest area. The car was heading directly toward the gas pumps; it didn't seem as if anyone was driving it.

As Bravo momentarily tamped the Citroën's brakes, Camille, who was on his side of the car, pulled open the rear door. Even as she jumped into the Citroën's backseat he took off, the car slewing alarmingly on the wet blacktop.

"We'll never make it," she said breathlessly. "She's going to go up in a fireball with the assassins."

Bravo could see that Jenny was twisted up in the raincoat and, though she struggled to get free, couldn't extricate herself. Then the Mercedes ran over something and the bump swung Jenny around, slamming her head against the blacktop. Her eyes rolled up in her head and her body went limp, twisting grotesquely.

"The door's the only answer," Bravo said.

"You're insane! To get me close enough you'll risk running her over."

"She'll be dead if I don't try," he answered grimly. "Roll down your window and get ready."

Narrowly missing another car on his right, Bravo took up position just off the Mercedes's right flank. Now for the hard part. Focused solely on Jenny, he depressed the accelerator, creeping up on the other car. Fortunately, he had physics on his side; the force of the Mercedes's passage was pulling Jenny's body in toward its undercarriage, giving him slightly more room to maneuver. On the other hand, he was forced to push the Citroën to an unsafe speed; the gas pumps were only several hundred yards away. He forced himself not to think of the beating Jenny was taking. Instead, he concentrated on the outline of her body as if she were part of a puzzle he needed to solve. And yet he hesitated to bring the Citroën closer to her. "*You'll risk running her over,*" Camille had said, and she was right. But he had very little time; he needed to act *now.* Desperately, he maneuvered the Citroën so that it was parallel, then matched the Mercedes's speed and trajectory. It was still heading straight for the pumps, and there was nothing he could do to stop it. He risked glancing sideways, glimpsed the driver slumped over the wheel.

"Come on!" he yelled at Camille. "I can't get any closer!" Jenny could be under his wheels in a heartbeat.

Already kneeling on the seat, Camille now stretched her torso out the window. Balancing her hips on the bottom of the window frame, she reached out and grabbed hold of the Mercedes's door handle. Jenny was directly below her, cocooned so thoroughly in the raincoat she couldn't see her face. She pulled the handle once, cursed mightily, tugged again.

"Now!" Bravo cried.

Camille jiggled the chrome handle and the door unlatched partway, but the same law of physics that kept Jenny's body close to the Mercedes was making it difficult to open the door.

"Camille! For the love of God!"

With a tremendous effort, she wrenched the door open. Abruptly released, Jenny's body rolled across the rain-streaked blacktop. Her face was bone white, and Bravo couldn't tell whether or not she was breathing.

He stood on the brakes so that the Citroën screeched to a halt. Camille threw the door open, gathered Jenny up. Even before Camille swung the door shut, Bravo had accelerated.

All at once, they were upon the gas pumps. Bravo turned the wheel hard to the left, and the Citroën's tires squealed in protest as it fishtailed. People were screaming and running in every direction. Bravo turned into the skid, then accelerated sharply. The car leapt forward like a race-horse at the opening gun. Just behind them, the grille of the Mercedes slammed into the nearest pump, taking it right off its foundation. Gas spewed upward, and with a great sucking whoosh and a fierce burst of heat, the car and the station went up in a nightmare fireball full of twisted metal shards and greasy black smoke.

A great fist rocked the Citroën so severely it threatened to roll over. Then a piece of metal, black and twisted, struck the sedan as it was about to reenter the A11, and Bravo was forced to steer in a white-knuckle stagger, barely missing two cars as he entered the traffic stream, until he had the car under full control again.

"How is she?" he asked anxiously as he made his way through the maze of traffic.

"She's unconscious, that much is certain." Camille was using her hands to feel for a pulse. "She's alive. Her heartbeat is strong."

"Thank God," Bravo breathed. The police hadn't arrived yet so far as he could see, but it wouldn't be long, he knew, until they did. In the rearview mirror the greasy fireball was finally subsiding, but now the flames could be seen licking upward into the rain-laden sky.

"Hand me my phone. It's there right beside you," Bravo said, a bit out of breath as he drove. "I have a call to finish."

"My love, how are you?" Camille asked.

When he took the cell phone from her, his hand was trembling visibly.

11

SEVERAL MILES ON, CAMILLE MADE HIM PULL OVER, AND they switched positions. Bravo walked on stiff legs around the back of the Citroën. He bent down, extracted part of the Mercedes from the Citroën and with a muffled cry hurled it away. He climbed into the back seat, settling Jenny's limp form beside him, her head cradled in his lap. He gently drew wisps of hair off her cheek. In the process, his fingertips caressed the soft flesh behind her ear.

In the rearview mirror, Camille noted how his hand lingered on Jenny, how his gaze had a faraway look. At length, she said softly, "My love, please close the door. We must move on."

In a half daze, Bravo complied. His gaze returned to Jenny, his thoughts as dim and nebulous as the fog that had crept in on the heels of the rain.

"Bravo," Camille said in that quiet voice that never failed to command attention, "the Mercedes had a German license plate."

"I saw," he said automatically.

"We must now consider the possibility that we are wrong and Jordan is right."

She drove quickly and efficiently to a hotel that lay on the landward side of the causeway that stretched out to Mont St. Michel like an entreating hand. It was here that, over the centuries, pilgrims came from all over to worship at the monastery of the Archangel St. Michael, whose statue rose from the pinnacle of the medieval stone abbey at the top of the rocky islet, five hundred feet above the English Channel.

Bravo felt the way those ancient seekers must have felt when they arrived here—exhausted, sick at heart, in need of a miracle. He held Jenny closer to him as Camille got out and went into the hotel. They'd need a miracle, he thought, to get rooms here at the height of summer.

He watched her returning, walking purposefully toward him, a small smile on her face.

"Come, my love," she said as she opened his door. "Our rooms are waiting for us."

THE room was clean and neat. It was modern and anonymous, but owing to its position on the third floor its picture window overlooked the channel and the magnificent sight of the Marvel, as Mont St. Michel was sometimes called by the French, now nothing more than a ghostly shadow in the dense and swirling fog. There was a sling-back sofa and matching chair upholstered in a dark tweedy fabric beside the window, with a low wooden table between them. In the middle of the rear wall was the door to the bathroom, and to their right was the bed, flanked by a pair of night tables and lamps. The floor was polished wood, the walls the color of sand. The light streaming in was pallid and watery, entirely without definition, so that no shadow was cast anywhere in the room.

Bravo sat on the bed, holding Jenny in his arms, while Camille used hot water and a washcloth to bathe the back of her head and her hands where they were abraded. He hoped that the raincoat that had trapped her had also protected her from more serious damage while she had been dragged by the Mercedes because right now they were afraid to subject her to the handling required to take it off.

Camille applied one of the antiseptic creams she had bought, and Bravo gently laid Jenny on the bed, pulled a light blanket up around her.

"Camille, we have to find a doctor. Surely the longer she's unconscious the greater the danger."

Camille sat down beside him on the bed and, leaning over, carefully lifted Jenny's lids. "Her pupils aren't dilated—she appears to be sleeping, nothing more."

"But—"

"Come away now, my love." She rose and took his arm. "What she needs most now is rest—as do we all."

"I don't want to leave her."

"And you won't." Bravo was too distracted to notice the small pause.

"You must take some time now to look after yourself. Go wash up. Don't look so concerned, I'll watch over her."

Bravo nodded. As soon as he was in the bathroom, Camille carefully and methodically searched the room. She knew exactly what she was looking for, and when she found Jenny's possessions she picked through them with the expert eye of a pawnbroker. At first glance, nothing out of the norm presented itself. This was to be expected; Jenny Logan was a Guardian. But because she was, Camille knew she could not be totally unarmed. She had to have a weapon on her—one that she could take through airport security. And so Camille came at last to a compact, which was slightly oversized and a good deal heavier than any compact had any right to be. Opening it, she found not foundation powder and a pad but a small folding knife. She wasn't fooled by either its size or the mother-of-pearl scales. Activating the switchblade mechanism, she was rewarded with the lightninglike appearance of a wicked-looking stainless-steel blade. With the digital camera in her cell phone, she shot photos of the knife open and closed, dialed a Paris number and sent the photos off. Wiping down the knife carefully, she returned it to the compact moments before Bravo reappeared.

"How is she?" His hair was still dripping wet.

"No change." She gestured to the sofa near the window. "Why don't we sit here where we can easily keep an eye on her."

Outside, the fog had settled like a blanket of snow. The centuries-old image of St. Michael slaying the dragon curled at his feet was visible, but of the massive fortress-isle below it nothing could be seen, so that the fierce and avenging archangel appeared as if borne through the air on vaporous wings.

Camille allowed Bravo to sit in silence for some time, then she began to speak: "Tired as we both are, we must make some decisions. Was this the form of attack you escaped from in America?"

"More or less, yes." Bravo was sitting forward, flexed elbows on drawn-up knees. He seemed hollow-eyed, his face empty.

"Then Jordan was right. The Germans—"

"The Wassersturms have nothing to do with this!" he exploded. Rising, he returned to the bedside, stood staring down at Jenny's pale face. Her freckles had all but disappeared; a faint spiderweb of blue veins was visible at her temple.

Camille gave him some time with her, but not too much. She rose and went quickly to his side.

"Bravo, I'm terribly confused," she said softly. "Isn't it time you told me what's happening?"

When he didn't respond, she turned him around to face her. "Why won't you confide in me?"

"I want you to leave right now."

"What?"

He took her by the elbow and led her to the door. "Get in the car and go back to Paris."

"And leave you here like this? You can't be serious!"

"But I am, Camille. I'm deadly serious."

She made to break away from him, but he held her all the tighter. She struggled for only a moment, then she was still. They stared at each other in an odd contest of wills that mimicked the impassioned struggle between a headstrong teenager and his mother.

"This is no game, Camille. These people are out for blood—"

"*What* people? Do you know who is behind this? Bravo, you're frightening me."

"Then I've succeeded. Camille, I've put you in enough danger as it is. I'd never forgive myself if something happened to you."

"And what about your friend, Jenny Logan? You would risk losing her?"

At that moment, a sound came to them, like the soft mewl of a cat that hadn't been fed. They both turned, and Bravo let Camille go as he rushed to the bed. Jenny's eyes were open; they were looking blankly around the room.

"Bravo?"

"I'm here." He took her hand as he sat beside her. "And so is Camille."

As Camille came into her line of sight, Jenny said in a cracked voice, "Where am I?"

"In a hotel," Camille said with a smile. "You're perfectly safe here."

Jenny's eyes settled on Bravo. "The Mercedes?"

"Destroyed, utterly," he said. "It hit a gas pump and went up in flames."

"God. . . ." Her head turned to one side and a single tear rolled down onto the bedspread.

"Thank you for saving my life," Camille said, kneeling beside her. "Your courage is extraordinary."

Jenny looked at her but said nothing.

Camille leaned against the night table. "You must rest and regain your strength. We have brought you to Mont St. Michel. It is a sacred place, Jenny. A place for healing both the body and the spirit. It has been so ever since the first abbey was built in the eleventh century. But the very site itself is holy. The monastery was founded in 708 by St. Aubert, the Bishop of Avranches, who was visited in dreams by the archangel Michel himself. Ever since then Mont St. Michel has been a magnet for people in need from all over the known world. Be at peace now, you need time to recover. Call me if there is anything you want and I shall bring it."

She rose and, smiling, told Bravo that she was going to lie down for a while.

Bravo waited until she closed the door behind her, then said, "How are you feeling?"

"Like I was run over by a freight train."

"You very nearly were," Bravo said, "or something very much like it." He took a breath. "Jenny, did you see who was inside the Mercedes?"

"I had only the briefest glimpse and that was . . . I keep getting flickers of images. There were two figures."

"Male or female?"

"The one with the gun—he was a man, I'm sure of that. He had a long, narrow face, dark hair and eyes, mid-thirties or so." She closed her eyes for a moment. "Everything's spinning around."

"Here," Bravo said, "see if you can sit up."

He helped her put her back against two pillows. Then he gave her some water. Jenny stared down into the bottom of the glass as if it were a sorcerer's bowl in which the images of her encounter with the Mercedes could be conjured up.

"THE driver was a man, as well."

Standing in her room, smoking a cigarette, Camille had to admire the ingenuity of the microcircuits on the listening device she'd planted on the underside of the night table as she knelt down. Her conversation with Jenny had been a diversion while she pressed the tiny device into the unpainted plywood.

"Yes, he was," Bravo said. *"I saw him slumped over the wheel after you*

shot him dead. I think we can reasonably assume that your recollection of the other man is accurate." A small noise interrupted the flow, then Bravo's voice returned. *"The Mercedes had German plates. Camille thinks that Jordan might be right about the Wassersturms being after me."*

"Surely you don't think that."

"I don't," Bravo said, *"but I suppose it would be best to be certain."*

"The Wassersturms are a blind alley, and a potentially dangerous one," Jenny said in a voice audibly more firm. *"We can't allow anything to interfere with finding the cache of secrets."*

"Dear God, no, we can't have that," Camille said into the ensuing silence. When she was certain that the conversation was at an end, she took out her cell phone and tapped in a number.

"Bravo doesn't know where the cache is," she said when her son picked up the phone. "On the other hand, he isn't going to tell me a thing about the devilish labyrinth Dexter has set up."

"Did you actually expect him to?"

"There was always the chance."

Jordan laughed, a piercing, thoroughly nasty sound. "How disappointed you would've been if he'd proved himself such a fool!"

"He's his father's son, after all, isn't he?"

There was a small silence.

"He won't go for the Wassersturm story, and neither will Jenny. I told you," she said, abruptly changing the subject. "That was Osman Spagna's idea, wasn't it?"

"What if it was?" Jordan said somewhat defensively.

"I don't like that man, Jordan. I've told you before. Get rid of him."

"I didn't think Bravo would go for the Wassersturm story, either, but that wasn't the purpose," he said, avoiding an answer he did not want to give. "We needed to build your credibility with them."

"Yes, it's an old confidence trick. The girl didn't like me from the outset, now there's a bond of trust between us." She paused a moment. "About the Mercedes, there were no survivors."

"Survival of the fittest," Jordan said. "If they were good enough Jenny wouldn't have been able to kill them."

"How did you know Jenny did it?"

Jordan laughed again. "I have to have some secrets, Mother, even from you, otherwise I'm just too good a boy."

"Make sure there aren't any more," Camille said sternly as she broke the connection.

SILENCE.

Jenny, her eyes half-closed, whispered, "Why are you looking at me that way?"

Without answering, Bravo disappeared into the bathroom. A moment later, she could hear the water running. The sound soothed her and her gaze drifted to the picture window, beyond which only the largest form—that of Mont St. Michel itself—could be seen, though indistinctly, no more than a shadow towering from the salt beds of the unseen tidewater. The long afternoon had progressed, but within the white void of the fog there was no sound, no movement, not even a hint that the sun continued to cross the sky. It was as if time itself stood still.

Settling herself, Jenny felt small sticking pains as if beetles roamed over her body, biting her with their pincers. She made incoherent sounds deep in her throat, as people often will when their dreams get the better of them.

After an indeterminate time, she opened her eyes to see Bravo standing over her. The water sounded like a cataract, burbling and rushing as if anxious to get from one place to the next. She had the strange impression that the tide had risen high enough to seep through the foundation, swirling upward to wash into the room and now lapping at her thighs. Her fingers worked the bedspread, searching for evidence that she had floated free of terra firma.

Without a word, Bravo scooped her off the bed and carried her into the bathroom. Once inside, he did not stop but stepped over the lip of the tub. Steam was rising, and it was wonderfully warm. He laid her in the water and, taking up the hand-held faucet, ran the hot water over her. Then he began to untangle her clothes. At first, she felt as if the beetles had returned, and she resumed her sounds of distress, but when she was more herself, she understood that her own blood, drying, had made her clothes stick to her and it was this that caused the pain when she'd moved in bed.

Slowly, layer by layer, he unpeeled her. Her blood was dissolving, and it was not an unpleasant sensation. She thought of an orange, whose bitter rind must be stripped away to reveal the sweet fruit beneath. She gazed up into Bravo's face and saw herself reflected in his eyes. She was half naked, and somehow she was neither angry nor embarrassed.

On the other hand, she felt compelled to say, "Why are you doing this?"

As his hands continued with their work, he looked at her for what seemed a long time. "Because," he said at last, "I almost lost you." His fingers, nearly finished, stroked her bare flesh. "Because you mean something to me."

"What?" The hot water cascaded over her, over both of them as he knelt facing her. "What do I mean to you?"

She saw what he wanted to say in his eyes, felt it in the way he cradled her, in the heat rising between them. Her arms came around him and because she couldn't help herself she pulled him toward her. She felt him against her and she was lifted up, not only her body but her spirit. She recalled what Camille said about the healing power of Mont St. Michel.

She felt the steady, strong beating of his heart. A wildness had taken hold of her that was strangely familiar, the deep, soul-shattering yearning that had gripped her before her mother had sent her away to school.

The floodgates, so long held in check, opened. Her head moved forward, her lips opened, and she surrendered herself to everything she wanted, everything that was coming.

WHEN they emerged from the bath, the fog had lifted entirely. It was that time of day, beautiful, mysterious, when the sky is infinite and full of light from an unseen source, when far below, the darkness of evening has already begun to gather, spreading its midnight-blue shadows across roads and cobbles, low walls and foundations, weighing them down, fastening them to the black earth.

They sat side by side, gazing out the window at the Marvel with its two-level walled village curled like the defeated dragon around its feet. The enormous monastery, which was constructed entirely of granite, had foundations that were laid 160 feet above sea level.

"As you probably know, the abbey is Benedictine," Bravo said, "but in the fourteenth and fifteenth centuries it was fortified in the manner of a military installation. In fact, Mont St. Michel's position in the channel made it an important outpost when France went to war with England. Immediately, it became both strategic and impregnable. Its defenses have never been breached."

On the wall just above the window were sculpted a cockleshell, a horn and a staff.

Jenny ran her fingertips over the bas-relief. "Do these symbols have a meaning?"

"They're the insignia of Mont St. Michel," Bravo said, "known to every pilgrim who made his way to the islet from the thirteenth century on. This was before the causeway was built, you understand, when the high tide completely cut off the islet from the mainland. Many people drowned in the uncertain tides. It's difficult to know which was more treacherous, the tides or the sea floor. The staff was used to probe for quicksand on the journey out to the abbey, the horn would be used to sound the alarm if the pilgrim was lost in lowering fog or rising water, and the cockleshell was stuck in the pilgrim's hat when he left Mont St. Michel, a symbol that proclaimed his safe and successful journey."

"I wish I had a cockleshell." Jenny put her head back against the sofa.

"Do you want to sleep?" Bravo asked her.

"No," she said, a small smile on her lips. "I'm hungry."

"What should I bring you?"

But her eyes were already closed. In a very short while her breathing became even, and Bravo, rising, brought the blanket over, covering her from feet to neck.

12

ST. MALO OCCUPIED THE WESTERNMOST PART OF A SMALL
cape that jutted out into the English Channel. The cape was more or less
in the shape of a dog's head, St. Malo being the muzzle. They arrived
just after 12:30 in the afternoon. The inner core of the city was ancient
and beautiful, fortified by a thick stone wall. Around this had been
thrown up concentric circles of twentieth-century housing, cheap and
ugly, where many of the residents lived and worked. The tour buses,
however, drew up in the vast cobbled car park outside the gates to the Old
City, where they disgorged their contents of excited, video camera–
toting tourists, wanting to tape the highlights, eat crepes and continue to
the next stop on their whirlwind tour. There were Germans and Swiss
and Austrians, Spaniards, Italians, Britons and, of course, Japanese. As
hostile as warring parties, they clannishly formed into tight knots as if
afraid to come into contact with each other. They moved in swarms, under military banners resentfully brandished by their guides.

Camille pulled up adjacent to several of the buses. She looked at
Bravo sternly and said, "Are you certain this is what you want to do?"

He nodded. "Absolutely."

"Bon."

"You'll do as I asked and return to Paris," Bravo said a little anxiously.

"I told you at breakfast I would." She kissed Bravo and Jenny both on
either cheek and advised them to enter the city amid the forming crush
of tour groups.

This they did. As they passed through the ancient gates to the Old
City, Bravo glanced over his shoulder, but the Citroën was nowhere to
be seen.

Amid all the video equipment and digital cameras, the GPS Bravo had taken from Kavanaugh's car was inconspicuous. He punched in the coordinates his father had provided.

They stayed within the knot of the tour group for five or six minutes, but when it began to move out to its first destination, he went to their left. "This way," he said, heading through the narrow shop-lined streets. He led them through the maze of the Old City, heading generally northwest toward the seawall.

St. Malo, more or less midway along the Côte d'Emeraude, the Emerald Coast, was built on the rocky and often wild coast of Brittany, France's north shore. In the old days, it had harbored both merchant sailors and marauding corsairs. At that time, many of the European countries were at war, and the high seas was open territory. The kings of France, Spain, Holland and England did what they could to encourage private owners to arm their ships to attack enemy vessels. The French privateers were known as corsairs after the king's permit, a *lettre de course,* a formal authorization to carry out their business under strict regulations. Their booty was divided into equal shares split between the king, the ship owner and the crew.

The city was founded by Father MacLaw, a Welsh bishop who fled Wales to Brittany in 538, *Malo* being the French pronunciation of his name. Despite its advantageous location, the city did not attain real prominence until it was adopted by corsairs, who, growing rich and powerful, fortified it against their enemies both on the sea and on land. By 1590, the St. Malo corsairs had become so influential that they dared to declare the city a republic independent of both the federal and the municipal Breton governments.

Throughout the sixteenth, seventeenth and eighteenth centuries, St. Malo acquired considerable wealth, not only from its maritime trade between the Americas and Europe but from its so-called Newfoundlanders, whose fleets fished for cod in the chill waters off the east coast of Canada. However successful these intrepid fishermen were, the bulk of the city's riches and fame was the result of the constant raids of its feared corsairs.

If one knew what to look for, St. Malo's rich and storied history was visible all around in the stone houses, the fortified walls, the brightly colored corsair pennants. Striding along cobbled streets, Jenny and

Bravo reached the formidable seawall and now mounted the stone stairs set into its inside face. Gaining the top, they looked out onto the Gulf of St. Malo, beyond which were the gray-blue backs of Jersey and the Channel Islands, rising from the channel like breaching whales. The day was fair and what little breeze came to them was as soft and downy as a feather pillow. The summer sun blazed down from a clear sky. Because of yesterday's rain the normal heat haze had not yet reasserted itself. Every object stood out, sharp as a knife blade, and the vista seemed endless, the thick swath of sun-dazzle as solid-seeming as a pale stone road through a cobalt wood.

"There," Bravo said, pointing. "That's the spot!"

"But for miles and miles there's only water here," Jenny said. "Could your father have etched the wrong coordinates?"

Bravo shook his head. "He knew just what he was doing."

"Then how do you explain this?" Her arms swept out to encompass the infinite waterscape. "And what about the last four numbers—one, five, three, zero—what do they signify?"

Bravo glanced at his watch. "I don't know about you, but I'm hungry. Let's go down and have lunch at that pretty little café we passed."

Jenny looked at him sharply. "You know what the last number sequence means, don't you?" She shaded her eyes from the sun with the flat of her hand. The color had returned to her face, the spray of freckles across her nose clearly visible again. "Tell me."

"I don't want to spoil the surprise," he said with a laugh.

They sat in the tiny stone courtyard of the café, beneath a gaily striped umbrella, not three yards from the seawall. They could smell the tang of the brine and the sharp mineral scent of the ancient stone blocks. Jenny ate with little appetite. She drank no wine but insisted on iced coffee.

She wanted to talk about Camille Muhlmann but said nothing, afraid of Bravo's reaction. Fear of another sort, terribly familiar, was slithering through her belly like a serpent. Their sublime moment of intimacy should have changed everything, but when she had awoken this morning, her self-made wall had reasserted itself. Worse, she didn't trust her own feelings. After all, she admonished herself, she'd been no more than half conscious—perhaps the whole thing had been nothing more than a fever dream.

Seeing her shiver, Bravo said at once, "Are you all right?"

"I'm fine." There was a patch of sunlight on his face, making the electric-blue color of his eyes even more extravagant. "You don't have to keep asking me. Really."

"But you looked—"

Her face flushed with sudden anger and she shot him a poisoned look. "For God's sake, don't scrutinize me! Paolo Zorzi trained me—and trained me well—for this life. Do we have that straight?"

The remainder of the meal was passed without either of them uttering another word. The happy burble of voices, sudden bursts of laughter, clink of wine-filled glasses, amorous glances passed between couples at neighboring tables all served to depress her so thoroughly that before dessert and a refill of her iced coffee she was forced to closet herself in one of the two minuscule stalls in the café's bathroom so that she could burst into tears undetected. Dexter Shaw had charged her with protecting his son. Bad enough that Bravo had already seen her in a weakened state, she was certain he would lose all respect for her if he knew that she'd sunk so low.

AFTER lunch, they mounted the seawall again and stood in the same spot as before. Again, Bravo pointed. "Look!"

As they watched, they saw a ghostly shape rising slowly out of the sea.

Jenny, glancing at her watch, said, "One, five, three, zero. Fifteen-thirty—it's military time! Three-thirty in the afternoon."

Bravo nodded. "My father was referring to the tide tables. See there, the ebbing tide is bringing his *piscina* to us."

The ghostly shape began to resolve itself as the water of the bay continued to recede. Soon it became clear that they were looking at concrete walls.

"A swimming pool!" Jenny exclaimed.

"Yes, and a damned clever one, too. Look, it's three-sided to hold the sea water and allow anyone coming from the shore to enter, so that people have a place to swim all afternoon long while the tide is out."

They went a little way along the seawall until they came to a flight of steps on its far side.

"Come on," he said.

Clattering down the steps, they emerged onto the beach. Immediately, they were struck by the reflected heat and a stronger scent of brine, along with the odors of aquatic decay, suntan oil and pleasantly perspiring bodies. Down the beach some way was a shack selling raw oysters, *frites* and cold drinks. The beach was filled with people—women in skimpy bikinis or bare-breasted, men talking, arms folded across their chests. Three children kicked a multicolored striped ball into the surf, where bathers were coming and going.

Bravo and Jenny removed their shoes. He rolled up his trousers and she lifted her skirt, wrapping it like a Turkish towel around the tops of her thighs. Then they walked across the sand, wading out toward the swimming pool, which was still rising from the restless waters of the bay.

Using the GPS, Bravo guided them deeper into the water, which rose to their thighs. When they reached the left wall of the pool, Bravo moved along it to the farthest point. He ran his fingers down the inside of the wall as far as they would go.

"Anything?" Jenny asked.

He shook his head.

NOT far from where they stood, Camille leaned against the seawall. She had on a scarf that completely covered her hair, and she had bought a man's felt cap whose shallow brim she kept low on her forehead. Her elbows were on the top of the seawall, and her hands gripped a pair of powerful binoculars through which she peered at Bravo and Jenny. She watched with extreme concentration as Bravo handed the GPS, his passport and his cell phone to Jenny and then sank beneath the water.

WITHIN three minutes, Bravo reappeared. Water streamed off him and his shirt clung to him like rags.

"There's a small, square door flush with the wall," he said as he wiped water out of his eyes. "The problem is that the door has no handle."

"Does it have a lock?"

"That's the other problem," Bravo said. "It's utterly unconventional."

"I know a bit about locks," Jenny said. "What does it look like?"

"It's a tiny square. Do you know of any kind of key that would open a square lock?"

Jenny shook her head, frowning. "But your father wouldn't have led you here unless he'd provided you with a way to open the door."

"I only have the one key he entrusted to me," Bravo said. "I promise you it's not going to open that peculiar lock."

"What else did you find in the boat compartment?" she said.

He dug in his pocket, produced the Zippo, the cuff links and the enamel lapel pin. He stared at them for a moment, trying to think as his father would have thought. The Zippo was far too big and the pin was the wrong shape, but the cuff links were cubes—and they were more or less the right size. He picked up one of them and stared at the groove pattern around its side.

"You're right!" he said excitedly, showing Jenny the grooves. "This isn't simply a cuff link—it's a key! The key to the underwater door!"

He went under the water, but soon—too soon—reemerged.

"It slides into the lock but won't turn."

"The groove pattern is wrong," Jenny said. "Try the other one."

AS Bravo submerged again, Camille trained her attention on Jenny. Camille felt that she knew Bravo well enough. After all, she'd had years to absorb all the ins and outs of his psyche. It was critical now that she be able to do the same with Jenny, and her time frame was by necessity terribly compressed. Even her mole inside the Order hadn't known who would assign the Guardian to Bravo, let alone which Guardian it would be. To be truthful, she had been surprised that it had been Jenny.

In any event, if she was to carry out her plan, namely to herd Bravo and Jenny like cattle, separate them, make them desperate, then she needed to be able to get inside both their heads. What interested her now was that though they had spent the night together, Jenny was still maintaining a certain distance. In fact, from her expression and body language, Camille was sure that she was angry—but whether it was with Bravo or herself she could not yet say. Was she frigid or, possibly, gay? This was an important question for Camille because it was her experience that sexuality was a major determinant of human behavior. Camille had been in the next stall when Jenny had locked herself in and started to sob. She felt sure that this was a key moment to getting beneath the Guardian's skin and was frustrated that she hadn't learned what had caused Jenny to break down so hard.

Watching her now with the sun in her eyes, her hair gleaming, her shapely torso emerging from the white glare of the water, Camille found it in herself to admire the woman's recuperative powers, but what she was really concentrating on was the next phase of her plan to peel back the layers that all human beings erect to protect themselves and lay bare the vulnerable points she could exploit.

IT was as blue under the water as the arching rock face of the Grotta Azzurra. The pale legs of waders, the hairy bellies of swimmers, Jenny's thighs—everything appeared distorted, save for the door in the concrete wall. Brushing it with the flat of his hand brought out a shine, and he could see that it was some kind of metal—stainless steel, perhaps, to repel the effects of the salt.

As if in slow motion, he extended the cuff link into the lock, turning it forty-five degrees at a time until he was able to press it all the way into the lock. He turned it and pulled. Nothing happened. He turned it the other way, pulled again and the door swung open. With his other hand, he reached in, felt something and immediately pulled it out. It was a small packet sealed in plastic. He checked to make sure there was nothing else inside the box, then he relocked it, extracted the key and, with a strong kick, breached the surface.

THE moment he surfaced, he opened his fist just enough for Jenny to see what he held, then together they waded back to shallower water. They moved some distance away from the swimmers, finding a small patch of open water. As Bravo was about to open his fist again, Jenny put her hand over his and moved so that her back was to the shore.

"It pays to be cautious," she said. "We've been spied on more than once, and even though I finished off the Knights in the Mercedes, we can't be certain there wasn't a backup team in place. In fact, knowing how the Knights work, I'd be surprised if there wasn't. Given the stakes, I'll bet they're bending all their resources to keep us in range."

Bravo took a surreptitious look around. "Then why stand out in the open altogether?"

"No point in telegraphing how vigilant we are. Let them think we've forgotten all about them."

Bravo frowned, then nodded. As usual, what she said made good sense. In the shadow thrown by their closely bent heads he carefully opened the watertight wrapping and unfolded a sheet of paper. Inside was a gold coin of a male figure in a beatific pose, one hand raised in benediction. On the sheet of paper was written in his father's neat backward-slanting hand, "A scene of light and glory, a dominion/That has endured the longest among men."

Jenny looked at him questioningly. "What does it mean? More code?"

"In a way," Bravo said thoughtfully. "The quotation is from Samuel Rogers. It was a favorite of my father's, but only my mother and I knew that, I doubt that even Emma knows." He recited the two lines as if they were a prayer. "Rogers was writing about Venice."

"Obviously, that's our next stop," Jenny said. "What about the coin?"

Bravo held it between his fingertips, feeling its deep ridges. He turned it slowly, examining both its face and obverse. "First off, it's not a reproduction. It's very old—ancient, in fact. I think it will tell me where in Venice my father is sending us."

"You mean you don't know?"

"Not yet." He smiled into her concerned face. "Don't look so gloomy, I'll find the answer. When it comes to my father's codes I always have."

His heart beat fast. He was holding the confirmation in his hands. He was on a long journey, one that would keep him connected to his father even after death, for they had played this game often enough during Bravo's childhood—a game of codes, each one exponentially more difficult to crack than the last. At least, that was how it had seemed to Bravo when he was growing up. Now he knew that the lessons his father had taught him in code breaking must have been leading up to this moment. Had Dexter Shaw foreseen his death? Surely not, surely he'd been ensuring that when the time came he'd have a successor.

Bravo closed his fist around the coin. It had been warmed by the sun and by his own blood. The coin, the paper with the quotation, even the Zippo lighter had taken on far more importance. They were not simply the last remnants of his father's life. As cold and dead as he was, they carried the heat of life, the joy he'd experienced each and every time his father had challenged him to match wits. These clues brought him closer to his father than he had been since his childhood—a time when the world had made sense, when he and his father were tied together by the ever more complex and puzzling series of codes, as if they were the only two people in the universe.

Bravo and Jenny moved slowly back to where their shoes lay baking on the pale sand and sat for a time, watching swimmers in the *piscina*. From a plastic portable radio next to a bare-breasted sunbather came a plaintive pop song by Mylene Farmer. A group of children played in the sand, digging and building a wall from time to time undermined by the water. A pair of German women, pale-skinned and hollow-chested, walked the surf, talking of a pair of shoes they'd seen in a shopwindow. The scent of crepes and wine mingled with the salt tang. The heat of the sun baked into them, drying their clothes, the water evaporating to gritty salt on their skin.

At last, they pulled on their shoes and left the beach and its unique *piscina*. As they mounted the seawall, Bravo pulled out his cell phone and called the airline, making a reservation on the last flight to Venice.

"I suppose I shouldn't have sent Camille away. We need transportation back to Paris," he said when he severed the connection. "We'll walk into the new city and ask someone for directions to a rental car office."

The Old City was dense with tourists, slowing their trek through its packed streets, but at last they caught sight of the main gate.

"Now's the time to be on our guard," Jenny said.

Bravo nodded and began to walk toward the gate, but he swung around as her hand gripped his arm.

"I'm going first," she said and almost at once raised a hand to stop his intended protest. "It won't matter what argument you use, the outcome will be the same." Her gaze was as steady as it was serious. "You think I'm not up to it, but I promise you I am."

"You did a helluva job protecting me and Camille on the motorway," Bravo said, matching her serious tone. "I guess I didn't tell you that before."

"No," Jenny said, "you didn't."

She let go of him and strode purposefully past. He followed her as she snaked her way through the throng of sightseers streaming through the gate and out onto the cobbled road beyond which stretched the bus-filled carpark.

They had to pause, waiting for a gap in the slow crawl of cars backed up along the road. The air was stifling with the accumulation of sun, baking stone and exhaust emissions. People were everywhere: tourists in twos, fours, and larger groups; bicyclists on errands or just out for exercise; children laughing, crying or screaming; exasperated parents tugging at their little hands. Sweet scents came to them of ice cream, sticky candy and cheap cologne. Jenny turned, saw coming toward them a group of perhaps fifteen children between the ages of eight and nine. They were accompanied by three adults, one at their head, one behind, and the third walking alongside.

A gap was opening up in the traffic flow and she was turning away when she saw movement in the corner of her eye. The third adult had broken into a lope, leaving the group of children behind. The other two adult supervisors were paying him no mind, which told Jenny they didn't know him, he'd been using the children as camouflage.

Grabbing Bravo, she plunged headlong into the gap in the traffic, but they were no more than halfway across the blisteringly hot road when she saw the bicyclist bearing down on them. It was a two-pronged attack.

There was no more time for speculation. The cyclist had a length of wicked-looking polished wood in his hand and was lifting it in preparation of delivering a blow. She had to act *now*.

Pushing Bravo aside, she stood tall, waited for the downswing of the stick and, moving her arm in parallel to its arc, grabbed it and, at the same time, drove the cocked elbow of her other arm into the cyclist's throat. She kicked the front wheel and the bicycle went over, taking its rider with it.

"Run!" she shouted to Bravo. "Run!"

Together, they took off along the road in the same direction as the traffic flow. Horns blared and voices were raised in outrage as they darted in and out between the cars. Risking a glance behind them, Jenny saw the first man had grabbed the fallen bicycle. He swung aboard and took off after them. In one hand he brandished a large gun.

They ran as fast as they could, but because they had to watch out for the lurching cars, stopping and starting as they brushed against them, it was slow and perilous going. The cyclist was gaining on them rapidly. Jenny looked around for alternate escape routes, but the crowd pressed in at every direction. They'd be sitting ducks for the cyclist, unless. . . . She moved them into the thickest part of the throng, using the people around them as a shield.

But at that moment, another, even greater danger presented itself. A silver BMW X5 SUV appeared in the carpark, racing toward them from the opposite direction.

"The vise is complete," Bravo said without rancor.

There was no time for evasive manuevers—the oncoming BMW was upon them. In a moment, Jenny thought, they'd be dead meat, and there wasn't a thing she could do about it.

13

JENNY, TENSED AND DETERMINED TO DO WHAT SHE COULD
to protect Bravo from the Knights' attack, saw the driver's head pop out
of the side window.

"Get in!" he shouted.

Even while she was wondering what Anthony Rule was doing here,
Bravo called out, "Uncle Tony!"

Rule risked a quick glance at the cyclist and at once saw the raised
gun. "Get in, the two of you! Hurry!"

Jenny opened the SUV's door, placing her body as a shield between
Bravo and the gunman. A shot rang out, piercing the window, shattering
the glass. Jenny pushed Bravo's head down behind the metal as she bun-
dled him into the backseat. The instant she jumped in, Rule took off.
With a fierce blare of his horn he stopped two oncoming cars in their
tracks and caused a minor fender bender as the vehicle behind them
couldn't stop in time. He turned the wheel over, they jumped the low
concrete divider between the road and the car park and, with more
room to maneuver, he accelerated into the vast cobbled apron behind
the line of tour buses. By this time they'd left the gunman far behind, a
fact remarked on by Rule as he checked the rearview mirror.

"I'd have run over the bastard if I'd been alone," he said. Then he
chuckled low in his throat. "But if I'd been alone he never would have
been here, would he?"

"Speaking of which," Jenny said tartly, "what are *you* doing here?"

"Wait a minute," Bravo said, "you two know each other?"

"You're welcome," Rule said to Jenny as if Bravo hadn't asked the
question. Then, when he saw her frown, his eyes flicked to Bravo in

the mirror. "What was I thinking? She's the Ice Goddess, after all."

"The Ice Goddess. That's what the other Guardians call me," Jenny muttered darkly.

"You give them sufficient cause," Rule said.

"Oh, yes," she said, rising to the bait, "it's always my fault, isn't it?"

"And here's a newsflash for you, kiddo, it isn't only the Guardians."

"Why should I give a crap?"

Rule shrugged, as if to say that if she didn't want to take his advice, it was of no moment to him.

Bravo observed this dialog with a growing sense of astonishment. Not only did his father have a life kept secret from him, so did Uncle Tony.

"Shaken up, Bravo?" Rule said, as if reading his thoughts.

"Give me a minute."

Rule drove them out of the rear of the car park and into the new city, turning this way and that as if he were in a video game, making sure their enemies couldn't follow them. Of course, it made perfect sense that Uncle Tony was a Gnostic Observatine. Bravo had always called him Uncle Tony not because he was related but because he was so close with Bravo's father.

"You still haven't told us what you're doing here," Jenny pursued doggedly. "It can't be coincidence."

"Coincidence doesn't exist in the Voire Dei, does it, kiddo?" Rule shook his head. "No, I was following the trail of the second key."

"The second key?" Bravo said.

Uncle Tony nodded. "There are two keys to the cache. Your father had one, Molko had the other. Molko was taken by the Knights, tortured and killed. We have to assume they have the second key."

"So it has turned into a race," Bravo said.

"In a sense," Uncle Tony said. "Except that the Knights don't yet know the location of the cache. Only your father knew it."

"That's why I was being tailed all the way from New York to Washington," Bravo said. He thought of Rossi making sure they wouldn't be shot when they fled Jenny's house, the rubber bullet with which Jenny had been shot at the cemetery. Now he had confirmation of his theory that the Knights hadn't been sent to kill them; they needed to find out the location of the cache. "But Jenny and I took care of that before we came here."

"What you need to understand," Rule said, "is that the Knights of St. Clement are like a hydra—lop off two heads and four more take their place."

"They can't have a bug on Bravo," Jenny said. "He's got nothing on him he had in Washington, not even his clothes."

Bravo leaned forward, his forearms across the back of the driver's seat. "Except for the few things my father left me, and no one except me had any knowledge of where they were or their significance."

Jenny nodded. "They must be using another method to track you."

"What do I do, then?" Bravo said.

"Keep to the plan. Trust your father. That's all you can do," Uncle Tony said. "Meanwhile, Jenny here has your back."

He accelerated past two cars stuck behind a laboring truck. "Sorry about your dad. He was one of a kind—a great man and the best friend I ever had."

"Thanks," Bravo said, "that means a lot to me."

"I know you were Dexter Shaw's oldest friend inside the Order," Jenny said. "Is that why you're here?"

"And you thought it was to check up on you," Rule said with a not unkind snort. He was a tall, rangy man, with the rough and ruddy skin of an outdoorsman. His hair was going gray at the temples and was brushed forward in the style of a Roman senator. "Well, I don't blame you. Kavanaugh took it into his head to light out after you." A livid scar, slightly raised and ropy, ran down the left side of his jaw like an exclamation mark. "I'd say 'poor Kavanaugh,' if only the bastard had deserved it."

Jenny looked at him for a moment, then turned away to stare out the window.

Rule pursed his lips as if he had just tasted something rotten.

"Kavanaugh made a mistake, let's leave it at that," Bravo said. He had grown increasingly uncomfortable with their occasional verbal slaps, and he meant to put a stop to it. "Right now, what we need most is a lift to Paris. We've got a flight out of Charles de Gaulle at nine p.m. for Venice."

Anthony Rule nodded. "Only too happy to be of service." Though he was in his late fifties, time had been kind to him. He had lost none of the casual good looks that had naturally attracted women all his life. "Bravo, to be honest, Dex's death was a shock to me, but it was hardly a surprise. I think by now you must know what I mean. Dex knew he was marked for death, knew his murder was possible, perhaps even inevitable. That's the brutal nature of our war against the powers of evil and corruption. I wish it could be otherwise, but until the Knights of St. Clement are annihilated, it can't. It's as simple as that."

"It seems to me that an enmity that has survived for centuries would be anything but simple," Bravo said.

"Listen to the expert." Rule shook his head. "Instead of waxing philosophical, you should be concentrating that brilliant mind of yours on how the Knights have been able to keep tabs on you."

"My father—and Jenny's—both believed there was a traitor inside the Haute Cour," Bravo said. "Do you?"

Rule shot a quick glance at Jenny in the rearview mirror. "I see you've been doing your job in other ways as well, kiddo."

Bravo noticed that Jenny had returned from her sullen contemplation of the road. At last, Uncle Tony had her full attention.

"Do you have any idea who the traitor is?" Jenny said.

"That was Dex's obsession," Rule said darkly. "As for me, my attentions are elsewhere. I have no opinion."

They were on the motorway now, heading back to Charles de Gaulle airport. Rule exited the motorway and, slowing considerably, joined the traffic on the secondary road. He took one of his periodic reads of the cars in the side mirror and made two quick turns. "Okay, we're clean."

They were now on a long, relatively straight stretch of road that was perfect for keeping an eye out for tails.

"They want our secrets, Bravo," Rule continued. "But they especially want one secret—the one your father was guarding with his life."

"But I don't even know what that secret is."

"Of course you don't. Jenny doesn't know what it is, and neither does the majority of the Order. But I do." The entrance to the motorway came up fast on his left. Rule was already in the left lane, but there was a broken-down car blocking the entrance and he zoomed past without being able to get on.

Jenny had already turned her torso half around so that she could look through the rear window.

"What's going on?" Bravo said.

Rule sat a little forward, his body tense. "We've got a problem."

"Picked up another tail." Jenny moved slightly closer to Bravo on the backseat to improve her view. "White Mercedes coupe three cars back."

Rule nodded. "That's the one, but my concern is that it might not be the *only* one."

"What makes you say that?" Bravo asked.

"The broken-down car that was blocking the motorway entrance," Jenny said.

"It kept us on this road," Rule said. He turned the wheel hard, and the X5 skidded slightly. He pressed the accelerator to the floor, and they were thrown backward into their seats.

"Now we'll really see what this can do," Rule said. "I have a twelve-cylinder engine in here that should let us do everything but take off."

Up ahead, Bravo saw a red Audi move over to the left and accelerate to match their speed.

"It's a box, all right," Jenny called out.

Rule nodded again. "They've got us front and rear. Better fasten your seat belts, children."

He wove in and out of the traffic, cutting his lane-changing within a hairsbreadth of disaster. He was deliberately going faster than the traffic flow, and now it was easy to see the two Knight vehicles—the Audi in front, the Mercedes behind.

All at once, the Audi slowed. Rule stepped on the brakes, skidding slightly, and he shifted down to compensate. An instant later, they were slammed by the Mercedes, and he accelerated directly at the Audi. The Audi, smaller and lighter by far than either the BMW or the Mercedes, skittered to life, staying in front of them.

"This isn't good," Rule said. "I have to assume they want us on this road for a reason."

No sooner had he said this than he saw the semi idling up ahead. Its rear doors gaped open, a steel ramp extending down from it.

"That's why they put us in a box," Rule said. "They want to herd us into the semi."

To their left loomed the off-ramp to the motorway. Rule waited until the last possible instant, then he swerved for it. A gray Renault was lumbering along the exit ramp when the driver saw the BMW X5 on a collision course. The Renault's horn blared furiously even as it slewed out of the way. Rule accelerated up the off-ramp and onto the motorway.

They had lost both the Audi and the Mercedes, but now the BMW was heading the wrong way. Horns sounded and brakes screeched as disbelieving drivers struggled to get out of the way without slamming their vehicles into other cars or the guard rails. Mercifully, there was a breakdown area that Rule used to make a screeching U-turn, pulling out into the disjointed traffic flow before his passengers had a chance to catch their breath.

They were by this time northwest of Chartres, and at the exit for the town of Dreux, Rule cut across the entire motorway to take the off-ramp. As he slowed the X5, he pulled out a cell phone and made a brief call, his voice so low that neither Bravo nor Jenny could hear what he said.

Within six minutes they were in Dreux. It was a small industrial town filled with hulking foundries, refineries, sprawling factories where televisions, boilers and chemicals were manufactured. Not surprisingly, it was an ugly and vaguely depressing place, despite its trees and flower beds. The stern and forbidding Gothic St. Pierre's Church was one of the few surviving medieval buildings to remind those with a sense of history that Dreux had once belonged to the counts of Vexin and the dukes of Normandy.

"All the counts of Vexin were members of the Order in their time," Rule said. "In this way, Dreux still belongs to us. These are my people, I can vouch for every one of them."

They were met outside St. Pierre's by a slim young man in jeans and a T-shirt, whose eyes were completely hidden by a pair of glasses with reflective lenses. Ignoring Bravo and Jenny completely, he exchanged keys with Rule. He went straight to the BMW and drove off.

The interior of St. Pierre's was cool and dim. The air was faintly tinged with incense and massed voices raised in hypnotic liturgical chant. Rule led them to a particularly gloomy side chapel dominated by the emaciated figure of Christ, body bent backward, eyes raised heavenward.

They stood close together, listening for hurried footsteps or stealthy movement in the shadows. Bravo felt the Voire Dei close around them, as if they had sunk beneath the Bay of St. Malo. From time to time, he saw small groups of tourists, or a priest striding past on some unknown business, and he was struck by how removed he felt from them. It was as if they existed in an old, dim print he was being shown. And he thought Jenny was right, he could never go back to their reality.

At length, Rule took off his sunglasses and said very softly to Bravo, "You must listen to me closely because I suspect that there may be no other time for me to tell you what your father entrusted me to say. The secret the Order has guarded for centuries, the secret Rome has wanted above all others is this: We have a fragment of the Testament."

"Testament?" Bravo said. "What testament?"

Rule's eyes flashed with a kind of fervor Bravo had never before seen. "The Testament of Jesus Christ."

Bravo's heart seemed to give a painful lurch against his rib cage. "Are you serious?"

"Never more so," Rule said.

A priest walked by, saw them and nodded with a smile. All three fell silent until he had disappeared from view.

When Rule spoke again, his voice was both lower and more urgent. "Tell me, Bravo, in your studies have you come across the Secret Gospel According to Mark?"

"Of course," Bravo nodded. "In 1958, a scholar discovered it in the library of the Mar Saba monastery near Jerusalem. He found a hand-written text on the endpapers of a 1646 edition of Isaac Voss's 'Episto-lae genuinae S. Ignatii Martyris.'"

Rule grinned. "Full marks, as usual."

"And they come into Bethany," Bravo recited from the Secret Gospel. "And a certain woman whose brother had died was there. And, coming, she prostrated herself before Jesus and said to him, 'Son of David, have mercy on me.' But the disciples rebuked her. And Jesus, being angered, went off with her into the garden where the tomb was, and straightaway, going in where the youth was, he stretched forth his hand and raised him. . . ."

Rule laughed. "Of course, your eidetic memory."

"Basically, the Secret Gospel has been derided by Bible scholars because it depicts Jesus as a miracle worker, which runs counter to formal Church doctrine. It describes in detail how Jesus resurrected not only Lazarus, as is told in the eleventh chapter of Clement, but this boy and others as well."

"That's correct," Rule said. "And so dangerous was the Secret Gospel deemed that it was secretly suppressed by the Church in the fourth century, and then destroyed. Or so they thought."

"This is one of the secrets in the cache my father was guarding?"

"That's right," Rule said.

"Are you saying that you think it's true?"

"I know it is," Rule said, "because the fragment of the Testament of Jesus Christ confirms it. This is why it is vital that it and the other documents so closely guarded for centuries not fall into the hands of the Knights of St. Clement, for they will surely destroy all trace of them as if they had never existed."

"If what you're saying is true," Bravo said, "then why are you holding on to this secret? It's not only a religious artifact—it's an archeological miracle, a part of history. Why not reveal it to the world?"

"Bringing the Testament to light would violate our basic tenets, and this we will not do."

"I don't understand."

"It's not only the Testament that we possess," Rule said. "We also have the Quintessence."

"What?" Bravo had started, as if pricked by a needle.

Rule nodded. "You heard me."

"The fabled fifth element," Bravo breathed. "Medieval philosophers were convinced that the celestial regions were composed of earth, air, fire, water and the Quintessence—the essence of life itself. I always assumed that the Quintessence was a myth, like alchemy and turning water into wine."

"It's quite real, I assure you," Rule said.

"But what exactly *is* it? Can you see it, feel it, taste it, or is it beyond man's ability to observe and to quantify?"

"In His Testament, Jesus describes it as an 'oil,' but that term may or may not bear a resemblance to what we think of as oil." Rule leaned in, lowered his voice. "What makes the fragment of the Testament so explosive, so potentially dangerous to the Church, is that in it Jesus writes that it is by means of the Quintessence that he resurrected Lazarus and the others."

"But that goes against Church doctrine. The scriptures say that Jesus resurrected Lazarus by His divine power."

"Indeed, that has been the accepted interpretation since time immemorial," Rule said. "But the Testament of Jesus Christ clearly states that it is the Quintessence that brings Lazarus back to life. Christ makes no mention of a divine power."

Bravo was stunned. "Wait a minute—"

"Yes, yes, you see the mind-boggling implications. If it was the Quintessence that resurrected Lazarus and not Jesus's divine power, then the stories of him being a healer, the stories that the Church has systematically repressed, are true. And it might also be true that when he died his disciples resurrected him using the Quintessence."

Bravo's mind was reeling. At last he understood. "The entire structure of the Catholic faith would crumble because it would call into question whether Jesus was, in fact, the son of God."

"This is why over the centuries kings have been assassinated, regimes have been toppled, countless lives have been lost, blood has been spilled." Periodically, Rule tried to decode the shadows beyond the columns. "Your father told me he read the Testament, authenticated it. There is no doubt it's a fragment of the Testament of Jesus Christ, none at all."

Bravo stood absolutely immobile. To someone with his training, the idea of finding even a fragment of the Testament of Christ was akin to suddenly unearthing the Holy Grail. And, on top of that, to have the Quintessence, as well! The very possibility that Uncle Tony was right took his breath away.

"If the Order has had the Quintessence for all this time, if it actually exists," Bravo said, "then why didn't you use it to heal the sick and infirm?"

"That precise point was the subject of much heated debate in the twelve hundreds between Fra Leoni, the Keeper, and Fra Prospero, the Order's *Magister Regens*." Rule kept shifting his gaze to areas of the interior. "Two reasons for keeping the Quintessence secret prevailed over all the others: One, man was not meant to be immortal, or even to have his lifetime unnaturally extended. Two, news of the Quintessence would bring out the worst in people. What do you suppose would happen? A stampede, a panic in the general populace. But it would never get that far, because the rich and the powerful would contrive to steal it, to keep the secret for their own benefit, to extend their own lives. By applying the Quintessence at intervals they would live virtually forever."

Bravo's mind was moving at lightning speed. This was why the Knights were in a sudden lather to find the cache—the Vatican was pushing them to find the Quintessence. The pope was gravely ill. Was he ready to die? If so, the Quintessence was his only hope. The closer the pope came to death, the more pressure the Vatican would put on the Knights, the more of their power would be wielded. He'd have to remember that. Even in this day and age, the Vatican's power was a net flung far and wide across the globe wherever Christ had been introduced.

"And so power, already concentrated, would become ever more so," Rule continued. "And then there would be governments, rogue individuals, terrorists who would wish to use the Quintessence for their own ends, rather than for the betterment of mankind. Unmitigated disaster." He shook his head sadly. "No, the Quintessence is too powerful for mankind—it only seems like a gift, but that's the nature of all corrupting influences."

"If you feel that way, then why not destroy it?"

"It's not up to me, is it? But any archeologist will tell you—I'm sure you know this and are testing me—it would be criminal to willfully destroy such a miraculous artifact from the time of Christ. Jesus himself held the Quintessence in his—"

Some movement Rule had been looking for must have occurred because he said, "Come now, quickly, quickly!" and with his arms he guided them deeper into the shadows of the chapel. Groping along the plaster of the rear wall, he found a small glass knob and, pulling on it, opened a small door.

Pushing them into the dark doorway, he said, "This passageway will take you to a side entrance. There are a number of turns, but the door to the outside will be at the far end, not along either wall."

"Who did you see?" Jenny said.

"It doesn't matter," Bravo said. "Come on, Uncle Tony."

"I'm not going with you." Rule put the set of keys the young man had given him into Jenny's hand.

"Oh, no you don't," Jenny said. "I'm not going to let you—"

"You'll do your job," Rule said shortly, "which is to protect Bravo with your life. Leave these people to me. Besides, you have a plane to catch, and if I don't provide a diversion you're never going to make it."

"I won't leave you," Bravo said. "You taught me never to run from a fight, and I sure as hell am not going to start now."

Rule put his hands on Bravo's shoulders. "I appreciate the sentiment, Bravo, really I do, but sentiment has no place in the Voire Dei."

"I don't believe that."

"You'll learn soon enough that I'm right." He gripped Bravo all the harder. "In any case, we all have our roles to play in this war, and yours is safeguarding the Testament and the Quintessence. You're the Keeper: at all costs, you must remember that."

Rule stared into Bravo's eyes. He had the knack of making you feel as if you and he were the only two people in the world. "Since Dex's murder and the deaths of the other members of the Haute Cour, we've been virtually leaderless and terribly vulnerable. If you fail to find the cache or—worse—if the Knights of St. Clement should wrest it from you, we'll be undone. They'll have in their possession all the secret knowledge we have acquired. With the promise of the immortality the Quintessence provides, they could create unprecedented havoc—they will have the wherewithal to entice key personnel within governments, economic combines or even terrorist organizations to do their bidding. They could become an unstoppable force, subverting world policy on every level."

Jenny closed her fist over the keys.

Rule nodded to her gratefully. "The car's a black Audi cabriolet— very sporty, good cover." He told them where it was parked. "Now go!"

He fairly pushed them into the darkness. Then he closed the door and, turning, prepared to meet the Knights he'd seen entering the church.

THE man with the gold teardrop stud in his left ear."

"I see him," Bravo said.

He and Jenny were standing in the dimness of the church's side doorway. Late afternoon sunlight, thick as honey, laid down long shadows. Across the street, leaning against the front fender of the white Mercedes, was the Knight with the gold teardrop stud in his ear. He was trying to look nonchalant, but his eyes were hard and flinty as they scanned each individual that came into range.

"Go to the car as if nothing's the matter." Jenny was all business now.

"The important thing is to walk at a normal pace—not too fast, not too slow—and don't look for him."

"He'll see me, and he'll come for me."

"I'm counting on it," she said. And then as Bravo was about to walk away, she added, "As long as he doesn't suspect you're on to him we're okay, understand?"

He nodded and left the protection of the recessed doorway, striding out into the white glare and the deep blue shadows that lapped at his ankles. His heart thumped hard and there was a buzzing in his ears that caused him to walk stiff-legged and a bit too fast. He caught himself and, with an effort, he relaxed, slowed down.

There was movement all around him, and he found the most difficult part was not to look in the Knight's direction. He thought of the essential mystery of film or TV actors that had fascinated him when he was a child: how had they trained themselves to ignore the camera completely. Now he was in the same situation, forced to ignore the man with the gold stud.

"As long as he doesn't suspect you're on to him we're okay, understand?"

He stepped off the curb. Checking for oncoming vehicles, he strode across the street. He could see the black Audi cabriolet, its cloth top up. So far as he could determine, there was no one around it. *But how can you be sure?* He kept going, his pace remaining constant, though his nerves were screaming.

Movement flickered in the extreme corner of his eye. It was coming from his left, the direction in which he and Jenny had seen the man with the stud in his ear lounging against the white Mercedes.

He's coming!

He kept his focus on the nearby Audi. He told himself that he trusted Jenny, trusted her expertise, trusted her plan. In any event, it was too late for doubts. He'd committed himself and there was no turning back.

Three steps, four, and then a hand gripped his shirt, the long, slender fingers curling, the nails digging into his flesh. He turned, saw a flash of metal—the gold stud—and, below, another metallic flash from the drawn gun raised into a patch of brilliant sunlight.

There was just enough time to take in the look of triumph on the Knight's narrow face before his black eyes rolled up. Jenny, who had come up behind him without making a sound, caught him under the arms just as he collapsed and together, she and Bravo half dragged the man onto the curb.

In response to the inquiring look a passing couple gave them, Jenny said, "Our friend had too much wine at lunch." The couple hurried on, in no mood to have their vacation interrupted.

Leaving the unconscious Knight propped up against an iron fence, Jenny and Bravo got into the Audi and drove away.

THEY reached Charles de Gaulle without further incident but with little time to spare, which was just as well since neither of them had any appetite for waiting around the airport for the Knights to find them again. In any event, Jenny, on somber lookout from the moment they exited St. Pierre, was convinced they hadn't been followed from Dieux.

All the way to the airport Anthony Rule had been on both their minds, though perhaps for different reasons. Rule had been like Bravo's second father and, in fact, on occasion had stood in for his best friend when Dexter Shaw had been unable to attend his son's school play or athletic meet. Rule, who was unmarried and childless, had openly reveled in his relationship with Bravo, imparting bits of wisdom or tricks for any and all of the physical disciplines the young boy was studying. So it wasn't difficult to understand why Bravo adored him. What seemed obvious now had never occurred to Bravo at the time: namely, that it was no coincidence that Uncle Tony was proficient in all the disciplines he was learning to master and only too delighted to help Bravo toward further success.

"It must have been interesting having Anthony in your life," Jenny said as they were cruising the parking lot, trying to decipher the confusing signs. The French seemed to have a fetish for making their airports as difficult to navigate as possible. "What was it like?"

"It was great." Bravo pointed to what looked like a space at the far end of the row. "He was like my father, without all the baggage between a father and son."

"Well, that was an answer I wasn't anticipating."

"What's with you and Uncle Tony, anyway?" Someone had parked a car over the dividing line and the spot was too small even for the cabriolet. "Do you mix it up like that with all your superiors?"

Jenny shrugged. "More or less, but I can tell you that none of them are like Anthony Rule."

"Don't tell me you have a thing for him."

She winced. "Not in the least." A spot opened up in the next row, and they pulled in. She sat for a moment, unmoving, staring straight ahead at nothing.

Bravo had seen that five-mile stare before, and he knew her mind was working overtime. By now he understood that she had a difficult time revealing anything of herself, and when she did, as she had at Mont St. Michel, she immediately withdrew into the anonymity of her self-made armor.

"It's okay if you don't want to—"

"Shut up," she interrupted in a rush. It was as if once she'd begun she wanted to make certain she said what was on her mind. "I respect Anthony tremendously—he and your father were two of the really good guys. Because of that, it's painful when he ridicules me."

"He ridicules you because he likes you," Bravo said.

"Really?"

He nodded. "He used to do it to me, too."

She had turned to look at him, to make certain he was being sincere. It gradually dawned on him what a the terrible price she'd paid for maintaining her position in the Order. She had developed an assumption that when she was with a man she was bound to be the butt of endless jokes.

On impulse, he said, "Dorothy Parker once said that ridicule might be a shield, but it's not a weapon."

She stared at him for what seemed a long time. "Well," she said in a soft voice, "I guess it's safe to say that Dorothy Parker was never a part of the Voire Dei."

She got out of the Audi on the pretext of needing to stretch her legs, but in reality she was afraid that the look on her face would reveal her true feelings. She had been surprised that he had understood the crux of her plight and terribly touched by his attempt to mitigate her anguish by putting it in the words of the famous author feared for her sarcastic wit by men and women alike. Right now, though, having been so recently vulnerable, she could not afford to allow her normal steely facade to waver.

Inside the terminal, they picked up their tickets. As they were going through security, Bravo's cell phone rang. On the other side of the checkpoint, he discovered that Jordan had called. The tone on his voice mail was thin and strained, not at all the sanguine Jordan Bravo was used to.

Jordan picked up during the first ring when Bravo called back.

"*Ça va, mon ami?*"

"None the worse for wear, Jordan."

"And your friend Jenny?"

"Right beside me," Bravo said with a frown. They were heading toward the gate and he was on the lookout for a bookstore. "You're the one who sounds bad."

"Ah, well, the Dutch have been working me over. Without you, I am lost. You're the one who knows how to handle them—you intimidate them, you see."

"The secret is simple, Jordan. The next time you meet with them you must be mentally prepared to walk away from the deal. If you are, they'll sense it and back down. They don't want this deal to fall through, trust me."

"I do, *mon ami*. I will do as you suggest." Jordan took a breath. "But this other matter—I am not encouraged by what Camille tells me. I think you should consider abandoning this quest you seem to be on."

"I can't, Jordan, I'm sorry. This is something I have to do."

"Camille warned me you'd say that. Then you must allow me to provide you with a higher level of security. Where are you now?"

"At Charles de Gaulle. We're taking an Air France flight that gets into Venice at 10:45 tonight."

He spotted the bookseller and, with Jenny at his side, headed toward it.

"*Bon.* I will make a hotel reservation for you and have you met at Marco Polo airport. A man named Berio. He'll be armed and will stay with you for as long as you're in the city."

"Jordan—"

"This is non-negotiable, *mon ami*. I'm not going to risk losing you— my business would collapse inside a year." He laughed, but quickly sobered. "Take care of yourself and of Jenny. You are vulnerable until you step onto the plane."

"Don't worry, Jordan, I'll be careful." He hesitated a moment. "And Jordan . . ."

"*Oui?*"

"Thanks."

He made several purchases at the bookseller, then they headed straight for the gate. By the time they arrived, their flight had begun boarding. It was with a palpable sense of relief that they surrendered their boarding passes and passed into the covered jetway.

THE flight was full. Under the pretext of using the bathroom Jenny went back down the aisle, checking each and every passenger, committing their physiognomy to memory. Returning to her seat, she buckled up.

"I think we're okay," she said.

"I wonder if the same can be said for Uncle Tony."

"I wouldn't worry about Anthony, he's extremely capable."

"So was my father," Bravo said bitterly.

That silenced her, which, it seemed, was how he wanted it. When they had been in the air for some minutes, he took the time to reexamine the items he had discovered in the compartment on his father's boat. He held the gunmetal Zippo lighter in the palm of his hand, slowly turning it over and over.

"When is a Zippo lighter not a Zippo lighter?" Jenny said, trying to reestablish contact.

As if in response to her semiserious question, he pulled off the gunmetal-colored sheath. Inside, stuck into the housing below the wick, was a snapshot of a small boy. It was faded and grainy, but the child's face was plain enough.

"You were such a cute boy," Jenny said, leaning over.

Without a word, he slid the casing back over the photo, pocketed the Zippo.

"Why d'you think your father hid the photo of you?"

"I haven't the slightest idea." At once, he knew he'd made a mistake, and in an attempt to assuage her quickening interest, he added, "It was a complete surprise to me. Didn't Uncle Tony say that sentiment had no place in the Voire Dei?"

"So far as I can tell, Anthony doesn't have a sentimental bone in his body."

"He loved my father, and he loves me," Bravo said. "Anyway, it seems to me that his lack of professional sentiment is an asset."

Jenny put her head against the seat back. "It all depends on your point of view." She closed her eyes.

"Do you think he was right?" Bravo asked suddenly.

"About what?"

"The Testament—and the Quintessence."

She opened her eyes. "You don't believe him?" When he didn't answer, she said, "Your father authenticated it."

"All by himself."

She stared at him, then shook her head. "I don't understand you."

"My father trained me to be a medieval scholar. That means I've got a healthy dose of skepticism when it comes to purported finds regarding Jesus Christ or the Virgin Mary or—"

She leaned over, lowering her voice. "But this is different, don't you understand? The artifacts came into our possession centuries ago—"

"How did the Order get them, where were they found, who passed them on to whom, these are all questions that need to be answered."

"Dammit, Bravo, the artifacts aren't being touted on the Internet by some sleazy archeologist out to make a splash. The Vatican has been desperate to get their hands on them—every pope down through the decades gladly would have given his right arm for—"

"I haven't seen either one with my own eyes," he said doggedly.

"Is that the only thing that will convince you?"

"Frankly, yes."

She stared at him, wide-eyed. "Where's your faith, Bravo?"

"Faith is the bane of scholarship," he said sharply.

"I don't understand. How could Dexter have brought you up without faith?"

He hadn't, of course, Bravo thought, but that faith had been tested, and broken, and he hadn't been able to pick up the pieces since.

"My God," she said softly, "you are difficult." She waited until she was certain he had no intention of responding, then she turned away and closed her eyes again.

Bravo slipped the Zippo into his pocket. One by one, he again examined the other objects, this time in more detail—the two packs of cigarettes he had slit open, the enamel lapel pin of the American flag, the cuff links. Every so often he would nod to himself and his lips would move as if he were talking himself through a complex set of formulae. With the passage of time, the hum of the plane faded into white noise that lulled his fellow passengers to sleep. His seat light, however, remained on. At length, with a kind of reverence, he put his father's effects away. They were far more than effects, of course; each one had a purpose, and he now knew or at the very least could guess those purposes.

He kept the dog-eared notebook on his lap, however, and now he carefully paged through it. In the back, he came upon a section with the curious heading: "Murray's Ear." Curious, that is, to everyone who might stumble on the notebook, save Bravo. The words made him smile. Murray was a character his father had made up when Bravo was a little boy. Murray was a seemingly endless font of stories that fascinated the child, but by far his most wondrous characteristic was his ability to produce gold coins from his ear, a piece of magic that never failed to delight Bravo as Dexter, in the guise of Murray, sat at the side of his bed at night.

Below the "Murray's Ear" heading was a list of four nonsense words—*aetnamin, hansna, ovansiers, irtecta*—each followed by a string of eight numbers. He recognized the words immediately as anagrams and at once set to work deciphering them, using the methodology his father had taught him.

When decoded, each spelled out a word in a different ancient language: Latin *manentia*; Sumerian *ashnan*; Trapazuntine Greek *vessarion*; and Turkish *ticaret*. For a moment, he sat back, studying the words. Their meaning was not readily apparent, even to him.

Then he looked back up at the heading, "Murray's Ear." Gold coins—money—of course! Now he recognized *Ticaret,* the last of the four words, part of Turk Ticaret Bankasi. These were the names of banks in different cities.

He set to work on the number strings. Again using his father's methodology, he printed them out backward, ignoring the numerals "0" and "6," which his father used as blanks to further confuse any would-be cryptologist. What he was left with was his own birth date and the birth dates of his father, mother, and grandfather. These, he decided, must be the individual accounts in the respective banks.

He did not know whether to be reassured or apprehensive, because either his father had thought of every contingency or, more ominously, he was expecting his son's journey to be both arduous and perilous.

Lost in thought, he put the items away and turned to the Michelin green guide to Venice he had bought at the airport bookstore. He'd been to Venice twice before, once with college friends and once during his tenure at Lusignan et Cie. As he read, he memorized pages here and there, refamiliarizing himself with the city whose history and heritage belonged as much to the East as to the West.

Beside him, Jenny feigned sleep. Paolo Zorzi, her mentor, had taught her from her very first day under his tutelage to look at the big picture. *"There is a tendency, especially in high-tension situations, to narrow your focus,"* Zorzi said. *"Of course, naturally enough, you're trying to find the smallest detail out of place. But you must never lose your sense of the big picture, because that is where your sense of right or wrong will come to the fore. If the big picture feels wrong, then you may be certain you'll find a detail out of place."*

All her senses were on high alert. There was something about the big picture that felt wrong. The trouble was, she had no idea what it might be. Too, the entire operation had been designed by Dexter Shaw, and when it came to Dex she knew that she couldn't fully trust her sense of right and wrong. He'd had that effect on her—he'd always had.

Really, she was such an idiot. When he'd come to her to assign her to Bravo, she'd made not one sound of protest. What in the world had she been thinking? Working with Bravo, becoming emotionally involved, was turning out to be the most difficult assignment she'd ever been given. Certainly, it was the thorniest, filled as it was with lies, deceit and dangerous pitfalls that were sure to crop up during virtually every conversation that involved Dex. Had he known this would happen? She couldn't get that deeply disturbing thought out of her mind, because Dex had a curious talent for anticipating the future. She'd seen compelling evidence of it more than once, but when she'd asked him about it, he'd merely shrugged his shoulders. One thing father and son had in common: they held secrets.

Silently, she cursed Dex for getting her into this, then, filled with remorse, was immediately ashamed of herself. Settling deeper into the seat, she tried to will herself to sleep. Her body ached in every place it could ache and in several more she'd never even considered. Her head throbbed in sympathy, and she rubbed her temples before she realized that she was supposed to be asleep.

Beside her, she could hear small sounds, and she wondered what Bravo was doing. He was an enigma, impossible to read. Every time she thought she had a grip on who he was, something cropped up to prove her wrong. Take that photo of himself as a child, for instance. You'd think he would have been happy to know that his father carried it with him wherever he went. Instead, she had sensed his instant withdrawal. But in truth, she knew he wasn't the only one to blame. Her own secrets loomed large, feeling like a chasm she was less and less able to cross to get to him.

With an effort, she turned her mind away from Bravo, and once again took that mental step backward, struggling to gain perspective on the big picture. Yes, it was true, she didn't like that big picture, but for the life of her she did not know why.

"I'M having second thoughts about whom I assigned to the Venice task," Jordan said to his mother.

They were gliding through the glittering Parisian night in one of Lusignan et Cie's fleet of limousines. In the low light, sitting side by side, they could be mistaken for brother and sister.

"Perhaps I should use Brunner instead," Jordan continued.

"From Lucerne?" Camille said, her voice unnaturally sharp. "I'm sure that was Spagna's idea. As I've said before, darling, this man has altogether too much influence over your decisions. Besides, Cornadoro is already en route to Venice to be their protector."

Outside, the Seine glimmered beneath the cool blueish light of a half-moon, glimpsed between the sentinel rows of horse chestnuts beneath whose leafy arms Bravo and Dexter Shaw had walked and spoken in secret for almost the last time.

"I can always recall him."

"The decision has already been made."

"You're not angry, are you, Mother?"

"Certainly not."

Camille took a moment to stare out the window at the lovers strolling the cobbled banks and the ornate bridges of the river. Oh, to be young and innocent and in love, she thought. Then, as quickly as she had conjured it up, she banished the thought from her mind, and she was in full control again. Those days were long gone, part of another life, when she had been a different person. Or had she ever been different? Lately, she found it difficult to know. She did not even know whether she would want that life back again because, in the end, it had been nothing more than a cruel mirage, slipping like sand through her fingers.

"I am surprised, however," she went on. "You know Cornadoro's reputation as well as I do. He's the best we have. The very best."

"As Spagna pointed out, he has an exceptionally strong personality and can be headstrong as well as willful."

"He's also extremely clever, utterly ruthless and absolutely loyal." Camille leaned forward, murmured a location to the driver, who immediately turned away from the Seine, heading into the Left Bank's upscale seventh arrondisement. "Now that Ivo and Donatella are gone, it seems to me that he's the perfect choice."

"He's not subtle enough to be able to lure the Guardian away."

"Sometimes women don't respond to subtlety. Surely you know his reputation with women," Camille said. "It's my considered opinion that in this area Jenny Logan is terribly vulnerable. St. Malo gave me the measure of the Guardian. Has Spagna even met her?"

"You have a point."

"This is anything but an ordinary operation, my love. A mistake now could prove irreparable." She looked out as they turned into rue de la Comète, searching for the shop lights.

"*Bien*. Cornadoro it is," Jordan nodded. "On one condition."

The limo had stopped in front of a shop whose hand-painted sign said *Thoumieux Couteaux*. They got out, Camille leading the way into the shop. It was small and cramped inside. The walls were covered with photos of knives, the small glass case at the rear displayed three neat tiers of elegant knives, all handmade.

"*Bon soir, Madame Muhlmann.*" The small man bustled out from behind the display case. He had a bald head and the long fingers, elegant as his knives, of a surgeon.

"Is it ready?" Camille asked.

"*Bien sur, madame.*" He smiled shyly. "Precisely to madame's specifications." He held a small knife in his open palm.

Camille took it. It was a small stainless-steel folder with pearl scales. She touched the hidden mechanism and the blade popped open. He slid across the counter copies of the two photos she had taken and sent to him via her cell phone. Consulting them, she satisfied herself that he had made an exact replica the knife she had found hidden away in Jenny's compact.

She thanked the knife-maker as she paid him. Outside the shop, she turned to Jordan. "What is your condition for using Damon Cornadoro?"

"I've told him to use the name Michael Berio. Jenny Logan will recognize his real name, I'm quite certain." Jordan smiled the secret smile he reserved only for her. It was an expression of intimacy, and of complicity. "You're right: we've waited patiently, planned for too long—at this stage we cannot afford any mistakes. You'll monitor him in the field, keep him on a tight leash. Just be careful."

"You know I will," Camille said, entering the limo with him.

The long black car edged away from the curb, turned a corner. In a moment, it had vanished into the stream of nighttime traffic.

14

BRAVO AND JENNY ARRIVED IN VENICE MORE OR LESS ON time. As Jordan had promised, they were met at Marco Polo airport by a man who introduced himself as Michael Berio. He was tall and very fit-looking, with wide shoulders, sturdy runner's legs and not an ounce of fat to be seen. His hair, cut long in the current Venetian fashion, was thick and prematurely white, curling at the nape of his neck. His face was wide, with prominent cheeks and jawline and unblinking eyes the color of the lagoon at night. He was dressed in loose black clothes and seemed to move on gimbals, in the manner of a martial arts expert. His eyes lingered on Jenny—not just her face, but her body as well.

He led them outside into the humid night. "I have a private *motoscafo* waiting for you," he said in a mild voice that belied his physical presence. And there it was, rocking gently at its mooring several hundred yards from the terminal doors, the mahogany facing gleaming, the brass fittings glittering in the moonlight.

As Jenny was about to step onto the motorboat Berio caught her around the waist and swung her onto the deck. He held her a moment too long, his eyes locked on hers, then he went to cast off the lines as Bravo came on board. The guttural sound of the engines echoed off the stone facade of the bulkhead, and they nosed out into the black water.

At all times of the day, Venice appeared suspended between sea and sky, but it was at night when it seemed like a city out of a fairy tale, its design resembling a gigantic seashell. Crossing the flat water of the lagoon at speed, Venice was twinned, its perfect reflection spread across the water like a mirage. The moon, painted as if by Tiepolo in the midnight pigment of the sky, burst across the water in ten thousand tiny scimitars, as if reminding these new guests of the city's Eastern roots, the fabulous trade with Constantinople that in centuries past had made the fortunes of the merchants and doges of the Serene Republic.

Here and there, stars glimmered, their light, along with that of the moon, frosting every detail of the Gothic campaniles, Byzantine basilica, Renaissance libraries, Flamboyant Gothic palaces.

Standing beside Bravo, Jenny could feel him relax. It was as if the outermost layer he had donned during their flight had been peeled away by the soft wind of the lagoon.

"I feel like I'm home." His voice was tinged with wonder, as if it was filled with the same starlight that made city, sky and sea gleam as one. He took a deep breath, let it out. "Smell that, Jenny? All the centuries, year by year, lie beneath the water, waiting to be resurrected."

He turned to her, saw her quizzical look. "Don't you understand? For centuries, Venice has been the Order's home. It's only logical that the cache of secrets would be hidden here."

They had slowed considerably as they entered shallower waters. The channel was marked by the signature striped poles of Venice. Ahead lay the first sweeping curve of the Grand Canal, which ran through the city liked the beckoning forefinger of the dissolute Casanova, once one of La Serenissima's most notorious residents.

On their left rose the magnificent basilica of Santa Maria della Salute. Bravo had always thought it fitting that this was the first major structure one came upon when entering the Grand Canal. Venice had about it a haunting beauty tinged with melancholy. Breathtaking La Salute, for instance, had been commissioned in 1622, in the waning days of the Black Death. The church had been built in gratitude to the Virgin for ending the plague that had ravaged the city's inhabitants.

But, in truth, it was the nature of Venice that was the source of its particular melancholy. Built as it was out of the *caranto*—the base of clay and sand—of the lagoon, the ineffable beauty of its waterways created a sense of impermanence, as if at any moment it would crumble and sink into the patiently waiting water. This was especially true during the *acqua alta,* when the lagoon rose into the city, inundating the *piazettas* and first floors of the *palazzi.*

On their left, white as a lace veil, the Doge's Palace appeared from out of the darkness, as if brought to life by the moonlight. More than any other single structure, this magnificent feat of Gothic architecture embodied Venice's dizzying reversals of perspective of sea and sky. The ground floor appeared lighter than air, the frothy confection of its many delicate arches, galleries and open arcades supporting a stolid fortresslike structure, complete with militaristic corner towers and capitals.

Each time he entered the Grand Canal, passing between La Salute and the Doge's Palace, Bravo had the eerie sensation of stepping through a mirror into another world where magic had always existed and still did.

The *motoscafo*, its sleekness somewhat sinister as it glided by St. Mark's Square, passed the sculpture of the winged lion of the Republic—one of fourteen depicted in varying ways in the square. Four of these creatures had appeared to the prophet Ezekiel, and the lion was subsequently adopted as the sign of St. Mark the Evangelist, under whose protection Venice had placed itself.

Somewhat further on, the boat slid to a stop at a small slip, where a fleet of porters in the gold and blue livery of the Hotel d'Oro waited to unload baggage. They seemed slightly confused when none materialized and more than slightly put out until Berio briskly slipped euros into their hands. Here again, the observant visitor could see that he was at the crossroads of West and East. While Venice was one of those cities where anything could be had for the right amount of money, it was also true that nothing could be gotten here without euros crossing the right palm.

Having been amply rewarded for wasting their time out on the dock, the phalanx of porters accompanied the three visitors into the hotel. The lobby was two-tiered (so its guests would not be inconvenienced by the *acqua alta*) and lit by the glow of fanciful chandeliers of golden fish and lamps of turquoise mermen and sconces of silver shell clusters conceived and manufactured by the master glassblowers of the island of Murano, which lay a small distance away in the lagoon. There was a pair of enormous fireplaces surmounted by carved marble mantels on which sat Louis XIV–style clocks of fired porcelain and ormolu. The settees and chairs were their match in ornateness and style, all filigreed gold, carved wooden cabriolet legs and mounded silk cushions.

Jordan had booked them one room, but since they had dealt with this situation before, they made no comment. Perhaps one room was all he could get: the hotel was filled to capacity. Berio left them, finally, after they had checked in, promising to pick them up in the morning and take them wherever they might need to go. When Bravo tried to tell him they didn't need him, he was insistent.

"Mr. Muhlmann's orders," he said, opening his jacket just enough for them to glimpse the grips of the gun slung in its shoulder holster. He grinned hugely before turning his broad back on them and walking with his rolling gait back the way they had come.

"What d'you make of him?" Bravo said as they went up in the elevator.

"Is he dangerous, or does he merely think he is?"

The doors opened and they got out.

"He couldn't keep his eyes off you," Bravo said.

"You're imagining things."

"No. It was how he looked at you, how he touched you." Bravo put the old-fashioned key into the lock.

"How did he look at me, how did he touch me?" she said.

"As if he was ready to eat you up."

Her eyes flashed. "You aren't jealous, are you?"

He turned the key, pushed the door open, and they went inside. The room was large and looked like the inside of an oyster shell—not only the plush furniture but the walls, as well, were covered in a moire silk fabric. To the left, up two low stairs, was the bathroom; fish swam across its tiles. He walked to one of the Byzantine-shaped windows, which overlooked the canal and the palazzi beyond. Starlight fired a thin crescent at the crown of the basilica of La Salute. The canal seemed to be made of jeweled moonlight and shadows, mimicking the pattern of the silk.

Jenny flopped onto the lush, high bed. "I think you *are* jealous."

Bravo looked back at her. "Of Vin Diesel?"

She laughed, watching him slyly as he went toward the bathroom.

"I don't know about you," he said, "but I feel like I need an excavating tool to get all the layers of sweat and grime off me."

The light came on, a butter-yellow glow, and then the water began to run. The door had a full-length mirror affixed to it, and by moving a bit on the bed she contrived to watch his reflection as he stripped off his clothes. She didn't want to watch—she knew what she'd feel at the sight of his naked body, but she couldn't help herself. His image, the sound of the running water brought back to her with heart-stopping force their erotic encounter in the tub outside Mont St. Michel.

Her eyes drank him in, the line and form, the play of shadow and light over his musculature. There was something about his flesh—the contours, the texture, the color, even the constellation of birthmarks on the large outer muscle of his upper left thigh—that drew her like a magnet. She was hot and cold, the feeling traveling through her with the astonishing energy of a bolt of lightning, leaving her weak. A bead of sweat rolled slowly down the shadowed valley between her breasts. All at once she could feel the grime on her—the crusty sweat-stink of travel and anxiety—like a rime of salt. Her thighs moved on the bed, and she pressed her palms together between them.

"Bravo," she said, but he couldn't hear her, he'd moved from her view into the fountain of water. It was just as well, she thought. She was not in full possession of all her faculties. She could not be held responsible. . . .

All at once, she couldn't bear to be on the bed a moment longer. On bare feet, she crossed the room to an inlaid fruitwood bureau. A bottle of wine stood on a silver platter, along with two glasses and a note. She opened the envelope, read the typewritten sentences.

Hearing him padding out of the tub, she said, "A present from your friend Jordan, how thoughtful."

Someone had forgotten the corkscrew. It was of no matter to her. She took out a round compact she'd had specially made for her. It had a lead lining to keep out X-rays. She opened it, removed a small folding knife with mother-of-pearl scales. At the touch of her thumb, the blade zipped open. With a deft twist of her wrist, she uncorked the bottle with it, poured them both wine. When she looked up, he was standing in the doorway in a swirl of steam.

"Pretty nifty."

She smiled, put the knife and compact away.

He was staring at her with a peculiar intensity.

"What?" Her hands were suspended in midair. "What is it?"

"I wonder," he said slowly, "if you'll come over here."

There was only a towel around him, its dampness hinting at the contours beneath.

"You're expecting me to keep my distance."

"Would I have any reason to think otherwise?"

Her expression was very serious as she brought the glasses to where he stood and handed him one. "I haven't had time to wash."

"All the better," he said.

The towel fell at her feet.

WHEN Damon Cornadoro—the man who had introduced himself as Michael Berio—returned to the Hotel d'Oro's dock, marked out with striped poles in gold and blue, it was deserted. But his *motoscafo* wasn't. Inside, Camille sat smoking, her long, bare, shapely legs crossed at the knee. She lounged, one elbow cocked back, on the white leather bench seat that lined the bulkheads on either side of the cabin.

"Are your charges tucked in safe and sound?" she said when he came down to her.

"So far as I can tell." He went to the bar, poured himself a drink without asking if she wanted one. "You didn't tell me the woman was so attractive."

Camille took a long drag of her cigarette, her eyes glittering. "Excited already?"

He swallowed half his drink. "That one could get a rise out of a corpse."

She got up, then, and walked over to him, placed her cupped hand between his legs. "Let's see, hmmm." Her eyebrows raised in mock surprise. "I do believe you're right."

He dropped his glass and as it shattered onto the deck crushed her in his arms so that she gave a little moan. Then he scooped one arm beneath her knees and, lifting her, set her down at the bow end of the cabin. It was their favorite spot, the seats curving in on themselves, forming an erotic V.

Camille, sitting on the leather, spread herself until one leg was on either seat. Then she hiked up her skirt, but so slowly the movement transfixed him. When her lower belly appeared in the light of the gently swinging brass lamps the breath caught in his throat, and a moment later he was on his knees in front of her.

He let her take a handful of his thick, curling hair, tilt his head back, exposing his throat. "How easy it would be."

He didn't ask her what she meant; he knew.

She took from the bodice of her blouse a small folding knife. It flicked open with the touch of her thumb to reveal a thin, wicked-looking stainless-steel blade. She handled it like an expert.

Leaning forward from the waist, she put the flat of the blade onto his shoulder. "Is it the sight of blood, or the copper taste of it that makes people faint, do you think?"

"I wouldn't know," Cornadoro said. "For myself, I was brought up on it. Blood is mother's milk to me."

She laughed and with a practiced flick reversed her grip on the knife, holding it against his bare flesh as his hands came up to grasp her. She gave a little cry. Of course, she would never use the blade on him, not really. A nick here and there to draw blood to the surface for its scent and feel was all part of their erotic scenario.

The boat rocked back and forth, whether from a passing vessel or from their rhythmic movements it was impossible to say. The lust built as it always did. He was panting to enter her.

"Tomorrow morning, when you go to the hotel," she said, "don't go in, and don't let them see you."

He paused, taken off guard. "But Signore Muhlmann said—"

"It is not your place to remind me what Signore Muhlmann said."

"He was very specific."

"So am I." She twisted her wrist and her fingers spiraled around him. "What will you do now? You are confronted with a dilemma. You can only follow one set of orders, you can have only one master." She brought him forward, and then to a complete stop. "To whom will you give your loyalty?"

Tiny spasms had begun in his hips as he strived to control himself. "Tell me now, quickly," he panted. His eyes closed, and he bit his lower lip until he broke the skin. "Who will win this war?"

"Is it a war you see, Damon?" Camille smiled. "Ah, that is the Roman in you. Romans have war in their blood, yes, they do, it comes all the way from the time of the Caesars, when you ruled the world." Gripping him all the harder, she tilted her head, regarding him with no little curiosity. "You have to ask yourself, how can I win this war? I am only a *woman*." She said the last word as if it were a slap in the face.

He looked at her, sweat running into his eyes, burning them. "You know what you are," he said in a voice made ragged by desire full to bursting, "and I know what you are."

"So." Her voice was serious, almost grave. "You have made your choice, have you?"

"To victory," he said.

"To the bitter end," she replied.

His bowed forehead pressed into the fragrant valley between her breasts. All at once, she released him and, with a great shiver, he lost control, ramming all the way into her. While he erupted, she tenderly caressed the back of his neck as if he were a child.

THE empty wine bottle stood on its silver tray along with the equally empty glasses. The lights had been extinguished in the room, but the curtains hadn't been drawn and spangles of light roamed the walls and ceiling. The lapping of the water could be clearly heard, as if they were at sea. Then the throaty sound of a boat's engine briefly intruded, Italian spoken as provisions for the hotel's restaurant were off-loaded. Some time later, the lapping returned.

Bravo and Jenny lay in bed, side by side, naked, but not touching. They breathed out the fumes of wine and memories.

All at once, Jenny giggled.

"What?"

"I liked that you were jealous."

"I wasn't jealous," he said shortly.

"No, of course not." She couldn't help herself and another giddy sound escaped her lips.

There ensued a small silence, the nighttime sounds of Venice stealing in again, somehow making them feel safe and protected, as if they were a long way from the rest of the world.

"Why did you like it?" he asked, then.

"Guess."

"I feel like I'm fifteen years old," he said.

Her hand moved, fingers curling around his wrist. "I'm frightened," she said into the darkness.

"Of what?" Her changes of mood were mercurial.

"Of what I feel when I'm near you." She bit her lip; it was unthinkable that she should tell him the origin of that fear.

"It's all right," he said. "I understand."

The problem, Jenny thought, was that he understood only what she had arranged for him to understand. Not that her being sent away by her mother—and why—was a lie. Not at all. It was simply that by telling him that story, she had deliberately led him astray—her fear stemmed from another quarter entirely.

Bravo was comforted, taking her silence as agreement, and this led him to let down his guard. "That photo you saw," he said at length.

"The one of you that your father kept with him. I wondered why—"

"It's not of me." He reached over, plucked the Zippo off the night table, opened it. He held the photo up; the child's face was barely discernable in the night-glimmer, as if the image was not really there or had already become indistinct. But perhaps that was because it was a black and white snap that had been hand colored. "It's of my brother, Junior."

"I didn't know."

"You wouldn't," he said. "Junior's dead."

"Bravo, I'm so sorry."

"It happened a long time ago, when I was fifteen, in fact." He put the case back on the Zippo, returned it to the night table. "One winter we were out ice skating. Junior was only twelve then. A group of older boys and girls skated onto the ice and I spotted a girl I had seen a couple of times before. I liked her, but had never had the courage to go up to her. You know how that is."

"Yes," she whispered. "I do."

"I saw her glance over at me and at once I started to go into a couple of double axels. Of course, I was showing off, but I thought I might never get the chance again, and ice skating was one of the things I did really well. While I was performing for her, Junior must have gotten bored—anyway, he skated off. He went further than he should have and fell through a thin patch of ice." There had been an eerie, evil report, the flat sound of a rifle shot or the sky cracked open. It pierced the clear dry air, pierced, too, his eardrums, a terrible noise he could neither forget nor speak about. At that moment he had realized that life was as thin as an eggshell. "He never surfaced. I pulled my skates off and plunged in. Honestly, I don't know what happened next—the water was so cold I was in shock. But the boys had come over and they pulled me out. I fought them until I was black and blue, two of them held my arms while a third sat on my chest and said, 'Don't be stupid, kid' over and over like it was a nursery rhyme. Still . . ."

Beside him, she stirred, as if the tragedy had made her heart beat so fast she couldn't stay still.

"I relive that moment over and over," he said, "and I can't help thinking that if they hadn't pulled me out I could have saved him."

"You know that's not true." She rose on one elbow, stared down at him, her eyes spangled. "Bravo, you know it's not. You said yourself that you were in shock. And your brother had his skates on—the weight must have pulled him straight down. There was no chance."

"No chance, right. . . ." His voice died away into the lapping of the water against the side of the hotel.

"Oh, Bravo," she whispered, "this is how you lost your faith, isn't it?"

"He was my younger brother. I was supposed to take care of him."

She shook her head. "You were only fifteen."

"Old enough."

"Old enough for what?"

"It all seems so stupid and self-centered now. I was never going to win over a girl older than I was by three years."

"How could you know that then? Your hormones were running wild."

He stared up at her. "Do you believe that? Really?"

"Yes." She put her hand on his chest, then she drew back, abruptly breathless at the fierceness of his racing heart. "Really."

Gradually the night enfolded them, and though the spangles continued their mysterious journey across the walls and ceiling, they slept, entwined.

15

THE PALE MORNING LIGHT WOKE THEM, OR PERHAPS IT WAS
the musical sounds of the boatmen's raised voices, ringing like church
bells over the water. Looking out the window, Bravo could see that the
canal was full of activity—boats, ferries and the like, the daily traffic of
the medieval city. Sky and lagoon knitted into one seamless whole, the
water everywhere, moving, endless.

Jenny joined him, and they stood for a moment gazing out at the vaporous morning through which the palazzi's rich colors—ocher, umber,
burnt sienna and rose—pulsed like an earthbound sun.

Showered and dressed, they went downstairs. They were grateful to
see that Berio hadn't yet made his appearance, and they went quickly
out of the hotel, into the picturesque *piazetta* lined with shops still shut-
tered. He took her to a small café on a tiny side street. It was dark and
gloomy inside, as if time had collected in the low rafters. He chose a
table near one of the small wood-framed windows that looked out onto
a canal.

While they waited for their breakfast to arrive, he opened the news-
paper he'd bought and, as was his habit, scanned it.

All at once he looked up. "It's official. The pope has the flu."

"If they've gone public, his illness has grown near-terminal," Jenny
said. "The Vatican cabal will be putting ever more pressure on the
Knights."

"Not to mention global resources and influence." He folded the
paper and looked at her. "We're running out of time, Jenny."

She nodded grimly. "We've got to get you to the cache before the
Knights can find it."

Pushing the paper away, he handed her the Michelin guide to Venice and told her to turn to a certain page. Venice was divided into seven *sestieri,* or districts, each one with its own character. She opened the guide book to I Mendicoli, an outer section of the Dorsoduro district, a working-class section little frequented by tourists. *I Mendicoli* meant "the beggars": its original inhabitants—fishermen and artisans—were extremely poor.

As she read, Bravo took out the coin he'd found in the underwater safe in St. Malo. He looked at it front and back, held it on edge, ran his thumb along the ridged edge, smiling. Again, he thought of the system of cryptography his father had taught him and was immensely grateful both for the lessons and his studiousness.

Jenny looked at him inquiringly. "What should I be looking for?"

"Turn the page," he instructed.

At once, she came upon a photo of the Church of l'Angelo Nicolò. Just below was a detail of a painting: *San Nicolò dei Mendicoli* by Giambattista Tiepolo.

"This is the centerpiece of the church," he said. "Now look at the face on the coin."

She did. It was a copy of the centerpiece, the face of San Nicolò.

Bravo turned the coin over, showed her the letters on its obverse: *Mh Euah Poqchaq Ntceo.*

His sly smile turned into a grin. "At first, I thought this coin was old, but then I saw these."

Their breakfast came and they ate ravenously, clearing the dishes away as quickly as they could.

Bravo wrote the nonsense words onto a scrap of paper. On the line below, he wrote a simple equation: $54 - 42 = 8$.

"There are fifty-four ridges on the edge of this coin," he told her. "There are, as you know, twenty-one letters in the ancient Latin alphabet. Double that, you get forty-two." He pointed to the first letter of the phrase. "My father started out using the code Caesar devised, moving each letter of the original message by four to encrypt it, so alpha becomes delta and so on."

"That's a pretty easy code to break," she said.

He nodded. "That's where the equation comes in. Only the first letter is substituted this way. From then on, eight is the key."

"So the second letter is substituted for the eighth letter in the alphabet."

"Yes, and then we work forward. The third letter of the text uses nine, the fourth letter ten, until we reach twenty-one. Then we go back to eight, and so on."

"So what did your father write?"

Bravo finished up the decoding, then showed her the result.

"In alms cabinet purse." She shook her head. "Do you know what that means?"

"I think we'll have to go to I Mendicoli to find out." He paid the bill and they left the cafe.

With the rising of the sun, dawn had dissolved into a morning already hot and wet. By now the children were at school and the college age art students on their way to classes in astonishing medieval buildings, sketchpads tucked neatly under their arms as they jabbered away on cell phones.

"God, it stinks," Jenny said as they passed over a canal.

Bravo laughed. "Ah, yes, the stench of Venice is an acquired taste."

"Count me out."

"Given time, you'll change your mind, I guarantee," he said.

Several times Jenny slowed, looking around as if unsure how to proceed, even though it was Bravo who was leading the way.

"What's the matter, don't you trust me?" he said. "You look like you're lost."

"I have a feeling we're being followed. Normally, I'd be able to check reflections in shopwindows or in cars' side mirrors, but here that's impossible. At this hour there are few shops and, of course, there are no cars. I've been trying to use the canals, but because it's in motion water is a notoriously unreliable reflective surface."

They moved on, in the midst of a shroud of anxiety. Smells came to them of fermentation—the lees of wine—the whiff of an unseen woman's perfume, the distinct scent of the pale Istrian stone, borne aloft as if on St. Michel's gauzy wings against the deep-green water, from which emanated the ever-present rankness of decay. Even in brightest day, there was about Venice an acute sense of mystery. One was always turning a corner, hearing footfalls approaching or retreating, coming from narrow alleys into ancient *campi* in which could be seen clumps of elderly men speaking in hushed tones or a dark figure, furtively exiting the square.

Their first stop was in San Polo, where the Rialto Bridge spanned the Grand Canal just as it had since 1172, when the first boat bridge was built. Up until the nineteenth century the Rialto was the only link between the two sides of the city. As they crossed, shops on either side of the bridge were opening, their doors thrown wide and tourist-friendly signs put in windows and beside doorways.

The Banco Veneziana was just past the Erberia, an outdoor market that dated back to the time of Casanova. Here were sold herbs and all manner of produce brought in each morning from the small out islands that dotted the Lagoon. The bright spicy scents of green herbs mingled with the heady odors of blood oranges, *castradure* (baby artichokes) and *spareselle* (pencil-thin asparagus), as well as perfumed sprays of fresh flowers. As they worked their way through the happily chattering crowds, Jenny, clearly uncomfortable, kept an eye out for tails, which was made more difficult amid the dense bustle of the wholesalers, packing up to make room for the arriving retailers.

The bank was in an arcaded building of the Venetian-Byzantine style—the front was a mass of slender arched and columned windows—that had been rebuilt following the great fire of 1514 that had devastated it as it swept through the city. Like many buildings in Venice, the architecture was full of ornamental filigrees, intricately carved stone statues and stylized Gothic cornerstones. Inside, marble walls rose up to a domed ceiling into which had been set a marvelous mosaic of Venetian ships at full sail.

Behind the high banquette, they found a slim, middle-aged gentleman. Bravo spoke to him for a moment, and he handed over a form on which Bravo was required to write nothing more than the account number he had decoded from his father's dog-eared notebook, not even his name.

The banker took the form and disappeared for not more than three minutes. When he returned, he opened a section of the banquette. He allowed Bravo through, but not Jenny. He was polite and apologetic, but quite firm.

"I trust you understand, *signorina*," he said. "It is the policy of the bank to allow entrance only to the account holder. It is a question of possible coercion, you see."

"I understand completely, *signore*," she said with a smile. And to Bravo, "I'll be outside, looking for our friend." She meant Michael Berio, whom she suspected of following them.

Bravo nodded. "I won't be long."

The banker led him across the marble floor, up a staircase into a small hushed anteroom. Beyond was the massive open door to the safety deposit boxes. Of course, the vaults of Venetian banks would be upstairs, rather than downstairs, to protect against the periodic floods.

The banker left him in a small chamber—one of six that lined the left-hand side of the anteroom—and some moments later returned with a long gray metal box, which he put on the table in front of Bravo.

"I will be just outside, *signore*," he said. "You need only to call me when you are finished." He left without a backward glance.

Bravo sat staring at the box for a moment. In his mind's eye he saw his father seated where he himself now sat, the open box before him, filling it in his mathematically precise fashion. Bravo reached out, put his arms around the box, as if he could feel the last traces of his father. Then, with a convulsive gesture, he threw open the lid.

JENNY stood in the shadows beneath the bank's arcade, peering out at the glare. She leaned nonchalantly against one of the arches and made a good show of looking bored as she sipped a small cup of blood-orange juice she had purchased from a cart just opposite. She savored the sweet-tart taste but nothing else. As her eyes worked the people crisscrossing the *campo*, she felt a kind of depression weighing on her, as well as a dull headache, as if Dex's ghost were sitting on her head.

The deeper she got into this assignment, the worse she felt. She asked herself again why she had taken it, but the answer was as obvious as it was deflating: Dex had asked her to take it, and she never refused him anything. Hadn't he proved that he knew what was best for her? That had included, she'd assumed, this assignment guarding his son, but assumptions never took into consideration the curve balls reality threw at you. And Braverman Shaw had turned out to be one helluva curve ball. *I can't let it go on like this. When am I going to tell him the truth?* she asked herself. *You have to let it go on like this,* she answered herself. *The moment you tell him, everything will blow up in your face and you'll have lost him.*

"Have you spotted Berio?"

Jenny whirled, startled. "Um, no, but that doesn't mean he isn't here somewhere, spying on us."

"He only wants to protect us."

They began to walk toward the Dorsoduro, leaving the knots of people behind. Their footsteps echoed off the walls and narrow cobblestone streets, whose colors were made illusory by the reflections from the canals.

"What was in the account?" Jenny asked.

"One hundred thousand dollars," Bravo said.

She gave a low whistle. "Wow."

"And this." After a quick check of the immediate environment, he pulled out the SIG Sauer P220. "It's fully loaded with .38s ammo."

Her eyes opened wide. "Damn, that semiautomatic could win a war."

"I guess that's what my father had in mind," he said, pocketing the weapon.

"Do you know how to use that? Maybe you ought to give the gun to me."

"I can shoot an apple off your head at a hundred paces." He laughed. "Don't worry, my father made sure I had plenty of practice with handguns."

FOR a city that prided itself in architectural marvels, the Church of l'Angelo Nicolò was remarkably plain. Founded in the sixth century by a group of displaced Genoese, it reflected to this day their essential poverty. Apart from a much needed renovation in the fourteenth century, including what became its signature triple-bay gemel window and the installation of a beautiful portico in the fifteenth century, it remained essentially as it had at its founding.

"Stuck away in this backwater *sestieri,* it was so far out of the mainstream of Venice's religious life that it had been systematically denied donations from wealthy parishioners and patrons," Bravo said. "Instead, L'Angelo Nicolò became the de facto sanctuary for the *pinzocchere*—religious zealots—who sought to do penance within its walls."

"How did it survive?" Jenny asked.

"Good question. One answer is Santa Marina Maggiore, the nunnery built just behind. Apparently, it was money from the nuns that paid for the renovation."

"That must have cost a fortune," Jenny said. "I'd love to ask the nuns how they managed such an amazing feat."

The interior was cool and gray and beautiful, the Tiepolo painting of San Nicolò awe-inspiring. They stood beneath the central apse surmounted by a Byzantine cornice from the seventh century. At this hour, they were virtually the only people in the church, but now and again they could hear small echoes of hushed voices like the lapping of canal water, a door opening or closing, shoe soles padding along the stone flagging.

Bravo saw a small figure coming through the apse, a priest, who he stopped.

"Excuse me, father, does this coin have any significance for you?"

The priest was an ancient man with a deeply creased face, his skin burnished by the elements to the texture of fine leather. His long white hair and beard were in need of barbering—in fact, he looked more like a mendicant for whom the area was named than a member of the Church. Despite his extreme age, his blue eyes—as electric as Bravo's own—were so clear and penetrating that they seemed to pierce straight through to Bravo's core. After a long, contemplative look, the priest smiled and took the coin. His fingers, too, belied his years, for they were as straight as those of any man one third his age—in fact, save for the skin of his face, he exhibited none of the telltale signs of time's ravages.

The unknown priest gave the front of the coin only a cursory glance, then his fingers, still as deft as a conjuror's, flipped it onto its reverse. He nodded to himself, then looked up, his eyes, bright with secret knowledge, might have contained a touch of humor or satisfaction.

"Wait here, please, *signore*," he said, bobbing his head.

He went off with the coin and soon disappeared behind a column. Silence, and the dust floating down from on high. Light splayed across the floor, colored by the marble, conjuring up the bouquets of flowers in the Erberia. Three nuns, hands lost within their black robes, passed slowly in procession, walking in perfect unison, as if to a tempo God had provided for them.

"Do you think that was wise?" Jenny said. "Giving him the coin."

"To be honest, I don't know," Bravo told her. "But it's done now."

Two priests, one taller and slender, the other shorter and stout as a wine cask, appeared, walking down the north transept toward them, their faces bent, shrouded in shadow, deep in discussion.

"I'm going after him." Jenny made a sudden move, which startled the priests, for they paused, whispering to each other. By this time, Bravo had stopped her. The priests resumed their stroll, but in a different direction now, away from them.

"Listen, Bravo—"

He made a curt gesture, silencing her. "When it comes to protecting me, you call the shots, otherwise this is my show, got it?"

She bridled, her faced flushed with anger. He could see that she was uncomfortable ceding control to him, and he realized that she still harbored questions about his instincts, his motivations and, even worse, his mental fortitude. No matter that they were intimate in bed, there was still a chasm of distrust between them, which caused him to wonder whether their physical relationship was anything more than a passing illusion. He had been so happy when he'd arrived in Venice last night—he'd been sure that he'd been nearing something he'd been longing for all his life, something so important and vital that at last he might be absolved of the guilt he had felt over Junior's death. And now he was possessed by the sudden sensation of looking down at himself from outside his body, as if he had entered a dream without knowing when or how. Nothing seemed certain anymore; thin ice was beneath his feet, and he felt on the verge of losing his balance and tearing through into the chill water beneath.

Much to his consternation, he found that he and Jenny were glaring at each other.

"You wouldn't be talking to Uncle Tony like this," she said.

"I would, whether you choose to believe it or not. Two people can make decisions, but only if one of them is dead."

His paraphrasing of the famous Ben Franklin saying broke the tension, as he meant it to, and she visibly relaxed.

"Just remember who's taking care of you," she whispered.

Another priest had appeared in the shadows below the triple-bayed gemel window and was beckoning to them.

"I'm Father Mosto." The priest held the gold coin in his hand. He was of medium height, with flat black hair that covered his scalp like a cap. His skin was dark as cocoa mixed with cream, so it was possible that his forebears were originally from Campania, in the south of Italy around Mt. Vesuvius. Perhaps there was even some North African or Turkish blood in him. Though he wasn't big, he gave that impression because he was broad—stoop-shouldered and barrel-chested—with a heavy, brooding face that looked out at the world with an innate suspicion from behind the forest of a beard.

"You're Braverman." He held the coin between his thumb and forefinger. "Dexter's son."

"That's right." Bravo accepted the coin back.

"I recognized you from a photo your father gave me." Father Mosto nodded. "You will come with me now and we shall talk."

When Jenny moved to accompany Bravo, the priest held up his hand. "This is between the Keeper and myself. You may stand outside the door to my rectory if you wish."

Jenny's eyes flashed. "I was assigned to Bravo by Dexter Shaw himself; I accompany him wherever he goes."

A storm of emotion appeared to gather in Father Mosto's face. "That simply is not possible," he said curtly. "You will follow orders. Any other Guardian would not need to be reminded of his duties."

"She's right, Father Mosto," Bravo said. "What I hear, she hears."

"No, it is not allowed." The priest folded his arms over his chest. "Never."

"It was my father's wish and my choice." Bravo shrugged. "But if you persist, we will walk out of here—"

"No, you must not." A small muscle had begun to twitch in the priest's cheek. "You understand why you must not."

"I do," Bravo said. "And yet I will, trust me."

Father Mosto stared at him with a certain degree of belligerence.

Bravo turned and, together with Jenny, began to walk away.

"Braverman Shaw," Father Mosto called from behind them. "You are perhaps not so familiar with the traditions of the Order. Females have no place in—"

He watched them continue moving away from him, and when he spoke again, there was a plaintive note to his voice. "Don't do this, I beg of you. It is against our ancient traditions."

Bravo turned. "Then perhaps it's time you reconsidered what is tradition and what is rote, what is useful and what never should have been."

The priest's face was dark as soot and he rocked a little on his feet, which were as tiny as a girl's. "This is monstrous. I won't stand for it. You are extorting—"

"I'm extorting nothing," Bravo said calmly. "I'm merely suggesting another way of approaching a situation, just as my father would have done if he was standing here in my place."

Father Mosto scrubbed his beard with his curled fingers, his venomous eyes on Jenny.

"Where is your vaunted Christian compassion, Father Mosto?" she said.

Bravo started, certain that she'd upset the delicate balance he'd so carefully created. But then he looked into the priest's face and noticed a subtle softening. Like anyone else, he was not immune to flattery. Too, she had judged the right psychological moment to speak up. Father Mosto saw that she wasn't as compliant or as foolish as he had supposed. Bravo understood, then, just how clever Jenny was. She had been following every nuance of the conversation and knew precisely when the priest was on the cusp of acquiescing. All that had been remaining was an affirmation from her, proving Bravo's position.

An expression, perhaps of resignation, settled on Father Mosto's face. "Come with me, both of you," he said gruffly, and he led them through a thickly painted doorway at the back of the church that was, in fact, part of a panel painting. It was so small that Bravo had to duck his head.

They found themselves in a downward sloping corridor that must have been running alongside a canal because the further they went, the damper it became. Here and there, water was seeping through the immense stone blocks. A door appeared to their left, just before the corridor reached its lowest ebb. Here there was a metal drain set into the stone from which a sewer reek now and again wafted.

Father Mosto unlocked the door to the rectory and, opening the thick iron-clad wood door, made to step over the threshold. Jenny, however, was looking down the corridor.

"What's beyond there?" she said.

When it became clear he wasn't going to acknowledge the question, Bravo repeated it.

"Santa Marina Maggiore." The priest addressed Bravo through pursed lips.

"The nunnery," Jenny said.

"No one is allowed in there," Father Mosto said.

When Jenny entered he was already behind his desk, a rather ornate wooden affair for a priest. One wall was taken up by a massive oak cabinet, its carved doors chained and padlocked. The only other pieces of furniture were a pair of uncomfortable-looking spindle-back chairs of a wood that was almost black. Above his head hung a carving of Jesus on the Cross. Owing to its lack of windows, the room, which smelled of resin and incense, was claustrophobic.

"I'm afraid I have bad news to impart," he said. "The pope's health has declined precipitously."

"Then I have less time than I had thought," Bravo said.

"Indeed. With the full backing of the Vatican cabal behind them, the Knights have the upper hand now, of that there can be no doubt." He clawed at his beard again. "You see why I was so distraught when you decided to walk away. You're the Order's only hope. Safeguarding our secrets is what will save us. The secrets are our power, our future—they are the Order itself. Without them, we will cease to exist, our contacts will vanish, and the Knights of St. Clement will run rampant." He grimaced. "You see the irony of the situation. We barter the secrets in order to do our work, but also to defend ourselves. Until you find the cache, we are powerless to use our contacts to help us fend off the Knights."

"There is something you must explain to me," Bravo said. "Jenny has assured me that the Order is secular now—apostate—and has been for some time. Yet here we are speaking to a priest, not a businessman or a government official like my father."

Father Mosto nodded. "It is due entirely to your father. While others in the Haute Cour moved away from the religious side of the Order, your father did not. It was he who kept our centuries-old network alive and flourishing."

"You mean he had secrets even from the Haute Cour."

"Your father was correct when he argued for the reinstatement of a *Magister Regens*. He looked at a wider field, saw a higher level that he urgently felt should be the Order's mission."

"What was it my father wanted the Order to do?"

"Alas, I have no idea. He didn't tell me, and my contacts with the rest of the Haute Cour are, as you can imagine, nonexistent."

Bravo nodded. "I wish my father was here. Now the Order is under attack from inside was well as from outside."

"The traitor, yes. The members of the Order realize the errors their leaders have made."

"Too late for my father."

"Ah, my son, we all owe Dexter an enormous debt. About the future he was positively prescient." Father Mosto put his hand on Bravo's shoulder. "The Order may be in disarray, Braverman, but if you can fulfill your father's mission, if we can survive this terrible crisis, I feel certain that at long last true change can be effected." He gestured. "But I am forgetting my manners. Please sit down."

The chairs were as uncomfortable as they looked. Bravo and Jenny settled themselves as best they could. Through his anger, his assessment of the new information, Bravo did not lose sight of his mission. He made a mental note to call Emma at the earliest opportunity. Maybe she'd gotten a lead on the mole, but as soon as he thought it he knew he was whistling in the dark. Surely his sister would have called him if she'd made even the slightest progress.

The priest spread his hands. "I suppose you've been told that the Order came here because there was no love lost between Venice and Rome, and that's true, so far as it goes." He sat forward, his fingers steepled. "There was, however, another, far more compelling reason. To understand it, we must go all the way back to 1095, when the call went out for the first Crusade.

"Venice is remembered almost solely as a city-state of superb politicians, and that's true—again, so far as it goes. 'Keep safe from stormy weather, O Lord, all your faithful mariners, safe from sudden shipwreck and from evil, unsuspected tricks of cunning enemies.' " His forefinger wagged back and forth. "Cunning enemies, you see? Even then. But I'm getting ahead of myself.

"The prayer I just recited is recorded in the earliest histories of La Serenissima, spoken on the Day of Ascension when the doges of Venice were married to the sea. Because the Venetians were, first and foremost, a seafaring people.

"When the call went out from Rome for able swords to travel to the Holy Land, you would think that those who responded were of a religious bent, wanting to earn their way into the next life. But no, only a handful were soldiers of the Lord; the vast majority of those who took up arms to fight for Rome were opportunists who saw in the wholesale slaughter to come the chance to carve out for themselves fiefdoms, states, even empires in the Levant, as the Middle East was then called."

He raised a hand. "I am well aware that both of you are familiar with this era, but I beg you to indulge me for a few moments."

He rose and came around to stand in front of Bravo and Jenny. It was clear that he was at his most comfortable lecturing. Both his manner and his speech were distinctly old-fashioned, as if he had come from centuries past.

"The doges of Venice were as initially giddy as their rivals in Genoa, Pisa and, latterly, Florence to acquire bases in the Holy Land. Until, that is, they were advised by members of the Order, who pointed out that it would be far better to let others fight and die over foreign lands. Their wise counsel was this: while your rivals fight for land, you use your navy to control the sea. The sea? the doges said. Why would we want to control such a vast and inhospitable place? Because, we told them, when you control the sea, you control trade, not merely in the Adriatic, but in all of the Middle Sea, which we now call the Mediterranean. Through your invincible navy you will set levies on all of the ships coming into Italy from any country, you will regulate trade so as to benefit Venetian business and thus gain more favorable trading terms for your merchants, who will prosper no matter the outcome of the wars.

"Of course the Order had its own reasons for wanting Venice to control trade in the Mediterranean. We wanted to gain safe passage to and from the Levant, because already we had in our possession secrets which hinted at others—far greater—that were buried or had been hidden in areas of the *Oltremare*."

"Yes, yes," Bravo said, "the Beyond-the-Sea—Cyprus, Syria and Palestine."

"Oh, not only there, but also along the southern lip of the Black Sea, in Trebizond."

He cleared his throat, a certain sign that he did not care to be interrupted. "So persuasive were we that for four hundred years Venice pursued the single-minded goal of superiority at sea. They could not use blockades because ships of that time were neither built or provisioned to stay at sea for long periods of time, so they concentrated on what they knew: convoying their merchant ships from port to port and raiding enemy ports and shipping routes in a cut-and-run fashion.

"By suggesting they use the masts of their warships as siege towers, it was the Order who helped the knights of the Crusades take Constantinople; by their esoteric knowledge of the land beyond the *Oltremare*, it was the Order that helped the Venetian brothers, Nicolò and Matteo Polo, father and uncle of Marco. Having heard through our web of highly placed contacts that the Genoese had aligned themselves with the Greeks, who had subjugated the Levant previously, to retake Constantinople they spirited the Polos and as many other Venetians as they could out of the city. Those they could not find or who would not heed their warning were subsequently captured and treated as pirates—were either blinded or had their noses cut off.

"A traitor aided the Greeks in their successful assault on Constantinople, and less than a century later it was another traitor within the court of David Comnenos, Emperor of Trebizond, that caused the city to fall to the Ottomans. We were there, too, the day Trebizond fell, and took from there secrets beyond compare."

"This is all fascinating," Bravo said, "but I came here for a reason. Where is—"

Father Mosto, having jumped off the corner of the desk, now held up his hand. "Listen to me, Braverman Shaw. Each time a traitor has appeared a terrible flow of deaths has resulted, and the Order has been severely set back in its mission. Each time we know that the Knights of St. Clement orchestrated the plan, seducing one of ours to their side. We are in such a period now, and this time our very existence hangs in the balance.

"As you have said yourself—as your father fervently believed—there is a traitor in our midst. What you perhaps do not know is that it was Dexter Shaw's task to ferret out this traitor, capturing him so that through his subsequent interrogation we could trace the conduit back to its source and destroy its head once and for all."

"Interrogation," Bravo said. "You mean torture, don't you?"

"The intelligence needs to be extracted by any and all means."

Bravo shook his head. "My father would never consent to torture another human being."

"The plan was his own idea," Father Mosto said. "It was born of desperation, but all of us in the Haute Cour—the traitor included, ironically—agreed. We're in a war, Braverman. Here, today, at this very moment, there is only survival or death." He made a sweeping gesture. "This is why I must insist that what transpires next be between you and me only."

Jenny jumped up. "I'm not a traitor."

"Braverman certainly believes you're not," Father Mosto said, "but today, at this moment, I do not have that luxury, I am full of suspicion for anyone who is not Dexter Shaw's son."

"How *could* I be the traitor?" Jenny said hotly. "We all know that he's a member of the Haute Cour."

"In league, perhaps, with a member of those who guard the Haute Cour."

Bravo looked at him. "You don't really believe that, do you?"

"Half of the Haute Cour has been murdered in a span of less than two weeks. Where was their vaunted protection?" Father Mosto shook his head. "The time for making simple assumptions or taking chances is past. Your father would understand, Braverman, and so must you."

Bravo stood, thinking for a moment. At length, he turned to Jenny and said, "Please stand outside the door."

"Bravo, you can't mean that—"

"I need you to make sure we aren't disturbed."

Her face hardened and then she nodded once, curtly. She left the rectory without glancing at the priest.

When they were alone, Father Mosto said, "Do you trust her?"

"Yes," Bravo said at once.

"Absolutely?'

"She was my father's choice. It was his express wish—"

"Ah, yes, your father." Father Mosto's fingers knitted together. "Let me tell you something about your father. He was prescient in a way none of us understood. I wouldn't say he could see the future, exactly, but he seemed to know how things were going to end."

"I've heard that."

"If, as you say, he led you to Jenny, then you can be quite certain there was a reason."

Bravo shrugged. "She's the best Guardian."

"She's not, but leaving that aside for the moment, even if she was, he brought you to her for another reason, something he felt or saw, something to do with the future he knew he was not going to live to see."

Bravo stared at him wide-eyed.

"You can't be serious."

"Oh, I'm perfectly serious, Braverman."

"I would not have taken you for a mystic."

"I believe in good and evil, in the immortality of the spirit, in God's strict hierarchical order. Mystics believe in good and evil, in the immortality of the spirit, in a higher power and in a strict hierarchical order of things, so in the most fundamental sense I do not think that we are so very far apart."

"The Church would view you as a heretic."

"And burn me at the stake? Three hundred years ago, I daresay they would have tried," Father Mosto said flatly. "But consider: both the priest and the mystic are aware that there is far more to this world than man and man's creations. I respect that, and so should you." He pursed his lips. "Where is your faith, Braverman?"

The echo of Jenny's question was like a shot across Bravo's bow and, shamed by his inability to answer such a vital question, he remained silent.

After a thoughtful pause, Father Mosto continued. "In any event, it is vitally important that you keep what I just said about your father's prescience in mind as you move forward through the labyrinth he created for you. That's how you see it, isn't it? A labyrinth."

Bravo nodded.

"Good. Because that's just what it is. A labyrinth to trap the unwary and the deceitful as you make your way through it. I knew your father well. I believe with all my heart and soul that he built this labyrinth to withstand every possibility. It sounds improbable—impossible, even—but as close as you may have been to Dexter Shaw, you couldn't have known him as I did. His mind—well, it didn't work like yours or mine, I assure you."

"I know, he and I had a cipher game that he created—"

"I'm speaking neither of ciphers nor of games, Braverman," Father Mosto said sternly.

Something in the priest's tone warned Bravo, and he leaned slightly forward, concentrating his entire being on what was being said. Father Mosto became aware of this and, so far as he was able, appeared pleased.

"As I said, your father was prescient. He became aware of the traitor inside the Order before any of us. In fact, in the beginning, some of them foolishly disbelieved him."

"But not you."

"No. He spoke to me about his suspicions first."

"Did he tell you who he suspected?"

"No, but I'm convinced that he knew."

"Then why didn't he act?"

"Because," the priest said, "I think he was afraid."

"Afraid? My father wasn't afraid of anything." Into the silence that ensued, Bravo said, "What was he afraid of?"

"The traitor's identity. I think it shook his confidence in his own abilities. It was someone he knew well and trusted completely." Father Mosto produced a folded slip of paper from his robes.

Bravo took it. "What's this?"

"The list," Father Mosto said, "of suspects."

Bravo opened it, scanned the names. "Paolo Zorzi's name is on here." And then the breath caught in his throat. "So is Jenny's." He frowned. "You said the traitor was someone he knew well and had trusted completely."

The priest nodded. "Dexter and Jenny had . . . some sort of relationship."

"Of course, they worked together."

Father Mosto shook his head. "Their relationship went beyond the professional," he said. "It was both personal and intimate."

THERE was something thrilling, Camille Muhlmann thought, about dressing in men's clothes—and a priest's at that! Her breasts were bound, and there was padding around her waist to make her look portly beneath the robes. Giancarlo, one of Cornadoro's people, had assumed that neutered ecclesiastical expression so familiar to her the moment he had slipped into the robes. But then it was Cornadoro's contention that Giancarlo wanted to be an actor.

"He's a film whore," Cornadoro had complained when she had announced her intention to use Giancarlo instead of him. "Whenever the American film crews come to Venice he's always following them around like a dog begging for a handout."

"Is he reliable?" she had asked.

"Of course he is, otherwise I would have kicked him out on his ass months ago."

It hadn't been difficult to ignore Cornadoro's rant. Giancarlo was expendable and Cornadoro wasn't, it was as simple as that, a mathematical equation she had come to with a minimum of effort.

The thrill of being a man had mounted as she and Giancarlo had walked down the north transept of the Church of l'Angelo Nicolò, watching the unsuspecting Bravo and Jenny as they stood near the gemel window. Bound and padded, she felt as if she was a knight in armor, impatient for the battle to commence, and a fierce joy shot through her like a boom of thunder.

She and Giancarlo had waited in the shadow of the white marble statue of Jesus, watching as Father Mosto led the pair back toward the rectory. They had set off after them at a discreet distance and on a more or less parallel path.

Now they were almost at the doorway in the mural when another priest materialized seemingly out of nowhere. He was very old and had long white hair and a scraggly beard badly in need of trimming. As he approached them, his black eyes seemed to pierce her to the quick, so that uncharacteristically she had a moment of panic, convinced that he'd seen beneath her disguise and had unveiled her as a woman. But then he passed on as if he had never seen them, and at last they were free to pull open the door and follow Father Mosto to his lair.

In the reeking stone corridor, she caught sight of Jenny outside the closed door to the rectory. She whispered terse instructions and, nodding, Giancarlo brushed by her.

She watched as he approached Jenny, nodding. Then he had passed on and she removed her shoes. When he was five or so paces beyond Jenny, he turned and seemed to ask her a question, "What are you doing here?" perhaps. It was, Camille had told him, imperative that he immediately put Jenny on the defensive so that she had no choice but to respond, engage him in conversation, narrowing her attention.

As Jenny turned to answer him, Camille flew down the corridor, her bare feet making no sound at all. As she came on, she calculated both the angle of the blow and the power to put behind it. Her eyes were focused on the occiput bone at the base of Jenny's skull, and this is where she struck Jenny, planting her feet, twisting from the hip, the power behind the blow coming all the way from her tensed right thigh, up through her pelvis and torso, infusing her right arm with just the right amount of strength to knock her unconscious.

She was prepared, catching the collapsing Jenny in her arms. She became aware of Giancarlo coming to help her with her burden, but she shook her head, and he stopped, waiting, patient as a dog.

For a moment she had Jenny to herself, back against her bound breasts, lolling head on her shoulder, throat exposed. It was a terribly intimate moment. She put one hand gently against Jenny's neck. Feeling the slow throb of the carotid artery, she extended a forefinger as if it were the blade of a knife. It would be so easy to end her life right here, right now, she thought. But that would be a mistake. The Order would only send another Guardian—one she didn't know—and the meticulous psychological process she had set in motion would have to begin again. This they could not afford. Jordan was under enormous time pressure from Cardinal Canesi to produce the Quintessence and the Testament. If they failed, their entire power base would be jeopardized, perhaps irrevocably. No, her way was the right way, of this she was certain.

Her hand was on the move again, roaming beneath Jenny's robe as if they were lovers in an amorous embrace. She extracted a cell phone, threw it to Giancarlo. Happily, she found the weapon. For a moment, light flashed red and green off the pearl scales of Jenny's switchblade. Camille smiled. She had gone to the trouble of duplicating Jenny's knife because there had been no way for her to know whether Jenny would have it on her or whether she would be able to find it when she needed it. Now she wouldn't have use for the duplicate, she thought, as she pocketed Jenny's switchblade beneath her own robes, but it would make a fine memento for the secret collection she had built over the years, small items, possibly even insignificant, save for the fact that each possessed a sinister intimacy, stolen as they were from Jordan, Bravo, Anthony and Dexter.

Her moment came to an end, and she nodded to Giancarlo. Together they carried Jenny into a small room down the corridor and set her down. Back in the corridor, she retrieved her shoes and put them back on. Dismissing Giancarlo with another set of instructions, she melted into the shadows.

As Giancarlo hurried back to the church, he heard from behind him the soft *snik* of the switchblade opening.

INSIDE the rectory, Bravo sat down suddenly, the hard edge of the chair bringing pain to the backs of his thighs. *How could she?* he thought. *How could she not have told me?* When he looked up, Father Mosto was watching him with a keen eye.

"I have no idea whether or not Jenny is the traitor, Braverman, but I do know that your father was too involved to make an objective judgement. It's my belief that this is why he sent you to her, so that you could take the next step he couldn't, so that you could discover the truth about her."

"But it doesn't make sense." Bravo shook his head. "Almost everyone hates and resents her. Wouldn't she be the first to come under suspicion?"

"In fact, she'd be the last person they'd suspect. Consider: she's reviled, made fun of, always in the spotlight, never in the shadows."

"Unless she's out in the field."

The priest said nothing, there was no need.

"Did my father talk to Paolo Zorzi about her? Zorzi trained her, after all."

"Remember that Zorzi is also on the list," Father Mosto said.

Bravo glanced back over his shoulder at the closed door. "Do you believe she's the traitor?"

"I . . ." the priest began, but immediately faltered. "I am afraid of her, because she was able to get to Dexter in a way no one else could—not even, I believe, your mother."

Something screamed in Bravo's head. "I can't believe it. My father was having an affair with Jenny?"

"I knew your father longer than anyone. It's a fact." Father Mosto's eyes brimmed with empathy. "You must find forgiveness in your heart, my son. Your father was an extraordinary man, he accomplished extraordinary things."

"But he never told us."

"Why should he? Dexter led two lives, Braverman, you know that better than anyone now."

"But Jenny's half his age." Bravo's head came up. "Are you—a priest—condoning what he did?"

"Do you expect me to condemn him?" He sat down opposite Bravo, so close their knees touched. "I was Dexter's friend, first and foremost.

I counseled him as best I could but . . . I needn't tell you that he was a man of secrets. He could compartmentalize his two lives—one didn't intrude on the other. For reasons I can't even begin to imagine, he lived deep inside himself."

He stood, put a hand on Bravo's shoulder. "One thing I know for certain: he loved your mother, deeply and completely. Nothing he did could change that."

Bravo nodded, silent, lost in his own muddled feelings.

"When we are children, we see our parents through a child's eyes. If they fight, we think they must hate each other. But when we become adults ourselves we discover that people—including our parents—are complex. It's possible to fight and still be in love. What you need to keep in mind is that your father never left your mother, never left you and your sister. When your mother fell ill, he was by her side the entire time. And when she died . . . my God, he grieved for her. A part of him died, I can tell you that."

Father Mosto sighed. "Difficult knowledge, Braverman, but it's better to know the truth, isn't it? All your decisions must stem from the truth."

Bravo looked up. "But Jenny and I . . ." He couldn't finish his thought. Had she seduced his father as she had seduced him in the hotel room in Venice? Of course, there had been their frenzied coupling at Mont St. Michel, but even then hadn't she reached for him? Yes, he had felt tenderness toward her, but she had reached for him, he'd felt her heat, seen the desire in her eyes. . . .

There was a world-weariness in the priest's eyes, and a certain sadness. "I beg you not to give her your trust as your father did. I beg you to be on your guard."

Too late, Bravo thought bitterly. *Too damn late.*

Father Mosto was silent, giving Bravo the time he needed as he struggled to clear his mind.

At length, Bravo rose. "It's time we discussed the reason my father sent me here."

The priest nodded, a look of concern on his face. "Of course."

"The alms cabinet."

"Ah, I suspected it was an object here in my rectory. Dexter spent many hours alone here in study and research." Taking out a key, Father Mosto unlocked the enormous wooden armoire, drew the chain off.

At that moment, a bell rang on his desk. For a moment, he ignored it, putting aside both lock and chain. Then, when it kept ringing, he said, "You must excuse me for a moment, I'm needed in the church proper."

AS Father Mosto turned the corner of the corridor, he saw that several of the lamps had been extinguished, and he made a mental note to re-light them on his way back. He hastened on, his mind on Braverman and Dexter Shaw, which is no doubt why he heard nothing. The assault was so silent, so swift that he felt nothing, until the knife blade sliced across his throat. There was a great pulse inside him, and he started vi-olently, as a gout of blood poured from him. He began to call out, but almost at once a blackness was lapping at his consciousness and he felt a curious lassitude, so that he wanted to sleep even as he attempted to struggle. But struggle against what? His life was rushing out of him with every beat of his heart.

His last thought—he had no last thought. He was dead before he hit the bloody stone floor.

WITHOUT waiting for Father Mosto to return, Bravo opened the heavy doors of the cabinet. The inside smelled of age and cedar; the walls of the cabinet were lined with panels of the fragrant wood. There were three widely spaced wooden shelves. He opened the alms box, ri-fled through the accounting ledger and other miscellaneous papers and files, all without finding what he was looking for. He stood there for a moment, puzzled, breathing in the spicy scent of the cedar. He was certain that he hadn't misread his father's cipher. Where was the purse?

Then something occurred to him. Though they appeared to be old, the richly scented cedar panels were relatively new—the scent of the wood faded over a matter of years, and this armoire looked to be more than two centuries old. Curious, he began a series of sharp raps on the panels.

His ear, attuned to tiny sounds, heard what he was hoping for—a particular hollowness. He dug his fingernails into the gap between the panels and pulled. Peeling back one of the panels, he discovered a small niche from which he pulled out a curious object. It was cool to the touch and shone in the lamplight. Further investigation revealed that it was made of steel—possibly sword steel—beautifully formed into the shape of a small beggar's purse. The domed top was without a handle. Instead he noticed a tiny square cutout. He'd seen that lock shape before.

Taking out the cuff links, he inserted the one that wouldn't open the lock in St. Malo. Sure enough, it fit. Just as he was about to open the beggar's purse, he heard a noise, the sharp bang as of a casement window flying open, followed by what sounded like a groan wrenched from a strangled throat.

In two swift strides he reached the door and flung it open. "Jenny? Father Mosto?"

An empty corridor stretched in either direction. It was eerily silent. Bravo could hear his heart beating, the rush of blood in his ears. A slow drip of water from someplace close at hand. Where the hell was Jenny?

Quickly pocketing the beggar's purse, he hurried down the corridor. At the first turn, he saw a large shape lying on the stone floor.

His heart skipped a beat. "Jenny?"

He ran, and skidded. The flagging wept with the damp of the canal and something more, something sticky and slightly viscous. Blood. A body in priest's robes sprawled grotesquely at his feet. Father Mosto's face, pale and almost greenish, stared up at him, his eyes fixed and glazed. His neck was slit and blood, having at first gouted out, still seeped. Next to him, in the widening pool of blood, was the murder weapon—a knife.

Kneeling down, Bravo examined it closely without touching it. It was a slender switchblade with pearl scales—the one Jenny had used to open the bottle of wine.

Jenny killed Father Mosto? He could hardly believe it. But if she was innocent, where was she?

Hearing a soft scrape, he rose and hurried after what sounded to him like the furtive patter of footfalls. The lamps in this section of the corridor had gone out, and the further he got from the body, the more steeped in gloom it became until he could barely see a foot ahead of him.

Still, he continued—what else could he do? All at once, he became aware of something behind him and whirled just in time to have his head snapped back by a blow to his forehead. Staggering back, he slammed against a slimy wall and was struck again.

He allowed another blow to strike, but this time grabbed the wrist of the extended arm and was startled to discover how slender it was, how smooth the skin. He was being attacked by a woman.

"Jenny," he panted, "why are you doing this?"

Another blow rocked him, but he refused to let go of the wrist, bending it sharply back, hearing the quick hiss of pain escape from between his adversary's lips. Brushing against her as he turned away from still another blow, he felt the swell of her breasts, and he turned her, about to slide his arm around her throat. But just then she slammed the heel of her hand into his nose. His head snapped back and his vision blurred as tears started from his eyes, momentarily blinding him. His adversary used her advantage to break his grip. He had a brief impression of a female figure running, then it was silhouetted blurrily against the white glare of daylight as she pulled open a side door and vanished.

Bravo shook his head, trying to clear it. Then he stumbled forward, reaching for the door. He found himself on a narrow street running beside the dank water of the canal. A mass of reflections, moving and rippling, rose up to him as if from a painting still being altered by an artist's brush.

Up ahead was the stone arch of a bridge. Sunlight struck his face like a blow, and squinting, he thought he glimpsed a female figure in the crowd hurrying across the bridge. Wiping the last of the tears out of his eyes, he shouldered his way through the mass of sweaty tourists, but he reached the apex of the bridge without having been able to positively identify Jenny. He stood there for a moment, his back to the throng, scanning the people in the square on the other side. All at once, he was swaying, his head swimming, not only from the glare and sodden heat but also from the blows he'd sustained in the corridor outside the rectory.

What other woman would have the physical power and expertise to fight hand-to-hand like that? And then, as if a picture snapped into focus, he remembered what Jenny had said when he'd shown her the Sig-Sauer: *"Maybe you ought to give the gun to me."* If she were the traitor, of course she'd want the gun.

He was so lost in this excruciating line of conjecture that he didn't notice the two men who came up behind him. Before he understood what was happening, they had pushed him over the side of the bridge.

He fell, landing on the deck of a *motoscafo*. Immediately, a sack was drawn over his head, and the boat took off. His feet were swept out from under him, someone was saying something urgently quite close; he ignored it and fought, but soon his arms were pinioned to his side. Using his forehead as a weapon, he struck out, colliding with one of his captors. He bulled forward, trying to press his advantage, but a precise blow that landed behind his right ear drove him into unconsciousness.

16

JENNY AWOKE IN UTTER DARKNESS. SHE GROANED. EVEN
touching the back of her neck set off a wave of dizziness and nausea that
made her cry out. She held her aching head for some time. What had
happened? She had been talking to that priest and then . . .

Woozily, she stood against a wall. It was cold and damp. She put her
hand out, encountered stone. Slowly, she moved along the wall until she
came to a door. She tried the wrought-iron handle, but the door was
locked. She retreated two steps, took a deep breath and slowly let it out.
She repeated the process three times, each inhalation and exhalation
deeper than the last. Then, gathering herself, she kicked the door open.
She staggered back and almost fell. The effort setting off another bout
of vertigo and nausea. This time, she turned her head to one side and
retched, vomiting up the contents of her stomach.

Out in the corridor, she was greeted by more blackness. It was then
she remembered her pocket flashlight. Digging it out, she switched it
on, played the beam this way and that. It took her a moment before she
saw the body. At first, she thought it was Bravo, and her heart lurched
painfully, the ache at the back of her neck redoubling. As she came
closer, she saw the curtainlike drape of a priest's robes and recognized
Father Mosto.

Cautiously, she went toward where his body lay twisted and bloody.
A sudden flash caught her eye, metal reflected by the light. Closer still,
she found herself staring at a puddle of blood turned black and shiny
as oil by the beam of light. In it, glimmering evilly, was a knife that
looked—no, it couldn't be! Checking her pocket, she found her knife

gone. She peered more closely at the switchblade on the floor. She picked it up, needing visceral confirmation.

Oh, my God, she thought, *it is* mine!

Someone had attacked her, stolen her knife and used it to slit Father Mosto's throat. But how did they know she was carrying a knife? No time and no way to answer those questions now.

"Bravo!" she called. "Bravo!"

Running back toward the rectory, she came upon the side door, which was open enough to allow a narrow triangle of light into the corridor. It seemed logical that whoever had taken him had used this to make their escape. Still, just to be certain, she searched the rectory. There was the armoire, its doors agape, an inner panel removed, but no Bravo. Cursing herself, she flew back down the corridor and out the door into the blazing heat.

Almost immediately, she noticed the commotion on the stone bridge that spanned the canal. People were all too willing to tell her about the man who had been pushed over the side of the bridge into the waiting *motoscafo.*

An old man dressed in impeccable Venetian fashion was incensed. "The terrorists spirited him off!"

"How do you know they were terrorists?" Jenny said.

"They kidnapped him, didn't they? What else could they be? And in broad daylight, can you imagine!" He made a rude gesture, his anger at its apex. "When did Venice become America?"

CAMILLE, watching Jenny from the concealment of a shadowed doorway, was still vibrating with the aftermath of the adrenaline rushing through her system. She desperately wanted a cigarette, but the nicotine would calm her, and she didn't want that just yet. There was nothing like a burst of extreme physical exertion to make you feel alive, she thought. To make you feel vital, to prove that you're still young.

As she observed the progress of Jenny's inquiries, she dabbed absently at the corner of her mouth with a folded bit of cloth. The cloth was already stained with her blood. Her body ached where Bravo had struck her, but it was a delicious pain, verging on the erotic, and the breath came hot in her throat. To be in physical contact with first Jenny and then Bravo, to feel Jenny's warm weight in her arms, to know that she was utterly helpless, and then to move on to Bravo, to know that the two had been lovers, to sense in their musculature the other, like a shadow or an indentation in a pillow with all its intimate scents, stimulated her like nothing else could.

Bravo had not, of course, been as pliant as Jenny. He had fought her, enabling her to assess firsthand the job his father had done with him; it brought him closer to her in a way she found enjoyable. Over the years she had probed and prodded Bravo, mainly through Jordan, in ways he'd never been aware of. It felt good to take the physical measure of him—more than good, it felt right, as if like a sorcerer she had been able to transform an image in a photograph and bring it to life. He was like a beautiful chair she had once coveted, with one leg torn away, tottering, ripe for a fall.

Of Father Mosto she thought not at all. He was of no consequence to her except as an object through which she was separating the lovers, isolating Bravo, revealing the vulnerable spot by which she would at long last destroy him.

JENNY, leaning on the stone parapet of the bridge, was assailed by doubt. She was in the middle of a nightmare, much of it of her own making. She had been so tied up in knots over her growing feelings for Bravo and her guilt in not telling him the truth about herself that she'd allowed her instincts to be dulled. She had forgotten who she was and so had been vulnerable to a clever attack by Knights in priest's robes, for that was the only logical explanation for what had happened. Now Bravo was in the enemy's hands—the worst had happened, and she was to blame.

On top of that, she was acutely aware of being under surveillance. She didn't know by whom. Though only an hour ago she would have assumed it was Michael Berio, now she refused to accede to any such leap of faith. The worst thing she could do was to go by old assumptions. She was in an entirely new game, and if she couldn't adjust—and quickly—the Order would lose everything.

Much as she hated to do it, she'd have to call Paolo Zorzi and admit her failure. She needed help. Reaching for her cell phone, she braced herself for the shower of invective he would direct at her. Then her blood ran cold; her cell phone was gone, too.

She closed her eyes, trying to will away the pain in her head and neck. Breathing slowly and deeply, she allowed the added oxygen she was drawing in to do its work. First things first. She needed to get out from under the surveillance. In Venice, she knew, she could walk for the entire afternoon and still not feel confident that she had lost her watcher. There were no vehicles to get her away, and the boats were all too open and slow to be of any use to her.

Then she remembered something she'd read while glancing through the Michelin guide. Rising from her position, she looked this way and that, as if unsure of which way to go—not so far from the truth. Crossing to the far side of the bridge, she went through the small *campo*, turning into a side street. She entered a store selling masks. While the proprietor rang up and wrapped a mask for a customer, she had a look around, examining the rows of leather masks that hung on the walls. As its artisans had done with glassblowing, marbled paper and Fortuny silks, Venice had turned mask making into a high art. Masks depicting characters, many from the commedia dell'arte, were worn during Carnevale, which traditionally began the day after Christmas and went to the day before Ash Wednesday. All laws were suspended during Carnevale, and everyone, high-born and low, mingled together—a practice born of the doge's desire to be able to walk the streets of his city and visit those he wished to lie with, in complete anonymity.

A horde of sad eyes, grotesque noses, grinning mouths peered down at her, and such was the skill of the artisans that each mask seemed alive with emotion: ardor, mirth or menace. There were also long cloaks of sumptuous fabric. These were called *tabarro*, the shopkeeper explained. When celebrants donned this, along with a mask and a *bauta*, a black silk hood and short lace cape, they were able to pass their own wife or sister without being recognized.

When the proprietor asked how he could help her, she asked for directions to Rio Trovaso, which, as it happened, was closer than she had thought. She quit the store reluctantly, as if leaving a party filled with fascinating new acquaintances.

It was not difficult to find Rio Trovaso, and she followed it until the intersection with Rio Ognissanti. Turning the corner, she came upon the *Squero*, one of the few remaining shipyards that built and repaired the city's ubiquitous gondolas. It consisted of three wooden buildings— odd for Venice—and a small dock that fronted the workshop itself.

At once, she went inside. One of the banes of Venice now worked to her advantage. Offering a good deal of money got her an outfit of workman's clothes. Not a single question was asked by the master shipwright who directed the work at the *Squero*—all the answer he required was contained in the euros she placed in his extended hand. The outfit included a cap under which she placed her hair. Pulling the bill low on her forehead helped, but for good measure, she took a piece of charcoal from the workshop and streaked her cheeks, rolling it between the palms of her hands to darken them, as well.

For another somewhat smaller sum, she had the shipwright take her by means of an interior passageway into the adjoining building, where the workmen lived. He led her through the ground floor and out a side entrance, walking several blocks with her as if she were one of his staff. They entered a café, and he left her there some moments later.

In her new disguise, she left the café, walking aimlessly, it seemed, for some time. In fact, she was checking for tags, slowly and painstakingly backtracking, doubling and redoubling through streets that were now as familiar to her as her own hometown, until she was satisfied that she was clean.

Then she returned to the area of the Church of l'Angelo Nicolò in I Mendicoli. She stood for a moment, taking stock of the environment. The street was dominated by police and gawking tourists. Obviously, Father Mosto's body had been discovered.

She wondering if the Knights still had the area under surveillance. They had lost her, that was for certain; would they keep personnel here? She thought not. They would know that she, having lost Bravo, would have no reason come back here. She had to figure that they would be scouring a circular section of the city with an expanding radius as time passed and they failed to find her. They would, in fact, be moving further and further away from this locus.

Setting off, she bypassed the entrance to the church, which was in any event clogged with police and forensic personnel. Instead, she turned the corner and passed into the next street. At the entrance to Santa Marina Maggiore, she stopped and, using the brass bell set into the stucco wall beside the indigo-painted wooden door, announced herself.

If the first order of business had been to free herself from surveillance, the second was to find succor and aid. She could think of no better place to find it than with the nuns of Santa Marina Maggiore.

The door was thrown open almost at once and she was confronted by a pale oval face riven by fear and suspicion.

"What is it, *signore*?" The nun was young; the horror next door made her query uncharacteristically abrupt and somewhat hostile.

"I need to see the abbess," Jenny said.

"My apologies, *signore*, but today it is impossible." She could not help glancing up the street toward the side of the church. "The abbess is very busy."

"Would you turn away a supplicant at your doorstep?"

"I have orders," the young nun said stubbornly. "The abbess is seeing no one."

"She must see me."

"Must she?"

At the sound of this deeper, more mature voice, the young nun started, and turning, saw another nun standing at her shoulder.

"That will be all, Suor Andriana. Tend to the herb garden now."

"Yes, Mother." Suor Andriana made a small genuflection and with a terrified backward glance hurried off.

"Enter, please," the older nun said. "Excuse Suor Andriana, she is young, as you can see, and she is a *converse*." Her voice was deep, indeed, almost masculine in tonality. She was tall and slender, with the narrow hips of a boy, and seemed to glide across the stone flagging by some mysterious means of locomotion. "My name is Suor Maffia di Albori. I am one of the *madri di consiglio*, the ruling council of Santa Marina Maggiore."

The moment Jenny stepped across the threshold Suor Maffia di Albori slammed the door shut and threw the huge ancient lock. Without a word, she led Jenny to a stone fount, below which was a basin of cool water.

"Wash your face, please," Suor Maffia di Albori said.

Obediently, Jenny bent over, cupping the water in her hands, splashing it up over her face, washing off the charcoal. When she turned, Suor Maffia di Albori handed her a square of undyed muslin, which she used to dry her face.

"Take off your cap, please." As Jenny did so, the nun made a sound deep in her throat. "Now you may properly introduce yourself."

"My name is Jenny Logan."

"And who or what are you running from, Jenny Logan?" Suor Maffia di Albori was not a handsome woman. She had no need for beauty, for she was possessed of a powerful face with a strong Roman nose, prominent cheekbones and a thrusting chin like a sword blade.

"The Knights of St. Clement," Jenny said. "Two or more of their agents infiltrated the church and murdered Father Mosto."

"Is that so?" Suor Maffia di Albori examined Jenny with the deep-set curious eyes of the intellectual. "Would you hazard a guess as to the method of Father Mosto's murder?"

"I don't have to guess, I saw him," Jenny said. "His throat was slit."

"The murder weapon?" Suor Maffia di Albori said rather coolly.

"A knife—a pearl-scaled switchblade, to be exact."

Suor Maffia di Albori took a quick and determined step toward her. "Don't lie to me, girl!"

"I know because it's my knife. It was taken from me." She explained briefly what had happened to her.

The *madre di consiglio* listened to the account entirely without comment or expression. Jenny might have been explaining how she'd lost the two euros Suor Maffia di Albori had given her to buy a carton of milk.

"And why have you come to Santa Marina Maggiore, Jenny Logan?"

"I need help," Jenny said.

"What makes you believe that you will find it here?"

"I was told to ask to see the Anchorite."

A deathly silence now fell between them.

"Who told you that?"

"The Plumber."

It appeared as if Suor Maffia di Albori's face had gone chalk white. It took her a moment to recover. "You are *that* Jenny?"

"Yes."

Suor Maffia di Albori said, "You will wait here. You will not move or speak to anyone but myself, even if spoken to, is that understood?"

"Yes, Mother," Jenny said as meekly as Suor Andriana.

"You are neither *converse* nor *monache da coro*. You are not obliged to address me as 'Mother'."

"Nevertheless, I will, Mother."

The *madre di consiglio* nodded. "As you wish." She turned away, but not before Jenny caught the tiny flicker of pleasure in her eyes.

Jenny, alone in the dark and musty anteroom, stood quite still, waiting as she had been ordered to do. There were no windows, and what little furniture there was—two chairs and a settee—looked as forbidding and uncomfortable as if they had been manufactured for the visiting room of a prison. The floor was a mosaic of the Crucifixion, dimmed now with age and perhaps the waters of the lagoon. Even so, it was clear that only the dullest of colors had been used, because in the convent bright hues were deemed unseemly and to be avoided. On three sides, arches led to an even gloomier interior.

A distant chanting started up, as Sexte, the noon prayer, floated through the nunnery. As always, her mind was filled with Dex. It was he who had told her of Santa Marina Maggiore, who had told her to ask for the Anchorite. Dex was the Plumber—it was, he had told her, how the nuns of Santa Marina Maggiore referred to him. When she had asked him why, he had given her that wry, lopsided smile of his that so endeared him to her.

"Like everything else of import, it returns to the Latin, plumb *being Latin for lead,"* he had said. *"In medieval times, roofs were made of lead, so plumbers were roofers. The nuns of Santa Marina Maggiore call me the Plumber because they believe I kept the roof over their heads."*

"Did you?" she had asked.

Again that wry, lopsided smile dented his face. *"In a way, I guess, in money . . . and in my belief in them."*

She wanted to know more, of course, but she hadn't asked him, and he hadn't volunteered any more. Now, against all odds, here she was at Santa Marina Maggiore, asking to see the Anchorite, not even knowing who or what the Anchorite was. But, she told herself, that was how it had always been between her and Dex—he said things, and she took them on faith. It was him she had faith in, ever since . . . But she didn't want to think about that, and with a violent mental wrench, turned her thoughts in another direction.

She opened her eyes. Below her, Christ's sorrowful eyes beseeched her. What was He calling for? Faith, of course. For a Catholic with faith, life was simple. The phrase "Have faith, it's God will" covered every situation, no matter how disastrous. Life, however, was anything but simple, and it seemed to her that the platitudes that escaped from the mouths of priests were like soap bubbles, unable to sustain themselves, collapsing almost as soon as they were spoken.

Sexte was almost done by the time Suor Maffia di Albori returned. Her cheeks were flushed, as if she was in a hurry to return.

"Come with me, Jenny," she said.

Jenny dutifully followed behind the *madre di consiglio*. Passing beneath the central arch, she went through a door, out onto a stone portico held up by delicate columns of pale limestone with trefoil capitals. The portico stepped down into a square garden, divided into four equal plots, each holding different plants. One grew green herbs, another, small fig, lime and pear trees. In a third, she could see the tops of carrots and beets, along with the deeply-hued glossy skins of baby eggplant and the frothy ruffled edges of chicory, while the fourth contained a series of tiny complex leafed plants she could not identify.

It was in this that Suor Andriana worked on her knees, turning over the soil with a trowel, pulling out weeds, carefully trimming the plants. She did not look up as they passed, but Jenny could see her hunched shoulders tense, and she felt a pluck of sympathy for the girl.

The walkways between the sections formed a cross through whose center they passed on their way to the private rooms of Santa Marina Maggiore. Jenny was familiar enough with nunneries to know that she was being accorded a signal honor—normally, no outsider was allowed into the inner chambers.

"It's best I prepare you for your interview," Suor Maffia di Albori said in her sober, vaguely masculine voice. "Perhaps you know that the majority of Venetian nuns came from the upper crust of society. The society inside—*our* society—is formed along strictly hierarchical lines. There are the *monache da coro,* the choir nuns, those of noble birth, and then there are the *converse,* the social inferiors. This was how it was in the fifteen hundreds, and here it remains so today."

They had by this time crossed the garden and had passed through another, larger archway, the portal to the cloistered grounds of the nunnery proper. This part of the structure was set back quite far from the street, closer to the church than Jenny would have imagined. But then Venetian architecture had a way of mimicking the city's streets, which often bent, curling back on themselves. It was inevitable that one got lost in Venice; that was part of the city's pleasurable distinctions.

Sexte had ended and it was very still inside the building, with only the barest suggestion of echoes now and again reaching them, like the soft lapping of the lagoon against ancient pilings.

From a smallish egg-shaped anteroom they entered a long, narrow hallway, completely without ornamentation or color. It had an arched ceiling and electric lamps in wall niches where once torches must have flickered.

At one point, they passed what looked like a coat rack—a long wooden bar into which had been bolted a series of wrought-iron hooks. From each hook hung a long narrow leather strap, one side of which was coarsely matted horsehair.

Unable to control her curiosity, Jenny reached out to touch one, but Suor Maffia di Albori took her hand away.

"Those belong to the nuns, they are private." Her dark eyes regarded Jenny for a moment. "You don't know, do you?" She took one of the straps off its hook, held it by one end. "This is what we call a discipline. It is, in fact, a flail. The discipline is used periodically. Every night during Lent and during Advent three times a week. At other times of the year, twice a month." With a deft flick of her wrist, the flail arched over her head and with a sharp report struck her along the spine. "You look horrified, but the process is imperative to relieve the inner tensions of the body. Like fasting, it better readies the spirit for devotion." With a kind of reverence, she put the discipline back on its hook.

"Before we go any further, it is important that you understand something. Venice is in many ways still a medieval city. It has very little interest in the modern world. Here, time stands still, and we are grateful for that gift. If you cannot grasp this, Venice will surely defeat you." With those last words, she turned on her heel and continued down the corridor.

Jenny took a last look at the discipline, swinging balefully on his hook, before she followed the *madre di consiglio* to the end of the hall, where it gave out onto another hallway running perpendicular to it, like the head of the letter *T.*

As they turned left, Suor Maffia di Albori said, "I am from the noble house of Le Vergini. I followed my two aunts and three sisters here, and took the veil while they watched." She turned. "When I was born, my parents asked themselves the same question that all parents of girl-children ask themselves: *maritar ò monacar?* Would I marry or become a nun?" Her voice was impassive, matter-of-fact. "I was neither shrewish nor in any way deformed by birth or illness or accident. But you see my face, what man would have me? Besides, in that regard I had very little interest in men. I had no choice but to take the veil, where, with a modest dowry, I was married to Jesus Christ. I did not mind, but it was not uncommon for families with many daughters to force some of them into nunneries as a way of saving them from having to pay much larger dowries to prospective husbands."

The ghost of a smile tinged Suor Maffia di Albori's mouth like lipstick. "I seem to be making a habit of shocking you."

"It's not that, but I must say that I feel a certain kinship."

"With a nun? But you're a Guardian."

"I live in the Voire Dei—I suspect the Plumber must have told you about—"

"Oh, yes." The lips pursed, drained of blood now, so that they were almost stark white.

"The outside world is as alien to me as it is to you and your fellow nuns."

"Is that what you think, Jenny?" The *madre di consiglio* made a curious little gesture that could have meant anything. "Well, then, it's as well you've come to visit us. It's as well I am taking you to see the Anchorite."

"Who is the Anchorite?" Jenny asked.

Suor Maffia di Albori placed an admonishing forefinger across her thin, bloodless lips. "It is not for me to enlighten you." She turned and continued down the hall. "You will see for yourself soon enough."

To Jenny, this seemed an unnecessarily melodramatic pronouncement. She felt Bravo's absence even more acutely, surely he'd know who the Anchorite was. As they proceeded down the hall, she was aware of a deepening gloom—sunlight had never penetrated this far into the convent. She was normally not prone to claustrophobia, but she had the distinct impression that the walls were thicker here and, further, that they were pushing inward, trying to close off this section of the building forever. It was unnaturally still; even the sound of their footfalls was curiously muffled, as if something unseen were trying to strangle it into silence.

At length, they approached what appeared to be the furthest reaches of the hallway, a dead end, as if the builders, having exhausted themselves coming this far, had given up. More curious still, there were no doors, just three barred windows—one on the left wall, one on the right wall, and one straight ahead.

The light was very dim, and Suor Maffia di Albori took down a torch from a niche and lit it. The illumination cast off by the wavering flame revealed a hall made of brick instead of stone blocks, as it was elsewhere.

Suor Maffia di Albori raised the torch as she approached the iron grille of the window straight ahead. "Come, Jenny," she beckoned, "you must stand close. Closer still. Now look inside and present yourself to the Anchorite."

Jenny did as she was bade, approaching until her nose was almost against the square iron rods of the grille. Some peculiar quality of the flame allowed her to see clear across the cell, to the crucifix on the wall. There was a cot and an old-fashioned washstand, nothing more. Except the shadows.

All at once, one of the shadows moved, so that Jenny started back. But she felt Suor Maffia di Albori's surprisingly strong hand between her shoulder blades, propelling her forward. And then, the animated shadow emerged into the flame light, and Jenny gave an involuntary gasp.

"I can only imagine the enormous pressure you've been under," Jordan Muhlmann said as he and Cardinal Felix Canesi stood outside the specially outfitted hospital suite in the private, guarded wing inside Rome's Vatican City. "Seeing to the pontiff's needs, keeping the press corps in the dark, suppressing the inflammatory rumors that his holiness is on the point of death, holding news conferences, creating 'new' speeches by piecing together snippets of the pontiff's unpublished remarks, as well as keeping our friends on the inner council calm."

Cardinal Canesi showed his teeth. "Everything is running smoothly enough and it will continue to run smoothly, God willing, if you do your part."

"How could I not?" Jordan said, smiling. "The special relationship between the Holy See and my organization has existed for centuries."

"Yes. It was the Vatican that brought the Knights of St. Clement into existence, it was the Vatican that underwrote your missions. You serve at our pleasure."

There was nothing threatening in Cardinal Canesi's tone, but then there needn't be. He held the weight of history and of holy tradition in the palm of his hand. He wanted to make sure Jordan knew from whose hand he was eating.

"And how is the Holy Father?" Jordan said.

"The pontiff is on oxygen. His heart is laboring, his lungs are slowly filling with fluid. I can feel his death, Jordan. It creeps along my own flesh on its way to take him."

Jordan's eyes blazed. "Death will not take him, this I swear, your eminence! We are making progress, the Quintessence will be in your hands within days."

"I am pleased by your faith and by your unswerving commitment, Jordan. I could not have hoped for a better ally." Cardinal Canesi was a homely man. His legs were bandy, his head was oversized; it sat on his rounded shoulders seemingly without benefit of a neck. "It is most gracious of you to take the time to come, to pay your respects in person. Your presence has lifted his spirits considerably."

"For him I would travel twice around the circumference of the world," Jordan said with a reverence that privately disgusted him.

"Before you enter, you must be gowned and your feet and hands covered." Canesi guided him across the hall and into a dressing room. It was small and windowless. A line of pale green gowns hung on pegs. The cardinal took two down, handed one to Jordan, and slipped the other on.

Out the small window, enormous crowds of the faithful came and went across the acres of marble, their foolish placards held high for the news cameras, their eyes lifted as their lips moved in prayer. Here was the power in faith, Jordan thought, the manifestation of Canesi's power. But it was a power from another, an antique age. It was cracked, worn, hollowed out. There was nothing left of it but the facade. The crippled girl guided by her mother, the emaciated man in a wheelchair pushed by his son, they had come here along with all the others to be healed, to be saved, but Jordan knew the truth: they were doomed, just like Canesi.

Jordan turned away from the window and its view on the chamber of horrors, his heart cold as a stone. He had his own problems, and they had nothing to do with God, or even faith.

Canesi said in a low, quavery voice, "How many are dead?" And then, almost immediately, "No, no, for the love of God don't tell me, I don't want to know."

Jordan felt the contempt burst like a grenade inside him, and all at once he saw the cardinal for what he was: an old man, grappling with the vexing problem of how to keep his power as his world changed. "Suffice it to say, then, that the Haute Cour has been almost fully compromised," he said.

"Almost!" Cardinal Canesi exclaimed.

"We are moving with all due speed." Jordan ground his teeth to be in the presence of such hypocrisy. "You understand, of course, that there is the matter of the puzzle Dexter Shaw created."

"Ah, now we come to the crux of the matter!"

Jordan realized just how much he despised this man. He stood for Rome—a city that was too chaotic, too crowded, too dirty for Jordan's refined tastes, and he despised Vatican City's hothouse atmosphere most of all. The entire might and power of the Catholic church was focused here like sunlight through a magnifying glass, but so was its essential weakness. A city-state unto itself, it had willfully kept itself at arm's length from the rest of the world. As a result, it existed in a reality of its own, out of touch with its far-flung constituents, painfully slow to react to change of any kind.

"Dexter Shaw had been a thorn in our side for years," Cardinal Canesi said. "As he consolidated his position inside the Order, as he gathered power to him, he created more and more problems for us."

"And for us, he wanted to be *Magister Regens*," Jordan said. "Which is one of the reasons we took him out."

"I do not want to hear those things!" Cardinal Canesi's face went chalk white. "Have I not made myself clear on this issue?"

"You have, your eminence, but as we both know, these are extraordinary times. So I trust that you will forgive me my small transgressions."

Canesi made a gesture, as if to absolve Jordan of the onus of small transgressions, but still Jordan's keen eyes saw his body betray him. The cardinal moved uneasily, like a bird who has puffed up his feathers in alarm.

"You know how I rely on you, Jordan."

"Of course, your excellency. And you know how I am relying on your contacts in this time of ultimate crisis. You won't hold back, will you?"

"Of course not!" Cardinal Canesi said hotly. "The pope has three days, perhaps four, the doctors tell me. They are working hard to stabilize him, but even if they do, without the Quintessence he will not recover."

When it came to Cardinal Felix Canesi, Jordan held no illusions. If for some reason events didn't work out as he wished, Canesi would require a scapegoat, and Jordan knew full well who that would be.

Having had more than enough of Canesi, he went back out into the hallway and crossed into the pope's suite. Like all hospital rooms, it smelled of sweet sickness and acrid disinfectant. He stayed for ten minutes, which was all the pontiff had strength for. The Holy Father's face was gray and terribly drawn, but there was still plenty of life left in those pale blue eyes. He had ascended to the apex of the Catholic church more than twenty years ago, and it was clear he was not yet ready to relinquish his power.

"I am Arcangela, the Abbess of Santa Marina Maggiore."

The Anchorite stared up at Jenny with piercing gray eyes that bulged slightly from their sockets. "So you are the Plumber's woman. A handsome one, you are, but so sad!" Her eyes seemed fixed, like an owl's, so that she was obliged to turn her head to look this way and that. She was old and very thin, her skin translucent as rice paper, the blue of the veins in her temples and the backs of her hands startlingly vivid. She had a face the shape of an inverted teardrop, with a wide forehead and a crooked nose. One side of her mouth drooped slightly, and Jenny wondered whether she'd suffered a minor stroke until Arcangela shuffled forward on one lame leg.

"An ancient injury," Arcangela said. "I was nine when I was caught in the *Acqua Alta*. I slid and fell and was crushed between a piling and the hull of a boat. My parents said I was careless and, worse, stupid, to be standing at the edge of the *fondamenta* during the flood, but I loved to watch the water rising because at those times it takes on the color of wine . . . or blood."

She had a wide mouth with expressive lips that moved seemingly of their own accord. "You have asked to see me?"

"Yes," Jenny said. "May I come in so that I may speak with you in private?"

"You may not," Arcangela said, "principally because there is no way in or out of my cell."

"What?" Jenny was taken aback. "Surely you aren't a prisoner, as Anchorites were in medieval times?"

The Abbess smiled, a slow, sly, wonderful grin that served to lessen Jenny's unease. "It is so. I have been walled in of my own volition because, like all Anchorites, the depth of my faith in Jesus Christ has compelled me to reject the world, and live here in isolation. So far as the world outside this convent is concerned, I am already dead. Father Mosto said the last rites over me just before I was bricked in. That was thirty years ago." She turned and pointed. "Look there, the other two windows in my cell. This one, to the left, looks out onto the altar of the Church of l'Angelo Nicolò, and this one to the right is where I'm fed and where I put the chamber pot when it is filled."

Jenny was somehow terrified by this description. "You mean you haven't seen the sky in thirty years?"

"Why would I do such a thing, you're asking yourself. It sounds like hell, you're thinking." Arcangela's pale eyes were alight with an inner fire. "Am I right?"

"Yes." Jenny, on the verge of being overwhelmed, could only whisper the word.

"Well, it's not faith alone, I can tell you," the Anchorite said. "Such faith is indistinguishable from madness."

She came closer, and Jenny could smell her—a rank, sour, animal smell. It was, Jenny imagined, how human beings must have smelled in the time of Casanova.

"You do not flinch from me—well, that is something," Arcangela said. "I am here, I have been here for thirty years to do penance, to pay for the transgressions my charges commit every day of their lives."

"But your charges are nuns," Jenny said. "What kind of transgressions could they commit?"

Pointing at Jenny, Arcangela addressed the sister. "Look at her, Suor Maffia di Albori. Dressed like our own Santa Marina!"

Jenny blinked. "I beg your pardon?"

Arcangela crooked a knobbed forefinger. "Santa Marina, eighth century, from the Bythian province of Asia Minor." She nodded. "Like you, she dressed as a man—in her case, a monk's habit—and lived among males all her life. We brought her relics here in 1230, when we founded this convent in her name, so that we could walk among men, talk to men, and so advance our Order's work."

"The Order?"

The abbess's eyebrows suddenly shot up like a release of energy or the beginning of an idea. "Ah, Suor Maffia di Albori, now she has begun to make the connections, to piece together the patchwork quilt of clues we have been patiently feeding her."

Jenny's finger's gripped the iron bars of the Anchorite's cell. "You are members of the Gnostic Observatines?"

"As you yourself are," Suor Maffia di Albori said at her side.

"But I was told that—"

"The Order didn't allow women," Arcangela finished for her. "And now you know the truth. From the day Santa Marina Maggiore was founded, our charges have dressed in monk's habits, passing out of this sanctuary and into the world outside. In this way, we made deals with nobles, bartered with merchants, gathered knowledge for the doge and for ourselves. It was we who furthered Venice's way in the world, it was through our contacts in the Levant that the Serene Republic grew rich and powerful."

"And you with it," Jenny said.

Arcangela's face clouded over. "Ah, now you talk like your male counterparts in the Order."

"Oh, no, I was remembering Bravo's comment that the convent had provided the funds for the church's fourteenth-century renovation."

"And how conveniently our generosity over the centuries has been obscured by the envy of some of the members of the Haute Cour—including the late Father Mosto—who want us disbanded, stripped of our power. All because I dared ask for representation in the inner circle."

"But you *should* be part of the Haute Cour," Jenny said.

"You believe that—and so did the Plumber. It was he who stood up for us, he who, when shouted down by the others, came to our aid and helped us without anyone else knowing."

That was just like Dex, Jenny thought, tears standing in her eyes.

"We have nothing of our own, else why would we have needed the Plumber's help?" Arcangela said. "We have never wavered from the tenets of poverty laid down by St. Francis for the Observatines. Of course, wealth in many different forms did, on occasion, come our way.

But always it was used to help others, for the furtherance of the Order. Our loyalty is unquestionable."

The forefinger was raised again. "And the work for which we are vilified is highly dangerous. When, in 1301, the first of our charges was killed in Trebizond on a mission of grave importance, Santa Marina Maggiore underwent a sea change. The day our sister in Jesus Christ was brought back here from Trebizond, the then abbess, Suor Paula Grimani, swore to become an Anchorite in penance. Within three days, the bishop of Torcello arrived to administer the last rites and the first of our abbesses was bricked in. The penance has become perpetual."

Jenny shook her head. "But to consign yourself to a living hell."

"Do you not understand the purpose of penance?" the Anchorite asked. "Perhaps I should have quit smoking or given up raisins. Do you think such deprivation adequate for the loss of a life?"

"Of course not, but you could have stopped. You could have ordered your charges to return here and never leave again."

"Yes, I could have done that," Arcangela said, "but then I wouldn't have been fit to be abbess. Then our trove of secrets would have been depleted centuries ago, and that would have been the end of the Order."

"So you did most of the work, and the monks took the credit."

"It wasn't as simple as that, the monks were always quite active. But they don't think as we do, do they?" Arcangela said. "And they don't have access to our resources. You see, for centuries Venice's prostitutes came here to pray, to seek penance and have the Virgin Mary absolve them of their sins." She shook her head. "You know, many of them are closer to God than the so-called legitimate citizens of the city."

Arcangela moved a little more into the light, which only underscored the ravines etched into her face. "It was the whores who had access, you see, to everyone from the doge on down, and it is we who had access to the whores. At night, they lie next to politicians, merchant-princes, even Holy Fathers, and the whispered confidences passed in the aftermath of their work came straight to us. It was the masks, you see. It was easy in a city of masks, where identities were hidden, for anyone, married or clergy—even the doge—to move unrecognized through Venice, to visit anyone he wished without fear of being found out. This is why it is often said that what the whores of Venice don't know isn't worth knowing."

"The monks must have hated that you had sources not available to them."

"Of course they did, and they made our lives miserable because of it. They knew the nature of our transgressions. They knew we could not complain or go around them—we could not bring that kind of attention to ourselves. We're females, after all, we cannot give confession or communion or sermons, so even we—who ventured beyond the cloistered walls to further our Order—are in a way all prisoners."

"Nothing has changed," Suor Maffia di Albori said. "It is as I told you."

"I remember," Jenny said. "I won't be defeated by Venice."

"Good, good." Arcangela moved until her clawlike fingers touched Jenny's. Her skin was as smooth as silk. "So, now I will answer your question."

Jenny frowned. "But I haven't asked you yet."

"No need," the abbess said. "An emissary of the man you wish to see has just arrived. Suor Maffia di Albori will take you to him."

"The man? Who—?"

"Why, Zorzi, of course. Paolo Zorzi," Arcangela said shortly. "Now go." She waved a hand vaguely. "I am unused to all this talk and my head hurts."

JORDAN passed out of Vatican City into the sprawl and clutter of Rome proper. It was well that his hired car was air-conditioned, Rome was sweltering. At the Piazza Venetia, he turned, inching past the Forum, which was so choked with tourists it was impossible to make out the lower stories. He rose toward the Campidolgio and passed over it and out of the *centro storico*—the heart of Rome—arriving at the Bocca della Verità and then on into the Aventino, a calm, leafy district of large old villas, studded with embassies and a scattering of upscale apartment buildings.

Jordan observed everything through the tinted windows, at a remove from the overheated chaos of the Roman afternoon.

He pulled out his cell phone and dialed Camille. When she answered, he asked her for an update on the situation in Venice.

"Have no worries. Everything is on schedule, my love," she said.

"Good, because Canesi's been flexing his muscles again." He barked a short laugh. "Unfortunately for him, his muscles have begun to wither away."

"What a pity."

"How is Signore Cornadoro behaving himself?"

"Perfectly, my love. And now I must ask the same of Signore Spagna."

"Osman is no concern of yours, Mother. Your focus should be on Bravo."

"When have you ever had cause to doubt my focus?"

Jordan felt an unpleasant quickening of his heartbeat, a response to the whiplike flick of his mother's displeasure. His anger at himself flared. "Results, Camille, are what matter now. Results. All other issues fade to insignificance. Your world is Bravo, and only Bravo. Everything now rests on your shoulders."

He ended the call with a mixture of anxiety and elation, before she could come back at him. Pulling up in front of a stately embassy building flanked by pencil cypress trees and coral bougainvillea, he deliberately turned off his cell phone. Emerging from the car, he was hit with a wave of heat that fairly staggered him. As he walked up the Istrian stone steps, the front door opened and Osman Spagna, bowing slightly, ushered him into the cool, air-conditioned interior.

"It is a pleasure to see you again, Grand Master."

Jordan nodded as he followed Spagna through the facade of the Cypriot embassy offices. In reality, there was no Cypriot embassy in Rome. Those duties were handled for Cyprus by the New Zealand embassy. This building, in fact, housed the headquarters of the Knights of St. Clement of the Holy Blood.

Spagna used a special key to unlock a door set flush in the wood paneling and, moments later, he and Jordan were seated at a polished tulip-wood table in a high-ceilinged room, with double doors at one end and at the other windows that looked out over manicured lawns and trees. The magnificent view, however, was not visible, as the heavy velvet drapes were drawn across the expanse of glass. The walls were devoid of any decoration; there was nothing in the room to indicate its use.

"The documents are complete, Grand Master," Spagna said, pushing across a folder for Jordan's perusal. "Everything is as you specified."

Jordan avidly read through the signed contract selling off the building they were in, the one that had housed the Knights for decades. "No one knows about this, you're certain?"

"Quite certain," Spagna said. He was a short, stocky man, with dark skin, a large nose and a ferret's cunning eyes. With his calculating, mathematical mind he was the natural counterpart to Jordan, the engineer essential to the empire builder. "As you can see on page five, paragraph seven, the language is quite specific. The buyer cannot reveal the transaction for three months after he takes possession. Since it will be his residence, this presented no problem for him."

Jordan sighed as he looked up. "At last we are leaving here, at last we will be free of Rome, the Vatican, and Cardinal Canesi."

Spagna nodded. "It is, indeed, the last step toward our freedom," he said. "You and I have spent the last decade using Lusignan et Cie's resources and contacts to secretly replace the power and capital that had been provided for us by the cardinal and his cabal of Vatican insiders."

This was why Jordan had come to Rome, not to kowtow to Cardinal Canesi or to pay his respects to the pope, but to gather in the last piece of his plan. "It's done then—my dream has become a reality. From this moment forward, the Knights are no longer tied to Canesi or the whims of the pope. We are free to forge our own destiny."

He rose and Spagna with him. Together, they threw open the double doors to an enormous conference room. As they crossed the threshold, the thirty-five individuals—businessmen, politicians, economists, financial managers, currency and commodity traders, think-tank members from twenty different countries—rose as one from their seats around the rosewood table and stood beneath a banner embroidered with the seven-pointed purple cross, the emblem of the Knights of St. Clement.

"Gentlemen," Jordan said, "I come with the momentous news all of us have been waiting for." He circled them until he was directly beneath the banner. In an instant, he had tugged at a corner. The banner fluttered down, piled around his feet. Beneath it was revealed a new banner: one which depicted a *Gyronny* shield: lines radiated from the central point outward, dividing the field into six triangular sections. At its center was a guardant Gryllus, a mythical beast, a monstrous grasshopper with the head of a snarling lion. This was the emblem of the Muhlmanns.

Jordan, his face flushed with victory, turned to the assembled. "The

Knights of St. Clement, as we have known them, are dead," he said. "Long live the Knights of our own making!"

A glorious destiny, he thought amid the rising clamor, made possible by the death of Dexter Shaw, by the slow dismantling of Braverman Shaw. Because when Bravo finally found the cache of the Gnostic Observatines, Jordan would take possession of it all, including the Testament of Jesus Christ and the Quintessence, which he never had any intention of turning over to Canesi. No, they would be his to do with as he wished. Even Camille did not know that he planned to anoint himself with the Quintessence and so become as close to immortal as Methuselah himself.

But he was not thinking of godhood now—that was for the future. For now, he contented himself with imagining the endgame, when Bravo would be on his knees, when he would tell him the truth. He wanted to see the shock and betrayal in Bravo's face just before he ended his life.

17

BRAVO WAS IN WASHINGTON SQUARE PARK IN GREENWICH
Village. He was sitting across from his father. Between them was a
square stone-and-concrete table in which was set a chessboard. He had
chosen the Giuoco Piano/Two Knights Defense as his opening because
it gave him two options instead of one. But after the sixth move he could
see that it was no good—slowly but surely, as always happened, his father was getting the best of him.

Dappled sunlight filtered through the plane trees and the sounds of
kids skating or throwing a Frisbee floated like balloons through the soft
late spring air. Pigeons—the flying rats of New York—strutted across
the hexagonal pavers, greedily searching for the stray crumb.

As Bravo was moving his knight to c3, Dexter said, "What would
happen, do you think, if you chose not to gambit your e-pawn?"

Bravo thought about this for a moment. He now knew the knight to
c3 was a tactical mistake—his father had in his way said as much. Following the strategy out, he saw the flaw, then he turned his mind to al-
ternatives, finally pushing his bishop to d2.

Dexter sat back, pleased. This was his standard methodology of
teaching his son. He never told Bravo what to do, but rather nudged
him to rethink his strategy, find the flaw himself and then, armed with
that knowledge, come up with a better solution.

After the game, they packed up the pieces, according to custom the
kings and queens first, the pawns last. Dexter said, "Remember when
you soapbox raced around the fountain?"

"That was some racer you made me, Dad. It let me beat everybody."

"That was you, Bravo. You were born with the desire to win."

"I lost, though, that one time."

Dexter nodded. "To Donovan Bateman, I remember it vividly."

"He shoved me and I fell."

"You came home with that knee of yours all bloody—and when you took off your clothes and your mother saw your whole side black and blue she almost passed out."

"But you patched me up, Dad, good as new. You said you were proud of me."

"I was." Dexter slid home the top of the black and white box that held the chess pieces. "You didn't cry, or even flinch while I was cleaning the gravel out of your kneecap, even though it must've hurt like hell."

"I knew as long as you were there everything would be all right."

Dexter put the box under his arm and they stood up. "I'd like you to come back home and stay for a while."

"Are you all right, Dad?"

They had cremated Steffi less than a week before, Dexter standing silent, head bowed, Bravo on one side of him, Emma on the other, as the coffin entered the massive retort. Dexter had wanted—perhaps needed—to see the process through from beginning to end, and they wanted what he wanted. The fire would be on, they were told, for two hours, so they went out to an old-fashioned luncheonette. It had a soda fountain with chromium stools along one side and vinyl-clad booths on the other. The old waitress wore black, as if in mourning, and the tiny black and white floor tiles were hexagonal like the machine in the crematorium that crushed the bones. They saw their gray, shocked faces in a mirrored strip that ran above the soda fountain. Strange to say, for that two-hour span the family was the closest it had ever been. They ate turkey sandwiches, which came with dressing and a tiny paper cup of cranberry sauce, and drank chocolate ice cream sodas and remembered Steffi. There was something about the reduction of the human body to its basic carbon form that was liberating. This was, at least, what Dexter told his children both then and later, when they scattered the two pounds of ashes into the fallow ground of the small garden at the back of their brownstone where, months later, irises, dahlias and roses would spring up in delight.

"It wouldn't be for long." His father looked at him and, for the first time, revealed all the pain Steffi's suffering and death had unleashed on him. "It's only that when I pass by your room at night I want to see your head on the pillow, that's all. Just for a while, okay?"

"Sure."

Dexter stopped beside a plane tree, his hand running across the sun-splashed bark, pied as the coat of their neighbor's mutt. "Sometimes, Bravo, late at night when I walk through the house I see her, or hear her coming through the door, her voice calling to me, so warm and tender, you know, like this sunlight. . . ."

IN the twilight that lay between unconsciousness and consciousness Bravo was reluctant to let his father go. As Dexter's face threatened to dissolve in the mist, Bravo thought of the Quintessence and his heart leapt at finding it, of applying it to his father's body, of seeing him resurrected. But almost immediately, he knew it was not to be. Resurrection was not what his father would have wanted. How could he know that so absolutely? Because he knew that his father must have had these selfsame thoughts after Steffi had died. He'd had access to the cache of secrets and, therefore, the Quintessence. Why not use it to bring his beloved Steffi back to life? Because he agreed with Uncle Tony, the Quintessence was not for humans. It went against the natural laws of life; using it would upset the careful balance of nature, resulting in un-knowable, and possibly disastrous, consequences. This was why the Or-der had so zealously guarded it for so many centuries, this was why he must not fail in the task his father had given him. He knew this in a vis-ceral way now, a way he could not have understood before. Because even though he knew it was wrong, he could feel the powerful lure, the possibility, improbable though it might seem, of having his father resur-rected, returned to life. They could complete all the hesitating conversa-tions that, as adults, they had left dangling, they could let down their guard, produce for each other explanations for their thoughts and ac-tions. They could at last begin to understand each other fully, and in each other's presence reach the serene state of forgiveness.

Rising at last into full consciousness, he rolled over and groaned. He felt that something basic was different and it took him a moment to re-alize the rocking of the water was absent, he was no longer in the *moto-scafo*. Opening his eyes, he discovered that the hood had been removed. He was in a small, cramped room with a simple cot and bedding, on which he was lying, an unadorned scarred wooden chest atop which sat a utilitarian white porcelain pitcher and bowl. On the wall above the cot was a wooden crucifix. He was in a monastic cell.

Light streamed through a window. Though small, it was open and unbarred—odd for a prison cell, for he had to assume that he had been captured by the Knights of St. Clement. Jenny's mission had been to kill Father Mosto and then lead him to the apex of the bridge where the Knights were waiting for him. He lay for a moment more, mulling over her treachery. She had fooled him, just as she had fooled his father. He vowed that would never happen again. If he got out of here.

Painfully, he rose and approached the small window. Outside, he saw a beautiful cloister and, beyond a stone wall, rows of finely cultivated trees. As if they had been waiting for his appearance in the window, two figures came into view. They were wearing monastic robes, hooded like Capuchins, but their faces were hard-lined and decidedly grim.

"I suppose you're wondering if they're guards."

He turned to find himself facing a heavyset man with blue jowls and curious eyes. He was nearly bald, with a tuft of fine, sandy hair running around the rim of his deeply tanned pate. He, too, was clad in monastic robes.

"They are," the man continued, "but not in the manner you think. They're here to protect you."

Bravo gave a harsh laugh. "Do you mean the men who threw me over the side of the bridge and beat me senseless, or are you talking about someone else?"

"My people rather overzealously defended themselves. I'm told you're exceptionally strong. A bull, they tell me."

"I don't believe you," Bravo said. "Whatever you Knights of St. Clement want from me, I won't give it to you, no matter what you do to me."

The man showed very white teeth when he grinned. "Well, I am most very pleased to hear that, Braverman Shaw. Spoken like a true Keeper."

"You know who I am, obviously. But I have no idea who you are."

"My name is Paolo Zorzi." His thick eyebrows rose. "Ah, I see you've heard of me."

"You're not Zorzi, or anyone connected with the Gnostic Observatines."

"But I am."

"Convince me."

"I understand your skepticism, and once again I applaud it." He dug something out from the back of his waistband. "Step number one." He held out the SIG Sauer that Bravo had taken from his father's safety deposit box.

Bravo looked at it, then at Zorzi's face. "Either it's not loaded or the firing pin has been removed."

The man who called himself Zorzi shrugged. "My friend, there's only one way to find out."

Bravo took it gingerly from the outstretched palm. He checked the firing chamber, the magazine clip and the firing pin. So far as he could determine, the gun was just as it had been when he'd taken possession of it.

The man cocked his head. "Really, how you obtained it is something of a mystery to me, but I must say I'm pleased that you are armed."

He gestured. "Step two, do you feel up to a walk?" When Bravo made no move, he crossed to the door, flung it open. Bravo could see that the stone corridor was empty of guards.

"Please. I will answer all your questions. My name is Paolo Zorzi. Really and truly."

They went down the corridor and out through a small round-topped wooden door with massive iron bolts running clear through it. Outside, they stayed in the shade. Despite the closeness of the lagoon, it was hot and fairly stifling. They continued walking and Bravo still did not see any guards. He began to relax a little—or was that what this man wanted? he wondered. In a moment, a small breeze sprang up, ruffling the dark water, cooling him.

"All right, Signore Zorzi, where am I?"

"On the island of San Francesco del Deserto. In the lagoon, not far from Burano. More specifically, you're in a monastery—a holy place, actually. In the thirteenth century, St. Francis was returning from the Holy Land, where he was preaching the Gospel. His ship was caught in a terrible storm and was on the verge of breaking apart when, suddenly, the tempest abated, and in the ensuing halo of piercing blue sky overhead, a flock of white birds appeared. They began to sing sweetly, leading St. Francis to this island."

Seeing Bravo wince as he sat down, Zorzi said, "You should see the bruises on two of my Guardians."

All at once, Bravo remembered the urgent voice close at hand on the *motoscafo*. He had not listened, he hadn't wanted to listen. Now he knew he should have.

"Why have you brought me here?" he said.

"Because when you ran out of the church you were in imminent danger. The Knights were in the process of surrounding the area."

Behind them, the monastery crouched, closely held, guarded as a fortress. One end of it was crumbled. Their passage disturbed the soft earth, and from beneath the weeds and grasses came the sweet scent of decay. "It seems I'm facing another danger, closer to hand. I'm speaking now of my Guardian."

"Who?" Zorzi's eyes got hard. "Jen?"

Bravo nodded.

"Nonsense. I trained her, but I think you must already know this, yes?" Zorzi's face grew dark, engorged with bloody rage. "So you mean to disparage me? She's my brightest student—a prodigy, one might say."

"Take no offense, something's happened to her. She killed Father Mosto and assaulted me. This was minutes after Father Mosto warned me that my father suspected her of being a traitor." He didn't tell Zorzi that the list Father Mosto had showed him also had Zorzi's name on it. Who was he to believe? Who was he to trust?

"But what you say is monstrous. She of all people—"

"She of all people, yes. Distrusted and abused by the Order, she had plenty of motivation to betray us."

Zorzi shook his head. "But not me, she would never betray me. There must be another explanation."

"Tell it to me, please."

There was no response from Zorzi, who turned away, hands clenched into fists. Far out, Bravo could see a boat, but through the heat haze it looked like a mirage or an ancient Roman trireme. The lagoon was as flat as a desert, why shouldn't it produce mirages? He thought of Jenny—the look in her eyes, the smell of her skin, the feel of her hair. The degree to which he had relied on her was only now becoming apparent, and this reliance had led him to let down his guard with her.

Had his father done the same? Had she gotten under Dexter's skin the way she had gotten under his? Father Mosto was certain of it. *"I am afraid of her,"* he'd said, *"because she was able to get to Dexter in a way no one else could."* Jenny had killed him, she was the traitor, as Dexter had feared. Looking into the lagoon, Bravo saw reflected the sky—or was it the sky in which he saw reflected the lagoon? Dizzied, he could no longer tell, everything he had assumed was inverted.

"After what I've done for her . . ." Zorzi's voice cracked. "I will interrogate her. And if she is guilty, then I will kill her myself."

"I'll be right beside you," Bravo said.

Zorzi turned back to him, his face now appearing more normal. "You'll do nothing of the sort, my friend. You are the Keeper, you know what your mission is. Nothing must deter you or even slow you down. You must find the cache of secrets and keep it safe from the Knights."

"But I don't know where the cache is."

"Don't you?" Zorzi pulled out the steel beggar's purse Bravo discovered inside the alms cabinet. "Step three." He handed it over.

"You took this from me?"

"For safekeeping only, I assure you."

Zorzi's arm was still stretched out and Bravo saw an eagle in midflight tattooed on his forearm.

Seeing the direction of Bravo's gaze, Zorzi chuckled. "I wear the eagle with pride, Bravo. Only six or seven families in all of Venice were allowed to display the eagle or the lily on their coat of arms. My family goes all the way back to the seventh century, further some say, all the way to the founding of Rome."

"Zorzi, yes," Bravo said thoughtfully. "Your family is one of the *Case Vecchie,* the old houses. The twenty-four founding families of the Republic."

Zorzi raised his eyebrows. "Now I am truly impressed. Few people know this, others disbelieve the claim. Nonetheless, it is valid and binding."

They walked a little further away along the shore. The sunlight beat down on the water of the lagoon, turning it to the color of molten metal. Shore birds swooped and called amid the rush beds. Further out were a series of *barene,* salt-flats—clay and sand, really—deposited over time by the currents, feeding ground for warblers and marsh harriers alike.

"I will leave you to read the tea leaves left for you by your father," Zorzi said, and he strode off toward two of his men some five hundred yards down the islet shore.

Bravo, grateful to be alone during this process, looked at the square lock. It was the same size and depth as the lock in the underwater safe in St. Malo. He inserted the second cuff-link key into the lock, turned it one way, then the other. The steel beggar's purse popped open.

Inside, he discovered a rolled-up slip of paper with another cipher handwritten on it. He studied it carefully. This one was naturally enough of a different and more complex nature than the modified substitution code devised by Caesar. Bravo could see that it required a code book, so it stood to reason that his father had supplied him one.

He took out the small, ratty notebook. It was the only possible place his father would have inscribed the code protocol. Climbing the seawall, he sat on the white stone, looking out into the fog-gripped lagoon. Water and sky were indistinguishable, all was reflection, and once again he was gripped by this sense of inversion, as if Venice itself was a lens through which he was now forced to look.

With an almost obsessive patience, he went through the notebook, searching for page, line and letter numbers, the usual sources for the key to this form of cipher. Of course, he could start by listing the letter frequencies in the encrypted text—for instance, in English *e* was the most used letter and *t* the second most used. Each letter of the alphabet had a percentage of frequency. Also, vowels tended to associate with one another—such as *ou* and *ie,* whereas consonants rarely did.

Letter-frequency decryption went all the way back to the ninth century. The Arabic scientist Abu Yusuf al-Kindi provided the first known description of it. However, al-Kindi's code-breaking method was most useful in lengthy messages—the longer the encrypted text, the better the letter-frequency method worked—and this text was short. Second, and more important in this instance, was that letter frequency changed depending on which language one was using. For instance, the two most used letters in Arabic were *a* and *l.* Bravo knew, however, that there would be no less than five different languages in the text. This was typical of his father, who loved nothing better than to take a classic cipher and stand it on its ear so that it would baffle even an expert code-breaker.

With his eidetic memory, Bravo could, of course, have used these methods to laboriously try to break his father's cipher, but he had neither the time nor the confidence that he would be successful. Therefore, he required the key.

Once again, he went through the notebook, this time from back to front. On one page near the middle of the notebook, he came across the note, "There must be a reason for all this movement." By itself, it meant nothing, but on the next page forward, he came across the same sentence reversed, as if his father was working out a new cipher. When it came to ciphers, his father loved inversions. Bravo might not have noticed this one had he not been leafing through the notebook from back to front. Taking out a pen, he put the two sentences together, one right beneath the other. There were letters that lined up: *t* and *e*, which was interesting if one were thinking of letter-frequency decoding, but Bravo knew this was just the sort of false lead his father loved to insert into his cipher keys. But it was a clue that the key was a variant of the 3DES, the triple Data Encryption Standard, developed in the mid 1970s. *E* was the fifth letter of the alphabet, *t*, the twentieth. Subtracting 5 from 20 left 15. Subtracting 2, for the two letters, *e* and *t*, left him with thirteen. *M* was the thirteenth letter of the alphabet. He turned his attention to the *m*, which was the sixth letter in the first sentence, the fourth in the second sentence. He added the two, then subtracted the number of matching letters that came before the *m*'s. The result was eight. He had his key.

Bent over, he moved through the cipher. When he was done, this is what his father had left him: "Remember where you were the day you were born and the name of your third pet."

He'd been born in Chicago, but try as he might he couldn't figure how he could possibly connect that with anything in Venice. At length, he went on to the next bit. His third pet had been a dog—a stray mutt so disheveled-looking he'd called her Bark. So he had one piece of the puzzle his father had meant for him to solve.

Remember where you were. . . . He was born in St. Mary of Nazareth Hospital.

But how could that help him? There must be over a thousand statues of Mary in the city, and, in any event, what possible connection could Mary of Nazareth have with the word *bark*?

He looked up. The afternoon had slipped away. A cool breeze, marking the onset of sunset, ruffled his hair. His shirt was stuck to his back. With a sigh, he closed the notebook and placed the coded paper back in the alms box. Then he clambered down off the seawall in search of Paolo Zorzi.

THERE was a moment when Anthony Rule felt lost at sea. As was typical in summer, an afternoon mist had risen, born of the heat and the humidity that lay over Venice like a shroud. He was adrift in the whiteness with only the pulsing disk of the sun visible as it heated the atmosphere. For a moment his hand rested on the wooden tiller of the *topo*—a light sailboat used for fishing—without trying to guide it in any particular direction. He felt a kind of fierce elation in being lost, absolutely invisible to the rest of the world, as if now he could be anyone he chose to be. The sense of freedom was enormous.

He had passed south of Burano with its lace makers' shops, so colorful they looked for all the world like the set of a merry operetta. He was a skilled and crafty seaman: he loved boats of all kinds and felt as at home on the water as he did on dry land. Getting the owner to trust him with his *topo* was only a matter of two hundred euros in addition to the normal hourly rate, which Rule knew was inflated. He paid the tariff in advance without bargaining. Better to have the owner think him stupid and forget him than to be clever and stick in the man's memory.

The *topo* felt good under him—solid and responsive. It had been made in Chioggia, where they were first created, and he felt comfortable in it, almost as if it were a part of him.

In Dreux, he had dealt with the Knights of St. Clement in the usual fashion, but ever since the rescue in St. Malo his mind had been focused on Bravo. After talking with him for five minutes, he had cursed himself for forgetting just how intelligent and resourceful his "nephew" was. That was when he'd decided to alter his mission. His elite standing allowed him this singular flexibility, and so he had followed Bravo and Jenny to Venice. Quite naturally, his concern skyrocketed when he observed Paolo Zorzi's preemptive move on the bridge near the Church of l'Angelo Nicolò. He knew full well Dexter's feeling toward Zorzi, and now that Zorzi had Bravo the situation, already tenuous, was on the brink of disaster.

All at once, Rule could see, like ghosts in the mist, the outlines of trees: the parkland of San Francesco del Deserto. Immediately, he furled the two sails and allowed the *topo* to drift forward on the current. No doubt the Franciscan order that inhabited most of the islet had no idea of Zorzi's presence—or perhaps Zorzi had paid off the right people. Rule had had enough dealings with him to know how adept he was at circumventing both laws and customs.

The one thing he didn't know—the crucial bit of intelligence that worried him—was how many Guardians Zorzi had with him on the islet. It had to be enough to keep him secure but not enough for them to become obvious to the Franciscans who lived here.

The islet was oddly more or less square in shape, and Rule had aimed for the side that was most heavily forested, the farthest away from the monastery itself. Here and there through the mist he could see the wall that ran around the edge of the islet, just beyond the narrow shingle of rock.

His thoughts returned to Bravo. How many times, in years past, had he and Dexter spoken of Bravo? Long ago he had lost count. But he was the one who had encouraged Dexter to train his son, over the protests of Stefana. The issue was volatile. Once, Dexter and Stefana had almost broken up over it, Dexter coming to stay with Rule for almost three weeks. Bravo had been seven, and Rule had visited him several times, bringing him gifts, taking him to the zoo and, once, to Radio City to see the Easter show. He had perpetrated the myth that Dexter was away on business, and Bravo had never questioned him. It was the first time that Rule had understood the true nature of his relationship with the child, and he was filled with profound emotion.

At home, Rule had said nothing to Dexter, content to allow him to come to his own conclusions. When it came to his family, Dexter was the last person to need advice, so Rule had provided something more meaningful than advice: companionship and comfort. The rest, he felt, would take care of itself. And it had: Dexter had returned to Stefana, and Bravo's training had continued with redoubled intensity.

Judging that he was in close enough, Rule prepared himself, clambering down into the middle part of the boat, where it wasn't decked over. The hold stank of fish. The *topo* was nearing the shingle. It would surely bring two of the Guardians—perhaps three. It didn't matter. He had come to get Bravo, and get him he would, by any and all means.

BRAVO found Paolo Zorzi a hundred yards away, leaning against the seawall, smoking languidly, as if he hadn't a care in the world. Yet he stood up quickly enough when Bravo softly hailed him.

Zorzi flicked the rest of his cigarette away, a bright spark fading into the mist. "Did you work out the code?"

"Unfortunately, no," Bravo lied. He was still mindful of Zorzi's being on his father's list of possible suspects. "I'll need a bit more time."

Zorzi spread his hands, smiling. "Not to worry. That's one thing we have here in abundance."

Beneath a misty, silver-blue sky, they headed back to the monastery. On the way, Bravo counted three Guardians; they regarded him with a curious mixture of boredom and anxiety.

"You must be hungry," Zorzi said affably. "Let's sit down to table and afterwards if you wish I can help you with the cryptography. I'm an old hand at that sort of thing, and I have a number of seminal texts I can lend you."

"I'd be interested to see the books," Bravo said neutrally. He had no intention of allowing Zorzi anywhere near his father's cipher. "And now that I think of it, I'm famished."

They passed another two guards, who flanked the side door, and passed inside. The smell of stone and candle wax filled the rather gloomy interior. The image of Jesus hung on the walls.

They entered a large room. The stone walls were thick and without adornment of any kind. There were no windows. The space seemed cold and forbidding, giving the impression of at one time being a stronghold or keep.

A heavy plank trestle table was set for a meal—though not obviously dinner, which would be taken much later in the evening. Still, tall white candles flickered in silver holders, and several dishes were laid out: a simple seafood risotto and *sarde in saor,* an ancient recipe involving marinating fresh sardines in vinegar-drenched onions. It was a typical mariner's dish, used to prevent scurvy on long voyages.

As they sat down, Zorzi poured wine from a bottle. He said, "What form did the cipher take—was it a transposition code or possibly one of your father's clever substitution variants?"

Bravo smiled. "The *sarde in saor* is excellent."

"Try the risotto," Zorzi said, again all affability. "You'll find it as good or better."

In fact, it was, and Bravo said so.

Zorzi seemed pleased, though somewhat preoccupied, it seemed to Bravo. Bravo was hardly surprised, as his suspicions were growing exponentially. He had now turned his mind to leaving here without either Zorzi or any of his henchmen following him. Even though he had yet to find the solution to his father's most recent cipher, he knew he had to get away from this island and from Zorzi as quickly as possible.

WHEN the *topo* emerged from out of the mist, the Guardian patrolling that section of the shoreline immediately called to two of his companions, as Zorzi's protocol dictated. Zorzi had told them that the guest must not be disturbed for any reason, only Zorzi himself was to be allowed access. An odd order, but they followed unquestioningly nonetheless, for that was how he had trained them.

By the time the others arrived, the prow of the boat was scraping against the shingle. The *topo* seemed to be carrying one passenger. They hailed it in the Venetian dialect, then in Roman Italian, and, finally, in French, without receiving a response. As they cautiously approached, they saw that the figure was hunched over, an old man clutching a cane apparently to keep him from falling forward.

Still, they were on their guard, and even more so as they boarded the *topo*, because at once the old man stood up, though still horribly bent over. He spoke to them, then, his voice so thin and quavery they were forced to approach him to hear that he said: "I didn't give you permission to board my vessel."

His face was hidden by a white mask, and he wore the traditional *bauta* and *tabarro* though it was nowhere near Carnevale. His dementia caused them to snigger.

"You, sir, are on the island of San Francesco del Deserto," the Guardian who first spotted the *topo* said. "You're trespassing on our property."

"But how could that be?" The old man's voice had taken on an ugly querulous tone. "You don't look like Franciscan monks to me."

The Guardian lost patience. He had better things to do than to contend with an old, demented Venetian who thought it was February. "You'll have to leave, old man."

"Who do you think you are, talking to me in that rude manner?" The old man raised his cane threateningly.

The Guardian laughed and grabbed the cane. "That's enough foolishness—"

In one stunningly swift motion, Anthony Rule drew back his arm, freeing the thin blade from its cane casing and, before the Guardian could say another word, thrust a foot of razor-sharp forged steel through his heart.

As he withdrew the blade, while the Guardian thrashed and frothed, the other two Guardians sprang into action. They came at Rule from the left and the right simultaneously. He feinted right, moved left, neatly spitting the second Guardian with his sword-cane. But now the third Guardian struck the hand that held the sword so hard it went numb, and the sword dropped to the deck.

The Guardian drew a gun and leveled it at Rule.

"Take off your mask and *bauta*," he ordered.

Rule did as he asked.

His eyes opened wide. "Signore Rule! What are you—?"

"I can explain everything."

The Guardian shook his head. "You will explain to Signore Zorzi and no one else."

"That's precisely what I won't do. I—"

"Be still!" The Guardian indicated the mask and *bauta*. "Drop them both to the deck. Now!"

As Rule dropped the *bauta*, he flicked the mask hard and fast. It spun into the Guardian, its sharp edge laying open the bridge of his nose. As the Guardian reared back, Rule moved forward. One hand wrested the gun out of the Guardian's hand while the other struck him in the solar plexus. He doubled over and Rule drove his balled fist into the side of his neck. The Guardian went down and stayed down.

Quickly and with an economy of motion, Rule stripped the Guardian of his clothes and, throwing off his voluminous cloak, pulled them on over his own.

———

"YOU don't want to show me the cipher." Zorzi shrugged, poured espresso from a small metal pot set above a flame. "Fair enough, you're the Keeper, it's your decision." He smiled broadly as he pushed one of the tiny cups over to Bravo. "Your father was tight-lipped just like you. In fact, I am struck by how similar you two are. He and I were close, when he was abroad I supplied him with whatever he needed—men, materials, you understand."

Bravo understood more than Zorzi knew. It was time to go on the offense, he thought. "He relied on you."

"Yes, of course. Absolutely. We confided in one another."

Bravo knew he was lying. For the first time since he'd found Jenny's bloody knife beside the corpse of Father Mosto, he felt on solid ground again. He knew where he and Zorzi stood. Carnevale was over, the masks had come off, good and evil were restored to their proper corners in the Voire Dei. Satisfied, he said, "Have you had any word on Jenny?"

Zorzi drank his espresso straight and in one shot, as if it were a *macchiato*. "We have discovered where she is."

All at once, Bravo had no interest in Jenny or in her fate. She had made her bed, now she could lie in it. She had gulled him, in much the same way, he imagined, that she had gulled his father. The traitor's identity had shook Dexter to his core, Father Mosto had said. *"It was someone he knew well and trusted completely."* Bravo felt suddenly sick to his stomach and wanted nothing so much as to rid himself of the rich food Zorzi had fed him. They were both traitors—Jenny and Zorzi, collaborating together to undermine the Order and bring it down.

"There is something I must ask you." Zorzi frowned. "I am wondering whether you have had any contact with Anthony Rule."

"Why do you ask?"

"Ah, then you *have* seen him recently."

"As a matter of fact I haven't seen Uncle Tony in more than a year." With his hatred as a catalyst, Bravo found that it wasn't difficult to lie to this man.

Zorzi shrugged, and Bravo now understood. The gesture of indifference masked what was important to Zorzi.

"I'm not prying, you understand." Zorzi licked his lips. "I simply ask because I don't trust this man. In fact, I believe he's the traitor in our midst."

"What makes you say that?"

"I hear the sharpness in your tone. I understand, of course—he's your 'Uncle Tony.' Perhaps it was a mistake to bring this up with you, but it was for your own good, and after all I had assumed you were sufficiently mature to be able to separate your personal feelings from the objective truth."

"The cipher," Bravo said shortly. "I'd like the work on it now." It was becoming more of an effort to keep his anger under control. He was finding Zorzi tedious and sinister. "I'd like to see those books."

"Of course." Zorzi could not keep the excitement out of his voice. He rose. "I'll only be a moment."

Was this the time to make his escape? Bravo wondered. He turned in his chair. But no, a Guardian stood in the open doorway, regarding him as if he were a sea bream newly drawn from the lagoon and set out for feasting. His fingertips touched the butt of the SIG Sauer. Of course, he could draw the gun, but then everything would change. He would be instantly pitted against all the Guardians. Worst of all, it would bring him and Paolo Zorzi into direct conflict, on Zorzi's own ground with his people all around him. Bravo did not care for those odds. No, the SIG Sauer was an instrument of last resort.

"What's your name?" Bravo asked at length.

"Anzolo," the Guardian said laconically. His eyes were hard as Istrian stone.

"Do you know where Signore Zorzi has gone?" He rose. "I'd like to ask him a question."

"You are to wait here until Signore Zorzi returns."

The Guardian stood against the door, blocking his way. There was no question: despite Paolo Zorzi's protestations to the contrary, Bravo was a prisoner.

18

THROUGH A STAND OF WILLOWY TREES, RULE SPOTTED THE two Guardians flanking the monastery door like a pair of sphinxes. One had a white scar under his chin, the other, taller, had eyes as gray as the Venetian mist. They looked implacable—also a little restless. Well, that would soon change, thought Rule, as he broke through the trees and strode purposefully toward them.

The moment they saw him, he knew something was wrong. Though they smiled and offered him a silent hail, he could see their feet spread out slightly, their legs flexed, their shoulders rounded as the muscles tensed. They had heard something—from one of the Guardians who'd boarded the boat? That seemed the only possibility. Rule imagined one of them reaching his cell phone before he died.

The element of surprise ruined, he sprinted straight at them. The thing was to get them moving. They came at him, challenging him, as he knew they would. Turning his back on them, he darted back toward the stand of trees. They might have guns, but like the Guardians on the boat, they wouldn't use them, for fear of alerting the Franciscan monks on the other side of the island.

In the trees, he engaged them, using the blade of the sword-cane as an offensive weapon, darting in and out, using the trees for defense against their short, slightly curved Byzantine fighting knives. He knew these weapons well—they could be thrown as well as thrust. The curved blade had a purpose—it would open up a wide swath of flesh even on a partially deflected slash. He had no room for error, which was just the way he liked it. Living on the edge was Rule's reason for being in the

Voire Dei in the first place. It was better than tightrope walking, more intoxicating than mountain climbing, more addictive than skydiving.

Lunging forward on one flexed leg, he deliberately exposed himself to the Guardian with the scar. Grinning fiercely, the Guardian swung his fighter with an evil whistling sound. Rule ducked, felt the blade whir past the crown of his head and embed itself in the trunk of the tree. He came up, leading with his left shoulder, his elbow cocked. But the Scar had anticipated him, had let go of the Byzantine fighter and slammed his fists into the side of Rule's head.

Rule staggered back, felt rather than saw the approach of the Guardian with the gray eyes. He grabbed a handful of Gray Eyes's garment and swung him around. White Scar had by this time wrenched his fighter free and now was swinging it in a swift, shallow arc toward Rule. The crescent blade buried itself in Gray Eyes's chest, and immediately Rule shoved him away, came after White Scar in a direct attack.

White Scar's eyes opened wide with the shock of wounding his own compatriot. That was all the time Rule needed. He stabbed outward, driving the blade of his sword-cane in from an extreme low angle. Scar coughed once, and blood bubbled out of his mouth. He looked down in astonishment and fell to his knees, his hands cupping his abdomen. He had forgotten all about Rule, who took the opportunity to kick him hard in the side of the head. The Guardian toppled over, unconscious.

Without a backward glance, Rule left them, entering the darkness of the monastery, unseen and unheard, like a wraith.

"HE'S coming," Alvise said.

"Well, now," Paolo Zorzi said, "events have taken on an entirely new shape, haven't they?"

"Three dead, two wounded."

"He'll pay for each outrage," Zorzi growled, "as well as for the rest."

The two men were striding down the hall from the refectory. Alvise, a Guardian with a firm hand and short legs, was hard-pressed to keep up with the long strides of his master.

"It is essential that we keep Braverman Shaw isolated in the refectory," Zorzi said, "now more than ever."

Alvise nodded and spoke briefly into his cell phone. "Done," he said.

"Now we must prepare for Signore Rule's unscheduled arrival."

"This will be a pleasure," Alvise said, but he fell abruptly silent as Zorzi took his arm and swung him around.

"If you underestimate this man, even for an instant, he will kill you."

Alvise, his face drawn and serious, said, "I will kill him before he has the chance."

Paolo Zorzi's mouth opened in a silent laugh.

SOMETHING had happened in the last thirty seconds, of this Bravo was certain. Anzolo had received a call on his cell phone, and his eyes had betrayed him. They had cut to Bravo and then had moved quickly, almost furtively away as he turned his back on the refectory. Bravo knew the call concerned him, that Anzolo was getting instructions—probably from Zorzi himself. It seemed clear that Zorzi had no intention of returning with the cipher texts—or possibly returning at all. During the meal he had made his last pitch to Bravo, trying the soft route of insinuating himself into the deciphering process, in order to discover where Dexter Shaw meant to send his son next. This ploy having failed, he had obviously decided to move on to the hard route. Bravo could only imagine what horrors that might entail. He had told Camille that this wasn't a game, that the Knights were out for blood—his blood.

The moment he stood up, Anzolo whirled around, a stiff smile stitched to his face. "Please sit down."

"I'd like to talk to Signore Zorzi."

"I'm sorry, Signore Zorzi is otherwise engaged."

When Bravo made no move, Anzolo took a step into the room. "Please sit down." His face hardened. "Your espresso is getting cold."

"I've had my fill of espresso."

Bravo was careful to keep an edge out of his voice. Nevertheless, Anzolo took another step into the refectory.

"I really must insist."

"All right." Bravo smiled easily as he took his chair, lounging slightly forward. He changed the tone of his voice. "Would you like a cup? There's plenty left."

"Thank you, no."

But the tension had gone out of Anzolo's body, which was Bravo's objective. He swung another chair around, leaning on it with his forearms. It seemed darker in the room now, the golden discs thrown off by the candlelight somehow smaller and dimmer. And then one candle guttered and went out, and it was darker still.

"Anzolo—you don't hear that name much."

"Oh, but you do in Venice, *signore*, it's our dialect."

"Really? What is the Italian equivalent?"

Anzolo's brow wrinkled in thought, then his face brightened. "Ah, yes, Angelo."

Bravo threw the chair sideways so quickly and so hard that Anzolo was taken completely by surprise. It struck him in the face, and he fell in a kind of swoon. Blood was spattered in a fanlike arc across the slats of the chair back.

Bravo was up and on him in an instant, but Anzolo was only lying there, regaining his equilibrium, and when he felt Bravo grip him, he jackknifed his torso. His knee went straight into Bravo's solar plexus, and Bravo doubled over as all the air was driven out of him.

Anzolo drove a fist into Bravo's side. "Don't fight me," he said.

Ignoring him, Bravo lashed out, connecting with Anzolo's rib cage, but he had no leverage, and Anzolo brought his weight to bear.

"I warned you."

He jammed his forearm against Bravo's throat.

IN a defensive half crouch, Anthony Rule crept through the monastery corridors. He had encountered no one and nothing, which was both puzzling and somewhat alarming. He had expected to come across at least a couple of Guardians.

Up ahead he saw a door on his left that was partially open. Approaching it with caution, he contrived to peer inside. A man was hunched over a table on which several thick books were open. He was paging through one. Then he turned to search through another stack of volumes, and Rule caught a glimpse of the side of his face. It was Paolo Zorzi. The muscles of Zorzi's broad back and shoulders bunched and rippled as he stretched and torqued his torso, as if he were a lion or panther. Rule thought about Zorzi's deep and abiding hostility toward him and knew it stemmed from his friendship with Dexter. The nature of jealousy, he considered, momentarily caught by the thought, was to be like a serpent, slithering this way and that through the thicket of other, more obvious emotions. But it colored everything, even the intentions of the most clear-eyed people.

Rule smiled, his lips a thin, cruel line. This was all too easy—no Guardians and now Zorzi presenting himself through a partially open door, his back turned, a perfect target. Rule could smell a trap even from this distance, and so he moved on, past the bait meant to tempt him. He wanted Zorzi, of course, but he had come for Bravo, and he wasn't going to leave without him. He held no illusions as to how dangerous it was for Bravo to be with Zorzi. It was Zorzi, he suspected, who had tried to undermine his relationship with Dexter Shaw, and now that Zorzi had Bravo he imagined the same thing happening all over again— Zorzi would try to poison Bravo against him.

The room Zorzi was in was windowless, a place where logic said they would be holding Bravo. Also, he could see that the texts were on ciphers and decoding—Bravo would be working on the cipher Dexter had left for him here in Venice. Chances were, then, that Bravo was inside the room, somewhere where Rule couldn't see him. In any case, Rule knew that he couldn't afford to ignore the possibility. That meant he needed to gain entrance to the room by means other than the invitingly open door.

He stole past and soon came to a left-hand branch that, he calculated, would bring him along the right-facing wall of the room. Risking a peek around the corner, he saw a Guardian standing beside a closed door that could only lead into the room.

Pulling the hood of his appropriated robe up over his head, he walked with the sword-cane hidden behind him and his head down directly toward the Guardian. The man, a young, slender Venetian with a face still in the process of maturing, said, "You're ten minutes early, but I could use the relief."

Rule threw a punch to his solar plexus and then, as the Guardian doubled over, chopped down on the exposed back of his neck with the edge of his hand. Rule caught the Guardian as he slumped into unconsciousness and dragged him further down the hallway into a corner, where he piled him into the shadows.

Returning to the closed door, he put his ear to it. He could hear a voice he recognized as Zorzi's and someone else replying, but the second voice was too far away for him to be certain it was Bravo's.

He breathed deeply and slowly, his fingers tightened on the hilt of the sword-cane. His other hand gripped the doorknob, turning it slowly to the left. He was opening the door slowly and silently when he felt a tiny flicker of pain in the side of his neck. He started, turning instinctively, his senses already swimming as if he were drunk, and saw a face leering at him like a Carnevale mask.

Struggling through the chemical fog of the drug, he understood what had happened, and he pulled out the tiny dart that had embedded itself in his neck.

"Too late." The leering face laughed.

A moment later, the world disappeared from view, and Rule toppled over.

BRAVO'S eyes were bulging and there was a burning in his lungs. He knew if he didn't get oxygen soon he'd lose what was left of the strength in his limbs. Once that happened, he would be helpless. He couldn't let that happen.

In his mind's eye, he saw his father, and he a boy of eleven, learning how to use his body, to stretch it past its assumed natural limits.

"Relax, Bravo," his father said. "When you try too hard, your body will resist you. Mind and body need to work together, like a team."

Instead of continuing to fight Anzolo, Bravo let his limbs go limp. He allowed his eyelids to flicker, his breathing became erratic. His reward was the grin on Anzolo's face as he bent forward to apply more pressure. That was when Bravo slammed his forehead into the bridge of Anzolo's nose. A fountain of blood gushed out, and Anzolo reared back.

Bravo twisted from his hips and Anzolo lost his balance. Bravo rose up and brought the full force of his fists against the other's ear. Anzolo went down and Bravo was on him.

"Where is Zorzi?" He slammed the back of Anzolo's head against the stone floor. "Tell me where he went!"

Anzolo told him.

Bravo released him and began to turn away. Anzolo grabbed at him in desperation, trying to gouge out his eye, but Bravo used the Guardian's own momentum against him, swinging his body around in a shallow arc, using the entire force of it behind his cocked elbow. He felt the clavicle shatter, and then the Guardian collapsed onto the refectory floor.

In an instant, Bravo was up and sprinting out the door.

"**THE** neurotoxin will only last two or three minutes," Alvise said.

"That will be sufficient," Paolo Zorzi said as he stared into Anthony Rule's slack face. Rule regarded him with the peculiar wide-eyed stare of the newly paralyzed.

He and Alvise had carried Rule into the room, setting him down on a chair to whose legs they had lashed his ankles. His hands were tied behind his back.

Alvise already had a knife out, its gleaming point pressed against the hollow at Rule's throat.

"How d'you like the feel of this, Rule?" he said. "How d'you think it's going to feel when I push the blade in inch by agonizing inch."

"Careful," Zorzi said mildly, as if he did not mean what he said.

"I want him to pay for each and every sin he has committed."

"I'm afraid that would take several lifetimes." Zorzi took a handful of Rule's hair. "Wouldn't it, Anthony?"

"You were asked a question." Alvise dug the point of the blade in, turning it so that a drop of deep-red blood was held on the forged stainless steel. "Rude of you not to answer."

"Your time has run out." Zorzi bent over him, staring into his ferocious half-glazed eyes. "You no longer have Dexter Shaw to protect you. You're alone and naked in front of your judge." He jerked on Rule's hair. "I will now pronounce sentence and Alvise will act as executioner, a mantle he is all too eager to don in your honor."

Zorzi's lips pulled back from his teeth. "You are guilty, Rule, guilty on all counts. And now I have the satisfaction of informing you that the sentence of death will be carried out."

Zorzi was aware of a blur of motion, and then Alvise was falling and there was blood spattering on him like rain. He jerked erect and looked at Bravo, who was pointing the SIG Sauer at him.

"What do you think you're doing?"

"Untie him," Bravo said, gesturing at Rule.

"That would be most unwise. You have no idea what you're doing, what a grave mistake you're—"

"Shut up and do it!" Bravo said. He stood far enough away from Zorzi that the other had no chance to reach him.

"I won't." Zorzi shrugged. "Go ahead and shoot me while you have the chance. No? I see, you haven't the nerve or the fortitude. Coward! Of what use are you to the Order?"

He rushed Bravo, who pulled the trigger of the SIG Sauer. Nothing happened: the trigger was frozen in place. Zorzi was upon him, slamming him backward against the wall. He was grinning grotesquely, like some evil ogre out of a Grimm's fairy tale. "The gun is useless, it won't fire, and now where are you, do you suppose?"

Bravo slammed the butt of the gun into the spot behind Zorzi's ear. Zorzi went down, just as Alvise had, and stayed down.

Quickly, Bravo untied Rule. "Uncle Tony, can you hear me?"

Rule's lips moved slightly but no sound emerged. His eyes were clearer and more focused.

"What did they do to you?"

"Neurotoxin." Rule's voice was thin and reedy, as if he hadn't used it for some time. "Delivered with a blow-dart."

"Can you stand up? Here, let me help you." Bravo put his arm around Rule and lifted. He grunted with the drag of the dead weight, all the bruises and contusions he'd sustained in his hand-to-hand combat with Anzolo burning into him like tattoos.

Then Rule began to regain some motor control, and he took more and more of his own weight into his legs and hips.

"How did you find me?" he said.

"I came looking for Zorzi."

Rule nodded, still groggy. He turned back toward Zorzi. "Kill him, Bravo. It's the perfect time."

"Uncle Tony, we have to get out of here now."

Still Rule resisted. "Do it, Bravo."

"No, Uncle Tony, not in cold blood."

"You'll regret it. The sonuvabitch will come after you."

"I'm not a murderer."

"This isn't murder, it's an execution." Rule held out his hand. "Give me the gun."

"Uncle Tony, no."

But Rule had grabbed the SIG Sauer and, aiming it at Zorzi, pulled the trigger. Nothing happened. Taking advantage of Rule's surprise, Bravo wrested the gun away from him. For a frozen moment they stood staring at one another.

The next instant, they heard a noise in the corridor just outside the door, and the two of them froze. Rule put his forefinger across his lips, crossed silently to the door, and without a moment's hesitation, swung it quickly open.

A Guardian with his hand still on the doorknob stumbled in, and Rule drove a knee into his midsection with such ferocity that he broke several ribs.

"Come on!" Bravo whispered, taking the opportunity to get Rule out of the room and away from Paolo Zorzi. As much as he hated the traitor, he could not be a party to his cold-blooded murder. Did that make him weak, a coward? Would his father have made a different choice? This was the Voire Dei, after all—he was far away from the civil and criminal laws that governed other people. But what about the laws of morality? Did being a part of the Voire Dei give him the right to abrogate those? Even if it did, he still had a choice in the matter and, for better or worse, he had made his.

The corridor loomed, silent and deserted. Rule showed him the way and they retraced his steps back to the side door. By the time they passed through it, he had regained much of his strength and all his animal cunning.

"However many Guardians are remaining will be combing the island for us," he said. And he was right, for as they approached the shingle where he had beached the *topo* they saw two Guardians keeping watch on it.

"How are we going to get off the island?" Bravo whispered.

"I have a plan," Rule said.

Uncle Tony always had a plan. As far back as Bravo could remember, Uncle Tony had a plan for every contingency. If you needed to get from point A to point B, he knew the fastest route, the most circuitous, the most devious, as well as the most sensible.

They moved off, Rule leading the way. The long summer twilight had ended and it had grown dark, but out on the lagoon strings of pale yellow lights marked the perimeters of the deep water channel. A gull passed by overhead, calling in its plaintive voice, and then it swooped down, skimming the water, which picked up tiny phosphorescent lights like glimmering bangles on the double bracelet of the channel.

As they passed the pitch-black outlines of pine trees, Bravo could see more lights, pouring from a section of the Franciscan monastery. The air smelled resiny, and then a whiff of the lagoon reached them—bleached stone and clams, salty weeds that twined in the depths.

As they approached, they could make out the cluttered sound of many voices.

"The Franciscans have turned the island into a tourist destination," Rule said. "Once a week, they have an evening tour. We can mingle with the crowd and hitch a ride on the ferry."

But when they arrived in the shadows cloaking the outskirts of the dock, they saw that passage on the ferry would be impossible. Three Guardians were patrolling the area, no doubt having given the Franciscans a plausible cover story as to why they needed to be there.

They crept around to their left in a rough semicircle and saw a *motoscafo* tied up on the other side of the large ferry. Moving from shadow to shadow, they circled toward it. A Franciscan monk was unloading the last of a pile of small barrels from the rear deck of the *motoscafo*. People continued to stream onto the ferry, which sounded its horn twice, as warning of its imminent departure.

As they watched, another monk appeared to help the other carry the barrels into the monastery. When they were both out of sight, Bravo and Rule ran to the *motoscafo* and jumped aboard. The two monks reappeared and picked up two more barrels. The last of the tourists had boarded the ferry, and now it gave another long hoot of its horn as its engines began to churn.

Rule climbed behind the wheel and fired the ignition. Bravo let go the lines holding the *motoscafo* at the dock. The monks had just disappeared into the monastery, and Rule took advantage of the moment to ease the boat forward. Their window of opportunity was short, the monks would reappear at any moment, but he resisted the urge to surge forward and instead matched his speed with that of the ferry. They moved out in tandem, the *motoscafo* hidden from the Guardians by the bulk of the ferry. A night heron crossed their path, silent as death, and as the land slipped away through the black, purling water they got one last bracing whiff of the pines on San Francesco del Deserto.

Then the yellow lights were upon them and they were in the channel, free.

———

AFTER many hours the celebration of the new Knights—the Knights of Muhlmann, as Jordan privately thought of them—was still in full swing. A twelve-course dinner catered by Ostaria dell'Orso, one of Rome's finest restaurants, along with five cases of vintage Brunello di Montalcino had been consumed. The assembled had settled in for Cuban Montecristo Coronas, snifters of cognac and dark chocolate truffles, each one imprinted with a miniature of the Muhlmann shield, flown in that day from Belgium.

Jordan, his belly full, his head alight with his victory, was just finishing his second glass of the luscious Hine 1960 when Osman Spagna tapped him discreetly on the shoulder. One look at his expression caused Jordan to rise and follow the short man into the room where he had signed the contract on the villa. Behind him Spagna closed the double doors. Jordan saw before him four of the most influential and wealthy Knights: a Netherlands diamond cartel merchant, an English MP, an American money manager and the president of a South African–Australian metals conglomerate.

"Gentlemen," Jordan said, approaching them. "What have we here?" He laughed. "A meeting of the minds?"

"We fervently hope so, Grand Master."

They left it to the English MP, which was a bit of a surprise. Jordan had expected the American to be the mouthpiece. But they had opted to take the smooth path, the gentlemanly action.

"We'd like a bit of a word," the English MP said in his mildest and plummiest tone. "In theory, we have no problem with the action you've taken—"

"The *coup*," the American said, arching forward on the balls of his feet.

"Something stinks in here." Jordan stared hard at the American. "Is it a mutiny I smell?"

The MP moved at once to smooth the feathers ruffled by the American's injudicious remark. "Nothing of the sort, I assure you. We all recognize you as Grand Master, we all believe you're the man for the job."

Jordan, waiting for the shoe to drop, said nothing. He was good at waiting, better than the four of them put together, he'd wager.

The MP, rail-thin and pasty faced, cleared his throat. "We do, however, envision a potential problem."

"A *large* one," the American interjected. He was a big, beefy man with a Midwestern accent and the overly aggressive stance of a football thug.

No one was willing to restrain the American, Jordan noticed, which meant he was the designated attack dog. Smart move on their part.

"And that would be?" Jordan said.

"Your mother," the MP said silkily. "It's no secret that she's wanted to take control of the Knights. We've tolerated her machinations out of respect for you, Grand Master, but now . . . now she's inserted herself into the field with Damon Cornadoro, and we wonder . . . well, we wonder whether she would be playing so active a role in this most crucial venture if she wasn't your mother."

A stifling silence now descended on the six men. The MP cleared his throat again, someone—the Netherlander perhaps—coughed nervously.

"It was my plan," Jordan said evenly. "You're questioning it now?"

"Not at all," the MP said at once. "However, reports have come to us of her activities and we think something needs to be done to rein her in."

"You don't know my mother," Jordan said.

"On the contrary, I think we know her quite well." The South African stepped forward, placing a thick dossier on the table. He watched Jordan as he opened its cover. Inside were a series of surveillance photos of Camille and Cornadoro locked in amorous embrace.

After a moment, the MP said, "This is a dangerous cocktail, Grand Master. Surely you can understand our concern."

Indeed he could, better by far than any of them. Damn her to hell! With a hand he scarcely felt he pawed through the mess of photos, one more explicit than the next. Careful to keep his expression neutral, he said, "I appreciate your diligence, gentlemen, but I already know about my mother's indiscretion." This was a lie, but a necessary one. These men must never know they knew more about his family than he did.

"Surely you can see it's more than an indiscretion," the MP said.

The American stepped forward. "I think what you smelled, Grand Master, is a conspiracy between the two of them."

"I have the situation well in hand," Jordan said, "I assure you."

"Excellent," the MP said. He was beaming now. "That's all we needed to know, Grand Master. We'll leave the rest to you." He pointed to the dossier. "Rest assured all copies have been destroyed."

Spagna opened the double doors, the murmur and aromatic smoke drifted in from the larger room, and the four, their business completed, headed briskly for the door. The last of the group was the American. As the others departed, he turned back as if in afterthought and, strolling back to Jordan, whispered so only he could hear: "You know what you have to do, don't you? What is it the English say?" He grinned. "Oh, yeah, 'Off with her head!' "

19

"SO HOW IS IT WITH YOU, SON?" DEXTER SHAW SAID.

Bravo looked down, then away. "Oh, you know. The same."

"We haven't seen each other in over six months. You've been at Stanford and I've been away."

Father and son were sitting at an outdoor Burmese restaurant off M Street. It was summer, and Georgetown was cooking. Bravo had come up to see him, and Dexter had taken the afternoon off. That evening, they were scheduled to hear the Washington Philharmonic, sitting in the president's box.

"Anyway," Dexter went on, "what I meant was girls." He sought to catch his son's eye. "Do you have one—a special one, I mean?"

"I don't know."

"You don't know?" Dexter cocked his head. "Surely you can't mean that." Then, after a long beat, "Ah, I see. You don't wish to tell me. It's all right, Bravo, if you don't want to share—"

"Share? Why should I share?" Bravo blurted out. "When have you ever shared anything with me?"

Dexter blinked. "I can think of any number—"

"Anything important, Dad." Bravo had been unable to keep the exasperation out of his voice. "And, come to it, when have you ever come out to Stanford—"

"A year ago October, I believe it was."

"Sure, you were on your way to, where was it?"

"Bangkok."

"Right, Bangkok. We were going to have lunch, go to the theater. I got tickets, and then—"

"My schedule changed. I told you, Bravo. I'm very sorry, but there was nothing I could do."

"You could have stayed."

"No I couldn't," Dexter replied, "I don't have that sort of job, I never have."

Lunch came then, and they both fell silent, grateful for the distraction of eating. Fragrant smoke from the charcoal oven wafted through the leafy garden, strung with colored paper lanterns. Laughter and the murmur of other voices, the clink of tableware against plates, traditionally garbed waitresses silently coming and going.

At length, Dexter put down his fork and said, "Honestly, I would be interested to hear about anyone special in your life."

Bravo looked up, and his father smiled at him, an expression that brought him back to when he was younger, to the best days of their relationship. Still, doggedly, he said nothing. He felt keenly the spite his father's on-and-off attention brought out in him, the disappointment at his long absences, his father's refusal to talk about them.

"All right," Dexter said, "then I'll tell you about my first love." He took a sip of beer, his expression turning even more thoughtful. "She was smart and quite beautiful, but the main thing about her was that she was going out with my friend. I'd met her at a party—a pretty drunken affair—and we'd started talking while my friend was in a stupor, head in the lap of another girl who was also unconscious.

"Anyway, we hit it off. We were both so embarrassed we didn't know quite what to do, for days after walking around in a painfully pleasant haze—you know the sort I'm talking about, neither of us could sleep or eat. All we could think about was, well . . .

"Finally, we couldn't take it anymore and we met on the sly. Afterward, I wondered whether that was what poisoned the relationship. It was rather fierce, not that it lasted very long, but it felt like forever."

Dexter's ironlike hands sat atop the table. "One might have thought that the deceit necessary to sustain the relationship would have worn me out, but, really, that was no problem for me. But what I found out . . . you see, as a young man I was lonely as only young people can be. I had temporarily—and rather thoughtlessly—severed my relationship with my parents, I was never a joiner, and so I was alone. This girl—I saw in her a way to make a connection, to come in out of the cold, as it were."

He laughed. "Human beings are so stupid sometimes, they think that sexual intercourse will alleviate their essential loneliness. In fact, sex only reinforces reality—it's a vivid reminder of how truly alone they are.

"You see, Bravo, it's not a question of whether one is alone or not, it's a question of what one does with one's aloneness." He cocked his head again. "Does one give in to sullenness and despair, or does one begin to learn about oneself? Without that knowledge, how can one begin to make connections with anyone else?"

"Is this another lesson?" Bravo said boorishly. "I'm not ten anymore."

"No lesson intended or implied, Bravo. I was only trying to tell you . . . to do what you wanted me . . . to share."

Bravo looked away, biting his lip.

"What I mean to say, Bravo, is that you and I . . . we're different from other people. We're . . . well, I guess you could call us outsiders—it's far more difficult for us to find ourselves. Sometimes I ask myself what I have to do in order to be saved."

"Saved?" Bravo's head swung around to engage his father's eyes. "Saved from what?"

"From evil," Dexter said. "Oh, I don't mean the kind of evil encountered in the Crusades, at Auschwitz and Buchenwald, Hiroshima, in Angola and Bosnia, I don't mean the astonishing cruelty of mankind. This evil grips the mind and won't let go. It is a nausea of the soul, when you think nothing you possess can save you. 'What am I doing here?' you think. 'What is my purpose?' "

He held his glass of beer between his powerful hands as if it were a stalk of wheat. "You and I, Bravo, are not what we had assumed ourselves to be. It's natural, I suppose, to ask, Why? The answer is: because there is a power inside us. Are we supermen? No. But perhaps we are like artists; we are not hollow men, as Eliot so accurately termed them, though that may be our first reaction. Like all artists of every stripe, our desire, then, is to escape—escape the horror of the mundane, to become something better, to lead others along the same path—to, in a sense, save them from themselves."

Bravo was held spellbound. He understood every word his father said, understood it with every fiber of his being, understood down to his very soul. The knowledge shook him to his core.

Dexter shrugged. "If you don't get it now, I trust that one day you will."

But I do get it, Bravo thought, and was about to tell his father as much, when Dexter glanced down at his watch.

Jesus, Dad, no. Don't do it. . . .

"I'm sorry, Bravo, but I have to get to the airport. I'm afraid I'm off again." Dexter pushed over two tickets along with a pass richly embossed with the presidential seal. "You take your girl—the one you won't tell me about—to the Philharmonic. Trust me, she'll love sitting in the presidential box."

Fuck the presidential box, don't leave me again. . . .

GLIMMERS on the water seemed to follow them in the gray churning wake. Sky and sea were painted the same shades of purple and black. The low islands of the lagoon were strung out like a gigantic cipher. It seemed to Bravo now, standing beside his Uncle Tony, the *motoscafo's* engine thrumming through the soles of his shoes, moving through this dark and misty lagoon of antiquity, that Venice belonged to his father. Lights of unknown origin played over the water, refracted and reflected into shapes of cold flame that illuminated the shallow inky waves, smooth as glass.

Bravo took out the SIG Sauer. He tried not to think of Uncle Tony snatching it from him, firing at Zorzi point-blank. Perhaps in the Voire Dei it had been the right thing to do, he didn't know. "I don't understand," he said, wrenching his mind away from black thoughts. "I checked it after Zorzi gave it back to me."

Rule glanced over. "Didn't fire it, though, did you? The trigger won't go all the way back. Zorzi sabotaged it before he gave it back to you."

Bravo had been so sure that the gun was working properly, but then he heard the flat, shivery crack of the ice breaking and he shivered. The last thing he needed now was a flight of fancy or an echo from the past. Setting his mind on the job at hand, he sat on the gleaming varnished mahogany deck bench and carefully laid down each part of the weapon as he dismantled it. When he got to the trigger mechanism, he discovered something that had escaped his first cursory inspection—something was stuck there, jamming the mechanism.

"You see?" Rule said.

Bravo unfolded the object, examining it carefully. "This isn't Zorzi's doing. My father left it for me to find. He taught me to break down a gun before you use it, that was rule one. I just never had the time."

Rule peered at it. "All I see is a ball of old cloth."

"Not any cloth." Bravo unraveled it. "Linsey. It's a very low-quality linen and wool mixture which was said to be the material used for both Mary's head scarf and Lazarus's cloak." He was remembering the cipher his father left for him in the steel beggar's purse: *Remember where you were the day you were born.* St. Mary of Nazareth Hospital.

Not Mary of Nazareth, he thought now. "Isn't there an island in the lagoon that has a church named after Mary of Lazarus?"

Rule nodded. "It was used as a way station for pilgrims on their journey to the Holy Land. The church is long gone now." He thought for a moment. "Lazzaretto Vecchio lies due south, just below the Lido." He turned the boat in that direction. "In the old Venetian dialect, Mary's name became *nazaretum* and eventually, in the way of all languages, further distorted into *lazaretto*. Over the centuries, the island has had many incarnations. In the fourteenth century, for instance, it was used to quarantine plague victims during the city's first great epidemic." Moving out of the channel into the lagoon proper, he put on speed. "It's still quite lovely, but nowadays, it's only a center for stray dogs."

Remember the name of your third pet. Bark.

Bravo laughed out loud.

JENNY, in the company of Paolo Zorzi's emissary, arrived on San Francesco del Deserto to find her mentor with a bandaged head and in a foul mood. She was nervous and upset, but by far her overriding emotion was one of guilt.

They sat in the refectory, which she found oppressive and gloomy. Candles guttered all around her, and there was soot in the air. To her surprise, there were four other Guardians in the room. She waited for Zorzi to speak, but he did not acknowledge her presence in any way. Instead, he stared down at a message he had apparently just been given. Jenny would have given anything to know what was in it. As her gaze redirected itself to Zorzi, she noticed his red-rimmed eyes. He looked like he hadn't slept in two or three days.

At length, he said, "Father Mosto was murdered."

"And Bravo disappeared," she blurted in response, "more than four hours ago, and you've kept me waiting all this time. How else will you punish me?"

Zorzi looked up, impaling her with his implacable eyes. "Speaking of Braverman Shaw," he said softly, "you never delivered the message I ordered you to give him, did you?"

"That Anthony Rule is the traitor? No."

"Why?"

She knew that velvet voice, and she winced thinking of the iron fist behind it. "Because I don't believe it."

"It's not for you to decide these matters!"

Already on edge, she started at the sharpness of his voice.

"I was right when I counseled Dexter Shaw not to assign you to guard his son."

"And you were the one who trained me." Jenny was unable any longer to hide her bitterness.

"Precisely my point."

"You were harder on me than you were with your male pupils, you made damn sure of that."

Zorzi ignored her outburst. "I never should have listened to Dexter. Every instinct at my command told me he was making a mistake."

He regarded her with a look he reserved for those who had disappointed him. She could feel that he had removed himself from her sphere, that whatever she might tell him—whatever excuses she might put forward—would now fall on deaf ears. He was done with her.

Jenny, absorbing all this, was filled with despair. She stood, her head pulled into her shoulders, which were slightly hunched, as if she needed to protect herself from the assault of his words. She had always thought that he'd believed in her; now she knew that had it not been for Dex's intervention, Zorzi would have rejected her as the others in the Order had wanted to do. His belief had been in Dexter, not in her.

Still, she was not yet prepared to give up. "Why are we sitting here when we should be trying to find Bravo?"

"I'd rather talk about you," Zorzi said. "Tell me what happened."

"I was guarding the rectory where Bravo and Father Mosto were talking. I was attacked from behind, overpowered. The next thing I knew, I woke up in a utility room. When I went out into the corridor, I found Father Mosto with his throat slit and my knife beside him in a pool of blood."

"Your knife."

"Yes."

"How do you suppose it got there?"

"That's obvious. Whoever assaulted me took it."

"How would they know you had it on you?"

Jenny's heart skipped a beat. She glanced around at the four other Guardians, who were hanging on every word that was said. For the first time she viewed her situation in another light.

"Is this an interrogation? Do you think I murdered Father Mosto?"

Zorzi rose, paced back and forth in front of her. "As you know, there is a traitor in our midst. Lately, as the death toll has mounted, it has occurred to me that there may be more than one traitor." He stopped and leveled his gaze at her. "You see what I mean."

"All I see is that I've got to go after Bravo," she said doggedly. "I screwed up; it's my responsibility—"

"I'm afraid I can't allow that."

"You think I'm a traitor," Jenny said in a strangled voice.

There was that look again, reasserting the distance he'd put between them, and when he spoke, his tone was cold and unforgiving. "You failed to protect our most important asset; that is unforgivable. As if that weren't enough, consider the situation from Bravo's point of view. He finds the body, the throat slit, your bloody knife beside the corpse, and you gone. What would *you* think if you were him?" Zorzi crumpled the message in his hand with a kind of cold fury that terrified her. "His position is the same as mine, he can't afford to trust you."

She stood up. "You can't just—" She stopped, turning as the four other Guardians came toward her. "This isn't right," she said weakly, and felt immediately foolish, because if she were in Zorzi's place she knew she'd do the same thing he was doing.

"Now I must leave," he said, "to try and clean up the mess you made." He turned back. "Pray for me. Pray that I find Braverman Shaw before it's too late."

With that damning accusation, he and two of the Guardians swept out. The heavy wood and iron door of the refectory slammed shut behind them.

Another wave of despair filled her, fueled by her sense of outrage and helplessness. She had lost the confidence of her mentor and was being detained by her own people, all because she had been implicated by her inattention, her schoolgirl crush, her own stupidity. Why hadn't she taken a page from Anthony Rule's book and kept herself free of emotional entanglements?

The two remaining Guardians stared at her with looks of mixed pity and hostility. She turned away. The hostility she could handle—she always had. It was the pity that unnerved her. To compound her stupidity, she took a wild couple of steps toward them. One backhanded her across the face while the other moved away, so he could cover her from a different angle. She staggered back, and the Guardian pushed her down into a chair and told her to stay there.

She glared up into his sneering face.

"This is how I always knew you would end up." He looked at her as if she were a cockroach he was about to grind beneath his boot. "You're a failure—worse, you're a disgrace." He spat onto the patch of floor between her knees before stalking away.

Jenny swiveled around and put her arms on the table. She thought of the mess she had made of her life. She thought of Ronnie Kavanaugh and of Dexter Shaw. She thought of the other path that might have been, the path that had been snatched away from her, in whose terrible aftermath Dex had appeared to save her. But had he saved her? she thought bitterly. For what? For this?

She put her head down on her forearms. Last of all, she thought of Bravo. She hadn't wanted to think of him, but now in her misery she could not help herself. He could have been the one to save her, truly and finally, as in the end Dex had been unable to do. She thought she understood now why Dex had wanted her to guard his son. With his uncanny prescience, he knew—he had to have known, she was certain of it.

All at once, she heard the low derisive laughter of her guards—her former compatriots—and the sound cut through her like a knife blade. She was immediately ashamed; they could see for themselves the weakness they had always suspected would one day lay her low.

Then, into her mind appeared the image of Arcangela—and with it the memory of the life she had led, of the almost insupportable deprivations she had endured so that her charges could carry out their work. *Sacrifice* seemed inadequate for the path she had chosen. Either way, though, it was her courage now that seemed to wind through Jenny's veins and arteries like a vine that, though abused by frost and axe, refuses to die. Instead, it grew green in the springtime of her emotions. And now she realized that Arcangela had given her something more precious even than the advice and support she had taken from Dex—the Anchorite had given her a chance to take back her life.

Now, through the lens of Arcangela's uncanny eye, she saw how she was repeating with Bravo the mistakes she had made with Ronnie and, to some extent, with Dex. She had fallen under their spell. Why? Because she felt that on some level they would save her. But no one had come to save Arcangela; she had the inner strength to save herself.

While she was with the Anchorite she had been awed and, to some extent, cowed by both the extremity of Arcangela's circumstances and depth of her inner strength. Now she realized that she herself possessed the same courage. It only remained for her to claim it.

Easier said than done, because here she was, a prisoner, with Paolo Zorzi doubtless on his way to find Bravo, and she had her head in her hands, weeping. No wonder the two Guardians were laughing at her. She was about to lift her head up, to defy them once again, when it seemed as if she felt the touch of Arcangela's hand on her defeated shoulder, staying her.

Wait, a voice inside her head whispered, *there's a better way.*

She remained where she was, her head on her forearms, and continued to weep. All the while, her mind was working in fifth gear. If they thought her weak, then let them believe it all the more, for once let their perception of her work to her benefit. This was what Arcangela would do, she was sure of it. Arcangela, who had used the means forced on her, the means no one else wanted, to achieve extraordinary ends.

She began to sob, her shoulders hunched and trembling visibly.

"Look at her." One of the guards laughed. "Better bring her a handkerchief."

"A towel is more like it," the other guffawed.

She heard the scrape of boot soles on the worn stone floor, the creak of old wood as one of the Guardians bent over her chair. She could smell him and knew precisely how close he was to her.

"Here, take this," he said shortly, "before you bring on the *acqua alta,* ha ha—"

She flung out an elbow, putting all her physical strength and her outrage into it. The cocked elbow landed square in his eye socket and he gave a cry, muffled by the hands clasped to his face. The second Guardian started toward her, but she had the first one around the throat, had his throwing knife out, and she brandished it.

The second Guardian checked only for a split instant. Then he grinned.

"Don't make me use this," Jenny warned.

The Guardian lifted his bladed weapon, the scimitar curve gleaming in the candlelight. "Do I look worried?" he said with a smirk. He came on, his weapon swinging back. "You don't have the guts."

Jenny threw the knife butt first. With expert precision, it found the place just above his nose. As he fell, unconscious, Jenny smashed the first Guardian's face into her upraised knee and he, too, collapsed.

JENNY ran through the darkness. As soon as she had cleared the sea-wall, she could hear the lagoon lapping at the shingle. Overhead, the sky had cleared. Stars, brilliant as Byzantine lamps, blazed down in splendor through the last wispy tendrils of mist. A stiffening breeze lifted stray tendrils of hair from her face, streaming them behind her. Her heart beat fast, but she felt lighter than she had in some time. She had her mission, and for the first time, it seemed, she was sure about who she was.

She ran toward the light that streamed from the cabin, toward the sharp odor of diesel fumes that billowed into the night. The *motoscafo* was still there. She saw Zorzi and several others in the last stages of preparing for its departure. For some reason, they had transformed the *motoscafo* into a police vessel, complete with decals and flag flying from the bow. As she entered the black water, the lines were cast off, and the burbling of the engines deepened in pitch.

She swam powerfully, her arms reaching out, her legs scissoring, and she came up alongside just as the engines produced a throaty roar. The bow lifted and she grabbed hold of one of the bumpers on the side as the boat got under way. She felt the sudden pull on her shoulder sockets and compensated, relaxing. She should have been out of breath, but she wasn't. She had taken control of her own life, just as Arcangela had meant her to do, and she was exhilarated.

20

BRAVO AND RULE CAME ASHORE ON THE JUTTING SQUARE of Lazzaretto Vecchio that was fully forested. The night was very dark, but some stars were out, and to the west a cloud was illuminated from behind in theatrical fashion by the moon. The cloud looked veined and muscled, like an ancient god awakening from the sleep of eons.

"The traitor has laid low for quite some time," Rule said, "funneling information slowly but surely to the Knights of St. Clement. But now, with you on the hunt for the Testament, he's had to show his hand."

"You mean Zorzi."

Rule nodded. "I'm afraid so." He switched on a flashlight he had found in the cabin of the boat. "He was one of your father's closest associates. He knows almost as much about Dex as I do. He's after you now. He's cunning, devious and extremely dangerous. In fact, there's mounting evidence that he's quietly turned all his Guardians against the Order. They obey him and only him. I'm afraid you can't trust any of them."

Rule spread a tarp used to protect the foodstuffs the Franciscans brought to the island over the *motoscafo*.

"We were lucky on the way over here," Rule continued. "The monks surely must have reported the theft of this boat to the police. We'll have to keep a sharp eye out for them when we leave."

They turned away from the *motoscafo*. It was sufficiently hidden from a cursory sighting from a passing patrol boat but certainly would be found by a closer search. They would have to be well away from here before that happened, Bravo knew, which meant he had very little time to find his father's next cipher.

"I'll show you where the ruins of the old church are," Rule said as they struck out for the interior.

"How did you know where I'd been taken?" Bravo said.

"I followed my suspicions. I've had my eye on Paolo Zorzi for some time."

"Now this is just like old times."

Rule smiled, his eyes briefly touching Bravo in that familiar way.

The trees were thick in this area, a lush wetness spread beneath them. The rich air smelled dank.

"I want to thank you," Bravo said.

"I should thank you for saving my skin with Zorzi."

"You would've found your own way out," Bravo said, "but that's not what I mean."

Rule shot him a quizzical look.

"The winter Junior died I was royally pissed off at you."

"As I recall, you made no bones about it."

"I'm sorry about that."

"Old news."

"No, it isn't. I was angry at you for taking my father away."

"Yeah, well—"

"No, listen, Uncle Tony, I need to say this. I was a kid then, I was only thinking of myself, my own pain. I wasn't thinking of how bad it must have been for my father." There was a small silence. He wished Uncle Tony would say something, add an affirmation. "You knew he needed to get away, didn't you? You knew he would break down if he didn't."

"He sounded so bad when he called I knew I couldn't let you see what might become of him. A child shouldn't see his father in such grief, it was hard enough on you as it was."

"Where did you go?"

"Norway. We went hunting, moose and red deer mostly. Your father was some crack shot. One day—it was snowing, I remember—we came across some tracks that were unfamiliar to me. Very fresh they were, otherwise the snow would've covered them. Anyway, Dex got excited. He made us track the damn thing until the snow grew blue as the sun neared the horizon. Just for this one look we got of it—a wolverine. Even in those days they were rare enough."

"Did you shoot it?"

"Are you kidding? Dexter was in awe of it, he put up his gun and just sat in the snow like a little kid, watching. And you know I think the beast knew we were there—or at least that Dex was there, because once it looked in our direction and flinched. But it never bared its teeth and it didn't run." They were in a small grove of slender, wind-whipped pines now, and Rule pushed a springy branch out of their way. "That was one memorable trip. I saw your father sink down to the depths and then rebound. Out there in the whiteness, communing with that wolverine, he found the salt of life again."

Bravo felt once again the terrible weight of his father's passing, but this time it was leavened with a brush as if from the wings of a great bird that had swooped out of the blackness of the night. *I guess you could call us outsiders—it's far more difficult for us to find ourselves. Sometimes I ask myself what I have to do in order to be saved.* Revealed to him now was yet another layer of what his father had told him that summer afternoon in Georgetown—the difficult truth that he himself had learned about human connection and the world of the outsider.

"You were always a good friend," he said, his throat and his heart full, "to my father and to me."

Rule cuffed Bravo affectionately. "Sometimes you remind me so much of Dex it's uncanny." He paused, then, sobering, "I know how Junior's death affected all of you—especially you. You did everything you could. It wasn't your fault."

Bravo shivered, hearing an echo of Jenny telling him the same thing. For a moment, he flashed on her as she had been in Venice—the hotel room, the shower, the bed. He heard again the voices of the deliverymen, floating up from the canal like morning vapor. He felt her caress, heard her whispering in his ear. Then he heard again the eerie, evil report of the ice cracking beneath his feet. She had caressed his father, had whispered in his ear just as she had with him. He felt a certain horror, a creeping along his spine, and he shivered again as they pressed on.

THEY came to the crumbling stone foundation of the church without seeing a another soul. Part of the building had latterly been turned into the dog kennel. One wall of the old church reared up, black and glistening, as crevassed as an old soldier's face. It had been broken in two.

"Now what? There's not much here," Rule asked as they surveyed the scene.

Bravo stared at the wall. *Remember where you were the day you were born.* Remembering St. Mary of Nazareth Hospital had brought him this far. Where was the hospital in Chicago? He strained to recall. Then he had it: 2233 West Division Street.

He went to the break in the wall—the division—and walked ten paces west, ten being the sum of the four numbers of the hospital's address. He knelt on the grassy ground at the base of the wall. Rule joined him and together they began to dig with their hands. Three feet down they found a parcel wrapped in oilskin.

Far out across the water, trembling lights from the Lido pointed like a crooked finger toward them. A gull cried several times, the plaintive sound diminishing into a sudden rush of air.

Mindful of the police search that had doubtless already begun, they headed back to the *motoscafo* at a quickened pace. Bravo unwrapped the package. Inside was a small silver Greek cross. Wrapped around it, like a beehive or a wasp's nest, was a skein of red threads.

"What do you make of it?" Rule said, peering over his shoulder.

Bravo shook his head.

They reached the boat without incident. The tarp was in the same position in which Rule had left it. Quickly, they stowed it and cast off. Rule handed Bravo the flashlight. While he maneuvered the *motoscafo* away from Lazzaretto Vecchio, Bravo switched on the flashlight and holding the Greek cross in its beam unwound the short lengths of red string. There were twenty-four. The area on the body of the cross that was now revealed had three words etched into it. Bravo knew that this was a two-key fractionation system cipher. One of the most famous field ciphers, it had been employed by the German Army during World War I. The first two words were the keys, the third word was the encrypted text. He opened his father's notebook to a blank page and began to work.

The cipher system was based on the ADFGVX cipher, which used a 6×6 matrix to substitute-encrypt the twenty-six letters of the alphabet and ten digits into pairs of the symbols A, D, F, G, V and X. The resulting biliteral cipher was only an intermediate cipher, however. It was then written into a rectangular matrix and transposed to produce the final cipher.

What Bravo came up with was a single word: *sarcophagus.*

"Where are we headed now?" Rule said at length. "Do you know?"

"Back to Venice," Bravo said, pocketing the notebook and cross. The red threads he dropped into the dark, ruffled water as if they were the last vestiges of his father, who had been here and, by this gesture, was here again.

DAWN was extending its long pearly fingers across the flat expanse of the lagoon. For a few moments they were alone on the water. The oblique light turned the surface into sheet metal through which their boat cut cleanly, like a honed knife. Birds called and circled, roused from the sleep by the dawn and the hunger in their stomachs. They swooped and called to one another as they hunted, submerging themselves briefly to snatch a fish between curved bills.

There were other hunters on the lagoon. As the *motoscafo* rounded the end of the Lido, they saw the police launch, and immediately Rule cut his speed.

Bravo came up alongside him. "What are you doing?"

"You'll see."

Rule had not changed course. In fact, so far as Bravo could tell, he was pointing the bow of the boat directly at the police launch. And now, though Bravo knew that the flatness of the lagoon in certain light could fool the eye and even create mirages, just like in the desert, he was certain that the police launch, having spotted them, had put on speed. He could see the bow lift and the new charge of foam fountaining behind it.

"Uncle Tony—"

"Have faith, Bravo. Have faith."

The police launch rocketed toward them, its speed and noise scattering what was left of the breakfasting birds. Bravo could make out the men aboard, though not yet their individual faces or their uniforms.

He heard a sound then, like the noise wind makes when it catches the rigging of a boat and tautens all its sails. But of course the motorboat had neither rigging nor sails, and then he realized that it was Uncle Tony, who was humming happily to himself. He was in his element, commanding a fast boat, about to go head to head, as it were, with adversaries. *This is what he lives for,* Bravo thought. *This is why the Voire Dei drew him like a flame.*

The police launch was closing at what Bravo considered alarming speed.

Rule stopped his humming long enough to say, "Hold on," out of the side of his mouth.

Bravo clutched the railing with both hands as Rule shoved the throttle forward and the *motoscafo* leapt forward. He had an instant's glimpse of the astonishment in the eyes of the policemen aboard the other vessel as the *motoscafo* suddenly bore down on them, and he felt a shock go through him. Then Rule had turned the wheel hard to starboard. He had threaded the needle with an expert's hand, and the *motoscafo* veered off with a breathless rush, its port side lifted as it slashed through the water, creating a wave that swept aboard the police launch like a shipload of pirates.

Then they were away, headed northeast, in the general direction of Venice but more closely aimed at another islet whose northern flank presented itself to them to starboard. Bravo, glancing behind them, saw the swamped police launch swinging around, and with a roar it put on all speed to follow them.

"There's something about that boat," Rule said. "It's longer and lower in the water than the launches used by the Venetian police."

"You're right. I recognized a Guardian. That isn't a police launch at all."

Rule nodded. "Zorzi's picked up our trail."

The islet was coming up fast on their right. It was deserted, full of reeds and birds and the clean-sweet smell of decay. They had to be careful now because the water was shallow enough in spots to ground the boats. Long sandbars rose here from the depths of the lagoon to provide feeding grounds for birds as well as natural platforms for clamming.

The sun was fully above the horizon now, looking red and bloated, as if ill with a fever. The light, stronger, shot across the water in wavering lines, making the islet seem further away than it was. The air was warming quickly, creating a period of disorienting perspectives and bewitching mirages.

"We can't let him stop us," Bravo said, leaning in so he could speak over the engine's heightened bellow. "You've got to get me to Venice."

Rule swung the wheel hard over. "Don't worry," he said grimly. "I mean to take Zorzi out of the picture once and for all."

IF Paolo Zorzi were any other kind of man he would have blown a blood vessel by now, but he hadn't worked his way into the upper echelon of the Gnostic Observatines by being impatient or impetuous. "All things in their season" was his unspoken motto, and even in this chaotic moment when the tenuous future hung in the balance, he remained deathly calm. He neither cursed himself nor his crew for having failed to respond adequately to Anthony Rule's kamikazelike tactic, but he did resolve not to allow Rule to surprise them again.

Now, as they once again raced after Rule, he took the wheel himself. Instead of following directly in Rule's wake, he quartered in from the port side, effectively pinning Rule into the shallow passage of water between his oncoming *motoscafo* and the northernmost corner of the islet up ahead. He grinned as he came on. With each second that passed Rule's options were becoming more limited. Soon, he'd be out of options altogether.

"YOU see what he's trying to do," Bravo said. "Pin us into grounding ourselves on the shoals close to the islet."

"In this as in all things, he is bound to be disappointed." Rule's voice was low and fierce. The wind had got between his open lips, pulling his cheeks back from his bared teeth.

"But you're heading right for the shallows," Bravo said.

Rule said, "Zorzi will be well pleased for the same reason."

In the deceptive light, he could not make out the distinctions in the color of the lagoon that in late morning through late afternoon mariners used to differentiate the deepwater channels from the shoals that could wreck them. Charts were all well and good elsewhere, but the combination of the changing light and the treacherous tides often rendered the maps useless in all but the few major deepwater passages.

Ahead, Bravo could see the islet coming up fast—the sea fields of quivering reeds, the glistening tide pools, a dark wave, the rising and falling of the birds over their nests, and just beyond, like a series of wavecrests, a pair of *barene*, salt flats that were actually sandbars, pale as a woman's throat, the smaller one closer. On the one farther from them a dozen or so men stooped, their feet and ankles hidden beneath the water as they went about their morning's work, gathering clams that would be consumed that afternoon and evening in Venice's restaurants.

Rule kept glancing over his left shoulder as if worried about the police launch vectoring in off the port quarter. He kept edging in closer and closer to the islet. The launch, having maintained full speed, had gained on them. Apparently, this was precisely what Rule wanted, for he made no effort to push his own throttle forward. This would be consistent with a captain concerned with grounding his boat.

The police launch was now—by Bravo's admittedly inaccurate estimation—only three boat-lengths behind them. As it had been before, it was all about timing.

"Uncle Tony," Bravo shouted, "they're drawing guns!"

Rule veered abruptly to starboard, seemingly into the heart of the shoals. Bravo shouted again, this time in apprehension. But instead of grounding, the *motoscafo* shot forward as Rule now put on speed.

"There's a deepwater channel here," Rule said. "It's unmarked because of how narrow it is. Also, it all but vanishes during the low tides."

Bravo, listening, had turned his body perpendicular to Rule's so that he could look ahead and behind with equal ease. The police launch, having had too short a time to adjust its course fully, had grazed the edge of the sandbar and was now heading in the wrong direction. However, at Zorzi's shouted order, the launch swung around in a tight arc, headed into the channel. It put on all speed as they went through the channel into the open water after the *motoscafo*.

The police launch must have had a more a powerful engine, because it closed the distance between them with appalling speed.

"They're right on top of us!" Bravo shouted, as the first warning shots were fired across their bow.

THE moment Zorzi's *motoscafo* had first put on speed, Jenny had drawn her legs up through the rushing water—no easy task in and of itself—curling her body into a ball as she tucked her feet into the webbing of the draped line that held the bumper against the side of the boat.

She might have thought it a minor miracle that she hadn't been discovered, except that everyone aboard Zorzi's *motoscafo*—Zorzi included—was so intent on finding their prey they had no eyes for anything else.

She heard their voices over the engine noise. Occasionally, she could even make out a sentence or two, though she struggled to make sense of what she picked up. Zorzi kept referring to Anthony Rule as "the Traitor," which though wrongheaded was, she supposed, consistent with what he believed. It was the Guardians' responses to him that she found puzzling. They spoke to him as if he and he alone were the head of the Gnostic Observatines.

RULE held fast to his northwest course, even with the launch gaining on them. More shots were fired, and then Bravo had drawn his SIG Sauer and was returning the fire.

"Forget that," Rule shouted, "and hold on."

An instant later, he had turned the wheel hard to starboard. At the same time he shoved the throttle all the way forward, asking for and getting every ounce of speed the engine was able to generate. The bow, and then the entire front end of the *motoscafo*, lifted free of the water.

Bravo tossed this way and that, could see that they were headed directly at the first of the two *barene*. The clammers, having caught sight of the chase, now stood, staring transfixed as the boats roared toward them. No one—Bravo included—believed that Rule would allow the *motoscafo* to ground itself. Surely, they reasoned, he'd break off, as he had when he'd made the run at the police launch, feinting at the last possible instant.

But that moment came and went—Bravo could feel it, and he braced himself against the polished wood. Three seconds later, the keel of the boat grazed the rise of the sandbar. Instead of grounding on the *barene*, Rule used it as a launchpad for the boat. The *motoscafo* took off into the air, rising in a graceful arc that took them over both sandbars.

"Yahoo!" Rule shouted as they struck the lagoon beyond both sandbars. The double screws bit into the water, and with a massive blast the boat took off, heading straight for Venice.

Bravo, looking behind them, saw Zorzi's launch had broken off and was bobbing at idle beyond the *barene*.

Rule fumbled in his clothes. "Where's that damn pack of cigarettes when I need it?" He laughed, half-giddy with their spectacular success.

"GUESS I can't bum one off you, can I?" There was a slight pause. "So where shall I head this thing? You must know by now where we need to go."

Camille, on a sleek black and white *motoscafo* on the Grand Canal, held the cell phone to her ear and waited, her blood humming in her ear. She was aware of a slight sensation of anxiety, which she put down to anticipation. The call from Anthony Rule had come in just as he promised, everything was falling nicely into place.

"*Castello,*" Bravo's voice said in her ear. "*The Church of San Georgio dei Greci.*"

"*All right.*" Rule's voice now. "*We'll make our way from the lagoon side via canals to the Fondamenta della Pietà. We'll be there, I estimate, in fifteen minutes. That suit you?*"

Camille, having heard enough, put her cell phone away and gave orders to the captain to take her with all due speed to Fondamenta della Pietà in Castello. Then she moved away to where Damon Cornadoro stood, a deep scowl on his handsome face.

"My dear Damon, you look positively sullen," she said brightly. "Please don't tell me you've succumbed to jealousy."

"Can you blame me? Rule was your lover."

Camille took out a cigarette and lit it. "What of it?"

"The affair went on for years. It has occurred to me more than once that you still have feelings for him."

"If I do, it's none of your business."

"But your son—"

"What about my son?" she said sharply.

"I always wondered . . ." He let her hang there suspended for a moment, her eyes riveted on him, her breath stilled, a small victory, to be sure, but a victory nonetheless. "I always wondered whether Rule was Jordan's father."

She turned away, her eyes dark, unfathomable.

The topic of her son's father was taboo, he knew that, so he came after her, almost as a supplicant. "I'm your lover now, Camille. Do you think I would share you?"

Camille blew smoke out through her half-open lips as she contemplated the magnificent palazzi passing by on either side of the Grand Canal.

"Camille?"

She wouldn't think of Jordan's father, she wouldn't. So, to calm herself, she turned her mind to other matters. It both fascinated and depressed her that men thought only in terms of possession. *I don't have that, I want it. Now that I have it, I will never let it go.* Of course, what made them predictable made them susceptible to her. So. What should she tell this lover of hers? Certainly not why she had taken Rule as her lover, certainly not that she still loved him in the manner she loved any object precious to her. In truth, Camille was never so lonely as when she was with a man. They were so easily satisfied, so quickly sated, and then what happened? Their quick-shift attention turned elsewhere, you could tell them to go fuck themselves and they never even heard it.

Inevitably, however, there were men who presented her with something of a challenge. Anthony Rule, for one. Turning him away from the Order of Gnostic Observatines had been a long, slow, arduous and often perilous path. It had been a deeply considered and meticulously planned military campaign. For all those reasons—and, of course, others—it was without question a crowning achievement in her life, and a stunning success coming on the heels of such a devastating disappointment. Over the years, the intelligence he had provided had been invaluable to her and to Jordan. And the most satisfying aspect was that it was he who had passed her this ultrasensitive intelligence.

"You have nothing to worry about, my love," she said now. "Anthony Rule is my past. You are my present."

Even over the noise of the engine she could hear Cornadoro's released breath. She almost laughed at how immediately he responded to the stroking. It was, by this time, something of a Pavlovian response. He wanted—no, needed—to believe her. Men, obsessed with proving to each other how strong they were, were essentially weak. She had proved this maxim time and again even with the hard cases like Rule and Cornadoro. Then there was Dexter Shaw—but there was bound to be one, she told herself in a quick gloss of the past. What was he but the exception that proved the rule? She consoled herself with the thought that men had such a narrow definition of coercion. What did men—who after all were most comfortable with a cudgel in their hand—know of coercion? The velvet glove was anathema to them. Though they responded to it beautifully, even, she might say, movingly, they continued to deny its existence. All the better for me, Camille thought. Which was why throughout history there always had been successful women, clever and resourceful, who used their forced servitude as a cloak of anonymity behind which they wielded their own form of velvet glove to devastating effect.

Camille held no sympathy for women who took a beating from their men, whether physical or emotional. Hardly surprising, since she had nothing but the deepest contempt for weakness of any kind. It was her opinion that weakness was what got them into the abusive situation and it was weakness that chained them there. There was no situation that the human mind couldn't work itself out of. She believed this with the single-minded fervor of a religious zealot. It was, in fact, for her a form of religion, so closely did she adhere to the tenet. It was the one idea she could accept as gospel.

They approached the Fondamenta della Pietà, and Cornadoro leapt ashore before the captain even tied up the boat.

"I will come to you soon," she crooned to Cornadoro as if he were a baby longing to suck at her breast. "In the meantime, make your way to the church. And for the love of God be on your guard for Zorzi and his Guardians. I have no doubt that he will kill you on sight, if you give him the opportunity, just as he will now kill Anthony Rule."

21

WALKING SOUTH FROM THE FONDAMENTA DELLA PIETÀ, Bravo and Rule found the Church of San Georgio dei Greci without difficulty. Three times, they had paused or taken small detours to ensure themselves that no one was following them. Though still early, the day was already hot and sticky. White clouds hung motionless against the sky as if nailed in place.

The church presented an elegant facade to the street down which they walked, a remarkably simple affair, at least in terms of Venice's hyperventilating architecture. The only Greek Orthodox church in Venice, it had been built in 1539 when there was a thriving Greek population, many of whom had traveled for centuries with the seafaring Venetians to the Levant and settled in important trading communities along the south coast of the Black Sea, where their religion became the dominant form of worship until the Muslim Ottomans drove them from Trebizond in the fifteenth century. Now there were less than a hundred Greek Orthodox in all Venice.

The interior of the church, with its high, barrel ceiling, seemed empty and cavernous. There were few people about—an old woman kneeling, her hands clasped, as she faced the enormous gilt cross, a heavy man with tousled hair in earnest conversation with a tall, cadaverous priest with a humpback under his long black cassock.

The lack of people seemed endemic, as if something vital had hollowed out the interior, keeping intact the magnificent architecture and sculpture but leaving behind, as after a receding glacier, the peculiar barrenness of a moraine—a landscape devoid of both plants and the earth in which they would grow.

Like all Greek and Russian Orthodox churches, San Georgio dei Greci had a notable iconostasis, a wall of icons that was Byzantine in origin. Historically, the iconostasis had served as a kind of threshold or fence, a symbol of the division between the sanctuary and the nave, between heaven and earth, the divine and the mortal, but over the years it evolved into a wall into which the individual icons were set. As with all religions, what had once been correctable was now quite literally set in stone.

As soon as the tall priest noticed them, he broke off with the heavyset man and came over to where they stood.

"My name is Father Damaskinos," he said in a voice that made it seem as if his mouth was full of gravel.

Italian wasn't his first language, Bravo thought, and so he replied in Greek, giving their names.

The priest's eyes opened slightly in surprise and delight. "You speak Greek very well, what other languages do you know?"

"Trapazuntine Greek," Bravo said.

Father Damaskinos laughed softly. He had shoulders like a wire hanger and the head, small-eared and large-toothed, of a leopard. His hunchback was slight, from some angles seeming not to exist, so that he appeared, like many others of his height, merely stoop shouldered.

He replied in the same ancient form of his language, "Then of course you must have come to the Church of San Georgio dei Greci for a specific reason."

"I've come," Bravo said, "to see the crypt."

"Crypt?" Father Damaskinos's narrow brow furrowed deeply. "You are misinformed. We have no crypt here."

Bravo turned to Rule. "Uncle Tony, do you know this man?"

Rule shook his head. "He is not one of us."

Father Damaskinos's black eyes seemed lit from within his leopard's skull. "One of us? What does this mean?"

"Bravo, we have no time for this," Rule said.

Nodding, Bravo took out the Greek cross and held it in his open palm. For a moment Father Damaskinos said nothing. Then he took it as gingerly as if it were a scorpion. He examined every inch of it, most of all the inscription.

At length, he returned the cross to Bravo's palm. "Where are the red threads?"

"Gone," Bravo said.

"Did you count them?"

"There were twenty-four."

This odd exchange had the terse, staccato tempo of a spy's recognition code.

"Twenty-four," Father Damaskinos said. "You're certain? No more, no less?"

"That's right. Twenty-four, exactly."

"Come with me." Father Damaskinos turned abruptly on his heel, leading them across the checkerboard floor, to a door at the extreme left side of the iconostasis. Inside was a tiny space, seemingly carved out of the church's stone blocks. Father Damaskinos took a torch from a black wrought-iron ring set into the wall and lit it.

"For obvious reasons," he said, "there is no electricity in the crypt."

They descended a spiral staircase, its marble treads so well worn they dipped in their centers. Because this was Venice, the crypt was not as far down as it would have been in cities built on dry land. It was damp and cold as a refrigerator. The stone floor was awash in water and, here and there, tiny shelled creatures marched up and down the slick walls, their multiple legs clicking like the pens of an army of clerks.

"Our crypt is a secret place, its existence zealously guarded."

The crypt was larger than Bravo had expected. Two rows of stone sarcophagi stretched away from them, separated by a narrow aisle. Into the lid of each sarcophagus was carved the likenesses of those buried inside. Some held crosses, but others clasped swords to their chests.

Father Damaskinos faced Bravo. "You are Dexter's son, are you not?"

"Yes. How did you know my father?"

"We had a friendship based on mutual trust, we believed in the same thing: the overarching power of history. Your father was a great student of history, you know. Occasionally, I would translate ancient documents that even he couldn't decipher. In return, though I never asked for it, the church received a monthly stipend from an account that Dexter set up for the purpose."

Father Damaskinos addressed Rule. "You appear surprised that

he would turn to someone outside his Order, but consider: for centuries, there has been an alliance between the Order and the Greek
Orthodox—the Orthodox Church having provided the Order with information and even secret documents in the early days when members
of the Order traveled to the Levant—Samsun, Erzurum, Trebizond.
This alliance was a natural one, born both of necessity and self-defense
since both the Greek Orthodox Church and the Order were enemies of
the pope."

They walked through the water, down the aisle. It was curious, Bravo
thought, that though this was the resting place of the dead, he could
sense more life down here than he had in the church above. Like his father, he had an acute sense of history. For him, history was a living thing
with an endless supply of stories, of lessons to apply to the present of
one's own life. He could remember innumerable times he and his father
had read historical texts—their favorites the living words of those who
had lived through history, unaltered and unexcerpted by historians with
their own perspectives, their own axes to grind. The danger in studying
history, Dexter had told him, was in not going to the source.

"So you have become part of the Voire Dei," Father Damaskinos
said, "and now nothing seems the same."

"I felt that way the moment my father died."

"I, too," the priest said soberly. "Your father was a unique individual.
I wonder whether you are like him."

"You mean his gift of prescience."

Father Damaskinos nodded. "Your father saw the battle that began in
the Voire Dei and spread to the world outside in, shall we say, larger
terms than the others. He saw that the battle had commenced on
political terms, that it had remained so for centuries. In the fifteen
hundreds it might have had the trappings of a religious conflict, but the
underlying motivators were strictly political. Centuries later, those, like
the Communists, who refused to recognize the changes afoot, who
couldn't see that the battle had shifted to economic terms, were doomed.

"The lust for economic supremacy is the engine that has driven the
Voire Dei—as well as the larger world—for more than twenty years
now. It, like the idea of political power before it, has become so en-
trenched in the thinking of the participants that they have become as

blind as the Communists to the changes at work. But your father knew—he saw that the imperative of economic superiority was slowly being eroded by the rise of religious conflict. The so-called economic reasons for the conflict—that is, the scramble for oil—were once again trappings. You see the importance of history? Beneath those false trappings is the religious motivator.

"Fundamentalism, you see? The Christians on one side, the Islamics on the other. It is no longer simply Israel the Arabs have to fear, but America with its increasingly powerful fundamental Christian constituency. This is a conflict that goes beyond the traditional scope of the Voire Dei, as we have known it, and yet it brings the Voire Dei into particular focus and prominence because what your father saw coming is an age of the New Crusades. Make no mistake, it is the future, and those who ignore its growing importance are doomed to be ground beneath its powerful heel."

Seeing the smirk on Rule's face, Father Damaskinos broke off. "You do not agree, Mr. Rule?"

"No, I don't. The Order is purely secular now, no one knew that better than Dex. The idea that he had become interested in religious infighting is absurd."

"And yet the pope still sends his minions after you—now with ever-increasing fervor."

"The pope knows nothing of this," Rule said shortly. "If he has those around him like Cardinal Canesi, so much the worse for Rome. Even so, Canesi has no religious axe to grind—it's the politics of power he has on his mind. Do you really think he gives a fig about the Testament of Christ? No, the Testament is his enemy. It negates the very power base he has built for himself. It's the Quintessence he's after, my friend. Only the Quintessence will save his sorry skin now."

"He will never get the Quintessence. The good Cardinal is doomed."

"He very well may be," Rule said. "But with the pope having only days to live, you can be damned certain he's going to do his best to destroy the Order first."

"How very against God you are."

"Over the years, Father, I've learned the high art of atheism."

"That is a pity," Father Damaskinos said.

"What a surprising comment." Rule didn't bother to hide his disgust. "I've had enough talk of religion and doom to last me a lifetime. Let's get on with it."

JENNY was finally on dry land, for which she could only offer up a silent prayer of deliverance. Her arms were numb, and her legs trembled like a foal trying to keep its feet. A sharp pain at the base of her neck seemed connected to the violent headache that had driven its spike between her eyes.

She crouched in the shadows, not far from Paolo Zorzi, who had gathered his Guardians as soon as they had scrambled off the boat at the *fondamenta* in Castello. Zorzi had his cell phone to his ear. Her position was such that the acoustics of the street brought her every word he said.

"Where are they now?"

He had marshaled, she had gathered, all the resources at his command, using his men at fixed points like the coastal watchtowers that kept track of marauding Corsair ships, like signal fires that transmitted dire news from city to city.

"The church," he was saying. "Yes, of course I know it."

He turned, his expression set, impatient, annoyed and, Jenny hoped, quite possibly chagrined. During the journey across the lagoon, she had discovered that he had been the one to capture Bravo, but Bravo, thank God, had escaped, along with Rule. It was Bravo and Rule they had been chasing across the lagoon. She had not been able to tell this before, curled on the opposite side of the boat. But now Zorzi and his traitorous Guardians had picked up their trail again, and from the sound of the conversation they might soon have them surrounded.

All she had to do now was to think of a way to stop them. She almost wept with the futility of it—what could she do, one woman alone and unarmed against this well-trained, disciplined cadre?

"There is no good news this day, save one thing," Zorzi was saying. "The crisis generated by Braverman Shaw has at last drawn our enemy out of hiding. Anthony Rule is the traitor, this information is incontrovertible."

Who was he speaking with? Not another of his cadre, as she had first supposed. *You're lying!* Jenny wanted to shout. You're *the traitor!*

She wished she could accost each and every Guardian and tell them the terrible mistake they were making. Instead, she had to crouch here, trembling like a fawn and watch her world go to hell. She couldn't let that happen, no way—

"It's a delicate operation, of course," he continued. "Bravo must not be further injured in any way. The trauma of his father's death—yes, though I was six thousand miles away, I take full responsibility. Yes, sir. But you must understand, the delicacy of this operation is extreme. Not only must we extract Braverman Shaw safely but we must do so without killing Rule. . . . Of course, I'm certain. What good will it do us to shoot him dead now?" He walked a little away from the knot of Guardians, closer, as it happened, to where she crouched in a shadowed doorway. "This is our chance to turn the tables on the Knights. Imagine the intelligence about them Rule must be carrying inside his head." Zorzi switched his cell phone to his other hand, his other ear, while he flexed the one that had been holding the unit. "No, sir, I will not handle the interrogation myself. You know my history with Rule; we've never seen eye to eye. How would it look if I handled his interrogation? No, that I will leave up to you, sir."

All at once, Jenny realized that she was shaking all over. What was wrong with this picture? Paolo Zorzi should have been advocating Anthony Rule's death—if only to protect himself. Not only was he advocating the capture of Rule, but he was refusing to lead the interrogation. What Zorzi was saying made no sense to her. And then, with a icy ball forming in her stomach, she realized that if Zorzi wasn't the traitor—if, in fact, he was telling the truth and, instead, Rule was the traitor, the conversation made perfect sense.

Jenny put her head against the door and closed her eyes against the spinning of the world around her. She felt sick to her stomach. Rule was the traitor—Rule, who had been so close to Dex his son called him Uncle Tony. It was perfect—so perfect that she wanted to gag. So many unexplained anomalies raced through her head. No wonder the Order had been losing ground to the Knights, no wonder they'd now been losing key men—including Dex. It had all been Rule's doing.

Without her being aware of it, her fingers curled, her hands turned to fists she planned to furiously employ at the first opportunity.

BRAVO became aware of Father Damaskinos's keen eye on him.

"When it came to the Order, your father had a particular interest, Bravo. I wonder if he shared it with you."

The priest spoke in such easy, even tones it was possible to believe that this was not a test. But only for a moment. Bravo smiled, because he liked Father Damaskinos, liked especially his caution in this new time of terrible peril for those in the Order as well as for those who befriended members of the Order.

"He spoke to me often of Fra Leoni."

"Yes, indeed. Fra Leoni was the last *Magister Regens* of the Order. Afterward, the so-called Haute Cour—the committee originally formed to advise the *Magister Regens* and see that his dictums were carried out correctly—evolved into an egalitarian ruling body." Father Damaskinos looked at Rule as if in defiance, but Rule was silent. "There seemed little about the Order's hallowed leader that Dexter did not know. He also knew that the only way for the Order to evolve, to become a major force in the modern world was to elect a new *Magister Regens*."

"Does one of these sarcophagi hold the remains of Fra Leoni?" Rule's interest had suddenly quickened.

"Now that would be something, truly," the priest said. "However, you must know that the whereabouts of the crypt was so zealously guarded over the centuries that it has now become something of a legend. In fact, no one knows whether it actually exists."

"My father believed it existed," Bravo said.

"That's right," Father Damaskinos said, "but I believe that even he had no clear idea where it might be."

"Do you know the names of those buried here?" Bravo said.

"Of course," Father Damaskinos replied. "These are all Venetians who secretly helped us in centuries past. Their names are engraved on my memory, which is, of course, the only place they exist."

Bravo asked him to recite the names. When he was finished, Bravo said, "Please lead me to the sarcophagus of Lorenzo Fornarini."

"Of course." Father Damaskinos led them two-thirds of the way down the crypt, pointing to a sarcophagus on the left.

The Fornarini were, like Zorzi, one of the *Case Vecchie*, the so-called old houses, the elite families that had founded Venice: the twenty-four. This was the meaning of the twenty-four strands of red thread wound around the Greek cross. The three ciphers taken together read: in the Church of San Georgio dei Greci is a sarcophagus of a member of the twenty-four.

"As your father knew very well, Lorenzo Fornarini lived at the end of the fourteen hundreds and was a Knight Templar," Father Damaskinos said. "He was at Trebizond when it fell to the Sultan Mehmed II. In Trebizond, however, he secretly renounced his allegiance to Venice and became a member of the Greek Orthodox church, which was why he was secretly brought here. Members of the clergy there declared him a hero. But he was denounced by Andrea Cornadoro, another member of the *Case Vecchie,* and a knight with an exceedingly evil reputation.

"He and Lorenzo Fornarini fought each other over three years and two islands before Cornadoro finally killed Fornarini. The priests preserved his body, wrapped it like a mummy and brought it back to be interred here. Like Fra Leoni, Lorenzo Fornarini was a hero to Dexter."

"Help me," Bravo said to Rule.

Together, they moved aside the stone lid just enough for Bravo to peer inside. He stared for a long moment at the skeleton of Lorenzo Fornarini. In the flickering light from the torch all time and space seemed obliterated, and he saw again the knight who had fought so valiantly against the Ottoman horde.

Then the spell was broken and, leaning over, he reached in. Between the ribs of the skeleton, he found a PDA, which was lying on something long and narrow. He removed both items. With the PDA was Lorenzo Fornarini's dagger, beautifully preserved in a chased steel sheath.

Bravo examined it, then turned on the PDA. Up came a long series of letters and numbers. His father had turned the PDA into a one-time pad—or Vernam cipher. Gilbert Sandford Vernam was an American cryptographer. In 1917, while working for AT&T, he invented the one-time pad cipher system, still the only cipher so secure that it had never been broken. The keystream of the Vernam cipher was the same length as the plaintext message and consisted of a series of bits generated completely at random, hence its invulnerability even to modern-day supercomputers.

They went back up into the church, noted the women's stalls above the entrance were empty, and sat there.

The problem Bravo needed to solve was where his father had secreted the one-time pad he would use to decode the cipher into plaintext. His first thought was that it was somewhere in his father's notebook, but after a quick perusal, he realized that the keypad would be too obvious there. He looked at the enamel American flag lapel pin, to no avail. Then he took out the pack of unopened cigarettes he'd found with the other objects. On its bottom was stamped a sell-by date and a lot number. However, the lot number contained symbols as well as letters and numbers. With mounting excitement, he counted the string—it was precisely as long as the keystream on the PDA.

He entered the lot number on the PDA's keypad and pressed the calculate key. The resulting decoded cipher was a riddle in ancient Greek.

"What can run but never walk? Has a mouth but never talks? Has a head but never weeps? Has a bed but never sleeps?" Rule read over his shoulder. "What does that mean?"

"It's a river." Bravo laughed. "When I was a child, there was an epic poem I loved that my father used to read me. It began, 'By the waters of Degirmen did King David lose his life / When he was betrayed and the Conqueror took all that was his . . .'

"David was the last of the Comneni, the storied family that for centuries ruled Trebizond, the wealthiest of the Black Sea trading cities. Degirmen is the name of the river that flows through Trabzon, as it's now known."

Father Damaskinos was nodding. "The Comneni were Greek Orthodox. David, the last of the line, was betrayed by one of his ministers, and Trebizond, long thought impregnable, fell in 1461 to the army of Mehmed II, sultan of the Ottoman Empire, known as the Conqueror."

Bravo looked at Rule. "The Testament isn't in Venice, as I had thought. I have to go to Turkey, to Trabzon."

"So the journey continues," Rule said with an obscure kind of weariness.

Bravo scarcely heard him. For the first time, he was struck full force by the sense of his father's unfinished life, and he touched a sorrow inside himself so intimate and painful he'd never suspected it was there.

THE Church of San Georgio dei Greci stood in the glare and musty heat of the Venetian morning. Paolo Zorzi and his Guardians had gathered in the blue shadows that were slowly being eroded by the brilliant sunlight. Someone, in a nearby *campo,* was singing an aria in a fine, untrained voice. The notes floated across the canal like soap bubbles, making the air glisten.

The Guardians were wide-eyed, their lips half parted with the forces of their breath. Jenny could see on their faces that curious mixture of anticipation, tension and anxiety as they geared themselves up for war.

She burned to walk up to her mentor and offer her services, but she knew better. The frame-up had worked this well: he no longer trusted her, and no matter what he might say to the contrary she had the evidence in his eyes to remind her that she could no longer trust him. He had lied to her about Bravo, and once the lies began they became a torrent and then, simply, the way things were. She had her own example to go by.

No, she realized, she was on her own now, cut off from the Order that had betrayed her. She'd never been a valuable asset to them, merely an accommodation between friends. In her current state, she could even work up a hatred for Dex for interfering, for treating her like a thing instead of a human being. He had sold her into slavery in much the same way Arcangela's parents had sold her. The Order or the nunnery, what did it matter? She and Arcangela were both imprisoned in cages carefully and ingeniously manufactured by men. The difference between them was that Arcangela had figured out a way to escape hers.

She started. Zorzi and his Guardians were on the move, approaching the church in a concerted and controlled wave, all entrances and exits covered, blocked and, finally, used. She waited until the last possible instant, until just one Guardian was left to go through the front door, and then she stepped up behind him, punched him hard in the kidney and as he reacted, slammed his head against the church's stone facade. She climbed into his robe, took his gun, and then, like quicksilver, she slipped into the church.

BRAVO saw movement out of the corner of his eye and Rule, with an animal's keen defense mechanism, felt the imminent peril.

"He's here," Rule said. "Zorzi."

Bravo pushed Father Damaskinos down behind the dark wood of the women's stalls and said quietly but firmly in Trapazuntine Greek, "Don't move, not for anything, do you understand?"

The priest nodded and then, as they were about to turn away, saw the SIG Sauer in Bravo's hand. Reaching beneath his black cassock, he pulled out a gun, handing it to Rule butt first.

"Even here, there are times when one needs protection," he whispered.

Rule nodded curtly, a gesture that reminded Bravo of a military salute, a coded recognition one soldier gives to another.

"Godspeed," Father Damaskinos said.

Rule brandished the gun. "God has nothing to do with it."

They crept partly out from behind the partition of the stalls. From this vantage point they could see the enemy crawling like maggots— Paolo Zorzi and four Guardians. But they knew there were others— there had to be—in other parts of the church not visible to them.

"They won't hurt you, or at least they'll try not to," Rule said grimly. "As for me, I'll be dead in the blink of an eye if I let them get a clear shot at me."

"Then we have to make sure they don't get a clear shot at you," Bravo said.

Rule laughed briefly and silently. He ruffled Bravo's hair, as he'd done when they were both much younger.

"This is what I admire most about you, Bravo. Your absolute loyalty is a refreshing change for me."

"You're saying loyalty has no place in the Voire Dei."

"I would never tell you that," Rule said seriously. "Never."

"NEVER," Camille had told him. *"You must not interfere."*

Damon Cornadoro was a sentinel in the shrinking shadows that still lurked around the church of the Greeks, semiderelict and of no value to him or to anyone he knew. He was not cut out to be an observer; his skills were best served in the furtherance of action. And, as he observed the Guardians moving in as they ringed the rear and sides of the church, he decided to ignore Camille's express order.

He knew the endgame had begun, and he would be damned if it would take place without him. He went into action, if he thought about it at all, because it pleased him; the lure of bloodshed was irresistible. But there was another reason locked away beyond his understanding. His willful disobedience stemmed from the look that had come into Camille's eyes when she took the call from Anthony Rule. He had felt their connection, even displaced by wireless electronics. He could see the slight tremor in her hand that held the cell phone, the sexual flush that came to her cheeks. Worst of all was the sighting of Rule himself in her eyes. She had been staring at him—Cornadoro—but it was Rule she was seeing.

And so he moved, rage and spite informing every movement, every decision. He made no sound in the dimness of the church, coming upon each Guardian unsuspected and undetected. He took them down with an economy of movement but with a terrible excess of pain. He never saw their faces, never cared to see them; his eyes were filled with someone else. He possessed the fixed gaze of a killing machine and was unstoppable.

Until, that is, he felt the familiar touch on his arm and, swinging around, found himself staring into her eyes.

"THE staircase is the key," Rule said. "For us, it's the only way in or out."

Bravo nodded. The spiral staircase up to the women's stalls was narrow. A creak from one of its wooden treads hidden behind a curving wall brought them up short.

Rule's eyes opened wide as he pointed a forefinger downward in the instant before he wrapped himself into a ball and tumbled down the staircase. Bravo, understanding the plan, followed him, the SIG Sauer at the ready. He heard the surprised grunt as Rule made contact with another body, and he leapt around the wall, saw the Guardian staggering back and slammed the butt of the gun into the man's temple. The Guardian collapsed, half on Rule, who immediately threw him off and sprang up.

"Nice going," he whispered.

"I saw four, plus Zorzi," Bravo said.

"Now three, plus. But it's Zorzi I have to worry about." They paused behind a wall to catch their breath and to reassess tactics. "I've always believed that the best strategy is the last one the enemy thinks of. Zorzi's got superiority in numbers and, he thinks, the edge of surprise. He can't help but believe that he's got us on the defensive. Therefore, we go on the offensive. We stalk him—and only him—as he's been stalking us. What do you say?"

What was Bravo to say? Rule was older, with far more field experience and an unblemished record of getting out of even the hairiest tactical situations. Besides, what he was proposing made sense: Bravo never liked the feeling of being back on his heels.

"Let's do it," he said.

Rule nodded. "We go everywhere together. We're a team, get it? No suddenly taking off on your own, no individual heroics—that'll screw everything six ways from Sunday."

They moved out from behind the wall, bent over and scuttling like scarabs until they were behind a massive column. In that time, Bravo saw that what few people had been in the church had been evacuated. The field had been cleared for battle.

Bravo saw another Guardian appear from behind a column twenty-five feet away. He was looking straight ahead, not in their direction. Rule grabbed his shoulder as he was about to move.

"An excellent way of cutting down the odds further, that's what you're thinking, isn't it?" Rule whispered in his ear. "But that's just what Zorzi wants us to think. The man's a decoy, a means to flush us out." He gestured in the opposite direction. "Remember, we're after Zorzi. He's the key. Once we have him, the battle's won."

As Rule dictated, they moved in tandem, quickly and cautiously. The sun was high enough now for light to pour in through the windows, creating patches of bright color on the floor and walls. The windows themselves were invisible save as a white glare. As a result, the shadows in the interior were as deep and dark as if it were midnight.

"We look for two together," Rule said, as they traversed the circumference of the interior. "In these situations Zorzi always has a Guardian watching his back."

"Clever thinking."

"No, it isn't," Rule said. "It's predictable and therefore a security risk." He pointed ahead of them. "But it does give us an edge."

Bravo saw the two figures, and a thrill of hatred went through him. Who knew how much intelligence Zorzi had passed on to the Knights, how many deaths were on his hands, including the murder of Dexter Shaw? Bravo felt his teeth slide together, grinding in rage.

He was in such a keyed-up state that when Rule said, "You take the Guardian, I'll take Zorzi," he almost said, "No, I want Zorzi for myself." But then he came back to his disciplined self. Now that they were so close to beating the odds stacked against them, he desperately didn't want to screw things up six ways from Sunday.

They circled around until they were on the left side of Zorzi and his Guardian bodyguard. They could see Zorzi talking urgently into his cell phone, no doubt repositioning his men as they quartered the church's interior. The bodyguard was watching his back. Doubtless they had found the Guardian that Bravo had knocked cold, and their nerves, already taut, had begun to vibrate.

There was less than ten feet between the enemies, and with Zorzi intent on his troop movements there would never be a better chance. Bravo and Rule leapt at the two men. Bravo slammed his fist into the Guardian's rib cage, then brought the butt of the SIG Sauer into play. The Guardian swiveled, forcing Bravo to turn with him. The Guardian drove a knee into Bravo's solar plexus and grabbed his hair, jerking his head up and swinging him around.

Everything happened very quickly after that. Bravo saw out of the corner of his eye two Guardians rushing toward him. One leveled a gun at him, and improbably, it seemed as if the other Guardian knocked the gun out of his hand and brought him down. His eyes, teary from the blow to his stomach, might have failed him for a moment, or then again, he might have been subject to a wishful mirage like those manufactured at times by the lagoon.

Then he was fully engaged with the struggle with his own Guardian, who had him on his knees. Bravo reached up, pulling the Guardian down, using his own momentum against him as he drove a blow directed at Bravo's head. The man, surprised, toppled head over heels and Bravo grabbed his ears, slammed his head against the floor. Panting, he rose to see Rule with his forearm across Zorzi's throat. He had him, the battle was won. It seemed Zorzi had in some sense given up, for he had seen Bravo. His mouth began to work, words tumbling out, rushed and barely comprehensible. Despite his caution, Bravo started to move closer, so that he could hear what the traitor had to say at the moment of his defeat.

But Rule had pulled the gun given him by Father Damaskinos, and now as Bravo looked on he shot Paolo Zorzi three times in the chest.

Zorzi's eyes opened wide, his body recoiled violently backward. Still, his eyes were on Bravo and he continued to talk, but his mouth was full of blood, there was blood everywhere and there were no more words left to say.

Rule, a gleam of triumph in his eyes, was just turning away from his last look at Zorzi's corpse when another shot sounded. Rule spun around. A sudden spray of blood as he was shot a second time, and he flew into Bravo's arms as if he were Icarus, who dared too much and was now fallen from the sky.

Behind Rule came the Guardian Bravo had seen before out of the corner of his eye. The figure was smaller than the others, and when the hood of the robe was pulled back, Bravo saw Jenny's face. Jenny with a gun in her hand, Jenny who had shot Uncle Tony.

Bravo could feel Rule against him, shuddering, struggling to breathe, which was odd because he felt so warm, warm and wet, never more alive than he was now in his convulsions.

"Bravo, listen to me," Jenny began.

The sweet-copper odor of fresh blood clogged Bravo's nostrils. Uncle Tony was in his arms, gasping, coughing blood, dying, and a red haze obscured thought and reason. He lifted the SIG Sauer.

"I don't want to hear your lies."

"I'm asking you to listen to the truth—"

"The truth is you shot Uncle Tony dead. Were you also responsible for planting the bomb that killed my father?"

"Oh, Bravo, you know better than that."

"Do I? I feel as if I don't know anything—about you, the Order, the Voire Dei."

"I took one down." She pointed to a fallen Guardian. "I took one down to protect you."

Bravo aimed the SIG Sauer at her. "I don't believe you."

"God, how can I convince you?"

"Liar. Don't even try."

She bit her lip because she was a liar. She had lied to him from the moment he'd come to her door and she'd never stopped, and now the truth had become so incendiary that she knew she had lost her chance with him.

Feeling her failure like a millstone, she dropped her weapon. "You won't shoot me like this, I know this much about you." She held out a hand. "Let me at least help you put him down."

"Don't come any closer!" he shouted. "If you move I *will* shoot you." It was as if the words were being forced out of him like drops of blood. His face was white and stricken.

"All right, Bravo. All right. But you must know that I didn't kill Father Mosto. I was framed."

"With your own knife?"

Jenny squeezed her eyes shut for a moment. *How else?* she wanted to say, but the explanation, the situation seemed at this moment too much for her. And, in fact, she lacked any evidence, not to mention the crucial answer of who had murdered the priest. Her hesitation was a mistake.

"Back away!"

The harsh tone of his voice made her jump. Her eyes flew open. There was so much to say, but the look of hatred on his face strangled her, turned the words in her mouth to stones.

"I should kill you dead for what you've done."

"He was the traitor, Bravo. I know you don't want to hear this, but Rule was—"

"Shut up!" If he hadn't still been cradling Uncle Tony he felt sure he would have struck her with as much force as he could muster. He wanted to see her on her knees, swaying, dizzy with the blow he had delivered, the weight of his enmity. He wanted to see her pay for her unspeakable treachery, but it was not in him to kill her in this way.

Slowly, keeping his eyes on her, he lay Rule onto the cold stone. The anguish he felt at leaving Uncle Tony here almost finished him, but no matter what horror had occurred he was determined to remain strong. He did this for his father and because in the core of him he still could distinguish good from evil, even in the hell of the Voire Dei.

"I'm leaving now," he said in a cold, detached monotone, the only voice he dared summon up. "If you try to follow me, if I see you again, I'll kill you. Do you understand?"

"Bravo—"

"Do you understand?"

The fury of his voice went clear through her, robbing her of coherent thought. "Yes." She'd say anything not to hear that tone of voice again.

By some superhuman force of will she held her tears in check until Bravo, backing warily away, melted into the shadows that seemed to reach out long tendrils to embrace him. Then her vision blurred and, swept up by an almost unbearable loneliness, she sank to her knees, feeling like a blind woman for the last mortal remains of Paolo Zorzi.

PART THREE

PRESENT DAY—
VENICE,
ROME,
TRABZON

22

IN THE SOUL-WRENCHING DESOLATION OF THE AFTERMATH,
Father Damaskinos emerged from the shelter of the women's stalls.
Leaning over the balcony railing he saw the human carnage and fell to
his knees, his head bowed in prayer for the dead and the dying. He had
no thought for the police or the laws of the world outside; the air in his
church—the house of God under his stewardship—was black with the
soot of mortal sins. The need for spiritual cleansing and forgiveness was
the only thing on his mind as he sank deeper in prayer, first seeking forgiveness for himself, for his own role in the madness below him.

But in the midst of his holy work, his head jerked up, his eyes flew
open, and slowly he rose and his gaze fell on a slim figure advancing
across the floor like a fawn crossing a forest glade. His heart gave a
painful lurch against his ribs, so that his left hand clawed at his chest.

It was the devil, the devil was in his church. All plans of forgiveness
fled like a flock of startled birds before an onrushing storm. His house
didn't need forgiveness, it required an exorcism. With this terrifying
revelation, Father Damaskinos turned and fled.

JENNY was numb with shock. But gradually she became aware that a
shadow had fallen across her. Someone was approaching. She lifted her
head and, turning, tensed herself for the inevitable Guardian attack.
But, instead, she recognized Camille Muhlmann. She breathed a sigh of
relief, the floodgates opened and she began to weep. Camille knelt beside her, enfolding Jenny in her arms, rocking her back and forth.

For Jenny, her abandonment was overrun by the blinding pain of the
past, which had begun with her meeting Ronnie Kavanaugh. It had

been in London, fittingly enough, in a casino belowground, where high rollers, Kavanaugh among them, spent the night with bejeweled toys on their arms. He had been on assignment, had been playing roulette and chemin de fer for hours. She had been on leave, after chipping a bone in her arm running down a Knight in a speedboat on the Thames.

When Kavanaugh had approached her, Jenny was startled, and she was understandably flattered when he'd told her he'd noticed her the moment she'd walked in. He'd asked whether she was a gambler, and when she'd said she didn't understand the impulse behind it he'd laughed. His eyes glowed with a kind of feral light she felt rather than saw. He wore a thick-striped shirt and a midnight-blue tuxedo of handsome cut. Gleaming shoes, almost like slippers, clasped his feet. He smelled pleasantly of sandalwood and sweat. A faint halo of cigar smoke hovered above his curly-haired head.

Their affair had started that night, she supposed, though she hadn't allowed him to take her to bed, as he'd desired. She wanted him—his elegance, sophistication, charm, not to mention his fiercely handsome face with its enticing hint of cruelty, all drew her like a moth to a flame. But she was also a little afraid of him, afraid that she couldn't handle him, that his energy would simply absorb her and that lying next to him she would cease to exist. Despite these fears—possibly because of them—within a day of their first meeting she had succumbed to him.

Their affair, torrid and breathless, lasted a little more than three months—a record, it turned out, for him. During that time she gave herself to him wholly, gave herself over to her own lust for perhaps the first time in her life, and there came a time—how quickly it had arrived chilled her—when she knew she'd do anything for him.

Anything, yes. But everything?

The day he broke it off, her period was already a week late. She cried for three days straight. Still, her blood didn't flow. Finally, she dragged herself to a pharmacy and, in the desolation of her hotel room, took the test. Then she went out, bought another and took it again. She couldn't believe it—she was pregnant.

In utter despair, she went to him, foolishly, hysterically—how on earth could she be expected to think clearly?—and told him, hoping against hope that he would be overjoyed, that he would take her back, that he would propose a future together. Instead, he hit her, backhanded her casually, cruelly, and told her to get it taken care of.

"What a mess you've made of things," he'd said. His voice did not drip with contempt; that would have implied emotion was involved. Much worse for her, it was cold and detached. "Haven't you ever heard of the pill? Too young, too stupid, I should've known." He shook his head, clearly disgusted by her hysterical sobbing. He bent down, hauled her to her feet. "I know a place, I'll take you there." His hand had gripped her jaw, made her look at him. "You're lucky, you know that? If anyone else inside the Order knew about this you'd be out on your ass, no excuses tolerated. Don't worry now. I'll take care of it and it'll be as if it never happened. Come on now, don't even think about it, don't be stupid again."

And so she hadn't thought about it again, until much, much later, until it was all over and there was nothing inside her but an empty place she was certain would never be filled. It wasn't until nearly six months later, on the island of Rhodes, awakened by the coming of dawn, the arrival of danger, that she understood what Ronnie Kavanaugh had done to her. Of course he wanted her to say nothing, get the "problem" fixed and they all would live happily ever after. It wasn't her career he was concerned about, it was his own. If word got out that he got a Guardian pregnant it would be bye-bye Kavanaugh, and that he would not have.

Why hadn't she gone to her father, why hadn't she sought his help? Because he had been helping her all her life: she was an adult now, and if she was in trouble it was up to her to battle her way through it.

She'd tried, she'd tried, but. . . .

CAMILLE, feeling Jenny's heart lurch against her own, held her tighter, murmuring in her ear. She felt the unfamiliar burn of tears against her eyelids, but they were for herself, not for Jenny. On the scrim of her mind, she saw the sprawled body of Anthony Rule, with an altogether unfamiliar blank expression, as if he were a wax model from Madame Tussaud's, some simulacrum that had been mistaken for Rule.

She summoned the specter of her own abandonment, and with some effort tears came to her eyes, rolled slowly down her cheeks for Jenny to see and to misinterpret. Wasn't it possible that she was the least little bit empathetic to the pain and misery of Jenny's abandonment? After all, she herself had been thrown away like an old rag after expending years to the mental care and feeding of the Knights of St. Clement. She had guided them from behind the scenes, using her breasts and her thighs, her lips and her fingers, busy pillow talk that translated into political know-how. But the moment she tried to step out of the shadows, the moment she had reached for the power itself, she had been rebuffed by the very same senior men who had absorbed her ideas in the dead of night and implemented them as the sun rose high in the sky. She had made them stronger, more powerful, extending their reach into the heart of the Gnostic Observatines—a place they themselves had failed to breach. Still, they had rejected her bid to lead them, without, she felt certain, even much of a debate. A knee-jerk reaction was more like it. And so she had crept back into the shadows, licking her wounds, had settled for manipulating them into elevating her son into the position meant for herself. Another pyrrhic victory, leaving a bittersweet taste in her mouth.

But no, that abandonment was nothing to the one she had felt when Dexter had left her. Her fall from Eden, the destruction of dreams, the end of all things. As for Anthony, he was gone from her bed, from between her warm thighs, from her web, but she had to admit that the thrill his lovemaking brought her was due not to his own skills but to the hot gush of revenge she enjoyed against not only the Order but Dexter each time he thrust into her and let go. Anthony was the mailed fist she wielded against the Gnostic Observatines. Anthony had belonged to her, only her. Even Jordan, who knew of Anthony's existence, had not known his identity. How well she had deceived Anthony—deceived everyone, including her own son. But then deceit was what she lived for. . . .

All at once, she felt Jenny's arms around her, the vibrant twanging of her nerves. Misery and pain, Camille's meat, the psychological state off which she feasted. Yes, Anthony was gone, but she wasn't alone. She had Jenny to gull and manipulate.

"It's all right, it's all right," she whispered. "I'm here now."

She rose, the weight of her new instrument against her.

"Jenny, what happened?"

With muscular aplomb she hustled Jenny out of the Church of San Georgio dei Greci, out into a muddled late afternoon glaze and the frenzied fanfare of approaching sirens. The police launches began arriving. She and Jenny needed to be gone before the operatives of society began swarming. "Michael Berio called me, frantic." Michael Berio was the alias Damon Cornadoro had used with Jenny and Bravo. "When you gave him the slip outside your hotel. Good thing, too. If he'd called Jordan, my son would have sacked him without another word."

She hurried with Jenny to a small café, where she ordered them double espressos and pastries layered with chocolate, to give them a quick energy boost.

When Jenny returned from cleaning herself up in the ladies' room, Camille took her hands, cold as ice. "Now tell me," she said softly. "I know today has been monstrous, a terrible ordeal. Just do the best you can."

Jenny told her what had happened—how she'd been framed for the murder of Father Mosto, how Bravo had been captured, how he believed her to be a traitor working with her mentor Paolo Zorzi, how she'd learned that Anthony Rule was, in fact, the traitor.

When she came to the part about Bravo not believing any of it, Camille said, "Of course he doesn't. Rule was like an uncle to him. Rule partially raised him."

The espressos and pastries arrived, and for a while the two were silent. The cups were painted porcelain, the plates chased silver. Inside, rosy-cheeked angels romped across billows of pink clouds. People came and went, voices were raised in laughter or in brief quarrels. On the far side of the canal, they could see the flash of the police launch and the dark shapes of uniforms, blocking out the fiery sun that slowly sank through the western sky. There was an efficiency about their movements, as if each was a cog in a machine. The thought lightened Camille's heart. She had been quits with society for years, but it was always pleasant to have her decision reaffirmed.

Seeing Jenny push aside her uneaten pastry, she said, "What's the matter, don't you like the sweet?"

"It's fine, I'm just not hungry."

"But you must eat." Camille took up Jenny's fork, handed it to her. "You must keep up your strength, we have a long road ahead of us."

Jenny's head came up. "What do you mean?"

"I mean we—the two of us—will go after Bravo."

Jenny's expression was bleak. "He said he'd kill me if he saw me again."

"You let me take care of Bravo, darling."

Jenny shook her head. "Camille, I'm so grateful for your help. This trip has turned into a nightmare."

"I understand, your friend—"

"No, you don't understand. I was assigned to protect Bravo, and now I've failed."

"Assigned? By whom?"

Jenny bit her lip. All her training cautioned her to keep her mouth shut. But under these circumstances, cut off from everyone and everything that had been her support system, she saw Camille as her only chance to redeem herself, to succeed in the vital mission Dex had assigned her, to stay close enough to Bravo to keep him safe from those who would kill him. In halting sentences, she told Camille a basic outline of the Order, and of their mortal enemies, the Knights of St. Clement.

"I knew there was more to this than Bravo was willing to tell me." Camille briefly gripped Jenny's hand. "I'm grateful you've confided in me, darling. Now I'll have a better idea of how to proceed."

How well she deceived Jenny, she mused, just as she had deceived Dexter—at least as well as she had deceived Anthony Rule. It was simply that Dexter had proved the tougher man to crack—too tough for her. He had melted, but only for a little while. She'd had hopes—real hopes—that the plan she had conceived would work, that she would seduce Dexter from his marital bed and from the Order, that he would divorce them both, Stefana and the Gnostic Observatines, that he would marry her, that he would turn over the cache of secrets. And she had come within a hairsbreadth of keeping him. Only the untimely death of his younger son, Junior, had turned him back to his wife and his two remaining children. If not for a crack in the ice, Dexter Shaw would have been hers.

"I see what I've done," he'd told her three months after Junior's death.

They lounged on a bench in Parc Monceau, amid the expensive landscaping that would soon turn lush. He had bought her chocolates, as if they were sweethearts, young as she felt in her mind. Spring was coming, she recalled, the cherry blossoms in first pale pink blush. But not for long; in a matter of days they, like Dexter, would be gone.

"Anthony took me hunting in Norway." His voice contained an odd note, she remembered, as if strained. "One day we came across the track of a wolverine—very damn rare creature. We tracked him all day in the snow, I couldn't let him go, I was half-crazed with the need to find him. But was it to kill him? No.

"I saw him, and in the same instant he saw me, and we recognized each other. And it was as if someone had held up a mirror to my face, I knew that an intimate connection existed between us. I knew that we were both dangerous, both capable of rending flesh, of inflicting enormous pain, and I knew that this was what would happen if we went on, Camille."

"What about me?" she'd cried. Now she knew, she'd heard it coming—that strained note in his voice—but she hadn't wanted to acknowledge it. She hadn't wanted to entertain the notion of failure. "What about the plans we've made together? The life—what about Jordan?"

"It was a risk, Camille. You knew it and I knew it."

When she had begged him to reconsider, he had landed his most stinging blow: "You're dangerous to me, like poison. Stay away from me, Camille. I mean it."

In retrospect, she recognized the studied coolness, with each word spoken the intimacy draining out of him like sand through an hourglass. With the confidence offered, he was already distancing himself from her. It was an old trick, one she'd used many times, and so later she cursed herself for letting him blindside her, because he was the one, the one for whom she might have given up everything—abandoned the Knights, her ambition, all that had sustained her. For him, and only him, would she have deviated from her meticulously designed plan. *Only for you, Dexter. . . .*

She had told Jordan how Dexter had cruelly abandoned her as soon as he was old enough to understand. She had him trained, sometimes by her own iron hand, and together they had schemed. Unsurprisingly, he was a clever boy—more clever, by far, than any of his classmates. He had outshone them like the sun outshines the moon.

After Dexter left it was Anthony Rule who became the object of her rage. If only Rule hadn't taken Dexter hunting, if only Dexter hadn't seen the wolverine. . . . All she wanted was to turn back time, to return to the moment before the ice cracked, before Junior dropped through and never reappeared.

And so with her mind fixed, Anthony Rule became her next target, and what a sweet prize he turned out to be! She'd had to go slowly—so slowly, in fact, that more than once Jordan lost patience with her. But then Jordan was always impatient. Where did that trait come from? she wondered. Surely not from her and not from his father, either.

Camille once again turned her formidable attention on Jenny.

"Don't worry now. We'll be like the angels," she said, "watching out for him and guarding him from harm."

On the other side of the canal the police launch had begun to move off, the investigators had finished their business. The tiny café had become more crowded. It was very hot. Twilight had come to Venice.

IT wasn't by chance that Bravo found Father Damaskinos; he saw the priest flee the church, as if having seen a ghost. Bravo couldn't blame him. There was a bloodbath on the checkered marble floor of his house of God. And it had been the priest who had given the gun to Anthony Rule.

Bravo stalked him as he would a petty criminal—a pickpocket or sneak thief. With his mind rattled by shock and grief, it was all he could think of to do. Much like a wounded animal, he was running on pure instinct. His higher functions, torn apart by what they had witnessed— Jenny's unimaginable betrayal, the life spurting out of Uncle Tony, the light going out of his eyes, the power and the solace he represented dimmed to ash—now ceded control of his movements and thoughts. Terror, disbelief, rage, revenge all bowed down before the necessity for survival.

Keeping the hurrying figure of Father Damaskinos in sight, he staggered through a small *campo*, where a clutch of old men leaned against the ancient stone wellhead in the center, a monstrous Cyclopean eye clouded by their cigarette smoke; over a severely arched bridge, reflections moving in mysterious and vaguely ominous ripples across the surface of the canal; down a narrow, crooked alley through which wafted unseen voices, a brief twist of an aria, an abrupt, harsh laugh, the gods of Venice commenting on his plight.

As he proceeded, he clutched Lorenzo Fornarini's dagger in a death grip. He felt marooned on an ocean from which there was no sight of land in any direction. A blind man in the Voire Dei, he had only this dagger and his father's last coded message to guide him, all else was deceit and lies, questions he couldn't answer.

He needed to leave Venice as quickly as possible, this was an imperative that stuck in his mind like a declaration of war. And he needed to take Lorenzo Fornarini's dagger with him. He had an idea, but he required the services of Father Damaskinos.

The hiding place Father Damaskinos chose was the Scuola San Nicolò. Founded at the end of the fifteenth century to protect the rights of the Greek community in Venice, it had latterly become a museum. Bravo followed the priest inside and was immediately surrounded by hundreds of religious icons, displayed on the walls in tiers and in glass cases.

Father Damaskinos was standing in front of a vitrine housing the icon of a twelfth-century saint. The gold-leaf halo shimmered above a long, heavily bearded face. Father Damaskinos's hands rose and clasped at his breastbone, and his bloodless lips moved in silent prayer so that, save for the halo, there was little to differentiate between the priest and the saint.

Bravo moved silently toward him. At this hour there was virtually no one else in the museum. Watery light filtered in through windows high up in the walls, casting cubes of pallid light, waking the icons from their long slumber.

Though Bravo spoke the priest's name under his breath, Father Damaskinos started as if pinpricked. He whirled, his eyes showing whites all around. He was clearly terrified.

"Bravo," he said, "you're alive, God be praised! I was so afraid—I didn't see—"

"It was a fiasco, Father. A complete disaster. Uncle Tony was killed, shot to death by . . ." He shook his head. His chest hurt as if it had been he, not Uncle Tony, who'd been shot. He wanted to scream until his throat bled. "Traitors. I've got to get away from the traitors."

"Yes, I understand." But Father Damaskinos seemed preoccupied, and he looked furtively around, as if at any moment he expected someone to burst through the museum doors. He had a pale, hunted look.

"But I must take Lorenzo Fornarini's dagger with me," Bravo went on quickly. He had his own terrors to deal with. "Father, I can do that if you write a letter affirming it as a religious antiquity being repatriated to Turkey."

"That is where you're going?"

"Yes, to Trabzon."

The priest nodded, but in a vague, preoccupied way that caused Bravo to speak his name once again.

The priest started, staring at Bravo as if he were an apparition.

"Father, what is it?"

Father Damaskinos's eyes snapped into focus. "Yes, yes, I will do as you ask, of course. But—"

Bravo looked at him enquiringly. "Yes, Father?"

For a moment, something dark appeared to pass before the priest's eyes, then like a cloud it was gone. "Nothing."

"Father, you did the right thing."

"What?" The one word escaped his lips like a gasp. It seemed his terror had tightened another notch.

"The gun, Father. Giving the gun to Uncle Tony."

"I don't know. God will forgive me, but I don't know. . . ." Father Damaskinos put his hand on Bravo's shoulder and with an effort pulled himself together. "Just be careful, my son. Be very careful. You're up against . . . the most dangerous opponent."

Bravo's brow furrowed and he shook his head.

Father Damaskinos wiped his lips free of the spittle that had formed there. "It's the devil, you see," he said with a soft exhalation of sour breath. "The devil has entered the field of battle."

23

AT THE TRABZON AIRPORT, WHERE BRAVO STOOD WAITING
for the suitcase into which he'd packed the dagger, the air was filled with
a blinding hail of Turkish and Arabic, falling on his ears like soft hammer blows, like someone chopping cabbage, like the ten million grains
of a sandstorm. He eavesdropped on nearby conversations, attuning his
ear to the harsh, rapid-fire music of the East. He hadn't heard Turkish
spoken in some time, and as he thought of answers to questions posed
by the men, women and children crowding around him at the baggage
carousel, he spoke them in Turkish and Arabic under his breath.

He snatched his bag off the carousel and took it into a stall in the men's
room. After assuring himself that the dagger lay undisturbed just as he
had packed it, he washed his face and hands. Looking up into the stained
mirror, he wondered who was staring back at him. A death's-head, it
appeared, as haunted-looking as Father Damaskinos in the Scuola San
Nicolò. He turned away, a bit frightened by what had happened to him,
what he was becoming.

Back in the crowded, echoing terminal, he took a long, lingering look
around with what he felt was a throughly justified knife-edge of paranoia. No one appeared to be paying him the slightest attention. With his
bag clutched in one hand, he went out into the humid night.

He took a wheezing, skeletal taxi into the city, which was built on a
steeply sloped shelf of rock that rose from the scimitar harbor front up
into the foothills of the hazy blue and ocher mountains that for centuries had acted as a miraculous natural barrier against a landward invasion. As Trebizond, the city had been tucked securely behind thick
walls, modeled after those that protected Constantinople.

Looking upward into the dark heart of the lamp-lit mountains, Bravo could feel the shape, the weight of Trabzon's history. When Constantinople fell to European armies in 1204 as a result of the Fourth Crusade, three smaller Greek empires emerged from the wreckage: Nicaea, Epirus, and Trebizond. Alexius I, a grandson of the Byzantine emperor Andronicus I Comnenos, made Trebizond the seat of the grandest and richest of the three. What the Comneni emperors understood the moment they and their army landed at Trebizond was the city's almost magical location. Situated at the beginning of the road that connects the southern Black Sea coast to Iran, as well as sitting at the gateway to the Zigana Pass through Erzurum and thence into the interior of Anatolia, its strategic importance could not be overstated. Thus the Comneni became the architects of Trebizond as a major East-West trading nexus, where Christianity met—and, during the fourteenth and fifteenth centuries, famously clashed with—Islam, for Trebizond was intensely coveted by the Greeks, who developed "the Fortunate City," the Latins, who traded through it, and the Ottomans, who considered it stolen from under their noses.

Through the cleft in the dark mountains he imagined the long, jangling train of tawny-gray camels snaking into the city through the narrow, well-defended valley of the Pyxitis, bringing untold riches to the anxiously waiting merchants and entrepreneurs of Venice, Florence, Genoa, as well as the Vatican, for in its day Trebizond had been home to many a warrior-priest.

The rattletrap taxi dropped him at the Zorlu Harbor Hotel, where he had booked a room overlooking the placid Black Sea. The night itself was inky with low-hanging clouds, starless, moonless. The unseen cries in Turkish and Arabic mingled with the desperate barking of the lean street dogs. Outside his window, boats slid past as if across a theater stage. He unlocked the glass door and went out onto the balcony, stood at the edge, inhaled the exotic scents of sumac and myrrh, turmeric and mint, absorbed the strange cacophony of the city. From an open doorway of a seaside club, the trill of Turkish music, the authoritative strum of oud and balzouki. The staccato bass of diesel trucks, the hyperventilating percussion of the motor scooters. Then could be heard the alto and tenor voices. In the ululations, the rise-and-fall toccata of the languages, he could hear hints of Venetian arias, Byzantine twists brought westward across the watery divide by caliphs and sultans, terrifying Seljuks and

Mamalukes. He heard what might have been a call to prayer and lifted his head. The black leviathan of an oil tanker was lumbering west. Across the sea lay Ukraine, a country more foreign even than this one.

He ate a meal of *dorade* grilled with olive oil and mint beneath a shower of charred oregano. He turned the white flesh inside out, away from the translucent infrastructure of the skeleton, a grid of mathematical ingenuity. Wouldn't it be marvelous, he thought, to create a cipher based on such an organic grid.

He slept then, though he hadn't meant to, sprawled diagonally on the bedspread, his rumpled clothes still on, the remnants of dinner piled on the white linen-covered cart.

In his sleep, he dreamed, and in his dream his father came to him once again. His father in his bath, the water rushing in, the steam rising, Dexter's head thrown back, his wet hair slicked away from his broad forehead. His father at his ease, but not vulnerable, never vulnerable.

He had shaved once while his father was in his bath.

"I suppose you've read all the news dispatches from Somalia," Dexter had said in a matter-of-fact tone.

"Yes." He knew that his father was referring to the deaths of American marines and the subsequent alleged massacre of Somali civilians that so incensed certain members of the United Nations and which the American administration vehemently denied.

"That's where I've just come back from, Bravo. Angola. Do you want to hear the truth?"

"The *New York Times* isn't reporting the truth?"

"They're reporting *a* truth," Dexter said, "just like *Time* and CNN and Reuters and everyone else."

Bravo had put down his razor. "How many truths can there be?"

"If one person believes a story, it becomes a truth—for him. That's why history is such a mare's nest: it's difficult to determine what happened as opposed to what people *thought* happened, *wanted* to happen, felt *should* have happened. The slant is everything, Bravo. The spin. Remember that."

Bravo watched whisker-laden suds swirl down the drain. "What happened in Somalia, Dad?"

"We got our butts kicked, that's what happened. The generals made a terrible miscalculation. Hubris, Bravo. It happened to the Romans and it happened to us. We thought of ourselves as unbeatable, we thought of the Somalis as a lower form of soldier. Then they tail-whipped us and because the secretary of defense got pissed off we went in and slaughtered—thousands—indiscriminately. Their crime was that they were Somalis, and we made sure they died for that crime."

"So Ambassador Perry was lying when he denied—"

"Perry was being the loyal mouthpiece for the administration. He told the truth just as it was written out for him by the president's policy wonks."

He had turned to his father. "You're sure about this?"

Dexter gestured with a soapy arm. "Look for yourself."

He saw a black folder sitting on the closed toilet seat and, drying his hands, opened it. Inside lay six photographs—aerial shots, taken from aircraft, of bodies, mounds of dead bodies, Somali bodies, not only soldiers but civilians. There was something sickening in the godlike view, the detachment from the human catastrophe. He found his hands shaking.

"You're the last person who'll ever see those," Dexter said. "In ten minutes I'll burn them to ash."

He had looked up, into his father's eyes. "Why did you show me these?"

Dexter sat up, the water purling off his shoulders and chest. "Because I want you to know the truth, because we live in the land of the blind and I don't ever want you to be blind. I want you to see what's around you, Bravo, even if it's painful, even if it's not what you want to see. Because doing the right thing is not the goal, doing the *best* thing is what you must strive for. If you learn nothing else from me, that will be sufficient. . . ."

Bravo awoke, gasping. Sweat ran down his face. It was morning. Sunlight streamed down onto the haborside, its reflection burnishing the north-facing windows. He threw off his clothes and stood under a cold shower until his flesh was raised in goosebumps, until he shuddered with the chill. It was when he was toweling off that his father's words ran through his head again like an electronic news ticker. Wrapping the towel around him, he padded back into the room and, sitting cross-legged on the bed, allowed the dagger to rest in his hands as if it were a sacrificial blade. He pulled the dagger from its scabbard. How many Saracen hearts had this blade sundered, how many Ottoman bellies had it torn open, how many Knights of St. Clement's ribs had it shattered?

The lamplight spun off the blade as he moved it but also revealed something else. Carefully, he placed the dagger on the coverlet and picked up the scabbard. It was lined with blood-colored velvet, a fabric not used by bladesmiths because the constant abrasion of the weapon being drawn and scabbarded would have soon destroyed the nap. And even if it had been used on this particular piece, the velvet would not have survived the centuries intact.

Scrutinizing the inside of the scabbard, he could see a small edge lifted slightly from the steel. Plucking at it, he found that the velvet lining pulled away easily enough, revealing the leather beneath, worn shiny, dark with oil and, possibly, blood. On the reverse side of the velvet, he found written in his father's hand a name: Adem Khalif, along with a phone number. Just below appeared two words, one above the other:

VINE

PURPURE

THERE was an *altane,* a roof terrace, outside Father Damaskinos's apartment. Nowadays *altane* tended to be used to dry washing, but in the past women would sit out on the terrace in a wide-brimmed hat. Though the brim kept their skin youthful and pale, the hat was crownless, exposing their hair to the sun, hair that had been soaked in a solution that helped the sunlight bleach it blond.

The apartment was a haven for the priest, a place high up—the third floor was high in Venetian terms—away from the constant consumerism of a city obsessed with consumerism. Father Damaskinos was especially relieved to be home after this nightmare day. He had eaten nothing since noon, but found he had no appetite for either food or drink—in his mouth was the salty-copper tang of human blood, imagined, to be sure, but no less terrifying for that.

It was the *altane* he was thinking of on this hot, humid night, and the moment he closed the door of his apartment behind him, he crossed the Byzantine carpet and threw open the window beyond which the terrace beckoned. As he did so, he noticed a shadow, large and blocky. He craned his neck to see what it might be and the shadow moved, startling him. All at once the shadow resolved itself into a human figure, a large man who grabbed him with two powerful fists and shook him until his teeth rattled.

He looked into a pair of eyes the color of the lagoon at night, a distinctive face, part of a long bloodline to those students of Venetian history.

"Cornadoro," he breathed, "what are you doing here?"

"Let's step into your parlor, Father." With an enormous bunching of muscles, Damon Cornadoro threw the priest back through the open window. With a lightness belied by his size, Cornadoro stepped onto the Byzantine carpet and hauled Father Damaskinos to his feet.

"Answers, Father," he said. "I require answers."

"To what?" The priest shook his head. "What could I possibly tell you?"

"The whereabouts of Braverman Shaw."

Father Damaskinos's eyes showed white all around and his nostrils flared as if he had scented the approach of his own death. Nevertheless, he said, "I have no idea—"

The last word was snatched from his throat, ending in a high-pitched sound not unlike that of a stuck pig.

"You scream just like a girl, you know that, Father?" Cornadoro's breath was thick with bile and liquor. He made a sudden grab. "You aren't a female under all those robes, are you, Father? Oh, yeah, I've heard all the stories." Cornadoro frowned, as if disappointed. "But, no, there's no need to look further, is there, Father, though of what use a cock is to you I can't imagine."

With a violent tug, he drew Father Damaskinos off his feet. "Now where is Braverman Shaw?" His eyes, pits of darkness, seemed merciless. "I won't ask again."

"I . . . I don't know."

Cornadoro kissed the priest on his hairy cheek. "Ah, Father, now you've made me happy."

He shoved Father Damaskinos into a chair, took a candle from the marble mantelpiece, lit it. He brought the flame close to Father Damaskinos's face.

"Father, I'll tell you something about me. I'm an old-fashioned man. Not for me the modern innovations of torture. I like the tried and true." With that, he grabbed the priest's hair, at once pinning him to the chair and pulling his head back. "Now in five seconds I'm going to set your beard on fire. You have until then, not a moment more." He jerked on the curling hair, making the priest's eyes tear. "Do not mistake me, Father. You will not get a second chance, I will fucking burn you alive."

"No," Father Damaskinos stammered.

"Five, four . . ."

"You wouldn't." In his terror, he had reverted to his native Greek.

"Three, two . . ."

"This cannot be happening. I refuse to believe—"

"One, zero."

Cornadoro brought the tip of the candle flame in contact with the edge of Father Damaskinos's beard. At once, the hair caught fire and, screaming, the priest arched up off the chair. Cornadoro kneed him in the solar plexus. The air began to stink.

"Stop! All right! Stop!" Father Damaskinos managed to get out. "He went to Trabzon! Trabzon, Turkey!"

"Too late." The wicked blade of a push-dagger protruded from between the curled second and third fingers of Cornadoro's right fist. "I told you you wouldn't get a second chance." And with a terrifying efficiency he slashed the priest's neck from ear to ear.

JORDAN Muhlmann called Osman Spagna the moment he stepped onto the waiting *motoscafo*. Behind him rested the Lusignan et Cie Gulfstream G-550 jet on the tarmac of Marco Polo airport. He had not told his mother he was coming to Venice, and of course, Cornadoro knew nothing of his whereabouts, either. He had people here keeping both of them under surveillance, people he should have used long ago. No matter. He would take care of everything, just as he had promised the Knights of Four, as he thought of them since their intervention on the night of his ascension in Rome.

Spagna said, "I assume you want to do something about the American." Spagna, used to cell phone conversations, would never use a name over the air.

"Indeed, I do."

With a sinister burble of its brawny engine, the *motoscafo* took off, heading for the lagoon.

"I can take care of that."

"Not that way." Jordan knew Spagna's meaning only too well; for a backroom engineer he was a bloodthirsty fellow. "Something better is called for here, an indelible lesson to be learned. I want the American obedient, not dead, otherwise I will simply have a hole to fill that I cannot afford now."

"Understandably," Spagna said.

The clammy night air clung to Jordan like a shroud, making him restless, and he moved to the side of the *motoscafo*. They approached the hotel landing where two of his Knights waited for him. "Let me see, he loves cars."

"What American doesn't?"

Jordan laughed. "Ferraris, isn't it?"

"Quite a passion," Spagna said. "He's got twelve."

"Not for long." Jordan's nose wrinkled as he stepped out onto the landing. *This stench is positively medieval,* he thought. Venice was like death, a rotting corpse someone had forgotten to bury. He shook hands with the Knights, but he couldn't wait to move on. "Personally, I don't care for Ferraris, too damned showy. Arrange something, Osman."

"Immediately." Spagna could not hide the glee in his voice. "He's got two vintage autos that he can never replace."

"Still, if I am any judge of character the loss will only just get his attention. Like all Americans, this one needs to be punched repeatedly in the head before he learns his manners." Jordan, his mind racing ahead, said, "As I remember, he has one child."

"A daughter, nineteen," Spagna confirmed. "And quite beautiful judging by the photo I have here. She is—how do the Americans say it? Ah, yes—the apple of his eye."

"America is a dangerous country, they tell me, the cities so full of violent crime—rapes and beatings, so forth." Jordan stepped away from his Knights, to the end of the landing, lowered his voice. "This is delicate, Osman. I don't want an investigation. A simple robbery, an encounter on a dark street, a working over, followed by an ambulance, a stretcher, hearts in throats, parents in tears, in the end a recovery of sorts, you know what is required."

"Indeed I do, sir."

Jordan put away his phone and went to join his Knights. He was unaccountably eager to get an update on what his mother and Cornadoro were conspiring behind his back. The first word whispered in his ear lifted his spirits considerably.

"I know where Trabzon is," he said. He was thinking of the Knights' attack on the Order's headquarters so many centuries ago, he was thinking about how history does, indeed, come full circle.

THE sky was low, grainy as a sleepless soldier's eye, grayed-over with militant clouds when Bravo left the hotel in his reeking clothes. It was already early afternoon—he had slept almost twelve hours straight. He went first to Ataturk Alani, the enormous central square of the city, heading due west from there down a street lined with clubs and clothing stores. It was an altogether ugly place, monstrous slab-sided buildings hulking like defeated wrestlers too dazed to get up off the mat. It could be said that Trabzon was a city of contrasts, but in a way that exploded his luscious visions of local history. The ancient and the modern rubbed shoulders in shabby splendor, but, unlike in Venice, the concrete imperative of the present relegated the splendid, blood-soaked past to the rusting alleyway trash bin.

Entering a shop with up-to-date clothes in the window, he bought himself an entire new outfit into which he changed before leaving the shop. His old clothes he relegated to a dust bin outside. Soon after, he made his way to Ortahisar, the Middle Fortress, the old section of Trabzon. Twice as he wended his way through the bazaar, he thought he was being followed, but one would-be pursuer turned out to be a Russian merchant eager to sell him a set of hand-painted nesting dolls, the other a boy on a bicycle who had nothing more on his mind than racing from point A to point B in the fastest possible time. Still, he could not help being reminded of the attack outside the walls of St. Malo from which Uncle Tony had saved him and Jenny. At the thought of Uncle Tony his eyes started to smart, and he wiped away tears of pain and longing.

When he had spoken to Adem Khalif on the phone, his father's contact had reported being out of the city. Khalif had suggested meeting for drinks and dinner at a café on the hill. Bravo crossed one of the two bridges that linked the oldest part of the city to the modern concrete one. The bridges spanned twin ravines, carved out of the bedrock long ago by the furiously gushing rivers—one of which, the Degirmen, was the last clue Dexter had left for Bravo in Venice.

The café was perched on a hill, as old and crumbling as its wooden neighbors. Adem Khalif was seated at a table in front and, spotting Bravo, he rose, lifting a brown arm in greeting. Khalif was a broad-backed man with huge shoulders and upper arms. His was not a handsome face, but it was powerful. He was dressed neatly in slacks and a polo shirt. Clearly, he was no priest.

Burly fishermen and slit-eyed oil company executives were their companions, smoking harsh Turkish cigarettes and eyeing a trio of exhausted looking "Natashas," ex-Soviet prostitutes, all rancid smiles and high, pointed breasts, fueling up for their nightly chores with strong coffee, *ekmek*—sourdough bread—local butter, and the ubiquitous black olives known as *zeytin*.

"So you are Braverman Shaw, your father talked about you constantly." Adem Khalif spoke perfect English, though with a slight British accent. When Bravo said he'd prefer they speak in Turkish, Khalif was overjoyed. His smile was lopsided and wide, bristling with the glitter of gold teeth.

They sat at a small round table of rough mosaic, near a wrought-iron railing. The rain, forecast by the angry clouds, arrived like a drunken guest, drenching the margin of the terrace beyond the protection of the faded striped awning. It was, if possible, more oppressive here than in Venice.

"Gloomy weather," Bravo said as he sat down opposite Khalif.

"This is summer on the Black Sea." Khalif shrugged. "One gets used to anything." He poured from a bottle of raki and they clicked their glasses together. Khalif watched Bravo as he drank the fiery liquor.

"No smoke coming out of your mouth, good, good," he said as he refilled Bravo's glass. He had an outsized presence, seeming to fill the café with light, with life. "You know, for me, it is always of great interest to meet Americans. America reduces other cultures to a state of transparency. In its place, it exports many things of bright colors: Britney Spears, Bruce Willis, anorexia, Fords bigger than Cadillacs, Hummers bigger than Fords. America has become a country of extremes, and so it engenders extreme responses. The rest of the world wants to either run under America's skirt or chop off its head."

"Which camp are you in?" Bravo asked.

Adem Khalif laughed. "Do you mind if I smoke?"

"Not at all."

"Well, that is a relief." He took some moments lighting up a Silk Cut. "These British brands, very difficult to obtain here. I go to a lot of trouble for my habit." He shrugged. "But then who doesn't, yes?"

Another bottle of raki appeared. When they were alone again, he hunched forward, his voice lower and somehow conspiratorial. "I am not a member of the Order. I was a conduit for Dexter Shaw—a resource for both practical knowledge and spycraft. I was, in a word, Dexter's eyes and ears on this part of the world." He took a bit of tobacco off his ruddy lower lip with the tips of thumb and little finger. "This is in answer to your question about which camp I am in, you see?"

Bravo said that he did.

"But now let me ask you whether you think it's wise for America to raise such extreme responses."

"I don't, no, particularly so because despite their power the extremists in America are a tiny minority."

"But like all extremists everywhere, what havoc they can cause, yes?"

"Absolutely." Bravo took more raki. "What was my father interested in out here?"

Khalif smiled. "The current state of mind of the Muslim fundamentalists, the extremists, as well as their movements. I was monitoring both for him."

"Do you know why?" Bravo asked.

"I never asked," Khalif said. "This is not something someone in my line of work would do."

"Would you hazard a guess?"

"It is coming on time for dinner, shall we order?"

Bravo asked Khalif to choose, which made Khalif happier still.

"You will love the food here," he said, "everything sparkles fresh from the sea." When the waiter had gone, he topped off their glasses. His gold teeth glittered. He looked like he should have a pegleg and a wicked cutlass between his teeth. "Guesses are inherently dangerous. Having said that, I will tell you what I believe was your father's concern.

"It had to do with America, and with Islam—with the fundamentalist religious elements who are diametrically opposed to one another, who want nothing less than to see each other wiped from the face of the earth." He looked around suddenly. "This place, this Trabzon, it doesn't look like much now, but the importance it once held for both East and West, for Christian and Muslim, is incalculable. It was the center of trade, and trade breeds wealth, wealth breeds warfare, just like religion. Here, still, in this slum, East and West mingle, trying to get the better of one another. Your father, I believe, saw the coming of the new religious war, the last Crusade, if you will, and he wanted very much to do everything in his power to stave it off."

"So that was why he wanted to be *Magister Regens*."

"Through the power of the Order, judicious use of its cache of secrets—oh, yes, I know of the cache's existence, though little, I'm afraid, of its contents. There is great power there, and influence, this much I do know. But it would take a special man, indeed, to take control of the Haute Cour, to be elected *Magister Regens*."

"There was also the matter of the traitor hidden in the midst of the Haute Cour. I imagine he would have worked dutifully to frustrate my father's plans."

"I would think he made circumstances more difficult for Dexter, yes."

"I found him," Bravo said. "In Venice. Paolo Zorzi."

"Zorzi! But this is incredible news." Khalif shook his head sadly. "I know Zorzi, and liked him, as did your father. I thought him intensely loyal."

"Then he did his job well," Bravo said.

"Did?"

"He's dead. Uncle Tony—Anthony Rule—shot him before he himself was killed by a second traitor, one of Zorzi's Guardians named Jenny Logan."

"My God, the tragedy is doubled and redoubled." Khalif rubbed his chin. "Heartfelt condolences, my Bravo, what a terrible series of shocks you've had." He lifted his glass. "A drink to departed friends."

They clinked glasses and drank deeply of the strong, harsh raki.

"And the inferno to our enemies, eh?" Khalif cried.

The glasses clinked again and this time they drained them dry.

The food came then, a veritable feast, seven plates or more, and they fell to consuming it. The steady rain had morphed into a fine drizzle that kept the concrete and roof tiles dark and gleaming. Lights had come on, steaming in the wetness. Illumination harsh as the local tobacco threw into prominence the bow-backed workers trudging across the bridges that spanned the ravines. The Natashas were long gone, presumably now hard at work seducing what tourists had wandered, halfstupefied, into their territory. An eerie hissing rose from the pavement, as if the drizzle were tiny pellets of ice. The low sky was the color of a deep and painful bruise.

Bravo was lost in thought. At length, he said, "I never realized how difficult my father's life was. He was battling the Knights and members of his own Order."

Adem Khalif nodded. "Your father had vision, this is undeniable. In this he reminded me of Fra Leoni, the last *Magister Regens* of the Order, but he lacked a certain—how shall I put this—a certain ruthlessness. I don't mean to give offense, I loved Dexter as if he were my brother, but his expertise lay in other areas. His genius lay in planning for the future. He wasn't the warrior required of a *Magister Regens.* What was required was digging deep into the lower echelons of the Order, that's where his support would have come from." Khalif's eyes twinkled. "It's a lesson his successor should learn."

Bravo put down his fork. "You mean me."

Khalif spread his hands. "Who else? You are Dexter's son, he chose you from an early age to follow in his footsteps."

"I've heard this before."

"Of course by now you have, but have you ever asked yourself why he chose you? It wasn't because you were his son, that wasn't Dexter's way. The Order was too important to him, it was his life. He chose you, Bravo, because he *knew.* He saw your future, just as, I firmly believe, he saw his own death. It is the passing of things, from father to son, the building of a legacy, do you see? This I know." He thumped his chest with his fist. "I feel it here."

"If my father had this so-called second sight, why didn't he know the identity of the traitor inside the Order?"

Khalif cocked his head to one side. "I hear your skepticism, Bravo, and I grieve at your lack of faith. Do you think second sight is like a flashlight that can be turned on and off at will? This adolescent idea is from the comics. Your father wasn't a superhero. He was gifted with something unknown and unknowable, it cannot be questioned or parsed. The more you try to understand it, the more enigmatic—and improbable—it seems." He shrugged. "But I cannot tell you to have faith, you must find it on your own."

There was silence between them for some time. Khalif went back to shoveling grilled octopus into his mouth. Bravo, his appetite vanished, turned away. Light thrown off by the buildings on either side lit the top of the ravines like a livid scar, but below was the utter darkness of the abyss, as if the ravines were bottomless, a crack clear down to the earth's core. On the bridges, the procession of people continued unabated. He observed a smattering of women now, young, pretty, perhaps more Natashas on a cigarette break. An old man walked beside a small boy, a large, square hand on the boy's narrow shoulder. The boy looked up, asked a question, which caused the old man's face to crease deeply in a smile that made him look twenty years younger.

"I need an answer," Bravo said, turning back. "Is there a building in Trabzon with a spiral staircase?"

Khalif, sucking at his teeth, thought for a moment. "In fact, there is. At the Zigana Mosque. Why do you ask?"

Why? Because *vice,* the first of the words Dexter had written on the velvet scabbard lining, was derived from the French word *vis,* a vine. In medieval times, a vice was a spiral staircase, as in the twisting of a vine's woody tendrils.

"Come, come," Khalif said, "you've stopped eating. It's a sin with such fine food."

The clear note of affection in his voice caused Bravo to turn back to him. "On the matter of faith, ever since I started on this journey, my father has come to me in dreams and at . . . other times. At first, I thought little of it, putting the visions down to a symptom, an aftershock of his violent death, but now I don't know, I feel as if . . . as if in a way he's still with me."

A huge grin spread across Adem Khalif's face. "On the matter of faith, my Bravo, I believe you're on your way to finding yours."

"SECRETS," Camille Muhlmann said. "We all have secrets, God knows I have a fistful of them."

She and Jenny rode in a jouncing taxi on their way into Trabzon from the airport, having caught the evening's last flight out from Venice, via Istanbul. High up, the sky was still indigo, but below the dark undercurrent of the night held sway, pierced here and there by lights, glimmering sickly yellow, as if irradiated.

"I had a lover who treated me badly—very badly." Camille shook her head with a grim and rueful smile. "What woman hasn't? One—at least one. But what I can't make out is *why*—why do we choose these men who will abuse us physically, mentally, emotionally? Is it because we feel we deserve to be punished, Jenny, or is it cultural, passed down from oppressed female to oppressed female? Is it true we can't help but feel the same way our mothers and grandmothers did?"

Jenny shook her head. "I don't think it matters. What's important is that we can change, that we make different decisions, *braver* decisions."

Camille raised her eyebrows. "Really? How do you propose we do that when men stand in our way no matter which way we turn?"

"It might be that we walk away from them, from everything they've built, everything they stand for." Jenny stared out the window for a moment, watching the fast accretion of concrete spreading over the green countryside like a pernicious skin disease. "I used to think that, anyway." Yes, she had, in the aftermath of her disastrous breakup with Ronnie Kavanaugh. In fact, she'd been sure of it. Then she had met Dexter Shaw, and everything in her life had changed. Or had it? Wasn't Dexter another of her male crutches? Arcangela would no doubt pity any woman with such a psychological need.

"But now, obviously you don't." Camille held up a pack of cigarettes, and Jenny nodded.

As Camille lit up, she said, "I would very much like to know what happened. Will you tell me?"

Jenny took the cigarette from between Camille's lips, took a long drag, let the smoke out slowly, then handed the cigarette back. "I discovered that the way to change things is to do all the things men do, only better."

"Beat them at their own game."

"In a way," Jenny said, "but only in a way. Their game is the only game, that's the hard thing to get set in your head because it's just not the way you want it to be. Then you have to learn to skin the cat another way."

"Pardon?"

Jenny smiled. "Sorry. 'There's more than one way to skin a cat.' In American slang the saying refers to a catfish, which is always skinned before cooking. What it means is that there's more than one way to get the job done."

Camille held out the cigarette and Jenny took another drag before giving it back. "I don't want to ever again be attracted to a man who can abuse me."

"What kind of abuse was it?" Jenny asked, as casually as she could with her heart pounding hard in her chest.

"Psychological," Camille said after a moment. "And I fell right in line with what he wanted. *Mon dieu,* what an obedient little girl I was!"

So was I, Jenny thought.

"It's humiliating to think of the traps we fall into, isn't it?" Camille observed.

"Especially because we fall so willingly, because it's so difficult to get out."

"And even pain isn't enough to extricate us."

"No. Often, it isn't." Jenny turned to Camille. "There was a time I applied to a convent. Can you imagine such a thing? For eight months I studied to take the veil. I was very young, I didn't understand, I had no friends, I was afraid of men, I was sure I didn't fit in."

"But, my dear, it's clear from what you say that you had no calling."

"That's what the Mother Superior said when she called me into her office."

"Lucky for you she was so discerning." Camille shuddered. "What a place to end up!"

"I was devastated," Jenny said. "I saw it as another failure."

Camille smiled. "The failure to understand God is the mark of a clear-eyed pragmatist."

Jenny laughed. She sat in silence for a time while the taxi rattled on and the radio blasted out staticky music that sounded like two people clashing ash can lids together while screaming at the top of their lungs.

"Down deep," Jenny said, "we're all obedient little girls."

She turned to Camille and, as if on cue, they smiled at each other.

WHAT *a perfect idiot you are,* Camille thought through her smile. *And we have our lovely Dexter to thank for that, don't we? He's the one who picked you up like a bad penny and made you shine again after the abortion—but to what end, darling? So you could be my plaything, so you could assist in the last phase of his destruction: the death of his son. And there were those—Anthony included—who were convinced that Dexter had the gift of second sight, that he could see the future.* Her smile widened and a tiny laugh escaped her.

"What's so funny?" Jenny asked.

"I was thinking that we are also bad girls, that we want what we want, that we should have what is due us."

"Yes, Camille, indeed we should."

Camille was quiet again, smoking her cigarette down to the end. The taxi had no windshield wipers but the driver, reclined casually in his seat, seemed not to notice as he peered through the rain-stippled windshield. Camille thought briefly of Damon Cornadoro, who had been seated behind them in the last row of the plane to Trabzon. Jenny had seen him, of course, on her way to the bathroom, and had told Camille on her return that she felt that much safer against the forces of the Knights of St. Clement massed against her. Little did she know that it had been Cornadoro who had obtained news of Bravo's next destination from the late, unlamented Father Damaskinos.

Now she was heading into uncharted territory. The Knights had no one in Trabzon—it was not part of their territory. That was when she had phoned Jordan.

"It's all right," he had assured her. *"Cardinal Canesi and his cabal are using every ounce of influence at their disposal. That means all the priests in the city and its surrounds will be our eyes and ears. I'll download a list of their names and contact numbers to your phone when we're done."*

Crushing out the butt beneath her heel, Camille turned to Jenny and said, "I know you have secrets, as we all do. *Alors,* it's your expertise—and quite possibly your contacts—that will enable us to find Bravo and keep track of him now," she lied. "I've done as much as I can through Lusignan et Cie's resources, but here in Trabzon, I'm frankly blind."

She took Jenny's hands in hers. "In this crisis, we have only each other, we must trust each other or we'll fail Bravo, and we cannot let that happen, *n'est-ce pas?*"

Jenny leaned forward, delivered instructions to the driver that Camille could not hear. A moment later, the taxi swerved to its left. They zipped past the stripped-out carcass of a car, accelerating in a new direction.

KHALIF and Bravo strolled the narrow, twisting streets of the Avrupali Pazari—*European Market* in Turkish—which was actually run by émigrés from the former Soviet republics. Russian or Georgian was spoken here, virtually no Turkish. Bare bulbs, strung from lengths of flex, lit up the colorful wares. There were no T-shirts or baseball hats, none of the commercial souvenirs that had become ubiquitous in Florence or Istanbul, more touristed destinations. Here the wares tended toward native crafts, rugs from all over Turkey, the hills of Afghanistan, even Tabriz, hand-beaten copperware, Russian nesting dolls. Dealers in imported vodka, local antiquities, Asian hashish plied their trade.

"As a student of medieval religions you're no doubt disappointed to see what's become of fabled Trebizond, eh?" Adem Khalif said. "Overrun by ex-Soviet citizens who consider themselves entrepreneurs—they're all chasing capital. It certainly has its amusing side."

"I can see why you got on so well with my father," Bravo said, "he always had a soft spot for philosophers."

Khalif chuckled. "Street philosophers, perhaps."

"I find it interesting that he didn't use you to keep track of the Knights of St. Clement."

"I didn't say that, exactly, but Dexter was keen to have an ear to the ground at all times, because he knew it's not only the elephant that can run you over."

"Meaning?"

"The Order is interesting and, in many important ways, useful, but as an outsider looking in it seems to me that its members are too concerned with the Knights of St. Clement and nothing else. Your father wasn't like that, he always had the big picture in mind. The constantly changing nature of the world—be it politics, economics, religion—was his meat. He moved in a far larger world than any of the others."

It had begun to rain harder again, in glistening silver lines, dots and dashes, like Morse code being broadcast from heaven. They were moving from street to street in a pattern Bravo tried to make sense of, but the labyrinthine twists and turns of the bazaar defeated all his efforts.

"Toward that end, he supplied me with massive amounts of equipment," Khalif went on. "Electronic eyes and ears of the most sensitive and sophisticated nature, so that I could record for him all the coded signals that day and night fly through the ether."

"*All* of them?"

Khalif nodded. "*Massive* amounts—you can't imagine. But he would come and sort all of it out. He knew what he was looking for, of this you can be sure."

"This wasn't official Order business?"

"Your father's alone." Khalif lifted a forefinger. "I'm bringing you to the Order's official representative now, so not a word. If there is any news you should know before you continue, he will have it."

They had reached a carpet shop. A young Georgian girl, no more than seventeen, was standing outside, hawking the wares. She had a slim body and dark eyes. Her thin hair was pulled back in a ponytail.

"Irema."

She kissed Khalif on both cheeks as he introduced Bravo.

"Father is inside," she said in Turkish.

"Is he busy?" Khalif asked.

"Always," she said with a shrug.

They passed through the narrow doorway, into a dim interior throbbing with Arabic dance music and dust. The walls were hung with carpets, which also lay in neat stacks in a checkerboard pattern across the floor, so that one was forced to take a winding path to the rear of the store.

Khalif grinned, flashing his gleaming gold teeth. "His name is Mikhail Kartli. You'll like him, once you get used to him." He put a warning hand on Bravo's arm. "This is a man, no matter his manner, who deserves your respect. He still fights the Azerbaijani and the Chechen terrorists. The Azerbaijan government wants whole areas to be renamed from the Georgian toponyms to the Azerbaijani—same with people's surnames. As for the terrorists, they continue to try moving their bases into Georgia. He spent six years defusing Chechen bombs. You'll see when you shake hands."

It wasn't easy getting within spitting distance of Mikhail Kartli. Cell phone to one ear, he was surrounded by a clutch of merchants, gesticulating like bond traders while calling out softly but urgently under the music, which served to mask their business from outsiders and passersby. As they approached, Bravo recognized not only Georgian but Russian, Turkish, Italian, Arabic being spoken. It didn't take long to realize that these weren't carpet merchants but traders in oil, natural gas, currencies, precious metals, diamonds, as well as arms and all manner of war materiel.

The heady stench of money was in the air, the confluence of sweat and greed, grime and blood, power and deceit. Here beat the heart of modern-day Trabzon, which, despite appearances to the contrary, was still a potent nexus point between East and West, currency and commodities snaking like veins and arteries into the four corners of the world, the flow of capital pumped with the speed of sound irrespective of race, religion or political affiliation.

While they waited, Bravo took a long look at the Georgian. He was as stubby as a pencil end, as tough-looking as a bale of razor wire. He had the wide-apart stance of a street fighter and carried his football-shaped head low in the bulwark of his shoulders, as if from long years of defending himself, his family, his country. His hair was thick, black and wild, fiercely growing low on his forehead. As a consequence, the paleness of his eyes, rimmed by long lashes, were startling.

In the middle of his personal chaos, he saw Adem Khalif and briefly inclined his head. Then his eyes slid toward Bravo, and they opened so minutely anyone else but Bravo himself might have missed the reaction.

Eventually, the music changed and the crowd thinned sufficiently for Khalif to lead Bravo to the Georgian's side, where he introduced them. Kartli held out his right hand, which consisted of thumb and forefinger only. Bravo gripped it, felt the pressure of the healed-over nubs that used to be fingers and thought of this man defusing Chechen bombs, thought of one detonating, taking part of the hand with it.

"Your father was a good man," Mikhail Kartli said laconically in perfect Turkish and, snapping his fingers, called for liquor. He took possession of the bottle, pouring the clear liquid into three water glasses. Bravo did not ask what it was. It was like liquid fire going down, and the afterburn tasted not unpleasantly of anise and caraway.

Kartli excused himself, finishing up the last pieces of his business. Then he turned the cell phone over to a younger version of himself—doubtless his eldest son—and they retired through a shadowed door in the rear.

A narrow, cramped corridor suddenly led out onto a bare poured-concrete terrace. An awning flapped above their heads. Rain pattered down on the crumbling city. Kartli stood spread-legged, a bantam fighter gazing down on the site of many victories. The small merchants with their painted dolls and their charcoal-braised cuttlefish, their burgeoning libraries of pirated DVDs of popular American movies looked up to him much as a small-arms dealer will genuflect before the trader in nuclear weapons.

He unfolded his arms, lit a thin black cigarette with a gold lighter. "This is not a civilized place," he said, seemingly to no one in particular. "To believe so has been the fatal mistake of many over the centuries, especially the Greeks, who came here first to tame Trebizond. The Venetians, as well, though they were more clever than the Greeks, because they were less trusting. But, in the end, Trebizond belonged to the Ottomans, and the Ottomans were not civilized, not at all. Look what they became. Turks! And then, more recently, there were the greedy Russians, speeding across the Black Sea as fast as their boats could ferry them." He shook his head sadly, throwing off the peculiar electricity of currency, as if even now he was manufacturing it somewhere inside his own body.

"Thank you for taking the time to see me," Bravo began.

"The pope is dying," Mikhail Kartli said over Bravo's last several words, "there is scarcely any time left."

"That's why I've come to you. My situation has become increasingly desperate."

Kartli turned to Bravo, the ugly black cigarette between his brilliant red lips. "You see, this is just the kind of situation the Order decided long ago to guard against. Do you think Canesi wants to save the pope's life for humanitarian reasons? Of course not. It's power, and power only. He wants to save his own skin. A new pope, clever and in his prime, surely would not tolerate their power, he'd sweep them aside like so much kindling."

A certain grit lay underfoot, like sand from the desert, like gold dust ready to be swept up and transshipped.

"How up-to-date is your news of the pope's health?"

"What do you take me for? An hour old, not a moment more." Mikhail Kartli's pale eyes bored into Bravo's. "You are in more danger than you can imagine, my friend. Elements have been awakened—new informers, the Vatican's eyes and ears—that I can neither identify nor control."

Kartli suddenly caught sight of the chased scabbard and the hilt of the dagger tucked into Bravo's waistband and his eyes narrowed. "What is this? Surely it cannot be Lorenzo Fornarini's dagger."

"It is." Bravo removed it to show him. "I've been to his sarcophagus in Venice."

"My God, Fornarini's dagger!" Kartli took another deep drag of his cigarette. "Through the priests at Trebizond, Lorenzo Fornarini was introduced to the Order, was converted to their cause, and swore allegiance to protect them, which he did with both courage and discipline, which as you can imagine impressed the fathers no end.

"Some years later, when they were attacked by the Knights of St. Clement, he was present outside the Sumela Monastery, at the last moment intervening to save Fra Leoni from Fra Kent, a traitor from within the Haute Cour. This was when Fra Leoni was the Keeper, before he became *Magister Regens*.

"Fra Leoni was wounded during his fight with Fra Kent. By the time he reached the cache of secrets his wound was festering, there was no doubt that he was dying. By prior arrangement, he was met by Fra Prospero, the Order's *Magister Regens*—in those days, both the Keeper and the *Magister Regens* held keys to the cache. Together, they made a monumental decision: they availed themselves of the secret of Christ's Testament. Following the directions set out by Jesus, the *Magister Regens* anointed Fra Leoni with the Quintessence, the sacred oil that Christ used to resurrect Lazarus and, according to the Testament, others.

"Fra Leoni was not only healed, but he lived another 350 years, eventually ascending to become *Magister Regens* and guiding the Order through dark and difficult times. Some believe that he died, finally, in 1918, during the worldwide influenza epidemic, but of course there are no records and so no way to know for certain."

At that moment, a bit of raucous electronic melody sounded and the Georgian pulled out another cell phone, flipped it open. He listened for a moment, then he said, "Do it. Do it now."

Closing the phone, he said to Bravo, "Someone known to you is approaching. One of my people has spotted Jennifer Logan, the traitor—oh, yes, word spread quickly within the Order. I have ordered her executed. I have someone standing by who will shoot her dead."

24

"NO," BRAVO SAID.

Mikhail Kartli smiled thinly. "You are in my house now."

"But if you kill her you'll never find out if she and Paolo Zorzi are the only ones to have infiltrated the Order. What if there are more? She's our best chance to find out."

The Georgian knew a good argument when he heard it. Flipping open his cell phone, he pressed a speed dial and said into the mouthpiece, "Stand down and deliver her instead."

His grin grew fierce. "I only hope that you have the courage of your convictions. I hope you have the stomach for articulated interrogation. Your father certainly didn't."

"There are other ways," Bravo said.

"Name one." The Georgian said this without an edge of menace, he simply wanted to know.

"The woman is desperate to get me to believe that someone else is the traitor. She wanted me to believe that someone set her up for the murder of Father Mosto in Venice, and I almost believed her, until she shot Anthony Rule dead." He did not mention his very personal hatred of Jenny for seducing both his father and himself. "I can talk to her, I can deal with her. She'll listen to me."

"In that event, I would be exceedingly careful. Have you thought about how she followed you here?"

Bravo stared at the Georgian.

"Did you tell Father Damaskinos you were coming to Trabzon?"

Father Damaskinos had asked him where he was going next, and Bravo had told him.

"Yes, of course you did," Kartli said, answering his own question. "She must have been the one who interrogated him and murdered him."

"Father Damaskinos is dead?"

"One of our people found him in his apartment last night and contacted me immediately." The Georgian spat again, more heavily this time, as if it was an uttered curse. "His face was burned, then his throat was slashed in a very particular manner."

"What do you mean?"

"It was made with a push-dagger. How do I know? A push-dagger is made for stabbing, not slashing, so when it's used for slashing the wound is unmistakable." Kartli paused for a moment. "I know someone who kills in this manner; he's a Knight of St. Clement assassin. He must have trained her. Does this girl carry a push-dagger?"

"I never saw one on her," Bravo said, "but all along the bitch has been full of surprises."

DO you think it wise," Damon Cornadoro said as he watched Jenny passing through the narrow streets of the European Market, "to allow her to go off to meet with Bravo alone?"

Camille studied his handsome face, admiring him as if he were a statue sculpted by Michelangelo. She put a slender forefinger, warm against his cool flesh, across his lips. "What's the matter, my love? Do you think she can persuade him to the truth, rather than the ever more plausible lie I have laid out for him?"

"Rational argument has nothing to do with it. There is chemistry between them, I felt it the night they arrived in Venice. When I lifted her on board the *motoscafo*, when I put my hands on her waist and drew her close to me I thought he was going to kill me."

Camille laughed. "*Mon dieu*, what an imagination you have, darling! They fuck and you see skyrockets."

Cornadoro shrugged his huge shoulders. "Now that he's isolated I want to make sure he stays that way."

"Oh, and whose idea was that, Damon, yours or mine? Don't you worry, when it comes to isolation I know all the ins and outs. He hates her now, she killed his beloved 'Uncle Tony,' just as I planned it."

She could feel his heat, the brief tremor as his yearning responded to the proximity of her body. On the pretext of keeping Jenny in view, she contrived to lean ever so slightly against him, so that the tips of her breasts, the small platter of her belly, the strong pillars of her thighs imprinted themselves briefly on his muscles. "Not all men are like you."

"Women rarely get what they want, Camille, though what that might be eludes me."

He smiled the smile that was impermissible, the smile that revealed his weakness to anyone who, like her, was clever enough to see it. His weakness she knew well, and it made her long for the heady days of Dexter, a man who grasped the big picture and never let go.

"But you—you're different—you know men better than any other woman."

"Better than they know themselves," she said casually. "That's the point, isn't it?"

"How do you do it? That's what I'd like to know."

She ran her nail across the stubble of his cheek, as if tracing out a scar. "Poor baby. If you have to ask, you'll never understand."

He grew angry then, which is what she wanted, his eyes blazing, his reflexes animal sharp. When he made to grab her, she danced lithely away. But she didn't laugh at him. With each of her men she knew where to draw the line, and she never transgressed. That was her secret. She had failed only once, with Dexter Shaw—not that Cornadoro would ever find out.

"*Alors,* you have the Husqvarna," she said, referring to the sniper's rifle. "It's time to take it to the rooftops."

THEY stood facing each other: Bravo and Jenny, amid the bustling, noisy, anonymous street. No one in their view paid them the slightest attention, but there were others, hidden from them, who were very much interested in what they said and did.

"I said if I saw you again I'd kill you," Bravo said.

Jenny spread her hands. "Here I am." She had to bite her lip to keep from screaming. How on earth was she going to make him understand?

"Are you armed?"

She laughed, a bitter sound she immediately wanted to spit out like the white under-rind of a lemon. "Do you imagine I'd shoot you?"

"You shot Uncle Tony—"

"Because he was the *mole,* he was the *traitor*—"

"You slashed Father Damaskinos's throat after you set fire to his face."

"*What?*" Her eyes opened wide. "What did you say?"

He came toward her, hating her and at the same time marveling at the naturalness of her performance. "Where is it?"

"If Father Damaskinos is dead you can be sure I had nothing to do with it," she said with a good deal of alarm.

"I'm no longer sure of anything." He'd had enough of her feigned innocence. "The push-dagger—where is it?"

"What the hell are you talking about?"

"I want it!"

"You're crazy! I don't know—"

Taking her by the wrist, he pulled her out of the dust and the grit into the shadows beneath a dilapidated awning. They appeared to be a couple in the middle of a minor dispute, that was all.

"Let go of me," she said quietly, balefully. Despite her best efforts, her anger at what she saw as his obtuseness was getting the better of her. What was the use of trying to explain what had happened to her? One look at his stony, closed-down face told her that he'd never believe her. He didn't want to. And it was this last realization that spun her down into the lowest depths of despair.

"Listen, you," Bravo said, "Mikhail Kartli—surely you know who he is—wants you dead. He had sent one of his men to shoot you for being a traitor to the Order—"

"I'm not a traitor—"

"Shut *up!*" He jerked her around and she nearly tripped a portly Turk negotiating hotly to buy a copper kettle. He ignored the Turk's brief alarm, ignored, also, the deep circles under Jenny's eyes, the unnatural pallor of her cheeks, as if the pith of her was disintegrating, as if something had devastated her from the inside out. Which was difficult, because it meant ignoring the painful lurch the sight of her gave his heart—despite her lying, her deceit, her murderous treachery he felt . . . God help him. Again, his heart contracted, and he wondered whether he could forgive himself for loving her still. "The only reason you're still alive is that I told Kartli I'd talk to you—that I'd get out of you whether there are any more moles inside the Order."

"I have no idea. You'd have to ask Anthony—"

Rule's name became a scream as he dragged her back into the street. It was his love, he realized with a shock that literally sickened him, that bore his rage on high. His hatred of her was not a professional hatred—he was ignoring Uncle Tony's admonition to disinvolve himself personally, to keep his head well above the rising tide of the Voire Dei's toxic sludge. He loved her and she was evil. How on earth could that be?

"It's to be the hard way, then," he said with exaggerated grimness. "I'll take you to Kartli. He has all manner of articulated interrogation in mind to make you talk." Her eyes found his, and the part of himself that loved her still shied away from her challenge, disengaging at the last instant, so that a stranger with his mouth said: "In other words, torture."

Jenny was stricken, felled as if by a bolt of lightning. "How can you—? God in heaven, how can you even contemplate such a monstrous thing? I'll fight you tooth and nail right here, you know that."

Something buzzed past her cheek, soft as a moth, causing her to gasp, take an involuntary step back. Just beyond her reach, the portly Turk lost control of the kettle, his arms splayed out, pitching forward into the copper merchant as the bullet caught him between the shoulder blades.

Instantly, the market erupted into a tsunami of shouts, gesticulations and pounding feet. People ran in every direction. The melee flung Bravo and Jenny apart, and Jenny took the opportunity to sprint away into the crowd. There was no point in attempting to follow her, for she was soon lost to his sight and he was borne away on the rising tide of panic.

"YOU told me—"

"I am a man of my word," Mikhail Kartli said firmly.

"And yet one of your men tried to kill her."

The Georgian stood with his arms crossed. A tattoo of a hawk with open wings showed on the inside of one wrist, a controlled burst of colors on the brown flesh. "Correction. *Not* one of my men."

"Then who?" Bravo demanded.

"You're doubting me?"

"I'm simply asking."

Kartli's brows gathered darkly and there was a hitherto unknown thickness in his voice. "No, you're accusing."

"That's your interpretation, not an accurate one."

Adem Khalif tried to extricate Bravo, to spirit him away from the rising peril. But Bravo shook Khalif off, stood his ground.

The three men formed a triangle at the entrance to the Georgian's shop. Around them were Mikhail Kartli's offspring—four adult sons, built like their father and no less muscular—and the daughter Khalif had spoken to on their way in. There was a different kind of tension now from the one Bravo had observed earlier. Kartli's clients were gone, the ones still needing to do business hustled away moments ago by the eldest son to whom Kartli had given one of his cell phones.

"Irema, your place is at home with your mother," Kartli said to his daughter.

"But, Father—"

Her protestation was cut short as one of her brothers cuffed her on the side of her head. She uttered no sound, but bit her lip until the blood flowed.

Kartli did not reprimand his son. Instead he said to Irema, "Go this instant. You will be punished, but not as severely as if you force me to send your brother as escort."

Irema glared at the brother who had struck her, and then with naked curiosity, momentarily turned her gaze on Bravo. A moment later, avoiding her father's murderous stare, she fled into the maze of the bazaar.

There was red dust in the street. It coated their shoes and the bottoms of their trousers. It had sunk darkly into the creases of their palms, mimicking dried blood. A kind of animal musk was rising with the dust and the tension, the scent of a pair of mountain goats about to lock horns. In the end, only one of them would be left standing, and they both knew it. This was the end that Adem Khalif was working mightily to avoid.

"Obviously, there has been a miscommunication, a misunderstanding," Khalif said in Georgian. "This is not the time to quibble over such trivial matters and, in any event, Mikhail, wouldn't it be wiser to take the discussion inside?"

No one paid him any mind.

"I could have gotten her to talk," Bravo said. "Instead, an attempt was made on her life and now she's lost to us—the opportunity is lost. I don't consider that trivial."

"She was lost through your inexperience," Kartli said imperiously. "You were the one with her in the field."

Bravo swung at Kartli. The Georgian took the blow on his shoulder, grabbed Bravo's wrist and began the process of breaking it.

Bravo slammed his fist into Kartli's stomach to gasps from the onlookers. Released, he inadvisably took a step forward, ran right into a left-handed uppercut from the Georgian that dropped him onto his backside. Kartli came on in a low brawler's crouch. Bravo, half-dazed, waited until as long as he dared, regaining his breath, before he drew Lorenzo Fornarini's dagger.

Kartli froze in mid-stride, but his four sons moved toward Bravo, until the Georgian held up a hand. His blazing eyes were on Bravo, not them.

"Have a care," Kartli said with a strange intensity. "I told you to make damn sure you knew when to use it."

As Bravo's fist tightened on the dagger's hilt, Khalif intervened again. "Listen, both of you, if the Order is divided against itself, then, truly, all is lost."

Kartli sneered. "He comes here, this American, with his hand out, asking for help. Then, in the same breath, he orders me to crouch at his side like a dog, then he accuses me. Like a dog, he strikes me, expecting that I should happily grovel before him." He spat heavily. "Should any of this be a surprise to me? The day dawns when the horns of the rampaging beast will gore even the most prudent of onlookers. This is the American way, isn't it, all over the world."

"This is the Voire Dei, Kartli, we're both—"

The Georgian cursed in Georgian and in Turkish. "What do I say to someone whose government has allied itself to the Moscow criminals who continue to persecute my people without mercy?"

"For the love of God—"

"Another point that must be clarified, American—whose God do you invoke, mine or yours?"

"We're both human beings."

"But we're not equal, are we? You wish to use me, just as your government uses the Russians for their own end."

Adem Khalif said quietly but urgently, "Mikhail, after all, Bravo is the Keeper, it's your duty to protect and to help him."

"Such arrogance in a Keeper. And now you side with him." Kartli hawked and spat into the dirt.

Bravo, grief and frustration once again flaring into anger, began to advance on Kartli, but Khalif grabbed him, held him back with a grip like iron.

"Don't do this," he whispered in Bravo's ear. "I warned you, this man is very dangerous, easily provoked." To the Georgian, he said, "Since when have you known me to take sides? I, who have broken bread with you, who have changed your children's diapers, who have sat in counsel with you. We are friends, Mikhail. Friends."

"Then back away from the American."

"Only to see you kill him," Adem Khalif said sadly.

"He drew a weapon in my house. He has committed a mortal offense."

"You were friends with his father."

"Dexter Shaw is dead," the Georgian said. "My obligation died with him."

"But the Order, your vows—"

"I have taken enough from these people." Kartli's hand flashed down. "It is finished."

"At least allow him to walk away," Adem Khalif said. "The death of Dexter Shaw's son will be a heavy weight to bear."

"Let him go, and step back," Kartli said simply.

Khalif did as he was told, but not before he managed to whisper in Bravo's ear, "Sheath the dagger and wait. . . . Wait."

And there Bravo stood, the dagger sheathed, alone, waiting. A terrible silence strangled them, the furious bustle of the street faded away as if it had never existed. And all the while the Georgian's eyes never left Bravo's. There seemed to ensue a curious contest of wills, silent, lethal.

Very slowly, Bravo pulled out the scabbarded dagger, held it out, an offering to propitiate Mikhail Kartli or, perhaps, his god.

"You seek to buy me off," the Georgian said. "How American."

"There is no price on this dagger," Bravo said. "It is yours."

Kartli shook his head, as if at something infinitely sad. "No, Keeper, where you travel you will need it."

Bravo lowered the dagger.

"Go now," Mikhail Kartli said.

Bravo turned, saw that Khalif made no move to go with him. The circle of the Georgian's sons parted as he neared it.

Just before he stepped outside the ring, leaving the Georgian's aegis forever, out into the streets of Trabzon, Mikhail Kartli said, "Pray to whatever god it is that moves you, for without him you are truly lost."

25

BRAVO SAT IN THE SAME CAFÉ ON THE HILL IN THE ORTAHISAR
quarter where he had first met Adem Khalif, hoping that if he stayed
long enough the Turk would come. The café smelled of burnt cigarettes
and cat urine, but the coffee was thick and strong. From his tiny table he
had an excellent view of the main arteries of the Old City, the ravines in
which all light was absorbed. He realized that he could not bear to be in
any section of the new city, grown like a gross shell around the jewel of
long-lost Trebizond. He wanted to recapture that fabled city, wanted to
walk its streets, hear the regal sound of Trapazuntine Greek being spoken, watch the stately round ships sailing in from Florence or Venice,
Cadiz or Bruges, ready to take on the exotic cargoes waiting for them in
Trebizond's bursting warehouses. And on the horizon, the sinister slash
of the black sails, the threat of the Seljuk pirates.

He pulled out his cell phone. In the middle of dialing Jordan's number, he stopped. Jordan was his closest friend in the world. Bravo had already asked him for help and Jordan had generously agreed, but now it
was too dangerous to involve him further. Bravo knew he didn't want to
endanger anyone else, especially his friend.

He put his head in his heads. He wanted another life, or at least to roll
back the clock. He pictured himself standing on the corner of Sixth Avenue in New York, watching his father walk away. If only he'd gone after
him. But, really, what good would it have done? Delayed what was already set in motion, nothing more. It was dispiriting, the idea that he'd
been helpless, trapped like a cog in a huge machine, grinding forward
with inexorable precision. . . .

"It's time to see your grandfather, Bravo."

He looked up, saw his father's weather-beaten face. They were in their house in Greenwich Village and he was nine years old.

"I know you don't want to go."

"How d'you know that?" Bravo said.

"Because you just asked Mom if you could help her dry the breakfast dishes."

Bravo set down the dish towel. He knew his father had made a joke, but just then it didn't seem all that funny.

Dexter put a hand on his son's shoulder. "Your grandfather wants to see you, he asked about you specially this morning."

"Doesn't he want to see Junior?" Bravo asked, thinking misery loves company. Emma was far too young to be brought to the nursing home.

"Junior's not feeling well," Dexter said.

That wasn't it at all, and Bravo knew it. He'd overheard his parents talking about it several weeks before. They'd deemed Junior too young to go, a decision that only added to Bravo's resentment.

The drive to the nursing home wasn't short, but to Bravo it seemed to take three minutes. Fleets of semis rumbled, factories belched smoke, and he had to roll up the window so as not to be overcome by the reek of chemical waste that smelled like burnt tires and cat piss.

The nursing home, somewhere in the unfathomable hinterlands of New Jersey, was a large Georgian redbrick building that seemed like one of those thoroughly unpleasant London institutions Dickens so brilliantly described. Bravo sat in the car, listening to the hot engine tick over like a mechanical heart, waiting for it to slow and, finally, stop. He stared straight ahead even after his father had clambered out, a sick feeling in the pit of his stomach.

"Bravo?" Dexter opened the passenger's side door and held out his hand.

Bravo, in his own way resigned, took it, and together they went up the cement walk to the front door. Just before it opened, Dexter said, "You love your grandfather, don't you?"

Bravo nodded.

"That's all you need think about, okay?"

Bravo nodded again, not trusting himself to reply.

The smell inside the nursing home was unspeakable. Bravo tried to hold his breath, just as he always did, but it was no use. He inhaled and felt himself gagging before he was able to settle his system down.

They found Conrad Shaw in the solarium, amid bright sunlight and the unnatural humidity of hothouse flowers and potted plants. As usual, he'd ordered his wheelchair to be set as far away from the other patients as possible. He was bald now, though up until ten years ago he'd had a thick shock of white hair of which he'd been inordinately proud. His thin flesh, speckled as a robin's egg, was carved by age and disease so close to the skull that it had taken on the color of the bone beneath. Once, he'd been a big man, robust and reckless, dapper and possessed of a raucous laugh he dispensed with great generosity.

The pity was that these gifts had been snatched from him all at once. The stroke that had felled him had been a serious one. Now his heart was damaged and he wore a pacemaker. His legs were useless, as was the right side of his body. His features sagged horribly, as if he was subject to a gravitational force of extraterrestrial virulence.

He had not adjusted well to his altered circumstance. It was as if all joy had been squeezed out of him. If he was pleased to see his grandson there was no way for Bravo to tell. His grandfather fixed him with his one good eye, gripped him with his one good arm in what Bravo came to think of as a death grip, as afterward he regarded the bruise.

"How are you, Grandpa?" Bravo asked.

"Where's my pipe, boy? What did you do with my pipe?"

"I haven't seen your pipe, Grandpa." Bravo wiped a bit of spittle from the flaky corner of his grandfather's mouth.

"Don't do that!" Conrad let fly the back of his good hand. "Broke it, did you?" He pinched Bravo's arm hard, his fingers like steel pincers. "Deliberate disobedience, knowing you."

"Dad, Bravo didn't take your pipe. You lost it last year," Dexter said, gently extricating his son.

"Lost, my ass," Conrad snorted. "I know when something of mine's been stolen."

Dexter closed his eyes for a moment, and Bravo could almost hear him silently counting to ten. "Forget the pipe, Dad, you know you can't smoke anymore." Dexter affixed a smile to his face and using his most diplomatic voice, said, "I know you're happy to see Bravo, you asked for him this morning."

"I asked for coffee with half-and-half this morning," the old man said irascibly. "If you think I got it you don't know a damn thing about this hellhole. It's a toilet masquerading as a hotel."

Every time Conrad saw Dexter, he begged his son to end his life. This was why Dexter had taken to bringing Bravo with him. The old man would never consider voicing his request while Bravo was around.

Bravo didn't react so much to the frighteningly swift decrepitude that had come upon his grandfather as to the terror, unvoiced but felt as only a child can feel it, of the old man's death wish. He deeply hated being dragged here against his will, having to see the waste that disease inflicts on even the strongest, most capable of men, of being hauled into close proximity with death when he did not even understand what death was.

"I don't want to go back there ever again," he said on the way home.

"That's what you say every time." Dexter's voice was deliberately light, as if they were bantering about some beloved topic.

"This time I mean it, Dad," Bravo said as forcefully as he knew how.

"Your grandfather doesn't mean any of those things he says, Bravo. You know that inside he's happy to see you."

Bravo looked away.

"What is it?"

Again, silence.

"C'mon," Dexter urged. "You can tell me anything, you know that."

"I don't want to die."

Dexter gave him a quick look full of fatherly concern. "You're not going to die, Bravo. Not for a long, long time."

"But Grandpa will."

"All the more reason for you to see him, as often as possible. I want you to remember—"

Bravo, in a sudden rage fueled by grief and frustration, shouted, "Remember what? A walking skeleton, something out of a nightmare?"

Dexter signaled and pulled over into the breakdown lane, where he stopped the car. Turning to his son, he said, "No matter how your grandfather looks now, he's the same inside, he's a man who has accomplished great things. He deserves your attention and your respect."

With a child's clear access to the truth, Bravo said, "I don't think he's the same inside."

This brought Dexter up short. He turned his head, one arm draped over the wheel, watched the lines of cars and trucks whizzing by. The car rocked in the fluted edge of their slipstream.

"You're right." Dexter Shaw sighed. "I've been fighting against it, but my father isn't the same inside, he's been brought low."

It was the first time Bravo had seen his father cry. It wouldn't be the last.

Bravo put his hand on his father's shoulder. "It's okay, Dad."

"No, it's not. I shouldn't be taking you every week. It's selfish."

"Hey, Dad—"

"My father was everything to me. To see him like this. . . ." Dexter shook his head. "But these are the consequences of life, Bravo. One has to own up to them, take them like a man."

"Then we will."

Dexter Shaw looked at his son.

"I mean, we're together, right?" The nine-year-old Bravo flashed a courageous smile. "We're men, right?"

LIKE a cool breath on his cheek, Bravo felt his father's departure, and he opened his eyes. The light had lowered, the lengthening shadows were the color of lapis. Still no sign of Khalif, and now Bravo knew that he wouldn't come. His coffee was cold and he called for another, along with something to eat. "Anything but *pulpo*," he told the waiter. He was up to here with octopus.

It was a mistake to have picked a fight with Mikhail Kartli. The imprudence of it shocked him even now. But there are times when control goes out the window and then you simply have to make the best of a bad situation. Take the consequences like a man.

His coffee came and he drank a bit of it, burning the tip of his tongue. With a clatter, he put the cup down and called Emma. He was eight hours ahead of New York. By all rights, he should have woken her up, but she answered immediately and there was no trace of sleep in her voice.

"My God, Bravo, where have you been? I've been trying you for the better part of a day."

"Out of cell range, obviously. Listen, I found the mole."

"You did? Who is it?"

"Was. Paolo Zorzi. He's dead."

"Zorzi?" There was silence for a moment, then Emma said, "I don't know."

"What d'you mean? He was one of the names on the list Dad made. Father Mosto showed it to me in Venice."

"Ah, Bravo. That list was one of Dad's ploys, nothing but disinformation, in case it somehow fell into the hands of a Knight."

He sat up straight. "You're joking, right?"

"Think about it a minute. This is Dad we're talking about. Do you really think he'd leave a list of suspects lying around, especially an unencrypted one?"

Bravo's head had begun to pound. "But Zorzi had me beaten, captured. . . . Are you telling me he *wasn't* the traitor?"

"No. What I'm saying is we can't be sure. The only list Dad compiled was in his head."

"But you were doing research for him. You know all the suspects. Was Zorzi one of them?"

"At one point, yes."

A cold ball of fear was congealing in Bravo's stomach. "What does that mean?"

"About a month before he was killed Dad had me stop all the background intelligence I was digging up."

"Why?"

"That's what I asked him. All he'd say was that he'd made a breakthrough, that he had to do the rest of it alone. I begged him to let me help, but he was adamant. You know how hardheaded Dad could be."

He certainly did know. "But why all of a sudden did he cut you out?"

"I've tried a dozen theories. None of them makes sense."

"What," Bravo said, "if the breakthrough involved a new suspect very close to Dad?"

"But why would he—?"

"Someone he didn't want you to know about—especially that he was very close to her."

"Her?"

"Jenny Logan—the Guardian. No wonder Zorzi was a prior suspect; it was one of his people who was the mole. She probably left clues leading Dad back to him. But it didn't work—or at least, not for long. I think he assigned her to me hoping she'd trip her hand conclusively and I'd find her out. Which is exactly what's happened."

"I don't know, Bravo, that's a lot of danger to expose you to."

"No more than what he'd been training me for."

"Still, it was a monumental gamble on his part, don't you think?"

"The stakes are high, Emma, I don't have to tell you that." He thought a moment. "What were you doing for Dad after he pulled you off the background checks?"

"Nothing all that important. Checking the Order's audio logs of their London-based intel. Honestly, I don't know why he wanted it vetted."

"Me neither," Bravo said. "But you know Dad, somewhere there was a reason. Can you manage—?"

"Blind, you mean? I've been trying to tell you since you called but you kept laying bombshells on me. Some of my sight has come back."

He let out a whoop of delight. "Emma, that's fantastic!"

"It's only in one eye so far and my vision's not that great, especially distances. It may never be, the doctors tell me. But I can see the computer screen well enough, especially with the great hulking magnifying lens I had made."

"Then you can continue vetting the London audio intel."

"But it's sooo boring," Emma moaned in her most theatrical voice.

"Look, I've recently discovered that Dad was working on fundamentalist movements in and around the Middle East. There's a long history of fundamentalist training and staging activity in London, as you know, so while what he's asked you to do might *seem* boring, it could have very serious implications."

"Okay, okay, you've sold me, but promise me you'll stay in touch more often. Where are you, by the way?"

"Best not to tell you."

She laughed. "Now you sound just like Dad."

"Get cracking on that London intel."

"Right. Take care of yourself."

"Emma, I love you."

He severed the line and put the cell phone away. By that time the food had come. He ate without tasting a thing. With the information about Emma and Jenny buzzing in his head he didn't know whether to laugh or to cry.

THE light was fading. Along Trabzon's crescent shoreline the sea was zebra-striped. Boats lay at anchor or in their slips, rocking gently as if they were children drifting off to sleep. In the heart of the Old City, Damon Cornadoro turned a corner, went down the block toward Mikhail Kartli's carpet shop. He had his orders and, like all loyal soldiers, he would carry them out to the best of his abilities, and he would succeed. With all the bewildering variables in the world, Cornadoro was grateful that his skills weren't one of them. He was absolutely confident in himself. He did not, like others, feel fear. The sensation was unknown to him—ever since, on a dare, he had stuck his arm in the flames of a Venetian street fire. He had been sixteen at the time, but street-smart beyond his years. Though a scion of one of the *Case Vecchie*, he preferred to slum. When he'd been challenged, he knew just what to do. He'd turned away, rolled up his sleeves and rubbed his hands together, as if preparing himself for the ordeal. In fact, that was precisely what he was doing, though not in the way any of the onlookers understood. He was coating his right arm with axle grease.

During this time he was keeping up a steady stream of boasting, daring more people to bet against him, furthering his odds. Classic misdirection, diverting the onlookers' attention from seeing how he was protecting his arm. Then, so quickly it brought a gasp to those crowded around, he thrust his right arm up to the elbow into the crackling fire, held it there for a full thirty seconds, before removing it. Holding up the arm, he laughed at the looks of astonishment on their faces, and jovially collected his winnings.

Now as Cornadoro came upon the Georgian's shop, he felt no trepidation, simply a desire to accomplish his task. Camille had warned him not to underestimate Kartli; Cornadoro had learned to take her warnings seriously.

The young girl Irema, the Georgian's daughter, who Kartli had ordered home during his altercation with Braverman Shaw, had not, in fact, done as her dear papa had ordered but had melted into the throng, hanging at the fringes, moving here and there, watching the shape of her father's anger. Cornadoro had noted this, and he would not forget. He passed her now as she at last decided that it was time to leave.

One of her brothers was folding small rugs, taking them off the rickety wooden stands outside the shop, preparatory to bringing them inside for the night.

"We're closed," he said without looking up or pausing in his work. "Please come back tomorrow morning."

"I must see Mikhail Kartli," Cornadoro said.

The young man glanced up. *"Must?"*

"I've come a long way to see him." Cornadoro stood his ground. "All the way from Rhodes."

At the last word, the young man stopped folding rugs. Something swam in his eyes—what was it? Fear, consternation, perhaps a bit of both. So it should be; Rhodes was the home of the Knights of St. Clement. Cornadoro was pleased.

The young man put down the rug. "Please wait here," he said as he turned on his heel and disappeared into the interior of the shop. Lights, the yellow of a mongrel's tooth, were coming on all over the city. New reflections turned the shopwindows into blind eyes.

Mikhail Kartli appeared in the doorway, spent a moment warily eyeing his visitor. At length, he emerged onto the street. "What can I do for you?"

"I think it's more what I can do for you."

Cornadoro stepped briskly forward but stopped when the Georgian held up his hand.

"First, your weapon of choice. The push-dagger, if you please."

Cornadoro laughed good-naturedly. "I commend you, Georgian, your intel is excellent." He produced the push-dagger he'd used to slit Father Damaskinos's throat, held it out, handle first. Kartli nodded and his son took it.

"For safekeeping," Kartli said. "It will be returned to you when you leave."

Cornadoro inclined his upper torso in a slightly ironic mock-bow. He now produced a small metal tin, which he held out to the Georgian.

"What is this?"

"A gift," Cornadoro said, "from one connoisseur to another."

"Open it, please," Kartli commanded.

"By all means." Cornadoro freed the latch, raised the box's top. At once, a delicately aromatic scent perfumed the air.

Kartli's eyes opened wide. "Bai Ji Guan."

Cornadoro nodded. "White Rooster Crest, a first generation tea, as you know, one of the four WuYi Mountain rock oolongs."

"Very rare, very costly," Kartli said, taking possession of the box.

Cornadoro shrugged. "If it pleases you, there's more where that came from." Inside he was smiling broadly; Camille had been right again, they'd scored a direct hit.

"Come with me," Kartli said, leading the way into the interior of the shop. Oil lamps had been lit, spilling pools of warm light across the magnificent tapestry of the rugs. The son brought coffee—no tea and no food. This form of the ritual told Cornadoro that the meeting was preliminary, the intentions of his host at this point neutral.

He sat on a pile of Tabriz carpets, accepted the coffee without sugar. After they had both partaken of the coffee, he put aside his cup. The son lounged in the background, text-messaging on his cell phone.

"You know me."

Kartli nodded. "Damon Cornadoro. Knight of St. Clement."

"Not so, I never took the formal vows."

Kartli cocked his head. "Am I wrong, are you not working for the Knights?"

"On occasion I do," Cornadoro acknowledged. "I am, however, an independent operator."

"Then we are the same, you and I. As of today, I have severed my affiliation with the Order."

This comment piqued Cornadoro's interest. Had he not observed the Georgian's falling out with Braverman Shaw with his own eyes, he would have been suspicious of such a radical change.

"One avenue closes," he said, "others open to take its place. It is said that Cherry Bateman trained you."

Cornadoro inclined his head. "Bateman is the avenue I chose—or perhaps it is more accurate to say that he chose me."

"Bateman is an American."

"I am Venetian and you are Georgian. What of it?"

"All across the globe," Mikhail Kartli said, "nationalism is on the march. It is a source of strength nothing else can match." He eyed Cornadoro shrewdly. "I think you know this."

"Cherry Bateman is an American by birth only. He is a citizen of

Italy, he has renounced America. He has renounced his son Donovan, who remains in America."

"This would make a difference."

"Of course. It is important to see things as they are, rather than as they seem to be." Cornadoro spread his hands. "You and Bateman. I could be mistaken, of course." He allowed himself a smile. "It wouldn't be the first time. But in the event I'm not wrong I would be prepared to arrange an introduction. You might find your time in the Veneto extremely constructive—as well as potentially helpful to the Georgian cause."

"And in return, you would want . . . what?"

"Information." Cornadoro smiled outwardly, even as he relaxed inwardly. He felt the unmistakable tug of the hook going in. "Information on Braverman Shaw."

26

WHEN AN ISLAMIC SAID "GEOMETRY IS GOD MANIFEST," HE meant it literally. The first-century mathematician al-Biruni codified geometry, called it *geodesy* and classified it as a philosophy both natural and religious, dealing with matter and form as they combined with time and space.

The interior of the Zigana Mosque, a beehivelike geodesic dome composed of pointed arches of honey-colored stone, was based on al-Biruni's sacred geometry. There was, indeed, a spiral staircase to one side that led up to the *minbar*, the sacred pulpit. It was constructed of a black wood, perhaps ebony, and was highly polished, shiny as glass.

Bravo stood looking at it for some time. The peculiar *geodesy* of the interior made the slightest whisper audible from clear across the mosque. He held everyone in his view. There appeared to be no threat, and gradually, as if he were swimming through clear azure water, a profound calm settled over him.

There were few people about. From somewhere, the melodic ululation of a prayer came to him, muffled by the space, further blurred by its own echoes. The door opened at his back and he felt himself stiffen slightly. Too late he realized that he should have immediately moved so as to keep an eye on who entered and exited. Two solemn men, thin and brown and bearded, passed near him. He could smell the spice of their passage. Shoulders touching, they walked down the aisle, away from him. No threat.

Taking a deep breath, he crossed the dusky mosque, through three identical pointed arches. At the elegant ebony corkscrew of the staircase, Bravo stood still as a statue, his head bowed as if he were preparing for the salat. In fact, he was thinking of the second word his father had written on the strip of velvet. *Purpure* was medieval English, the heraldic term for purple. However, it was not always possible to use color, so on black and white drawings it was indicated by lines drawn from upper left to lower right or, in heraldic terms, from sinister chief to dexter base.

The next cipher was at the base of the spiral.

JORDAN had his mother in his sights. Spying on her was an interesting experience; it caused him to wonder if she had ever spied on him. At this moment, he was willing to bet that she had. Through powerful field glasses, he watched her as she crossed the street in front of her hotel. As always, she was impeccably dressed—pin-striped tailored shirt, yellow linen skirt that showed off her long, beautiful legs. She slid into a battered landscaper's truck. Behind the wheel sat Damon Cornadoro, her lover, her coconspirator.

Jordan felt the murderous urge to take a gun from one of his men. He imagined himself getting out of this van with its blacked-out windows, striding down the street. He'd tap on the window of the truck and when Cornadoro wound it down, Jordan would shoot him dead. Blood and brains all over her fashionable blouse and skirt, her makeup ruined. He wondered if she'd have any other reaction. . . .

His cell phone rang.

"The American wants to see you," Spagna's voice buzzed in his ear.

"I imagine he does."

"He's extremely upset."

"I don't blame him." Jordan hadn't taken his eyes off the couple. Next to him, one of his Knights sat in front of a tape recorder, earphones clamped to his head. "Tell him I'll see him in due course. In the meantime, tell him I want a token of his fealty."

"Something of significance to the American," Spagna said, all ears.

"His daughter." Jordan made a gesture to the Knight sitting beside him. "Tell the American I'll take care of her rehabilitation, the best of everything, all expenses paid."

"He's sure to ask for how long."

"Tell him she will be with me for as long as I wish it."

Spagna chuckled. "He'll scream bloody murder."

"I am quite certain it will make him even more miserable than he is now."

He closed out the connection. In response to his signal, the Knight had passed him a set of earphones. Donning them, he heard every incriminating word his mother and Cornadoro said. Plus, they unknowingly brought his field intelligence up to date. The parabolic microphone aimed through the window by one of his Knights was working to perfection.

BRAVO kept one eye on the door as, occasionally, someone entered the mosque or left. Each time, he could feel his heart racing. He was not only worried about the Knights, but those who were loyal to Mikhail Kartli. He had offended the Georgian, and though Kartli had allowed him to walk away unharmed, there was no telling if or when he'd change his mind, give the order to have Bravo found and terminated. Bravo had no doubt that Kartli possessed both the power and the will to carry out the directive, and it wouldn't be only his sons who would jump at pleasing him—to anyone in his employ it would be a matter of honor.

As he knelt in front of the ebony spiral, he was never more aware of being alone in a hostile environment. He thought he had developed a kind of sixth sense when it came to the Knights, but as to Kartli's men, anyone and everyone who passed him a bit too slowly, looked at him a bit too long, moved when he did or glanced away when he tried to meet their eye was suspect. Under the heavy burden of these circumstances the only thing to do was to keep moving. If he stayed too long in one place he was surely a dead man.

He could feel the Roman ruins beneath his feet, as if they were tree roots running down into the living rock. He could hear the chanting of the priests in Trapazuntine Greek, see the entrance of the emperor in white silk and golden imperial eagles, crowned in his bejeweled imperial mitra, flanked by his Kabasitai, his imperial warriors, ceremonial golden swords lifted to honor him.

Movement off to his right caught his attention. Without turning either his head or his body, he saw the two bearded men, who looked even more solemn now as they knelt on small prayer rugs they had laid over the mosaic floor. They were on the opposite side of the mosque, just slightly behind where he knelt. Their foreheads were pressed against the rugs, which gleamed richly in the light, their deep colors burnished like polished metal. Something was wrong, something hidden in plain sight he was missing—what was it?

There came now at the nape of his neck a delicate prickling that advanced down his spine like a venomous serpent. All at once, he sensed a trap, its jaws closing around him, but glancing around he could find no imminent threat.

Still, he resolved to find his father's next cipher and get out as quickly as possible. Looking down, he studied the pattern of the mosaic floor at the base of the spiral. At first, it seemed the same as it was in other parts of the floor, but as he knelt down he could see various differences. For instance, here a green tile was blue, over there eight red tiles where elsewhere there were four, and at various intervals what were orange tiles in other areas of the floor were here white. Following these small anomalies outward, he found that they ended in straight lines and that, further, they corresponded precisely to the width and length of the "Goldenhead" painting, a moiré of Mother Mary, coated in gold.

He looked at the color changes—red, white, blue—and pulled out the enameled lapel pin, one of the items his father had left for him in the boat in Washington. He had already examined it, determined that the American flag had the wrong number of stars and stripes.

He looked up, saw that a priest in a hooded robe with a wide cinched waistband—an imam? he couldn't be sure—had appeared and was now talking to the two bearded men, interrupting their prayers. All three of them looked grim as pallbearers. There was something familiar about the priest, either in his physiognomy or in the way he stood, possibly both. Bravo chanced a quick direct look, but the priest had turned his back, and with the hood up he could make out no distinguishing characteristic. Perhaps, after all, he'd been mistaken.

Once again, he returned to his work, though his feeling of unease had increased exponentially. Having determined the area of the color-altered section of the mosaic, he now found the tile at the exact center. From this point, he moved up five tiles, the number of missing stars in the flag pin, then three to the right, the number of missing stripes. He encountered an ocher tile. Nothing there. Now he reversed the direction, went up five tiles, three to the left, where he encountered a green tile. Nothing. Next, down five, right three. This brought him to a black tile. Down five, left three: a brown tile. No red, white or blue tile, as he had been expecting. Now what? He moved, his shadow moving with him. Oblique light played over the mosaic, drawing his eye back to the black tile. Running his fingertip over it, he discovered that it was slightly rounded rather than flat like the other tiles.

With his forehead almost touching the floor in a position not unlike that of the prayerful bearded men on their rugs, he inspected the black tile more closely. It appeared to be made of a different material than those around it.

Inserting his nail into the space between the tiles he was able to pry it up with surprising ease. The stone was shiny, black as midnight. He rubbed the pad of his thumb over its surface for several seconds, then brought it near the floor, saw that it had attracted, by way of static electricity, a fine coating of dust.

The test served to prove his suspicion that this was not another mosaic tile, but rather a small piece of jet—more specifically *oltu tasi,* a stone used for jewelry and the like, which had been worked by the monks of the Sumela Monastery in the mountains just above Trabzon. From the cavity into which the stone had been set he plucked out a folded slip of paper.

It was at this moment that he became aware of movement off to his right. The priest had left the bearded men and was walking in deliberate fashion toward him. As he did so, he lifted one hand, cupping the fingers of his right hand to draw back the hood of his robe. Bravo was aware that the inside of the mosque had been overcome by a kind of unnatural hush; save for himself and the three other men it was, improbably, deserted.

The priest passed through a diagonal shaft of light and Bravo recognized Adem Khalif. Why had he been talking to the two bearded men? Whose side was he on—Mikhail Kartli's? It seemed that Trabzon belonged to Kartli, even though it was Khalif who was the native.

As if in confirmation of this hypothesis, Bravo saw the two bearded men rolling up their prayer rugs. Again, the light played off the rugs' nap, revealing all its sheen and rich colorations. And now, with a single indrawn breath, Bravo understood what had been disturbing him, what was hiding in plain sight: the rugs were silk—they were far too valuable to be used as daily prayer rugs. The bearded men hadn't come into the mosque for prayer, they were emissaries of Mikhail Kartli, the carpet dealer. Adem Khalif, making the only practical choice he could make, had allied himself with the Georgian. It was as he had feared: ally and enemy alike were after him.

Bravo turned and ran. He heard Khalif's voice raised behind him, but the sound was cut short as he sped around a cluster of columns, sprinted toward the door. The two bearded men were also on the run, trying to cut him off before he reached the front of the mosque.

He veered one way, then another, in an attempt to throw them off, but they came on. Risking a glance over his shoulder, he discovered why: Khalif in the imam's robes was closing in from the opposite direction. Again, he called out, but Bravo refused to listen, he would not be distracted. He had to concentrate on survival, and right now that meant making a clean escape from the trap.

A wooden bench was coming up too fast and he leapt over it, banging the trailing toe of his left shoe just as he went over the top. He twisted in midair, stumbled badly as he came down, lost several vital steps. One of the bearded men, taking advantage of his falter, launched himself into the air like a human missile. He struck Bravo in the small of his back, driving Bravo to his knees. The man reached out, seeking to end the encounter quickly, and Bravo slammed his cocked elbow into the bridge of the man's nose. Blood exploded, the man's grip on him vanished and Bravo gained his feet.

Adem Khalif was upon him by this time. As Khalif began to shout, Bravo plunged a fist into his solar plexus. Khalif groaned and doubled over. Leaping over him, Bravo was up and running again, between the twin columns flanking the entrance, out the door, down the steps and away.

Whirling out into the slate and gunmetal-gray evening, Bravo plunged into the crowds and almost at once lost all sense of direction. He allowed the flow to move him like a piece of jetsam thrown off a ship. At the moment, it did not matter to him where he went, as long as it was away from his enemies. Borne along on this human tide, he absorbed flashes of color, the scents of spice, strong coffee, anxiety and foreboding. The day was ending and, with it, all the mixed blessings and tiny setbacks that accompanied the preoccupations of each person he passed. The rhythms of languages and street argot fell on his ears like the beat of prayer drums.

The precious few moments of blissful anonymity passed through his fingers like sand. It wasn't long before he spotted one of the bearded men and, not far behind him, the other one, trying to stanch the flow of blood from his broken nose on the stained sleeve of his shirt.

Had they spotted him yet? He didn't know, he only knew they were heading in his direction. At once, he veered off to his right, out of the crowd flow. Yes, he was exposing himself for a moment, but he felt the risk was worth his gaining a safe haven.

He took a side street, trying not to break out into a run, to keep his pace more or less equal to that of the people around him. But the hard beating of his heart, the spurts of adrenaline rushing through his system made this difficult. And then, with an anxious glance behind him, he saw the two men shoot like sharks out of the surf on the main street, heading down the side street he had taken.

He plunged into the shadows of a narrow alley, stinking of garbage, creosote and offal. Dogs barked, heralding his presence, and the triangular head of one of them peered at him briefly before vanishing in a second explosion of barking.

He moved on, forcing himself to continue, even while he wondered whether he had made a mistake. No shops presented themselves, no doorways in which he could seek sanctuary. His smoldering fear burst into flame when he glanced back to see other shapes entering the alley. The bearded men? He heard the quickened pace of their footsteps. Who else but the bearded men?

He stumbled on, picking up his pace, hurrying around another corner, where the alley bent like an old woman's back. But scarcely a few meters on, he was brought up short. There, standing in front of him was Adem Khalif.

"YOU understand that this could backfire," Jenny said as they approached the entrance to Mikhail Kartli's house. "It's likely that Kartli has already heard the rumor that I murdered Father Mosto."

"In that case, you will implicate the priest," Camille said evenly, "absolving yourself."

"You want me to vilify Father Mosto?"

"I want you to help us find Bravo," Camille said quietly. "If that means lying to your contact about someone else's integrity I don't see that you have a choice."

Her manner was both forthright and steadfast. There was an iron will, a certain determination in her that reminded Jenny of Arcangela.

"What does it matter to Father Mosto, anyway?" Camille added. "He's dead."

"Kartli may not believe me."

"He will because you'll sell it to him." Camille lifted a hand, ran her fingers through Jenny's hair. "I have faith in you, Jenny." She smiled. "Don't worry, I'll back up whatever story you tell."

Jenny turned, knocked on the front door in a singular pattern not unlike Morse code. Camille took note with one part of her brain, but another part was thinking how amusing it was to fabricate feelings for someone you were manipulating. Artificial, slippery as oil, they could not sink their curved barbs into your flesh, could not hurt you in any way.

The door opened, revealing the lined, sober face of Mikhail Kartli. He ushered them into a small, rather dark sitting room, enrobed in heavy curtains. Lamps burned, illuminating a low ceiling, muscularly beamed. A series of small, exquisitely hand-knotted silk rugs hung on the wall, arranged as if they were paintings in a high-end art gallery. Camille glanced around as she sat on a heavy upholstered chair. He served them tea, dark and fragrant and steaming, from an old and well-used service on a magnificently hand-tooled copper tray. There was a selection of European biscuits from which they selected one each, more out of courtesy than hunger.

Camille had deliberately seated herself perpendicular to Mikhail Kartli so that she could watch him without seeming to do so. The Georgian was of great interest to her, since he had been the Order's mainstay in Trabzon, a city that had for many years gone unnoticed by the Knights of St. Clement. He had told Cornadoro that he was newly freelance, a soldier for hire. She sipped her tea, settling back to gain his measure while Jenny did the talking.

Kartli was speaking of mundane matters: the humidity, historical sites, the food—he recommended several restaurants. He would not, of course, ask them why they had come or how he could help them. That was not, Camille knew, how these people operated. They were cagey, you had to coax them out of their lairs. They needed to get the measure of you, as they might examine the glimmer of a creature plucked from beneath the ocean's waves.

With mounting interest she saw that, despite Jenny's stated fears, the younger woman was adept at speaking to Asians. Camille had discovered that as a rule Americans did not know how to treat either Europeans or Asians. To them, everyone in the world either shared America's values and customs or was of no import to them. Jenny's attitude was neither usual nor automatic. Camille adjusted upward her opinion of Jenny's abilities.

Kartli peered at Jenny from beneath hooded eyes. He had not moved during the introductions. Indeed, it was difficult to see the rise and fall of his abdomen, to ascertain whether he was still breathing.

"I'm going to tell you the truth," Jenny said now. "In Venice, I was set up as the fall guy for Father Mosto's death. My sin was not being alert enough to stop the attack on me, just before Father Mosto was murdered."

Kartli lifted the hand that until this moment had been propping up his chin. "You say you're telling me the truth." The hand waggled back and forth in equivocation. "You do not know me. What have I done to deserve this signal honor?"

"You're the Order's man in Trabzon," Jenny said.

"Therefore, I am trustworthy. But it seems these days no one, inside the Order or out, is to be trusted."

Jenny said, "I have nowhere else to go, nothing left to lose."

There was as slight pause.

"And this Father Mosto . . . ?"

"I don't pretend to know much about him. He's not important."

"A man's death—"

"What is vital for you to understand," Jenny pressed, "is that Anthony Rule was the Knight of St. Clement mole inside the Order—not me, not Paolo Zorzi."

Kartli's gimlet eyes never strayed from her face. "Paolo Zorzi was your mentor." It was not a question. "Difficult to believe he had turned against you, was it?"

"Actually, it wouldn't have been hard to believe at all," Jenny said. "He was perfectly placed."

"Yes, he was."

"But Rule would have been the smarter choice," she went on. "He was Dexter Shaw's closest confidant."

Kartli made no further comment, and nothing in his expression gave Jenny the slightest clue as to his thinking. Lacking such a guidepost, she had no choice but to plunge onward. "The bottom line is that we have to find Bravo before the agents of the Knights do, and keep him safe."

"I don't see how I can help you."

"You must have met him, that much we have surmised," Jenny said. "Like me, he had nowhere else to go in Trabzon."

"And I say again, I don't see how I can help you. I no longer work for the Order."

Jenny took a breath, as if she were about to move out into deeper water. She sat forward, her upper body angled toward Kartli, and Camille at once took note because a new, uncataloged tension had come into the muscles of her body, an expression of the deepest concentration flooded her face. She appeared undaunted by what Kartli had said.

"I want to tell you about Braverman Shaw," she began, and oddly enough, Kartli, though he might have wanted to, resisted the urge to stay her.

Jenny talked about Bravo in the most impassioned way, and Camille noticed something. Like a fly in a web, the Georgian's attention had been caught. Kartli, like Camille, had fastened onto the upwelling of genuine emotion as she conjured up Braverman Shaw for him.

This was of the most intense interest for Camille. Jenny was the vulnerable spot, the pivot point that would tip the scales and bring Bravo rushing to her, and now, for the first time, she began to understand the depth of Jenny's feelings for Bravo. Whereas before she had assumed a schoolgirl crush, a romantic infatuation brought about by intimate contact that could bond those in battle—she herself had had her share of fiery but short-lived affairs—now she heard the truth from Jenny's own mouth. Much to her surprise and consternation, Cornadoro had been right, after all. Jenny was committed to Bravo, truly, deeply, unshakably.

Camille took a deep breath, let it out slowly. This information changed everything.

Possibly Mikhail Kartli felt the same way, for he said, "I don't know where Braverman Shaw is."

Something passed across Jenny's expression. No more than a flicker, it was nevertheless picked up by Camille's keen eye. Friend or foe, this was how Jenny was coming to judge everyone she met. If they couldn't help her—or wouldn't—they became her enemy. For her the middle ground had disappeared, had been rendered meaningless by the betrayals she had suffered on this assignment. It would be wise to keep in mind her new way of looking at the Voire Dei, her rapid learning curve, Camille decided.

"In that case," Jenny said now, "I could really use a handgun."

"Luger or a Witness?"

"Is the Witness a Tanfoglio?" Jenny said. "I like the way the Italians make it."

Kartli smiled, as if she had passed a test. "The Tanfoglio Witness will cost you more."

"And extra ammo," Jenny said. "I aim to get my money's worth."

AS Bravo went into a defensive stance, Adem Khalif raised both hands palms outward in an unmistakable gesture of placation.

"I mean you no harm, Bravo, truly."

"What about those two behind me?"

"They mean you no harm, either."

"Bullshit. They belong to Mikhail Kartli."

"True enough," Khalif acknowledged, "but Kartli is no more your enemy than I am."

"Now I know you've lost your mind." It was maddening trying to keep track of both Khalif and the two bearded men at the same time, surely their intention. "I don't have to remind you that I offended Kartli. Mortally. He's out for my blood."

Adem Khalif inclined his head slightly. "So it would seem to anyone observing the incident."

There was a short pause, during which Bravo digested the implications of this comment. The feral dog had reappeared, no doubt lured by the prospect of fresh meat. One of the bearded men lofted an empty beer bottle in a low arc over Bravo's head, striking the animal in the side. It yelped in pain and vanished.

"Someone was observing us?" Bravo said.

"It was why Mikhail ignored my advice to take the argument inside his shop." Khalif ventured the ghost of a smile. "I wondered about that at the time. It is foolish to air one's business in public, and Mikhail Kartli is anything but foolish."

"True enough," Bravo nodded.

"I have more to tell you," Khalif said, "but, I beg you, somewhere more pleasant, yes?"

"What about the Glimmer Twins over there?"

Khalif's gaze shifted to the two bearded men behind Bravo. "Body-guards for you. Kartli's express orders. I wouldn't disobey them"—he shrugged—"though I suppose it is your choice."

Bravo waited a beat, considering. "I can dismiss them at any time."

"Of course."

Khalif's brown eyes met his without any hint of deception.

"All right," Bravo said. "Lead on."

A twenty-minute walk through the maze of the bazaar brought them to an unmarked door in a seedy building on a street sticky with beer. Here and there, garishly painted Natashas lounged and leered fiercely.

The door, its green field of peeling paint sadly faded, opened at Khalif's first knock, and they entered. The interior looked like Holly-wood's idea of an Oriental opium den circa 1950—red wallpaper, yel-low songbirds in bamboo cages, huge brass hookahs beside plush sofas, women in long, sleek, high-slit shantung silk dresses. On one wall, a painting of a lush naked woman, erotically sprawled on a divan, smiling with enigmatic malice.

The four men were completely ignored by the women, whose languid movement about the rooms reminded Bravo of exotic fish in a tank. Khalif nodded to an older woman with an inch of pancake makeup on her face, who directed them to a private room, then closed the door firmly behind them.

On the central table was a flagon of raki, eight bottles of beer, a de-canter of single-malt scotch and a fistful of glasses. Bravo and Khalif took seats. The Glimmer Twins remained outside, presumably flanking the door.

Khalif gestured at the liquor, but Bravo shook his head.

"Mikhail suspected that you were being followed," Khalif said. "Fur-ther, he felt there was only one way—sure and quick—to find out. He gave the impression of a serious falling out. I played my own part—unwitting, as it happens—of trying to be the mediator between two hotheads. His ruse worked. Not an hour after you left his shop, a man arrived. By that time I, too, had departed, though in the company of one of Mikhail's sons—to keep me from contacting you, or so I believed."

Khalif drew out a cell phone, turned it so Bravo could see the color photo on the screen. "Taken by one of Mikhail's sons. Look familiar?"

"Yes." Bravo frowned. "That's a man named Michael Berio. He met us in Venice, hired by a friend of mine."

"I'm afraid your friend's been duped—and so have you," Khalif said. "His real name is Damon Cornadoro. He's a member of one of Venice's *Case Vecchie*."

"One of the twenty-four founding families of Venice." Bravo nodded. "Like Paolo Zorzi."

"More importantly for you and for me," Khalif said, "he works for the Knights of St. Clement. In fact, he's their top assassin."

"Christ, and he's here."

"Here, and asking after your whereabouts. This is what Mikhail told me after his son summoned me back to his shop." Khalif opened one of the beers, took a deep swallow, set the bottle down. "Bravo, I must tell you that the fact that the Knights have sent this man after you is the worst possible news. He is powerful, determined, clever, and very very nasty. These traits have been bred in his bones, in his very blood."

"And now he's insinuated his way into my best friend's good graces." Bravo shook his head and took out his cell phone.

At once, Khalif stayed him. "What are you doing?"

"Calling my friend Jordan. I have to warn him—"

"The moment you do that, you alert Cornadoro you're on to him. Think, Bravo—is that what you really want?"

"If he's half as nasty as you make him out to be, you bet I do."

"And then what will happen, do you think?"

Bravo fought to put aside his anxiety over Jordan's safety. Fought to bring himself back to the here and now. "You're right, of course. The Knights will send someone else, someone we won't know about, someone we have no hope of controlling."

Khalif looked shocked. "Mikhail and I were talking about killing Cornadoro. Controlling him is—"

"Terrifying, yes, I agree. But killing him now will have the same effect as my calling Jordan. The Knights want what my father was guarding, what he's leading me toward. They won't stop with Cornadoro's death."

"Obviously you have something in mind." Khalif opened the decanter of scotch and filled two tumblers. "Tell me, please. We are in this together."

DAMON Cornadoro found Irema, the Georgian's daughter, at the Trabzonspor Club in the Ortahisar. It was named after one of Turkey's most famous football teams, and its decor showed their colors in pennants and photos signed by past and present team stars. All the serving girls wore team jerseys that came down to the middle of their bare thighs. Turkish techno music squalled from four large black speakers parked in the corners of the black-painted room. Television screens showed highlights of past games. The smell of beer and pot smoke hung like a pall.

Cornadoro sat at the bar and ordered a beer. Irema was sitting at a round table in the far left-hand corner with a number of her female friends. They were drinking and laughing. One of them, a heavyset girl with a flattish face, got up and danced while they laughed and clapped, and they bought her a beer when she sat down, flush-faced. It was all very innocent, which had immense appeal for him.

An hour and three beers later, he rose, went over to Irema and asked her very politely to dance. She looked up at him with her large, dark doe eyes, possibly to see if he was about to pull a joke on her—maybe he had come over on a dare from his buddies, maybe there was money riding on her response. But she saw only sincerity in his face—a handsome face, a face that was both sensual and sexual, a face that stirred her. She heard the laughs, the lewd encouragement from her half-drunk friends. Half-drunk herself, she held out her hand in a curiously formal gesture and allowed him to pull her gently onto the club's minuscule dance floor.

She had it in her mind to dance with him for one song, but the one song morphed into three, three melted into six, and on and on she danced, feeling their hips bump, their middles meld, their pelvises grinding as she moved ever closer to him.

"My name is Michael," he said, speaking to her in Georgian.

Her besotted eyes opened wide. "Just like my father."

"I am not your father," he said, swinging her around.

She laughed. "Oh, my God, no, you're not." She was breathless and flushed.

She told him her name and he said it was beautiful, that she was as lithe and graceful as the deer for which she was named.

She laughed again and held on to him as they spun, her arms around his neck trembling slightly with the onrush of her emotions. With her mother's delicate features and cool, porcelain skin, she possessed a freshness that was appealing. Her long black hair was pulled back in a ponytail, which whipped this way and that as she whirled around.

For Cornadoro's part, it was easy for him to make her believe he liked her—he *did* like her, in the way he liked virtually all women: their animal scent set his blood to boiling. There resided in him a certain insatiability that was like an itch he'd long ago given up trying to scratch. He wanted what was between a woman's legs, simple as that. And as superb a lover as Camille Muhlmann was, what she demanded of him was difficult for him to maintain: monogamy. He had never complied, not really. At first, he'd tried, but he'd failed so quickly—who had it been with, the dirty-blond American teenager on holiday or the sinuous Taiwanese five years younger than he had guessed or possibly someone else altogether, he could never be certain—that he'd never attempted it again. Instead, he had perfected his lies—no easy feat with Camille, something of a human lie detector—so that he could remain in her bed. He didn't want to lose that pole position, for many reasons, both carnal and political.

Camille was brilliant, no question, but the basic problem with her was that she was old. What he craved most was fresh meat, young and dewy and luscious in its innocence. Like Irema. Plus, he didn't like Irema's father, which gave the act of seducing her a frisson that made him lick his chops with anticipation.

As their dancing progressed he could feel her falling under his spell. It was a physical thing he experienced in his throat and his arms and his groin; it was like sex, like death. The blackness of the abyss was where he drew his sexual energy, it was what made it so feral, so irresistible.

He danced with her and, as he did so, he could feel that old familiar feeling creeping along his skin. He loved Irema and he made her feel it, though, of course, the source of it remained unknown to her. He loved her for the information with which she would provide him.

NO lights were on when he brought her to his hotel room. The glimmer of the city came through the jalousied window in pale horizontal stripes, illuminated her like a neon sign. He told her to strip and she did, slowly before his greedy, glittering eyes. Then he told her what else to do. She didn't seem to mind; in fact, she liked it. She was used to being ordered around, there was a high degree of comfort in the known, but he suspected from looking at her that wasn't what she wanted, not really. And tonight he was determined to give her what she really wanted.

Naked, she looked more like a girl, small breasts, slim hips, tiny waist. But her legs were long and nicely rounded, and her rump. . . . He had her continue to stand with her back to him, her arms at her sides. She was wholly unself-conscious about her nakedness, unafraid about what he might do with her. He had her trust, and this, more than anything, inflamed him.

He popped the buttons on his shirt pulling it off, and he was already so rigid that his trousers gave him a struggle. She turned in response to his growl of frustration and used her nimble fingers to unbuckle his belt, unzip him. As his trousers came down so did she, until she was on her knees. He ripped the band from her ponytail, twined his fingers in her loosed hair.

When he lifted her, her legs opened, her thighs gripping his hips as she gave a little moan. He felt her skin against him, warm, smooth as ivory, the bony hardness of youth still upon her. Enough to tip any man over the edge, but he held on, leading her up the sexual arc until, shuddering and groaning, she reached the apex. One wasn't enough for her, he'd known that from the start. Hot little thing. Like a star, intent on burning to a cinder. He waited her out, he was adept at that; in fact, the denial fired his nerve endings to the fever pitch he longed for, had to have.

But he needed her to feel that, too. She didn't have his reserves, didn't understand what was happening, trembled uncontrollably as he brought her to the final brink, then pulled them both back, over and over. Tears came and she clasped him desperately, implored him to finish it.

It wasn't until she said, "Why are you waiting, it's torture, I'm dying," that he ended it for both of them, so that she crawled up onto him, over him, seeking a way to be inside him as he emptied himself inside her.

Afterward, she asked for it again so quickly he almost laughed. She had never come down from her last orgasm, she was soft and warm as taffy, the black pupils of her eyes as dilated as if he had given her opium. This was the moment he had been manufacturing all evening, the moment to ask her for what he wanted while she wasn't thinking clearly, or at all.

"Of course I'll help you." She guided him back into her with a deep-felt sigh. "No one has ever asked me for help before."

"Not even your brothers?"

"All I ever get from them are orders." Her fingers cupped him, caressing. "You'd think they'd be more enlightened." She maneuvered herself above him, straddling his girth, stretching her thighs to their limits. The slight pain made the pleasure all the sweeter. "That's what we were talking about in the bar when you came over."

"They all feel that way, don't they," he said, "all your girlfriends."

"Oh, yes," she moaned, but he couldn't be sure that was an answer to his question because she was trembling again from head to toe and her eyes were rolling in her head.

He held onto her as she let go, feeling the frantic bucking of wild youthful energy as if it were a shot of adrenaline into his own system.

At last she was spent, or as near as she could get, but still she wanted to hear the phrase he had pumped out all night long, "Whatever you want, Irema. Whatever you want." When had she ever heard that from a man? In her secret discussions with her girlfriends, sitting in front of a mirror while she applied lipstick, in her dreams at night as she tossed and turned in fretful sleep. But in real life, from a flesh-and-blood male—one who held her, kissed her, caressed her, entered her with such tenderness, until she screamed at him to do otherwise? This night, never before. This night only.

Which was why she would do anything to ensure that it never ended, including convincing herself that everything he told her was true, *must* be true because of how she felt about him, because of what he had given her freely, and would do so again *whenever she wanted it.*

"Your father and I work for the Order." He held her gently, rocking her, just as she liked. "The only difference is he works in the field—in his case, here in Trabzon—while I am stuck in an office in Rome. For the most part. Every so often, I'm asked to go into the field to check up on operatives. But anonymously, you know. So your father must never know that I was here or that I was asking about his activities. It would cost me my job, with no opportunity to explain myself, do you understand, Irema?"

She nodded. Her heart was thumping as hard as if he were still thrusting into her. She vaguely understood that her father was more than a rug merchant. For one thing, there were the men who sought him out—they came and never left with a rug. For another, her father was far richer than any rug merchant of her knowledge. Also, people— Georgian, Russian, Turkish, whatever—inclined their heads to him when they passed him in the street. He commanded respect. So, though she had never been allowed in the shop during business hours, her eyes and ears had been open, picking up bits and pieces here and there, far more, she suspected, than her father knew.

"I've been here three days now, talking to his associates," he said, "and everything seems in order, except for one thing."

Irema stared at him. The thumping of her heart had turned painful— something bad couldn't happen to her father, it couldn't.

"What is the one thing?" she asked in little more than a croak. The grit of fear had parched her throat.

"Earlier today your father had an . . . altercation with another member of the Order." His face was stern, scaring her all the more. "This was a very important member of the Order, Irema, very high up in the ruling body."

"Very high up?"

He nodded. "*Very.* Your father sent him away, refused to give him the help he requested. I have to tell you that this is an extremely serious breach of protocol."

"Protocol?"

"My bosses are pissed off."

"Oh!" She put her hand over her mouth as she giggled delightedly.

"Irema." He took her hand away from her mouth. "This is no laughing matter, I assure you."

"Oh, but it is!" At last her heart was light, and she felt an exhilaration inside herself. She never could have believed it, but hers was the power to exonerate her father from false reports that would have doomed him with the Order. She had overheard enough, had pieced enough together to make a patchwork quilt, and although she had also heard her father tell her brothers numerous times never to tell outsiders family business, she knew this was different. She was helping her father with the people who paid him, who were the source of all the money, all the respect that he had worked so hard for. How could that be wrong? Also, this man and her father were allies. So she told her sweet lover what she knew:

"That altercation was a ruse."

"A ruse?" He rose up on one elbow, his shadowed face hard and craggy. "What do you mean?"

"My father would never be so rude to another member of the Order. I heard him talking on the phone to one of my brothers. It was all faked, in case someone was watching."

"All faked." Her lover lay back, his hand resting on her soft, soft belly. "Ah, Irema, my love. It was all faked."

Once he started to laugh he couldn't stop.

27

BRAVO SAW JENNY ON THE SPLIT-LEVEL TERRACE OF THE
Sumela Café, with the silver platter of the Black Sea spread out below
them. Adem Khalif had taken him here for a late-night dinner. Bravo
should have been exhausted, but he wasn't. He had read articles about
the so-called adrenaline high soldiers experienced in the heat of battle,
but until now he'd had no direct experience with the phenomenon.

Seeing her in profile, bathed in desolate moonlight, he recalled the
stricken look on her face during their brief encounter in the bazaar.
Then she turned and the nape of her neck was exposed to him, the long
sweep, pale in the moonlight, the gentle slope leading to the base of her
skull, the fine down of hair, the perfect vulnerable arc. For a moment all
his anger, rage and urge for revenge slipped away, and he was left
naked, as vulnerable as she seemed, with all his suppressed emotions
exposed.

Not only to him, apparently, because Khalif, standing with him
shoulder to shoulder, said, "Bravo, what is it? Do you know that
woman?" He drew a gun. "She is one of your enemies."

At a table not far away, the bearded Glimmer Twins, still with them,
raised their heads. They half rose off their chairs, their upper bodies
tilted slightly forward as if they were sprinters at the starting line.

"Put that away," Bravo said, without looking at Khalif, because Jenny
had moved a pace and now he could see that she was with another
woman: Camille, his Camille. What in the world was going on?

He began to walk toward the table where the two women sat, chatting
as if they were friends—no, something in their attitude convinced him
that the connection between them had become more intimate.

"Bravo, do you think this is wise?" Khalif said.

"Stand guard here," Bravo answered him. "Keep your hand on your gun, if you must, but don't try to stop me."

Khalif didn't, and though he was filled with foreboding he waved Mikhail's men to sit back down. He'd heard that tone of voice before, from Dexter Shaw, and he knew better than to interfere.

CAMILLE paused in midsentence, and Jenny saw the woman's eyes shift to a spot behind and just to the right of her. She turned. At the sight of Bravo her heart thudded in her breast and the sudden quick rush of blood to her head made her dizzy. She wanted to rise and hit him, as surely she would have in the bazaar had the bullet from the assassin's gun not struck the merchant beside her. She tasted blood in her mouth, and realized that she had bitten her lip.

"I want to speak with you," he said as he came up. "Now."

Her hands balled into fists, but then she realized that it was Camille he was looking at, Camille to whom he had directed his command. He hadn't looked at her, hadn't acknowledged her presence, as if she were a ghost occupying a place in another world.

Camille rose and said, "Of course, my love," leaving her without a backward glance.

BRAVO stood with Camille at the edge of the terrace. Low clouds obscured the northern horizon. High above, there was a palely glowing ring around the moon. Down the length of the light-strung terrace he was aware of Adem Khalif slowly sipping a glass of raki, watching them, exuding worry like musk. As for the Glimmer Twins, his image swam in their dark, avid eyes; they were itching to be needed.

"What the hell are you doing here?" he asked Camille in a ragged voice.

"What do you think? Keeping an eye on you, trying to keep you safe."

"It's you I'm worried about," he said angrily. "You shouldn't be anywhere near here. And certainly not with *her*."

"Who? Jenny?"

"Yes, Jenny. She's murdered three people: two priests and Uncle Tony. Are you out of your mind?"

"Listen to me, my love, you have to stop thinking of me as a helpless female." She shook out a cigarette, lit it, regarded him through the veil of aromatic smoke. "I wouldn't be here if I wasn't more than capable of taking care of myself." She blew out a spiral of smoke. "As for Jenny, you know what Sun Tzu wrote: 'Keep your friends close, your enemies closer.'" She looked at Jenny, smiled reassuringly into her face, before turning back.

"Sun Tzu had something else to say about the art of war," Bravo said. "Every battle is lost or won before it begins."

"Meaning?"

"If you don't know, you surely don't belong here."

"Ah, Bravo," she chuckled, "always testing me."

A breeze rose up from the coolness of the water, stirring her hair against her cheek. Music, trafficking in high spirits and a lover's touch, insinuated itself onto the terrace, reminding them how far removed they were from the rest of the world.

"I was prepared for this the moment I left Paris." She eyed him speculatively. "You think not?"

"I think it's damn odd you being here."

"Do you suspect me now? Of what?" She dropped her cigarette, ground it beneath her heel. "Dammit, Bravo, if I didn't love you so much I'd slap you. You're like a son to me. I mean to protect you, something Jenny only pretended to do."

Bravo rubbed the side of his head. He was exhausted, both physically and emotionally. His head pounded with a million different strands, possible paths he might take, he ought to take. The specters of what lay at the end of those paths haunted him day and night.

"Listen, we're friends now, Jenny and I," Camille said in a softer tone. "We're close, and getting closer. I know how to gain her trust, woman to woman. She tells me things."

"No doubt. Like she's innocent."

"Of course, but who's listening?"

"She's guilty as sin—and she's dangerous."

"I allow her to think I believe her, she lets down her guard. Perhaps tomorrow I'll know part of her plan."

"She'll never tell you what she's planning, Camille. She knows how close we are."

"She's been cut off from all her traditional sources, so she's slowly coming to rely on my advice. Why shouldn't she? I'll stay with her, I'll be *your* mole in the enemy camp." She put a hand on his arm, squeezed. "Let me do this for you, Bravo." She smiled and kissed his cheek. "*Alors,* don't worry so. She won't hurt me."

"She isn't the only one you have look out for," he said, lowering his voice. "That man Jordan hired, Michael Berio—his real name is Damon Cornadoro. He's a professional assassin."

"*Mon dieu, non!*" What a delicious thrill ran through her when she lied to him now; it was almost as deep a charge as lying to Dexter had been. "Are you sure?"

"Absolutely. He's been sent by enemies of my father to shadow me until I find what my father sent me to find. Then he means to kill me and take it."

"But what is it, my love? What could be so terribly valuable?"

"It doesn't matter. What matters is that you keep as far away from Cornadoro as you possibly can."

"I promise."

"Camille, for the love of God don't be flip. I have enough on my mind. I don't want to worry about you."

"Then don't," she said firmly. "I told you. I can take care of myself." She laughed softly, put her hand against his cheek. "I assure you, I will not become your damsel in distress."

He stared into her eyes and knew that she had made her decision; nothing he could say would sway her. He nodded, acquiescing, and pulled out his cell phone. "Then promise me you'll stay in touch, all right?"

She took out her own cell phone, nodded. "I promise." As he was about to turn away, she said with great concern in her voice, "Bravo, have you any idea yet where you're going next?"

"No," he lied. He didn't care what she said, he wasn't going to allow her to put herself any further in harm's way.

MIDNIGHT. Irema was home, safely tucked in bed, lips and breasts nicely bruised, drugged on sex and love, dreaming deeply of Michael. But Irema's father was far from home, far from the bed warmed by the lush body of his wife. Instead, he passed through the streets of Trabzon like a wraith. Music, reaching his cocked ears, failed to move him, drunken couples staggered by without seeing him. A solitary bicyclist crossed his path like a black cat. Smoking fiercely, he strode past two churches that had long ago been turned into mosques. Their magnificent Byzantine facades were dark as soot, faded now, as was almost everything in Trabzon. Cracks and crumbles showed everywhere. If he listened hard enough he could hear the buildings groan like the crippled veterans of long-ago wars.

His cell phone buzzed and he answered it. Adem Khalif's voice appeared in his ear like a djinn, talking of a plan to trap Damon Cornadoro. He was impressed by Braverman Shaw's plan, which, viewed objectively, had a certain merit. His mind spinning in several directions at once, he listened to the end, then agreed. "What route are you planning to use? All right, my people will be deployed before dawn."

He disconnected, called his eldest son and told him what was required. Then, because he was approaching his destination, he put away his cell phone.

Midway down a small, disordered side street stood an old but structurally sound building he had purchased many years ago. It looked no different than its slope-shouldered neighbors; it bore no sign on its peeling front, was surely mistaken by almost everyone for a private residence. Inside, however, it housed the Church of the Nine Martyred Children.

Kartli had named this tiny outpost of his Georgian Orthodox religion for the young pagan children of Kola who, of their own free will, had embraced Jesus Christ. They were baptized by the local priest and left their families to be brought up by Christian families, according to the ways of the Savior. Their parents came after them and dragged them back home, but when their children would not eat pagan food or drink pagan drink, when they instead spoke the words of Jesus Christ, their parents were so enraged that they mercilessly beat the village priest, drove him from Kola. One last time they asked their sons and daughters, many not more than seven years of age, to return to their pagan ways. When the children refused, the parents took up stones and beat their own children to death, as a lesson to the other children of Kola.

Mikhail Kartli paused to take in the holy surroundings. He was immensely proud of this church, glad of the name he had chosen for it, because it was a reminder of how the world really worked, of the terrible prejudices that ran like poison through the bedrock of mankind. Not that he needed such a reminder even here in Trabzon so far from home, but everyone else—including his children, especially wild Irema—did.

Nothing looked as it did in daylight. Shadows distorted all the shapes. Illumination came from two sources: a Byzantine oil lamp and a naked lightbulb. Like everything in the city the light was an uncomfortable juxtaposition of old and new—elements that should have been allies seemed to be enemies. The interior was sparsely furnished, appropriately bare save for the large portrait of the Virgin Mary, the iconostasis, the pulpit, a scattering of scarred wooden benches and, of course, the confessional. It was to this dark wooden structure that Mikhail Kartli came twice a week like clockwork to give his confession. Since the priests of the Church of the Nine Martyred Children were housed by Kartli at his expense, they were only too happy to oblige his habit, especially since the habit so eloquently expressed his devoutness.

At seven minutes after midnight, he opened the door to the confessional, settled himself on the narrow seat. Through the latticework of the carved wooden screen the profile of the priest was visible. He recognized Father Shota, one of his favorites. This pleased him. He and Father Shota had spent many hours talking of the history of their religion.

The Apostle Andrew, the brother of St. Peter, had come to Georgia to preach the Gospel, bringing with him the Holy Mother's Uncreated Icon—not created by the hand of man, an icon of divine origins. From that time forward, Mary became Georgia's protector. Over the intervening centuries the Georgian Orthodox religion had been heavily influenced by the Christians of the Byzantine Empire, so it was fitting to Mikhail Kartli, an ardent student of history, that he had brought the religion back home, completing the circle, the end returned to the beginning.

"Forgive me, Father, for I have sinned," he began.

And Father Shota replied, "Behold, my child, Christ stands here invisibly receiving your confession. Do not be ashamed and do not fear, and do not withhold anything from me; but without doubt tell all you have done and receive forgiveness from the Lord Jesus Christ. Lo, His holy image is before us—"

Without warning, the latticework screen shattered inward. Kartli, struck in the face by shards of wood, raised his arms defensively, and so received the priest into his hands as the man crashed through the aperture.

"Father Shota!" he cried.

Eyelids fluttering spastically, the priest tried to answer, but pink bubbles foamed in his open mouth. Kartli felt the slow creep of blood, warm and viscid, smelled the nauseating sweet-coppery odor. Cradling the priest's head and shoulders, searching desperately for the strength of vital signs, he was unprepared as the door to his side of the confessional flew open.

With barely a chance to turn his head, Kartli had a momentary impression, blurred and imprecise, of a grinning face. With a swift and vicious thrust, his maimed right hand was pinned to the back of the confessional by a spike impaled through the center of his palm. Oblivious to the pain, he tried to use his left hand to strike out at his attacker, but burdened with Father Shota's weight, he was essentially helpless.

Damon Cornadoro produced his push-dagger and grabbed a fistful of Father Shota's hair.

"No!" Kartli cried. "For the love of God, spare him!"

"Spare him? Why? He was the one who betrayed you. He told me where you'd be tonight." With the sickening precision of a surgeon Cornadoro slashed the edge of the push-dagger across the priest's throat. Putting his knee into the small of the corpse's back, he used Shota to pin the Georgian firmly in place. The priest's head lolled at an unnatural angle, his expression was one of terrified astonishment.

"How easily lies come to you, Georgian." Cornadoro leaned in. "Did you think I wouldn't find out?"

Kartli stared at him, stony, utterly silent. The initial shock was over: the barbarism could not affect him—he'd seen worse in his day—but the loss, he knew, would stay with him a long time.

"Don't you want to know how I found out?"

Kartli spat into the hateful face. He knew how to handle death-lovers, God knew he'd had enough experience. Show them fear and they lapped it up like cream. Cornadoro's mouth twitched in a parody of a smile.

There was something distinctly unsavory about the grin; with a repellent shock Kartli recognized the taint of lechery.

"It was Irema. Yes, yes. Your lovely daughter, your jewel." Cornadoro's head was inches from Kartli's face; his intimate tone brought home as nothing else could the stark horror of his words. "Her small breasts high on her chest, the dark nipples . . ."

Kartli convulsed, struggling against the pressure exerted against him. "You lying piece of filth!"

"The oval birthmark just over her left hipbone—like a tattoo, *better* even—*very* sexy, if you think like I do."

Kartli erupted, his eyes standing out, his face flushed with blood. "I'll kill you!"

"And the best part, Georgian, is how she *fucks*."

Cornadoro did everything but lick his chops. Dizzied, Kartli could feel the other's lust, the unequivocal affirmation, the lethal power of his words.

"Like an animal, wrapping her legs around me, begging for it over and over again. I swear she could drain a warhorse."

Kartli shouted as his ancient ancestors had surely shouted on the bloody fields of battle. With his left hand, he grabbed the end of the spike protruding from his palm and wrenched it free. Blood spurted, but he was beyond caring, beyond feeling anything. An animal himself, he was taken by blind rage. Somewhere in the back of his mind a voice of warning, of prudence sounded like an echo from another age, but it was quickly drowned out by the martial drumbeat of his blood.

"That's right," Cornadoro half sang in counterpoint to the threat of the spike. "That's right, come on."

The point of the spike pierced the muscle of Cornadoro's shoulder. The Georgian was powerful, stronger than Cornadoro had expected. Kartli tried to twist the spike, to sink it deeper, to open the meat of Cornadoro's shoulder. Cornadoro struck the Georgian's ear so hard his head bounced. Even in the strongest of constitutions such a concussive blow stopped thought and action in its tracks. Cornadoro tried to rip the spike away while Kartli's eyes showed white and he fought to stay conscious.

Running on instinct, on the need for survival, the Georgian lifted his knee from between the corpse's legs, buried it in Cornadoro's groin.

The Georgian drove the spike downward. Taking the brunt of it on his biceps, Cornadoro chopped down with the heavy, callused edge of his hand against the side of Kartli's neck, into the carotid artery. He applied pressure that ran all the way up from his feet, wrenching away the spike, reversing it, driving it into the Georgian's chest just beneath the breastbone. Kartli's eyes opened wide. He did not utter a sound, though Cornadoro knew he must have been in excruciating pain. His will to live was, even in Cornadoro's experience, extraordinary. A last gift was in order, a lifting of a mystery.

"I know what you're thinking, Georgian," Cornadoro said. "But it isn't religion or politics or nationalism that drives me."

"You're nothing, less than nothing because you have no belief, no faith, no soul." Mikhail Kartli's voice was a hoarse whisper. "With you it's all about commerce."

Cornadoro laughed, suddenly delighted. "On the contrary, as I told you when we first met, it's about the information. Secrets, the unknowable made known; everyone becomes vulnerable."

Kartli's fingers squeezed Cornadoro's neck, the last, desperate struggle, the terminal fight for survival, and with an almost superhuman effort he nearly managed to drive Cornadoro into unconsciousness. But the pressure on his carotid had weakened him past a vital threshold, cutting off blood and oxygen to his brain long enough to impair his coordination and reaction time. With a grunt, Cornadoro reasserted control, a control that, for Mikhail Kartli, would never cease.

"I have made you vulnerable, Georgian." Cornadoro clamped one hand at the nape of the other's neck. "I have defiled your daughter. You were dead two hours ago."

With his usual surgeon's precision, he swiped the push-dagger in a shallow arc that opened the Georgian's throat. Cornadoro studied Kartli's face as if he could in some way absorb the spark of life as it went out of the eyes. Then he wiped the push-dagger on Kartli's trousers and turned away. By the time he removed himself from the confessional, he had already forgotten both his victims.

28

AS THE POPE BREATHED SHALLOWLY IN HIS HOLY SICKBED,
as Cardinal Canesi paced the Vatican hospital corridor, continued to
burn up the cell airwaves with threats and false promises to every Turkish priest he could track down, Bravo and Adem Khalif set out for the
Sumela Monastery. Dawn, once a promising broken-shell pink on the
eastern horizon, had been swallowed whole by Black Sea clouds, hanging like a dank curtain, obscuring the mountaintops. The air was as
heavy as grease, stirred fitfully by a reluctant breeze. The sea, as they ascended, looked less and less real, appeared creased, solid, like a sheet of
aluminum foil.

Once, they would have risen toward the Zigana Pass on the backs of
sure-footed horses or stout donkeys laden with goods bound for the interior of Anatolia or, if they were enterprising enough, beyond, following the long and treacherous camel route all the way to Tabriz, in
northern Persia. In their case, Khalif's rattletrap car would have to do,
spewing sulphur-dioxide particulates every time he changed gears. The
car was full: in the backseat, the Glimmer Twins, heavily armed, con-
sulted their cell phones as if they were the Delphic Oracle. The phones,
wirelessly connected by satellite to the Global Positioning System, gave
them a god's-eye view of the trip. They were in contact with their
brethren, Kartli's people, deployed in strategic positions, monitoring
the traffic along the car's route through high-powered field glasses.

Bravo's cell phone gave a stuttering burr, but when he answered it,
the signal was gone, with no record of who had called. He thought,
then, of Emma, dutifully cross-referencing the London intel Dexter had
assigned to her. He found he very much wanted to talk with her, as if

hearing her voice would restore a semblance of the equilibrium he had lost with each betrayal, each death.

He held the slip of paper his father had interred beneath the tile of *oltu tasi* at the Zigana Mosque, along with his father's notebook. The cipher was a long one, a veritable bitch, and Bravo was having great difficulty decrypting it. Part of the problem was that the cipher seemed as if it was incomplete, but he knew that couldn't be.

Beside him, Khalif kept up a steady stream of stories from the Order's past, mostly about Fra Leoni. "Fra Leoni was both a genius and a saint, and here is why. Have you heard of Leon Alberti?"

Bravo glanced at him briefly. "Of course. He was the father of the Vigenère cipher, the greatest cryptologic breakthrough in more than a thousand years. He was also a philosopher, painter, composer, poet and architect. He designed Rome's first Trevi Fountain, and it was his book, the first ever published on architecture, that sparked the transition from the Gothic to the Renaissance style."

"And who do you suppose ensured that his book was published?" Khalif said.

"I have no idea." Part of his mind was still working on the perplexing cipher.

"His good friend and confidant, the man from whom he learned the philosophy of cryptography on which the Vigenère cipher is based. Fra Leoni."

His interest sparked. "So Fra Leoni was the cipher's godfather."

"Exactly so." Khalif nodded. "Shortly after taking over as *Magister Regens,* Fra Leoni discovered that a number of the Order's secret ciphers had been intercepted and decoded by the Knights. He knew it was essential that he invent an unbreakable cipher system, and he had the basis of an idea. Instead of a substitution cipher, he wanted to work on the notion of using two cipher alphabets simultaneously—the first letter of the message would be encoded using the first alphabet, the second letter encoded with the second alphabet, the third letter encoded with the first, and so on. He reasoned, quite rightly, that employing two alphabets instead of the traditional one would thoroughly confuse anyone attempting to break the cipher. To this end he recruited Alberti to aid him in his quest.

"This was around 1425, but Alberti died before he had completed his task of a fully formed method of encryption. Over the years, Fra

Leoni turned to others in the Order: a German abbot, an Italian scientist and, finally, a French diplomat, Blaise de Vigenère, who Fra Leoni contrived to have assigned to Rome. This was in 1529. Fra Leoni showed him Alberti's original treatise, along with the notations of the other members of the Order. It took Vigenère and Fra Leoni another ten years before the cipher was engineered to perfection."

"And for the next two hundred years or more it was unbreakable, so it must have served the Order well," Bravo said. "The British cryptographer Charles Babbage broke the Vigenère cipher in 1854."

"Ah, but his discovery was never published in his lifetime." Khalif rumbled off the road briefly to bypass a herd of goats, who looked at them with slitted demon's eyes. "It wasn't until the 1970s that—"

"Wait a minute," Bravo said, "you're not telling me that the Order had something to do with the suppression of Babbage's breakthrough."

"Charles Babbage was a member of the Order."

"What? Explain this to me."

"Under no circumstances." In a death-defying maneuver, Khalif pulled out into the oncoming traffic lane to surge past a truck whose diesel engine seemed on the verge of issuing a death rattle. "In this I must be your father's advocate. You have enough information to work out the solution for yourself."

The rearview mirror revealed that the Glimmer Twins were knee-deep in their own excited conversations. It was going well, then. Bravo tried not to be inordinately pleased, but he couldn't help himself. At last things were turning his way. Except for this damnable cipher his father had left him, whose key still eluded him.

Redirecting his thoughts to the problem Khalif had proposed, he said, "If I were Fra Leoni and had spent so much time and mental energy on creating this polyalphabetic cipher, if I was going to depend on it for the Order's secret communication, I'd want to make damn sure it couldn't be broken."

"How would you do that?"

"I'd use the same method I'd used to create it—put a team together to work on breaking it."

The twinkle in Adem Khalif's eye heartened Bravo; he was on the right track.

"And once they had broken it?"

"I'd make damn sure no one knew about it until I could come up with another, even more secure cipher. Which the Order must have accomplished in 1970."

"Quite right."

Bravo shook his head in awe. "And shortly thereafter, Babbage's discovery was made public."

"That was your father's doing." Khalif gave him a brief glance. "You know it was your father who invented the new cipher—the Angel String. Fra Leoni having died some decades before, it was your father who took up his torch. It seemed to me that he had an almost mystical bond with Fra Leoni." He shrugged. "Perhaps—I don't know this for a fact, you understand—your father managed to meet Fra Leoni. Don't give me that look, it's altogether possible, you know. When your father put his mind to something, he almost always succeeded."

The Angel String was his father's creation—he should have known that because his father had talked to him about how the Vigenère code was broken: a method was devised to determine the length of the keyword. The cipher was then broken down into sections corresponding to that number of letters. These manageable chunks were then analyzed for letter frequency. The whole idea of the next-level cipher, his father had told him, was to do away with the keyword. But then the encoder would be mired in a jungle of multiple alphabets without a place to start his encryption.

Then something clicked in his mind. Drawing out the lighter his father had left him, he opened it, slid out the photo of Junior. Odd that his father had chosen a black and white shot that had been hand-colored: red, blue, green. . . . In fact, now that he looked at it closely, Junior's face was yellow, not flesh-colored.

Turning to a blank page of his father's notebook, he jotted down the colors of the visible spectrum. It started with red and ended with purple. Assigning a number to each color brought him to 1543. So he was to use the first, fifth, fourth and third alphabets in that order. Referring back to the Vigenère grid he had used before, he began his decrypting.

Behind him, the conversation of the Glimmer Twins became more intense. He ignored it for as long as he could, until their excited chatter filled the interior of the car. By that time, he was halfway through turning the cipher into plaintext and was already deeply troubled by what he'd read.

Tearing himself away from his work, he turned halfway around in his seat.

"A sighting?" he said.

"Here's where we are," one of them, whose name was Bebur said, pointing to a screen glowing like a fusion reactor.

"And here's Damon Cornadoro," Djura, the other, said. Beneath the bandages, his nose was dark and swollen where Bravo had struck him in the Zigana Mosque. "His truck is a half kilometer behind us."

"Excellent. The plan is working."

"Not exactly," Bebur said. "Mikhail gave orders to shoot him on sight. Somehow, he managed to completely elude the ambush. He's still behind us."

"WHAT did he say?"

"I told you last night," Camille said as she drove the rented car through heavy traffic.

"I've been thinking about it, all night, as it happens," Jenny said. "I don't believe you."

Camille glanced carefully at her, trying to gauge the anger that had been building inside her. The idea was to turn it against Bravo, not to let it bleed onto herself.

"Why on earth would I lie to you?" Camille hit the horn as she maneuvered around two ancient autos, whose drivers were screaming at one another.

"You said it yourself. Bravo is like a son to you. You'd sacrifice me to protect him." Jenny turned to Camille. "What you don't seem to get is that I want to protect him, too."

"Even after what he's done to you? Accused you of murder, of being a traitor. Even after he's threatened to kill you himself?"

"I love him, Camille."

"He's given up on you," Camille said. "He said as much last night."

"It doesn't matter."

Camille shook her head. She was genuinely perplexed. "I don't understand you."

"Isn't that what love is all about? A feeling that transcends difficulties, misunderstandings, disappointments, seeming betrayals?"

For the first time in her life Camille felt stymied, at a loss for words. Her confusion stemmed from her memories of Dexter. Her anger at him, at his betrayal, had been monumental, all-consuming. Now, facing Jenny's immutable emotion, she was forced to confront the flicker of her own. She had loved Dexter, yes. She had been gripped by a fever that had threatened to turn her inside out, turn her from her avowed purpose. It had, in fact, frightened her so thoroughly that she had shut down the feeling, gritted her teeth, gotten on with the job of turning him against those he loved the most. Only it hadn't worked. She had failed, which was bad enough. But, far worse, there had come a moment when she recognized that she herself might turn against those *she* loved most. For him. For him.

She slammed the wheel with the heels of her hands.

"What is it?"

"Nothing," Camille said thickly. "Nothing at all."

Lies. Lies, lies and more lies. It was Dexter she had cared for, only Dexter. And Jordan? She'd had her chance to love him, but instead she had fed him bile and hatred with her milk. She had raised him for one purpose: to be her instrument for revenge on the Knights as well as on the Order. She wanted to bring them all down. Now it was too late. He had moved too far from her, as far as the dead moon was from the earth. When it came to Jordan, she could feel nothing at all.

"I don't believe you." Jenny's eyes searched Camille's face. Again, the murmur of Arcangela's voice resounded in her mind, the echos of courage, vigilance, daring, perseverance. These were, she realized now, the same qualities that Paolo Zorzi had sought to pound into her with every blow he had struck at her. All at once, she felt renewed strength flow into her from a source she never before had known existed inside her. She saw Ronnie Kavanaugh, and Dexter, too, in their rightful places. They, along with Paolo Zorzi and, of course, her father, had been part of her rite of passage, elements of the crucible in which the person she was now had been forged—in pain and misery, both of which had only made her stronger in the end. She knew that now, with a certainty that pierced her through and through.

"What aren't you telling me?"

Camille, alert as a hunting dog, glanced at Jenny. Another thunderbolt came at her. Something had happened while she hadn't been looking.

Jenny was no longer the lost, vulnerable, betrayed woman she had seemed just a short time ago. Camille felt the danger prickling along her arms. The silken hairs stirred at the back of her neck. Jenny would no longer simply accept her lies. She would have to do something that went entirely against her grain: she would have to tell her the truth.

"I envy how you feel about Bravo," she said, fighting a certain nausea. Telling the truth always turned her stomach. "Because I can't feel any of that. I'm dead inside, Jenny. Dead."

"Camille, what are you saying? I know you love Bravo—and you must feel the same about your son."

Camille stared hard at the traffic snaking up the steepening hill. She felt lost, and alone. What of it? She had her purpose—her decades-old plan—to snuggle up to. Vengeance was a warm and cozy curl-up. Best of all, vengeance couldn't betray you.

"Listen, what Bravo and I spoke about last night—I offered to be his mole with you, to report to him about you."

"You didn't defend me, you didn't tell him the truth?"

"He wasn't in any mood to listen, trust me."

"But why play into his horrific delusion?"

"It was the only way I could get him to tell me where he was going next."

The lie felt good on Camille's tongue, like melting butter. In fact, it was Cornadoro she was following, but, of course, she had no intention of telling Jenny that. Telling the truth in the service of her vice she could tolerate. Other than that, never. Never again.

LIKE a remora stuck to their side, Damon Cornadoro wasn't going away, Bravo reasoned, until or unless they put him away. This strain of logic had a certain unmistakable appeal. *There's no point in trying to outrun him or hide from him. I've tried that, and it's worked against me,"* he had told Khalif last night.

When Khalif had suggested a decoy car, Bravo had shaken his head. *"We're following the wrong train of logic. What we need to do is to make his extraordinary expertise work for us."*

So he had proposed his plan and Khalif had relayed it to Mikhail Kartli, who had approved it. Or so Bravo and Khalif had believed. Apparently, Kartli had had his own ideas. His people had tried to gain their revenge on Cornadoro prematurely by ambushing him and had failed. Worse, Cornadoro now knew they were on to him. Going after him now would be like putting their heads into a wasp's nest.

If that weren't enough, the Glimmer Twins in the backseat were restless, their mounting anxiety palpable.

"It's essential that we keep to the original plan." Ostensibly, Bravo was speaking to Khalif, but everyone in the car knew he was addressing the Glimmer Twins. "We've worked out how to take him at the mosque, and that's what we must do."

"We have a better idea," said the Glimmer Twins in almost perfect unison.

Djura opened a long canvas bag that lay across their feet and took out a pair of McMillan Tac-50 rifles, each equipped with a Leupold 16x sniper's scope. The rifles used huge 12.7-millimeter ammo that, even with a near miss, would tear a human being apart. With a sickening jolt Bravo thought of Mikhail Kartli's order to have Jenny shot to death in the bazaar.

"Let us off a hundred meters ahead," they said, their intent perfectly clear.

"Your people failed at that once, what makes you think—"

Before Bravo could continue, his phone pulsed against his hip.

"Emma."

"Thank God I got through." She sounded breathless and not a little frightened.

"What is it?"

"You were right to have me keep on with the assignment Dad gave me. Vetting the London intel wasn't make-work."

She swallowed so hard Bravo could hear her.

"It turns out he wanted me to help him with ferreting out the traitor, after all."

"Hold on." He told Khalif to pull over. "Don't let them do anything stupid," he added as he got out of the car. With some trepidation, he walked a little away, put his back to them. He watched the ghostly creep of the sun behind a bank of misty cloud. "All right, go on."

"I assume you know that for the last several years Uncle Tony had been working out of London."

"Of course," he snapped. "Emma, what did you find?"

"Everything seemed okay, until I got to Uncle Tony's weekly intel report—the most boring, routine stuff."

"The ones no one would look at twice."

"Right. Except Dad." The sound of her breathing was communicated along the signal. She was so distant, and yet she sounded as if she was in the car with Khalif and the Glimmer Twins, every tiny sound revealed to him, sharp and painful as a nail being driven home. "It seems as if there's a cipher hidden *inside* the coded weekly intel digest Uncle Tony was sending to Washington. It's not one of ours, of that I'm certain. I think Dad had found it and was in the process of deciphering it when he was killed."

Bravo, the breath knocked out of him, staggered a couple of steps before he leaned against a poplar tree. Once again, he heard the terrible sound of the ice cracking, felt in his soul the pain of another loss. Uncle Tony was the traitor. Someone so close to him that Dexter's world must have been turned upside down when he unearthed the identity. Just as Bravo's now was. Like his father before him, his reality had been upended, his sense of good and evil tested. The love Uncle Tony had shown him, the games they had played, the advice he had offered—all lines an actor speaks on stage. He had wormed his way into Bravo's heart, used him as cover to plant himself deeper and deeper in the Order's core. It was impossible to believe, and yet he had to believe it because it was true.

And then he was hit between the eyes with another truth.

"Bravo?" Emma said in his ear. "Are you still there?"

He put a hand to his forehead. He felt as if he was about to lose his mind. "Emma, I was so sure that Paolo Zorzi and Jenny were the traitors." He had mistreated Jenny, accused her, cut her off, threatened her. He had refused to listen to her side of things, he hadn't recognized the truth when she had offered it to him. The bitter taste of self-loathing was in his mouth. "How could I have been so wrong? Jenny's innocent."

"Zorzi could still be guilty."

"I don't think so. It was Uncle Tony who built the case against Jenny. He deliberately misled me. He wanted me to believe Jenny was the traitor in order to keep himself from being found out." The specter of the blood-spattered scene in the Church of San Georgio dei Greci rose up in his mind. "Oh, Christ, now I understand everything. When Uncle

Tony shot Zorzi, Jenny must have realized that Uncle Tony was the traitor."

He saw Jenny again as she had been on the restaurant terrace in Trabzon, the elegant sweep of her neck exposed, cooled by moonlight to the color of alabaster. He recalled with a guilty ache how he had deliberately snubbed her in order to warn Camille about her and Damon Cornadoro. Most of all, his own shameful threat echoed in the theater of his mind: *"If you try to follow me, if I see you again, I'll kill you."*

"Of course she shot Uncle Tony," he said now. "Knowing he was the traitor, seeing him shoot my mentor to death, I would have done the same thing." *But what about Father Mosto and Father Damaskinos?* he asked himself. *Did she kill them or had she been set up?*

"Dad found out Uncle Tony was the traitor, that was the breakthrough he talked about." Emma was working it out as she spoke. "All he was lacking was rock-solid proof, which is where I came in."

"Tony's plan was brilliant, don't you agree? No need for dead-drops or unexplained trips, no deviation whatsoever in his normal patterns." He thought for a moment. "Have you discovered where the cipher was going when it was pulled off the electronic transmissions?"

"I would have to have copies of the real-time transmissions," Emma said. "All I was able to do, after tons of sifting too tedious to go into, was compare the transmissions at the point of origin and the point of destination. That's how I came up with the discrepancy."

"Can you send the cipher to my cell phone?"

"That I can do."

"Along with the frequency Uncle Tony used to send the transmissions."

"They varied week to week, but I can send you a list."

"Good," Bravo said. "Do it now."

"You have an idea, don't you?"

Khalif got out of the car, an anxious look on his face. He was gesturing back toward the car, the Glimmer Twins were no doubt itching to fire their Tac-50s.

"I think I do."

"You keep sounding more and more like Dad."

Why did everyone tell him that? "Emma, I have to go."

"Wait, Bravo—there's something else I found out, something you should know. Dad was involved with Jenny."

Bravo closed his eyes. He didn't want to hear confirmation of Father Mosto's suspicions, and yet he heard himself say, "Involved how?"

"I . . . I don't really know. But it's a fact that he rented an apartment for her in London."

"How long did he keep her?"

"Bravo, please calm down. There's no hard evidence he had an affair with her."

Bravo pressed his thumb and forefinger into his eyelids to try to stop the vicious headache that had erupted behind his eyes. "How long, Emma?"

"Eleven months."

"Jesus. He *was* keeping her."

Silence. So he issued the challenge: "Give me another explanation, Emma."

More silence. Khalif had begun walking toward him.

"I really do have to go."

"I know. Stay safe, Bravo."

"You too."

"Keep me posted." Her laugh had a stinging ironic edge. "I don't like being in the dark."

"Neither do I." Were those tears in his eyes? "Thanks for the due diligence, from me and from Dad."

Bravo, walking back to the car, met Adem Khalif halfway. "You told me that my father liked to have his ear to the ground, that you were his eyes and ears in the Middle East." Consulting the text message that had appeared on the screen of his cell phone, he showed Khalif the list of numbers. "Did you monitor and record traffic on any of these frequencies?"

Khalif squinted into the small screen. "There are too many here. We'd have to go to my office to check."

"Despite what those two are thinking," Bravo said with absolute assuredness, "we have to go there now."

"Bravo, I have to repeat what you've already said: it's not a good idea to deviate from the original plan."

"Too late for that," Bravo said grimly. "Your friend Kartli already blew the plan to kingdom come."

KHALIF'S office was two-thirds up the steep Trapezuntine hillside, an apartment in a modern high-rise, one of five identical balconied towers, white proletarian milk cartons, known as Sinope A Blok. A winding drive led up to the main entrance. On either side of the black asphalt, sheared cypresses were ranked like saluting Soviet militiamen. Pink Colchian crocuses, thinly planted as if in afterthought or in grudging protest, waved in wan greeting. While Bravo and Khalif sat uncomfortably in the ticking car, the Glimmer Twins reconnoitered the property, moving in and out of the scimitar shadows of the rustling trees. Of particular interest to them were the maintenance men high up on movable scaffolding, sandblasting the side of the building.

"I don't know how anyone lives here," Khalif commented, "the construction is Soviet style, so poor they're always having to replace sections of the facades or reface entire lines of terraces."

He shook out a cigarette, lit up. Snorting smoke, he said, "Don't worry about those two, you can trust them with your life."

"Even the one with the broken nose?"

"You're thinking like an American." Khalif picked a fleck of tobacco off the tip of his tongue. "You surprised Djura. Before you attacked him, he was certain you were a coward. The pain means nothing to him, but your decisiveness does."

Bebur appeared, a cell phone clutched in one hand, a Mauser in the other. He was ashen faced.

"You've found someone?" Khalif asked. "What's happened?"

"It's Mikhail," Bebur said in an eerie monotone. "He's been killed, murdered late last night in our church, along with one of the priests." His expression was fixed and concentrated, his back ramrod straight, his stance wide, his limbs slightly flexed, his hands open and at the ready. In short, he was a soldier who'd received a field promotion. "His wife awoke to discover he hadn't come home last night. That in itself was not alarming, but when he failed to appear at the shop, failed to answer his cell, his sons called around and went to the church. Understandably, they are in a frenzy."

Bravo got out of the car. "Who did it?" Standing, facing Bebur, he looked at him as if for the first time, soldier to soldier. "Who killed Kartli?"

"Damon Cornadoro."

Khalif tossed his cigarette out the window, slid out from behind the wheel to stand beside Bravo. "You know this for a fact?" he said.

Bebur nodded. "Both of them were finished with a push-dagger. Cornadoro's signature." He turned as Djura trotted up.

"All clear," Djura said. "So far."

Bravo started. "Did you say a push-dagger?"

Bebur nodded. "Yes, you can tell—"

"I know, the push-dagger is made for stabbing, so its slash wound is unique." Kartli had told him when he'd relayed the news of Father Damaskinos's murder. *"His throat was slashed in a very particular manner,"* Kartli had said. *"It was made with a push-dagger. I know someone who kills in this manner; he's a Knight of St. Clement assassin."*

The last piece of the maddening puzzle fell into place. "Damon Cornadoro," Bravo said.

The three of them were staring intently at him.

"What?" Khalif said.

"It wasn't Jenny who killed Father Damaskinos in Venice, it was Cornadoro." Now he had his proof, she'd been telling the truth all along. He recalled her stricken expression when he'd told her that Father Damaskinos was dead. He'd been so angry he'd automatically assumed she'd been playing a part. Now he knew her reaction had been genuine. Logic led him back to Father Mosto. Jenny had claimed that she'd been framed for his murder. Cornadoro was more than capable of such a scheme, and he'd been in Venice at the time of Father Mosto's demise.

Bebur said now, "Mikhail's sons demand immediate revenge."

"They wanted us back at the shop for instructions." Djura looked Bravo in the eye. "Now we will do what we have to do, with no interference from you."

"Cornadoro is smart, very smart, you know this," Bravo said. "Killing him was never going to be easy, but now that he knows our intent, you'd be fools to confront him directly."

Djura lunged at Bravo, his hands up and grasping, but Bebur stepped in front of him.

Khalif threw up his hands. "Are we to be enemies now for real?" he cried.

"We are not enemies." Pushing back against Djura, Bebur eyed them. "But don't mistake our loyalties. We will not follow your orders."

"Even if they make sense?"

"We will not wait for the mosque." Djaba pointed to the terraced high-rise. "Up there we'll have the perfect vantage point."

Khalif nodded, and Bravo knew better than to protest. The decision had been made; for good or ill, the die had been cast.

Watching them retrieve their rifles from the backseat of his car, Khalif spat onto the concrete. "Don't underestimate them."

"I don't like it, it's an emotional decision."

"No, my friend, it's a business decision," Khalif said. "In killing Mikhail, Cornadoro crossed an unforgivable boundary. The sons have no choice. To protect themselves and their interests, their revenge must be swift and merciless. Otherwise, scenting weakness, the vultures will follow and eventually the sons will lose everything Mikhail worked so hard to build."

UP on the eleventh floor, Bebur insisted on unlocking the front door. Djura brushed by Bravo with no hint of animosity or grudge; his hostile reaction had been purely of the moment. Once they had assured themselves that the apartment was secure, they allowed Khalif and Bravo in. Bravo watched as they stepped gingerly out onto the terrace, which overlooked the front drive and, far below, the blue expanse of the sea. Despite their bravado, their continuing sense of responsibility toward his safety was touching.

After conferring among themselves, Djura came back in, heading out the apartment's front door, presumably to cover the building's rear service entrance, while Bebur hunkered down, peering through his rifle's sniper-scope in anticipation of seeing Cornadoro's truck.

Bravo called out and, as Djura turned, he crossed the living room.

"I appreciate everything you've done." He held out a hand. "I'm glad you have my back."

Djura looked him straight in the eye and without changing his expression one iota took Bravo's forearm in his heavy grip. Bravo did the same. Saluting like ancient Romans on the soon to be blood-soaked battleground of Erzurum or Tabriz.

KHALIF led Bravo into the kitchen.

"Fancy a beer?" he said, hand on the refrigerator door handle.

"You've got to be kidding."

Khalif laughed. Depressing a hidden lever, he pulled on the door and the entire refrigerator swung open, revealing a hidden suite of rooms. As they stepped through, Bravo saw that the refrigerator was hinged on two sets of concealed gimbals.

Khalif's workspace was cold as the interior of the refrigerator through which they had come. It was sealed, HEPA-filtered, entirely self-contained. Heavy blackout drapes hid the windows so completely that not even a crack of daylight seeped through. Banks of electronic equipment, much of it incomprehensible to Bravo, lined two entire walls from floor to ceiling. It was like a twenty-first-century library: devoid of books, for that matter of any printed material, overflowing nonetheless with information that kept arriving invisibly, as magically as the water-filled buckets of the sorcerer's apprentice.

Khalif seated himself at the center of this metropolis of intelligence. Bravo, beside him, read off the list of frequencies Emma had sent. As it happened, Khalif had electronic copies of them all. Hardly surprising, given what Bravo had recently learned about his father's methodology in tracking down the identity of the traitor inside the Order.

The next step was to isolate Uncle Tony's rogue cipher, the parasite deep inside the intestines of the main carrier report. There was no point now in trying to decrypt the ciphers—that would come later. What he wanted to ascertain was who had taken the encrypted message as it was en route from London to Washington.

This proved simpler than he had imagined, since Khalif quickly discovered an electronic file—composed by Dexter Shaw—of all the retrieved rogue ciphers. Clearly, Dexter had been working on decoding them. There was no record of how successful he had been, though Khalif searched the database thoroughly.

Impatient, Bravo said, "Let me take a look."

Khalif slid out of the way and Bravo, fingers dancing over the workstation keyboard, returned to the original carrier reports as they had been when they'd left Uncle Tony's London location. First, he engaged the audio spectrum-analyzer to pinpoint the moment the rogue cipher had been plucked out of the main text, but when that failed he was forced to think a bit more in depth.

Surely his father would have followed his line of reasoning. He would have used the spectrum-analyzer and any number of other electronic aids in his attempt to find the precise moment the rogue cipher was taken. And he had failed. Bravo sat back, silently contemplating the wall of gadgetry, as sophisticated as a spaceship's control panel, which winked and blinked back at him like some dumb animal. He needed to return to the beginning, to find another line of reasoning that wasn't so obvious—*that had not occurred to his father.* He needed to make the dumb animal moo.

There was another way, there was always another way. He sat still as a statue, immersed in furious contemplation. Forget about finding the precise moment of acquisition, that was a dead end. It occurred to him then that there was no need to stay within the Order's frequency, that was the beginning of the dead end. If he was to truly return to the beginning, he needed to listen *outside* the frequency.

He asked Khalif to analyze the surrounding frequencies from the beginning of Uncle Tony's report. Khalif obliged, but again the readouts showed nothing but the norm. The damn dumb animal still refused to moo.

DJURA, carefully wending his way through the cinder block bowels of Sinope A Blok, loaded Tac-50 beautifully balanced in his hand, was feeling good. An unwanted weight had been lifted off his shoulders. Being shackled to the American had rankled, gotten under his skin like a burr he couldn't reach. A warrior the American might be, but he was not family, not blood; he could betray them at any moment, as all Americans were known to do when the lure of money, power, cultural hegemony beckoned to them. Their corruption was complete, from the flesh down to the soul. Their naked greed, the measureless avarice would, in the end, prove to be their undoing, of this Djura had no doubt. But until that end arrived with the suddenness of an apocalyptic thunderclap, their gluttony was a contagion—at all costs to be avoided.

That Mikhail and his sons were capitalists bothered him not at all. They made money, yes, lots of it, but, like him, they had faith, which led them to use their wealth to help their people back in Georgia, rather than keep a revolving stable of young women, rather than buy out Tiffany's or the nearest Rolls Royce dealership.

He had seen what remorseless corruption came from the sprawl of the American lifestyle. How could he not? It was all around him, as if he swam in a sea infested with plastic bags filled with iPods of American music, DVDs of American films, cassettes of American TV shows, all in loud and joyful praise of celebrity and consumerism. Not that Djura didn't enjoy a pink Internet peek of Paris Hilton or Pamela Anderson, astonishingly exposed in various positions of sexual congress. The illicit nature of the moving images detonated like bombs on his retinas, providing a thrill he could not begin to define, let alone understand. But that was it; having taken these bites out of the rancid confection of American culture, he was certain his appetite had been sated. Unlike his brother Gigo, who had swallowed it whole and was now importing drugs and "Russian wives" from his five-bedroom triplex in the eternal golden sunshine above Miami Beach.

Gigo also had a cocaine habit as large as a Lincoln Navigator. Djura, passing the row of trash bins that stood near the rear entrance, shook himself. He hated the fact that he knew what a Lincoln Navigator was, knowledge unwanted but that nevertheless seeped into his skull. Evidence against the imagined purity of his life.

Which brought him back to Damon Cornadoro, corruptor on a grand scale. Djura would gladly take the American over Cornadoro, though probably he'd wind up shooting them both. They were infidels. Beneath the surface gloss, how much difference could there be between them?

Checking that the safety on the Tac-50 was off, he slowly pushed open the metal door into the open air. The morning was hot and sticky. Birds sang, insects whined, the hiss of traffic on its way up and down the hillside overspread his concrete bower. A car drove up, letting off a woman and a child. The woman was dressed in Western clothes, though to Djura she appeared Muslim. Her hands were filled with shopping bags. The child—a small boy—was busy licking an ice cream. The car drove off and the woman and child headed for the front entrance to Sinope A Blok. A man, dark-skinned, middle-aged, appeared, smoking a cigarette and talking on a cell phone. He strolled down to the curve of the driveway and stood in a patch of sunlight. A moment later, a car swung into view and he got in. The car pulled away, the sound of its exhaust echoing off the soundboard of the high-rise.

The heat abated a bit. A sea breeze all the way from Sevastopol, still stinking from Russian atomic submarines, tossed the tops of the sheared cypresses like the turbans of bowing imams. Speaking of imams, here came one, long beard aquiver, hurrying along the path toward him. In his wake, an ungainly woman, enveloped, as was proper, from the crown of her head to her sandaled feet in an *abaya* and a traditional Muslim head scarf. It would not be beyond Cornadoro to desecrate the holy state, to disguise himself as an imam, Djura thought. In fact, it would be just like him.

Squinting through the wan sunlight, Djura tried to take a closer look at the oncoming imam. But this chore was made difficult by the woman whose form obscured the imam's face, the part of him that interested Djaba.

Suspicions roused to full flower, he braced himself against the doorway, raised the Tac-50 into firing position. The imam was big—big as Cornadoro. And he had roughly the same build. This, Djura decided, was his target, but he would not fire until he was certain. Killing a Muslim imam was unthinkable, a disaster that would cause more damage to Mikhail's sons than they were prepared to handle. And so, tense and anxious, he waited with his forefinger curled intently around the trigger. In his mind, he already heard the satisfying sound, the thick, wet *splat! splat! splat!* of the bullets rending Cornadoro's flesh from bone. And the best part was that he wouldn't have to be close with him—unlike Mikhail, he could avoid the flat, deathly sweep of the push-dagger.

The imam was in range now. He said something sharp to the woman, who nodded in subservient fashion and dropped back several paces, her head down. Lucky for Djura, because now he had a clear look at the imam's face, and he exhaled a deep-drawn breath and his finger relaxed on the trigger. It wasn't Cornadoro, after all.

The imam's eyes barely registered Djura as he swept imperiously through the door. Djura's eyes barely registered the woman as she followed the imam, and so he missed the movement of her right hand as it appeared from beneath her voluminous *ayaba*, the blade of the push-dagger protruding between the second and third knuckles—knuckles larger and more callused than any female hand.

Djura became aware of the flat sweeping motion and, too late, tried to move. His arms were expertly pinioned behind him. The huge imam! At that instant the push-dagger entered his lower belly. He gave a brief cry as the *ayaba*-clad woman unwound her head scarf. He saw Damon Cornadoro's eyes burning into him.

"Where are they?" Cornadoro said with a twist of his wrist that caused Djura terrible pain. "Give me the information or your passage to Paradise will not be assured."

29

BRAVO, STARING AT THE WHITE-ON-GREEN SQUIGGLES, rubbed his temples with his fingertips. He was all too aware of time passing, time when he and Khalif should have been at the Sumela Monastery. Had he been wrong, was he going down another dead end? Was he doing what he'd accused the Glimmer Twins of doing? Was he making an emotional decision? No, he couldn't let this go. His father sat at his side, his energy pinning Bravo to his seat. *There is an answer. Use what you know, Bravo,* Dexter Shaw whispered inside his head.

"Play the frequencies again, both at once," he instructed Khalif. "But this time turn off all the readouts."

"What?"

"I want to listen—only listen. Do you understand?"

Khalif set the two frequencies to running simultaneously. A complex melody of beeps, hisses and squeals filled the room. At first, the cacophony sounded like a longed-for response to a SETI transmission—communication in an alien language—or the aural equivalent of the incomprehensible scrawling of an autistic child, both of which contained a message, no matter how deeply buried.

Bravo closed his eyes. If the electronic animal remained dumb, it was up to the human senses to solve the riddle of where the rogue cipher was going. The ear filtered sound and noise day in and day out. It was created to decipher the important sounds from the background wash of the world.

For him, it was only a matter of time before the layers of noise were stripped away and the melody presented itself. This was his business—or, at any rate, part of what he was good at. He could coax out the hidden with his senses—in manuscripts, in human speech, in the feel of forgeries purporting to be genuine archeological finds, in the scents of age and reason, despair and dissolution.

Now, in Khalif's postmodern bunker, having begun the process of winnowing the wheat from the chaff, he discerned the melody. And having defined it, listened to it, locking in its mathematical pattern, its sine-wave rise and fall, he heard the anomaly.

"Stop," he cried. "Stop it right there."

Opening his eyes, he had Khalif turn on all the readouts, even the ones that seemed irrelevant or spurious. And there it was: the dumb animal went "Moo."

"WHY are we following Michael Berio?" Jenny said from her seat beside Camille in the small red sports car. It was a Soviet-made vehicle, and therefore wasn't a sports car at all but a Russian travesty. "Your own man."

"His real name is Damon Cornadoro. You know it, don't you?"

"My God." Jenny's face had drained of color. "The Knights' hired assassin? I've seen more than a dozen photos purporting to be him, all of different people. Christ, how could I not have known?"

"Don't blame yourself," Camille said. "He fooled me as well." Of course this wasn't true, no one fooled Camille, but from the moment she had understood the connection between Jenny and Bravo, she knew she'd have to change her plan. Isolating Bravo was no longer the object; co-opting him was. For that, she knew she'd need Jenny's help, which required her to spin a whole new web of lies.

Camille tossed her head. "You're the expert, you tell me—how dangerous is this Cornadoro?'

Jenny glanced at her nervously. "How about eleven on a scale of one to ten."

"That bad?"

"You heard the backfiring before, the squeal of tires? And then, a bit further on—"

"The accident that delayed us, yes, what about it?"

"I took a long look. That was no accident," Jenny said grimly. "So I doubt those sounds were backfires."

"What are you saying?"

"I think Kartli's men attempted to attack Cornadoro—an ambush, perhaps. I'd bet anything they were rifle shots we heard, and the squeal of tires was the target ramming the attacking cars. I've read Cornadoro's dossier—that sounds like him."

Camille considered. Trust was what she was soliciting from Jenny, and empathy was the path she had chosen to that trust. If she didn't feel it, Jenny wouldn't either.

"If, as you say, Cornadoro was the target, then it's safe to assume that Bravo was involved in the ambush," Camille said. She had had time to reason out her course of action during the bumper-to-bumper that led up to the police swarming like ants around the aggressively wrecked cars. She had craned her neck to see the blood, without any luck. "He needs to know that Cornadoro escaped and is still on his tail." She thrust her cell phone at Jenny. "Call him and tell him."

Jenny didn't move a muscle. "Me?"

"Why not?"

"You know why not. He still believes I murdered his Uncle Tony, still believes I'm working for the Knights."

"Then now's the time to show him that you're on his side." She gave Jenny a small smile. "My dear, listen, he hasn't believed a word you've told him. He told me so himself." She nodded. "Look, there's Cornadoro's truck up ahead. We haven't a moment to lose, he's already left it. Courage is what's required now. Number three."

"All right." Jenny nodded, took the cell phone. Heart hammering in her chest, she punched in the speed-dial number.

"Camille—"

The sound of his voice struck her like a physical blow. "It's Jenny, Bravo."

"Jenny, I—"

"No, don't hang up." A certain terror gripped her at the thought that she would blow this one chance to prove herself to him. "Listen, listen, I'm with Camille," she said in a rush. "We've been following Cornadoro—"

"You what?"

She winced at his shouted response but pressed on, determined. *Courage.* "There was an ambush, two cars were involved, I don't know how many men, though you probably do."

"It was a total screwup, Kartli's idea, not mine, but he's dead now—Cornadoro killed him just like he killed Father Mosto and Father Damaskinos."

An indrawn breath was all she could manage. Her head was swimming.

"I know Uncle Tony was the traitor."

"Bravo, Bravo!" She bent over, almost ill with relief. "But how—?"

"Jenny, I have to go. Really."

"Wait, wait! Cornadoro is coming, he's still coming."

"Where are you now?"

"At some huge high-rise housing complex."

Sinope A Blok.

"IT'S a number," Khalif said, staring at the readouts. "A phone number."

Bravo, his cell phone still cradled in one hand, said, "Cornadoro is here."

Khalif pointed. "Take a look at it while I go tell Bebur."

As he went through the refrigerator door, Bravo took a close look at the number. It wasn't a London number, not even an English number. There were two prefixes: a country code and a city code, and he recognized them both: Munich, Germany. A warning bell went off in his head, a deadness was growing inside him, a sick feeling, intimation of a new and monstrous reality.

Khalif returned, pulling the hidden door shut behind him. "He hasn't seen anything suspicious," Khalif said as he retook his seat. "He said he'd call Djura to warn him."

Bravo hardly heard him. "Give me the overseas code for Munich, Germany," he said, because they would be different here than in England.

He dialed the number, and when he heard the deep male voice on the other end of the line, he felt as if the floor had given way beneath him. Nightmare came rushing at him with a ghoulish grin.

It was Karl Wassersturm's voice he heard in his ear. It was to the Wassersturm brothers that Uncle Tony had been transmitting the rogue code. From his eidetic memory he unspooled part of the conversation he'd had with Camille on their way to St. Malo:

"The Wassersturms were in a rage when their deal was terminated," Camille said in his mind. *"Jordan is worried that they're out to take their revenge on you. What's gotten him so upset is that he spent three days in Munich working on another deal with them simply to calm them down."*

"He shouldn't have done that; there's no reason to trust them."

Camille laughed. *"You know Jordan. If he can get his terms, he'll make a deal with the devil."*

But the thing was, what had stuck in Bravo's mind, what he hadn't been able to make sense of, was that Jordan should have known better than to do business with the Wassersturms no matter what kind of terms they offered. They were bad news—tied into illicit arms dealers and, possibly, terrorists—bad to the bone.

"Karl, it's Jordan." He spoke in German, summoned up Jordan's intonation, his French vocal quirks.

"Why are you using this line?" Wassersturm said in his gruff, nononsense manner. "We agreed to leave it solely to relay the . . . information."

Here was the reason, the connection between the Wassersturms and Jordan, revealed in all its ghastly glory.

Grimly, Bravo said, "You missed this month's, didn't you?"

"You know, like clockwork always." The anxiety in Karl Wassersturm's voice was palpable. "You get the information minutes after I pull it off the transmission, almost no delay, that's how you set things up. It isn't my fault, I swear. No transmission came through this month."

"If you're holding out on me, Karl, I swear—"

"But, no, Jordan, absolutely not. The thought never entered my mind. You told me, didn't you? It's your cipher. I don't understand it, you warned me it couldn't be broken, what good would holding out do me?"

"None at all," Bravo said in Jordan Muhlmann's sternest voice. "See you remember that, Karl. I'll be in touch."

He threw the cell phone across the room. Overwhelmed by the personal horror—the unimaginable betrayal—staring him in the face, he put his head in his hands.

CORNADORO'S truck was empty when Jenny and Camille pulled up behind it. Jenny, the Witness handgun she had bought from Mikhail Kartli at the ready, got out, made a thorough search. By the time Camille joined her, she had found something interesting.

She hauled the battered metal box out of the well below the truck's front seat. "Look at this," she said, flipping open the top. Inside were three layers of theatrical makeup; bits of hair in different colors for eyebrows, mustache, beard; small plastic cases containing colored contact lenses.

Camille, fingering the selection of prosthetic noses, chins, cheeks and ears, said, "What does this mean?"

Jenny had already grabbed her phone, was pressing the speed dial over and over, without success. "Shit, he's not answering." She began to sprint toward the high-rise.

Camille knew exactly what the contents of the box meant—she'd seen Damon in a number of his disguises and knew he was an expert at changing his appearance, the reason the Order had never been able to obtain an accurate photo of him. Hurrying after Jenny, Camille considered her options. She could, of course, stop Jenny right now, just as she had done in the corridor of the Church of l'Angelo Nicolò, just before she'd murdered Father Mosto. But that would be the height of folly. She needed Jenny now as the lure to bring Bravo to her. What she didn't need was Damon tramping around, killing people right and left. Up to this point, he had been useful, that was true enough, but the situation in the field had changed drastically, and any general unable to alter the plan of battle as the fighting saw fit would inevitably go down to defeat.

"My best friend is an actor. I've seen those kits before," Camille said, coming up on Jenny's right shoulder. "I saw what was missing, I think I know what he's going to look like."

CAMILLE had been right, Bravo realized, though in a way she couldn't possibly know. Jordan had, indeed, made a deal with the devil. He hadn't been scammed by Damon Cornadoro; he'd *asked* for Damon Cornadoro. Jordan, his best friend, was a Knight of St. Clement—not simply a Knight but the leader, because he was the architect, he was behind everything: Dexter's murder, the concerted attack on the Haute Cour, the pursuit of the Order's cache of secrets.

Bravo groaned. To top it all off, he'd been working at Lusignan et Cie, for Jordan, toiling away for years in the enemy's shell corporation. What if Jordan had given him tasks that destroyed businesses secretly owned by members of the Order? Oh, God, had he himself been doing the devil's work?

He didn't want to believe it, *couldn't* believe it wholly, not yet—it was too huge, too terrible, it was unthinkable. And yet, the evidence was irrefutable. This couldn't be happening, not to him. But, in this instance, denial was lethal. Bravo knew that, and he shook himself, urging himself to come to terms with a truth he never could have imagined he'd one day be forced to face.

How to understand the nature of a human being who could be so false, so two-faced: your best friend, your most implacable enemy. It was as if the sun had suddenly begun to rise in the west or the oceans had turned to stone. But when he took a mental step back, like it or not, he was struck by Jordan Muhlmann's brilliance: what better place for Jordan to camp than on his enemy's doorstep, what better vantage point from which to observe and to plot the order of battle?

And with this realization came the beginning of acceptance—a sadness so piercing it left a pain in his chest.

He lifted his head, a sudden terrible thought bubbling up to the surface: what if Camille knew everything, what if she was part of Jordan's scheme? Why not? They were close, she worked at Lusignan et Cie, she would do anything for her son, she had told him so herself. Even the devil's business? He didn't know. Her shocked reaction to learning of Cornadoro's identity seemed genuine enough, but how could he know with any certainty?

He felt the swift, bitter flood of paranoia. He heard his father's voice, as if from far away, coming nearer with each beat of his heart. *"Paranoia is a skill to be developed in certain professions,"* Dexter Shaw had told his son. *"The most useful thing about being a paranoiac is that you won't be shaken by failure."*

What profession had his father been talking about? the young Bravo had wondered. Now he knew. He'd have to be wary of Camille, gauge her reactions in a different light until one way or another she proved her loyalties.

A tremendous percussion shook the walls and rattled the electronics on their steel shelves. It sounded as if a bomb had gone off in the part of the apartment beyond the hidden door. He jumped and Khalif leapt to his feet. Ominously, three reports followed one upon the other—shots from a handgun, there was no mistaking the sounds, no doubt at all. A moment later, something hard slammed into the front side of the refrigerator.

Khalif hurried to the bank of electronics and, as the pounding started up rhythmically, quickly and methodically pressed a series of buttons.

"I'm wiping all the hard drives," he said, as much to himself as to Bravo. "I have all the critical data backed up elsewhere." Then he drew back one of the blackout curtains. Pushing two raw metal levers up freed the plywood panel he had attached over the window. Together, he and Bravo took the panel down.

Khalif threw open the window to a blast of noise and a mini-tornado of concrete dust from the sandblasting. Below was a sloping concrete ledge, no more than a decorative stripe on the milk-carton facade. It was so narrow there would be no room for error. One misstep would send him hurtling to his death below.

The crashing on the other side of the refrigerator was louder, more immediately threatening.

Bravo hesitated only a moment before he followed Khalif out onto the ledge. Khalif had already begun to edge to his right, toward the corner of the building. To Bravo, it seemed like a long way away, though it couldn't be more than a hundred meters. Where was Khalif headed? To a window in another apartment on the floor? That would only postpone the inevitable.

Bravo watched Khalif and, like him, refused to look down. Instead, he concentrated on keeping one hand against the concrete block of the building facade, putting one foot in front of the other in the straightest line possible. A sudden gust of wind swirled up the sheer building face, rippling against his left flank, causing him to stop and steady himself until it died back.

Khalif reached the corner and vanished around it. Screwing up his courage, Bravo followed, his hands gripping the corners, and he slid around it.

Beyond, he could see the workers' bamboo scaffold. His view was distorted by the shroud of plastic sheeting the workers had erected in a futile effort to keep the concrete dust at least marginally controlled. Bravo could make out two figures in overalls, faces goggle-eyed behind masks that kept their lungs clear. One of them was hunched over, wielding the heavy sandblaster, working slowly and deliberately. The other, just beyond him, was bent over the rope railing of the scaffold, presumably calling to the workers below down. They looked like old men; their hair was white with dust.

Khalif had reached the edge of the scaffold. He swung the plastic sheeting out of the way. As he stepped over the rope barrier, the worker nearest him turned, awkwardly waved one arm, warning him away. Khalif ignored him and the worker put down the sandblaster.

Khalif was trying to explain the situation, but the generator that powered the sandblaster was still pumping out noise at deafening decibels, and it was clear the worker couldn't hear him. By this time Bravo, too, had swung onto the scaffold. The two men were now so close that Bravo lost sight of the worker behind Khalif's broad back. It was natural then for Bravo's gaze to fall on the second worker. He was still bent over the railing, but now, without the interference of the plastic sheeting, Bravo could see his bloody hands, his bloody mouth, his bloody neck, ripped from one side to the other.

Bravo leapt forward. The first worker was removing his mask, a natural gesture as far as Khalif was concerned. Obviously, the man wanted to hear what Khalif was saying. But Bravo knew the movement was a ruse—a misdirection—for while Khalif's gaze was drawn to his face, the worker had produced a push-dagger from a pocket of his overalls.

"The worker," Bravo shouted, "it's Cornadoro!"

Khalif stepped back, but Cornadoro was already swinging the push-dagger, the arc of the blade sweeping in on the Turk's chest. Khalif swiveled, leaning heavily into the rope barrier as the blade ripped through the light linen of his shirt, baring his flesh. But the blade kept going, its arc continuing, until its target became clear.

The honed steel sliced through the rope barrier against which Khalif had tumbled. His arms shot out as he lost balance. Bravo threw himself forward, reaching out for Khalif's hand. Too late, he snatched at dead air. Looking over the side, he saw Khalif, clutching the end of the cut rope, swinging back and forth under the scaffold. Eleven floors below, he caught a glimpse of Jenny and Camille running toward the building.

Bravo took one lunge at the rope in hopes of hauling Khalif up, but Cornadoro swung the push-dagger, forcing Bravo to roll away from the edge, away from the only position from which he could save Khalif from falling to his death.

Lashing out with his right foot, Cornadoro drove Bravo's body beneath the rope barrier at the inner edge of the scaffold and into the side of the building. The scaffold rocked, banging against the concrete facade as Bravo struggled to keep from falling through the gap between it and the building.

Cornadoro struck him as he got to one knee, then grabbed him, pulled him off his feet. Their faces were very close. Bravo could smell the animal stink of the man, could feel the heat of his bloodlust and something else, something cool and detached: the total absence of fear.

"I want the cache of secrets." Cornadoro's voice was like a file sawing against Bravo's flesh. "Where is it? I want it. Where is it?" He flung Bravo against the side of the building. "Give me the information, or by Christ I'll rend you limb from limb. I'll leave you no man at all, or worse. When I'm done you won't even be human, you'll beg me to kill you."

From the first, Bravo had tried to get to Lorenzo Fornarini's dagger, but when he'd struck the concrete wall the knife had shifted, and now he couldn't reach it no matter how hard he tried. In any event, there was no time now because Cornadoro, swinging the push-dagger like a reaper, was about to make good on his threat.

The point of the push-dagger rushed in at Bravo. He tramped heavily on Cornadoro's instep, and as the bigger man reacted, he went straight for the inside of his wrist, digging thumb and forefinger into the nerve and tendon bundle. The push-dagger clattered to the bamboo beneath their feet.

With an animal growl, Cornadoro rabbit-punched Bravo in the kidney, then drove his knee into Bravo's chin. Bravo went to his hands and knees. Cornadoro smashed his fists into Bravo's spine. Bravo collapsed onto the sandblaster.

It was the machine's vibrations that kept him from slipping into unconsciousness. As Cornadoro stooped down to deliver the paralyzing blow, Bravo grabbed the sandblaster and flipping onto his back, aimed the nozzle at his tormentor, pulled the trigger.

Cornadoro bellowed, staggered back, and Bravo got to his feet, pressing his attack. Cornadoro let him commit himself before using powerful arms, elbows first, to knock the sandblaster away. Now Cornadoro clapped one huge hand around Bravo's neck and pressed on his carotid.

Bravo's arms flailed, he gasped for breath, but the blackness of the abyss was all around him, obliterating his senses one by one.

BOTH Jenny and Camille saw what was happening eleven floors up on the scaffold. For Jenny, her worst fears were being realized—Bravo was going to die, and she would be too late to save him. Camille, too, felt the unfamiliar stab of fear. Just as Jordan had predicted, Damon had overstepped his authority. What did he think he was doing attacking Bravo? Unless he wanted the location of the cache of secrets for himself, unless he thought he could torture the location out of Bravo. The fool.

And so both women ran, side by side, both locked in their own fears and anxieties. No doubt that was why neither of them saw the man hurtle out of the trees where he had been hiding. He leapt onto Jenny because she was the one with the gun. He tackled her, digging his heels in while twisting his upper torso, using her own momentum to bring her down so hard that the heel of her hand struck the concrete rim of the walkway and the gun skittered away from them both.

Camille stood less than eight meters away. She knew the man—the Albanian, one of Jordan's hand-picked Knights of the Field. The implications of his being here, spying on Damon—and on her—were as immediate as they were dire. Jordan no longer trusted her; he meant to get the Order's cache of secrets for himself. Camille experienced a moment of indecision, unusual for her. She could either help Jenny against the Albanian or try to save Bravo, she couldn't do both. Picking up the Witness, she turned and ran.

USING his last ounce of strength, Bravo slammed his knee into Cornadoro's groin. He had the angle, the angle at which the genitals are at their most vulnerable, when the proper force could produce the maximum damage.

The moment he connected, bone against soft tissue, the big man bellowed and let Bravo go. The primitive part of the brain, the part a human being used to keep himself alive, told him that he'd never survive alone on the scaffold with Damon Cornadoro, so he'd done the other thing. Without hesitation, he vaulted over the scaffold's side.

He fell.

But not far. He grabbed onto Khalif, wrapping both arms, heavy as lead weights, around the Turk's waist. Together, they swung in dangerous arcs, while Khalif groaned at the strain on his arms, shoulders and back. Above them, Cornadoro was on hands and knees, his eyes were watering and his head was wagging back and forth like a wounded bull. Then, ignoring all pain, he scooped up the push-dagger and began to saw at the hanging rope—Bravo and Khalif's lifeline.

"My shoulder is dislocated, I can't get to him," Khalif said. "But you have a chance. When I let go, grab the rope and pull yourself up."

"Are you crazy?" Bravo said. "You're not sacrificing yourself for me."

"Why not? It's my life," Khalif said. "Besides, you'd do the same for me."

CAMILLE ran until she had a clear shot up through the folds of plastic sheeting to the scaffold on the eleventh floor. Kneeling, she raised the Witness, bracing one hand on the other, forming a steady tripod. She got Damon in her sights, took a breath, exhaled. Her forefinger tightened on the trigger.

BRAVO, fighting to keep Khalif from dropping off the rope, scrambled up the Turk's body, grabbed the rope and clamped his legs around Khalif's waist, holding the man fast.

"These heroics will do you no good," Khalif said as he tried to free himself from Bravo's embrace. But at that instant two shots sounded from below, a spray of blood struck them, hot and strong, and Cornadoro staggered backward across the scaffold. They glanced down to see Camille in her marksman's position. Then Jenny had joined her and the two women were running toward the pulleys that controlled the scaffold's vertical movement.

"Jesus Christ," Bravo said, as the scaffold began its descent.

"God is good," Khalif breathed.

A moment later, a body fell past them, spraying them in the face and chest with more blood—Damon Cornadoro on his long journey to hell.

30

THE FIRST FACE BRAVO SAW WHEN HE OPENED HIS EYES WAS
Jenny's.

"Where am I?"

"In the back of Damon Cornadoro's truck." Jenny held a cool towel
to his forehead.

"What happened?"

"Cornadoro's dead—Camille shot him and he fell from the scaffold."

"I saw that." When he moved he could feel the deep ache in every
muscle of his body. "Where were you?"

"I was going hand-to-hand with someone Camille told me works for
Jordan, but that makes no sense, does it? It's why she insisted we get out
of there before he knew what was happening, why I stole the truck." She
grinned. "I hot-wired the ignition."

They were pushed together as Camille took a turn at speed.

"But about this thing with Jordan," Jenny said, "Camille must be
devastated. I don't know how she's going to get over it. You'd better
have a talk with her as soon as you feel up to it. Anyway, you passed out
as we were bringing you down. We just dropped Khalif off at the hospital; he's got a dislocated shoulder for sure, but there also may be a
break in his right ulna."

"Camille's driving?"

She gave him a small smile. "Isn't she always?"

"Where to?"

"The Sumela Monastery. Khalif told us that's where you were
headed, right?"

He closed his eyes. It was happening just as his father had predicted in his last cipher: he was not going alone to Sumela. All at once, he felt as if the puzzle his father had left him had gotten the better of him. He felt the urge to stop running, to give his brain a rest. Most of all, he wanted to sleep, not get up for a week or two.

He fought the unnatural lassitude, struggling to clear his mind and marshal his thoughts. He felt sure he could trust Camille. If she had been working with Jordan she never would have shot Cornadoro. Besides, now it appeared as if Jordan had sent someone to spy on her and him—the man Jenny grappled with. Which meant Jordan was growing ever more powerful, ever more willing to take risks. The pope lay on his deathbed, only the Quintessence could save him. Meanwhile, Bravo was feeling the tightening of the vise the Knights and the Vatican had prepared for him. He was nearing the end of his journey, and now he held no illusions. Jordan would do anything, risk anything to get his hands on the cache of secrets and the Quintessence. The twisted vines of the Voire Dei had almost worked themselves into a recognizable pattern. Almost.

He closed his eyes for a moment, allowing the jouncing of the truck to lull him.

"Bravo, Bravo," Jenny said with some urgency. "Camille called Khalif. He said that in Macka there is a modern clinic for the increasing number of hikers and rock climbers who backpack into the Black Mountains at all times of the year, even winter. There's a trauma center there, we can stop—"

"No," he said at once, his eyes snapping open. "We must go on to Sumela."

Their eyes locked, and at length she nodded, but he could tell she wasn't happy abut it.

He wished Khalif was with him. But now there was something he had to do on his own.

"Jenny—"

She stopped him with a hand on his cheek. "We can talk about this later."

"No, I have to tell you. I didn't trust you, I didn't believe you when Cornadoro hung Father Mosto's murder on you, I didn't understand when you shot Uncle Tony. There was no way then I could have believed—"

"Anthony fooled everyone, Bravo. Even, until the very end, your father."

It was only now that he noticed the dark circles around her eyes, her hollow cheeks, the blue veins at her temples, as if her skin had thinned to parchment. But these marks of exhaustion and emotional pain did not mar her beauty. Rather, they allowed him to see the newfound steely quality she had acquired while they were apart. Very soon, he knew, he'd have to ask her what had happened to her, how this change had come about. "There's something else."

Her fingertip brushed his lips. "Can't you let it rest for now?"

"I've waited too long already. Father Mosto told me that you and my father were having an affair. I was so angry I couldn't see straight. That's what clouded my instinct, my judgment of you—"

"But, Bravo, I never had an affair with Dexter."

Bravo felt a roaring in his head. "I don't understand. The flat he set up for you in London. . . ."

"Ah, you know about that." She sat back, her eyes turned inward.

He took her hand in his. "Don't lie to me about this, Jenny. Just the truth, only the truth."

Her eyes were firmly focused on the past. "The truth, okay." She nodded, but she couldn't bring herself to begin. Then she took a deep breath, let it out. "I had an affair, but it wasn't with your father."

"Who, then?"

"Ronnie Kavanagh. He got me pregnant then browbeat me into having . . . having it taken care of. He threatened me, warned me that if I didn't it would be the end for me in the Order. I was young, devastated, confused. I did what he told me to do. But it nearly finished me, psychologically. It was your father who took care of me—he was so kind, so understanding—and here I was terrified he'd give me away to the Haute Cour and, like Ronnie said, I'd be out on my ass. But he kept my secret. He talked to me about the baby, about what it meant to lose a child, but I never knew until you told me about Junior."

"He would never have told you himself, especially not in your state of mind."

"No, of course not," she said. "Instead, he told me endearing stories of fairies and elves."

"Did he tell you about the elf who could turn water into fire?"

Jenny's eyes lit up. "Yes, and the one about the fairy who wasn't invited to the Midsummer Night banquet—"

"And in retaliation put a spell on the fireflies hired to illuminate the party so they turned into wasps."

They both laughed softly.

Jenny sighed as she allowed the memories their due. "On days when I was really bad, he would tell me jokes of talking animals—clever, sinister and loving—that made me laugh despite myself."

"The zebra who bet his stripes, and lost—"

"The parrot who captained a pirate ship—"

"The greedy terrier who ran his company into the ground."

She laughed again, delighted as a child, and Bravo could imagine how his father had been taken with her, how he might have seen her as a surrogate child that eased the misery of Junior's death.

"And then there were the books we read together," Jenny continued, "historical novels of unimaginable hardship, loss and ultimate triumph. I knew what he was doing, and it worked. He was so empathetic, so attuned to my depressions and black moods I should have known, or at least suspected, he'd gone through his own tragedy. Over the year he took care of me I came to love him. Not so surprising, I guess. But I loved him like a father, and he never had any designs on me. On the contrary, he was the only man who made me feel safe—up until you."

"What if I have designs on you?" Bravo said.

Cheeks flaming, Jenny looked down at him. "I'm different now, I'm counting on it."

THE Sumela Monastery, set into the bedrock of the sheer mountainside, rose into the cobalt sky like the fortified portal of a Roman citadel. They lacked delicacy and finesse, these golden buildings; defenders of the faith, they seemed built for war.

"A war is what we'll have now," Camille said.

"There's no other way?" Bravo asked her.

"Sadly, my son has made his choice," Camille said. "With the pressures at play, the stakes so high, I doubt he could change his mind now, even if he had a mind to do so."

The three of them stood in the arched shadows of the ancient aqueduct that long ago had provided water for the monastery. Nearby was Cornadoro's truck, which Camille had parked on the narrow, twisting street some distance from the rank of tour buses, disgorging flocks of people armed with name tags, water bottles and digital cameras. No one seemed interested in their presence, but now each of them, infected with paranoia, studied the horde with obsessive interest.

Bravo turned to Camille. "I thought Jordan was my friend." He had explained, in as bare-bones a way as possible, the history of the Knights of St. Clement and Jordan's involvement in it. "How could he have betrayed me so callously?"

"He's a consummate actor, and for that I must take the blame." Camille stared up at the series of arches that carried the aqueduct on their brawny shoulders up the sheer cliff. "He never knew who his father was, but it's only in retrospect that I see how bitter he had become. I think now that it put a shell around him, turned him inward upon himself. But it would have done him no good had I told him; he'd have gone off on a futile and disappointing quest." She bit her lower lip. "Poor Jordan. We can't regain the past, much as we might want to."

"No point in recriminations," Bravo said.

"Yes, what's done is done, *n'est-ce pas?*" she said bitterly. All at once she fell into Bravo's arms. "Ah, Bravo, my only child has betrayed me as unforgivably as he has you."

"We should go on," Jenny said as she urged them out from the shadow of the truck, "as quickly as possible."

"Yes, yes," Camille said, coming back to herself, "tell us what we must do, Bravo. We're both here to help you."

JORDAN Muhlmann had switched from the van to an air-conditioned car for the drive up into the mountains. Lucky for him, since the trip entailed three hours of jouncing as the snaking road became steeper, full of hair-raising switchbacks, and just past the town of Macka, when they'd turned off to the left, the road, steeper still, became a shambles. He had three Knights with him, few enough to be unobtrusive, sufficient, he judged, to get the job done.

He had been here before—irony of ironies, with Bravo himself. Three summers ago. They had taken what was to be a two-week vacation in Ibiza, but after six days of immersing themselves in nonstop hedonistic bliss they had decided to leave the two beautiful blondes who, like greedy remoras, opened their mouths on sweaty dancefloors, trendy all-night lounges, swampy hotel beds, damp sand dunes. They left the women without a word and had run away from the predatory island to the end of the earth, which, for them, had been decidedly nontrendy Trabzon. A depressing slum, whose only saving grace had been the Sumela Monastery.

Now here I am again, Jordan thought, *back at Sumela with my old friend as he ends his journey in search of the Order's cache of secrets. Christ, it was here all along.* Irony, indeed. But irony was hardly unknown to him. On the contrary, sometimes it seemed to him as if his entire life was one grotesque irony. Take his relationship with Bravo, for instance—what could be more ironic than that? Friends, they had been friends: shared secrets, intimacies, close encounters with the opposite sex in Ibiza, Paris, Stockholm, Cologne and elsewhere. However, everything he had shared with Bravo had been a lie—even the girls. Jordan had a penchant for having two at once, something someone as straight-laced as Bravo would never understand or condone. Besides, his mandate with Bravo had been to get as close to him as he possibly could. What was the phrase his mother had used? *"You have to get under his skin in order to know him, and you need to know him in order to manipulate him."*

The precarious trip proved beneficial, though Jordan felt as if he were moving through a minefield laced with hidden trip wires. Everything they said to each other contained the possibility of disaster. Everything had to be withheld from Bravo. Everything. . . .

His cell phone burped. He knew who it was even before he looked at the caller ID.

"Mother," he said with a smirk he was happy to conceal from her.

"What are you doing, darling, having me followed?" Her voice was as rich as butter. "Your man almost ruined everything."

"I should think it was Damon Cornadoro who holds that dubious distinction."

Silence on the other end of the line; he'd rarely been able to cause her to miss a beat.

"Admit it," he continued. "I was right about Cornadoro. In the end, he could not keep to discipline."

"It was the Quintessence that corrupted him."

She said it as an admonition—not in retrospect about Cornadoro, but to him. He knew it, and it infuriated him further.

"You and Cornadoro. . . ." His voice clotted with emotion.

"What about me and Cornadoro?" his mother said blithely.

"I know he was your lover. What kind of pillow talk—"

"My pillow talk only goes in one direction, darling, you know that." But her voice had grown steely. "You're not becoming suspicious of me, are you? Because that would be a waste of your precious time—"

"My man was on surveillance because I was suspicious of Cornadoro," Jordan said. It was a half truth, anyway. He had gotten a firm grip on his emotions; no more stupid outbursts from him that would give her a clue to his current frame of mind. "You can't blame me for that."

"Certainly not, darling. On the contrary, I applaud your prudence."

"And I applaud your clear-eyed ability to shoot your lover."

"It was hardly difficult, there was never any emotion involved. Cornadoro served a purpose—when it came to an end, so did he." There was a brief pause. "But I do resent being spied upon, and especially by that horrid Albanian."

Jordan glanced over at the driver. "That horrid Albanian is sitting right here beside me."

"What are you saying? Jordan, are you in Trabzon?"

"No, I'm in Sumela, Camille." With three Knights of the Field: the Albanian, the German and the Russian, formerly of the FSB, but he wasn't about to tell her that. Now his voice turned steely. "I'm here to pick up the pieces, to make the corrections you have been unable to make."

"Idiot!" she said in his ear. "Everything has gone precisely according to plan. Bravo trusts me completely, as does Jenny. I'll be in on the end when he opens the Order's cache."

"No, Mother, that honor is mine." He signaled to his Knights, got out of the car.

"If you show yourself now, all will be lost," she said. "The minute he sees you he'll understand everything."

Jordan signed for his Knights to fan out. "Don't concern yourself, Mother. I'll make my appearance at the right moment." He watched his Knights moving up toward the monastery. "Shock tactics, something I learned on my own." He began to walk toward the steep stone stairs that led to the buildings themselves.

"Even your being here—you're making a mistake, Jordan."

"You let me worry about that."

"Dammit, I've spent decades orchestrating this—"

"The last four years I've nurtured Bravo because you told me to, because of what I never had, because of what you promised me."

"Don't be a child, darling."

He felt as if he had been stuck with a cattle prod and, with an animal growl, leapt up the stairs.

"I'll have my revenge, Jordan." The steel reappeared, like the claws on a cat. "Don't spoil it."

"Is that a threat? I sincerely hope not, because I hold the ace of spades, the information you've gone out of your way to keep from Bravo. The one—"

Her gasp produced a little thrill that ran right through him.

"So, enough of this posturing," he concluded. "Get out of my way, Mother, get out of my way now."

31

THE SUMELA MONASTERY WAS ANCIENT, DATING BACK TO
the fourth century after Christ. Founded in honor of the Virgin Mary by
two Athenian priests, it was named Sumela, from the Greek *melas*, meaning black. Whether the founders were influenced by the Karadaglar—the
Black Mountains—in which they built their monastery or by the color of
the icon of the Virgin Mary they brought with them remained an unan-
swered question.

Bravo had cause to think on this enigma as he and the two women
moved past the complex, which housed the Rock Church, several
chapels, kitchens, student rooms, a guesthouse and library. After renovation in the thirteenth and nineteenth centuries, the monastery was finally abandoned in 1923, following the three-year Russian occupation
of Trabzon.

Now it was nothing more than a tourist attraction. But through
Khalif Bravo knew the Order had been here. Through the twelfth century, King Alexius III and his son Manuel III had contributed to the
wealth of Sumela, had used it as one of their eyes in the Levant.

The mystery of Sumela's name mirrored the mystery of his father's last cipher: a long set of instructions, unambiguous and yet
mysterious—the most mysterious of all of them raising more questions
than it answered.

Beside him, Camille hiked silently, tirelessly. If Bravo hadn't been
shown evidence of them already, he would have marveled at her physical competence and stamina. Behind them both came Jenny, backtracking, quartering through the trees and underbrush as they made their
way up the mountainside, further and further from the tour groups.

Just past a particularly rocky stretch, she called them to a halt in a small copse of pines.

"I saw something," she said softly. "I think it was the man who tackled me on the grounds of the high-rise."

Keeping his father's last message in mind, which he needed to do at all times now, Bravo was unsurprised. "Circle back," he told Jenny. "See if you can get around him."

"He's Jordan's man," Camille said. "I'll go with you."

"I think that's unwise," Jenny said.

"Why? Don't you think I can be of help?"

"It's not that."

"What, then? He's unlikely to be alone. I know Jordan better than either of you."

"She's right." Bravo kept his gaze on Jenny. "I need both of you at my back now, all right?"

Jenny nodded.

"Meanwhile, I'll continue on," he said. "According to my father's instructions the cavern where the cache is buried is about a kilometer northeast of here. Come as quickly as you can."

THE Albanian had a long memory. He could resurrect every man who had ever attacked him, every man he had killed or maimed. The number was more than a few, less than a shitload, as he liked to joke with his fellow Knights of the Field when he was half drunk. But in all that time he'd never come up against a woman, let alone been bested by one—until he'd attacked Jenny. Furious, he was out for blood—her blood. Before this day was done, he'd hold her bloody head in his hands, this he had vowed to himself.

He moved through the forest without sound, as he had been taught. He could smell the pine sap, the leaf mold, the must of mushrooms, the sweetness of ferns and wildflowers. He listened, automatically filtering out the small sighs of his own breathing, the inner sound of the blood pumping behind his ears. He was scenting for Jenny as a bloodhound hunts a body—the quick or the dead, it made no matter to the bloodhound, but it mattered plenty to the Albanian. The scent of his quarry had not left his nostrils; it lingered there, as if mocking the surprise she had delivered to him. Her smell had become the smell of his own defeat.

He saw her first, just a flash that might have been the quick-winged streak of a bird taking off from the underbrush, but he was downwind of her and her scent came to him, distinct as ammonium carbonate. With a grin in his face he set out after her, hunched over, running low and quick, taking as direct a route as he dared. The faster he came upon her the better. His hands curled into fists, then flexed outward, stretching his leathery fingers. He saw her again, and he corrected his approach, veering a bit to the left. She had seen something or someone—perhaps the Russian, who had taken the sprinting lead—and was after it with a single-minded intensity that gave him an advantage. He sprinted forward, taking his opening. He meant to make the most of it, to make her pay, to bring her down and, between his thighs, to beat her senseless. He couldn't take too long—there was the Russian to think of. He didn't want the Russian to get all the glory, he wanted to be in on the end, when the cache of secrets was opened.

With this on his mind, he rushed forward. Jenny heard him at the last instant, began to turn even as he buried one fist into her kidney. Her eyes opened wide, the breath was knocked out of her and she fell, rolling and gasping.

The Albanian laughed, then, couldn't help himself, a short bark appropriate to the hunting dog that he was, shaggy-haired, muscular, red-meat-loving, loyal. He dropped onto Jenny, his arm cocked for a follow-up stunner to the bridge of her nose, when she reared up, crashed her forehead into the point of his chin. His head snapped back, his teeth clashing. Blood filled his mouth from where he had inadvertently bitten his tongue.

He reached down, but she swatted his wrist away with a remarkably powerful jab and, lifting one hip, tried to displace him, to regain some leverage. But he wouldn't let her, his superior bulk weighing her down. And now, while he struck her with one hand, his other clamped itself around her throat. He pressed down.

Then he heard a percussion—a gun firing. He looked down at the blood leaking out of his chest. He felt nothing, however—no pain, nothing at all. It was as if he had been anesthetized. His grip did not loosen on the Guardian's throat. Her face was congested with trapped blood, darkening the skin, and her eyes were bulging. He felt, then, the whisper of someone coming up behind him and he waited, waited, while the world slowly pulsed to his laboring heart, his damaged lungs. Still, he felt nothing at all, and so at the last possible instant, he twisted his torso. Now the pain came, excruciating, blinding pain, but he ignored it as he struck out with his free hand, knocking the gun out of Camille Muhlmann's hand, grabbing her, jerking her off her feet. His grin grew wider—two birds with one blow. He took his hand off Jenny's throat, curled the fingers into a ball, cocked his arm. That was when he heard the *snik!* of a blade opening, saw the ripple of sunlight as it ran across the edge of stainless steel. Then she had plunged the knife into his throat and he began to thrash like a fish out of water.

JENNY, eyes watering, choking on her own breath, was showered with the Albanian's blood. Half unconscious, she didn't immediately know what had happened. Not until she saw Camille appear, gun in hand. The first thing she thought of was how grateful she was not to have asked for it back. Then, with mounting horror, she saw what the Albanian did, how strong and determined he was even after being shot. The taste of her own death was in her mouth. Still, the moment the Albanian withdrew his hand, she raised herself on her elbows. He had turned away from her to attack Camille. She was about to strike him in the vulnerable spot on his neck where a major nerve bundle was located when she saw Camille drive something into his neck. The knife was in front of her face, she saw it and there was no mistaking what it was: an exact duplicate of her own switchblade, the one used to slit Father Mosto's throat. In that instant so many things clicked into place: why she had been bothered by the big picture, Rule's nonresponse when she had said that the Knights must be using another method to track Bravo. Most of all, who had knocked her unconscious in the Church of l'Angelo Nicolò and then slit Father Mosto's throat.

Then she saw Camille looking at her, and by her expression knew that she understood what was going through Jenny's mind.

"Camille—"

But it was too late, Camille was already lunging at her, and the blade sank into her.

AS Bravo wound his way upward, he could hear the soft splash of the Cauldron, the spring deemed sacred by the Orthodox Greeks. Through the trees and clumps of crocuses, Grecian anemones, and snowdrops he made out stone ruins and the remnants of carved marble columns from another era.

The land fell steeply away now, into a small valley amid the towering Black Mountains, at the end of which was the cavern. Birds flew, diving and twittering, while honeybees hovered over wildflowers, droning away at their endless work. The long afternoon had reached the zenith of its heat, even here so high up. The merciless sun beat down without the intervention of cloud or mist, the sky was that particular depthless blue peculiar to high altitudes, appearing vulnerable as an eggshell.

As he was crossing the valley, he heard from behind him the report of a single gunshot, echoing off the surrounding cliffs. He paused and almost turned back, then, but he remembered his father's explicit instructions, he remembered his mission, what he had vowed to protect at all costs, and with an effort and a heavy heart he put Jenny and Camille out of his mind, hurrying across the remainder of the flat ground.

Up ahead, he could see the mouth of the cavern, amid a number of others, guarded on either side, as his father had written, by two pencil cypresses. As soon as he entered its shadow he turned and, crouching down, looked out across the small verdant valley. At first there was nothing to see but the birds and insects, but the afternoon was waning, and it was in the lengthening shadows that he first spotted the movement. An arm, a shoulder as big as a haunch of deer came into view from behind a tree trunk. Then the side of a football-shaped head, a black eye, a face he identified as Russian through its dour expression, the manner in which the eye took in the valley in quick, precise vectors. Bravo moved then, rising to his feet, and the Russian's gaze centered on the mouth of the cavern. He'd seen movement, a slight difference in the depth inside the shadowed mouth. Bravo retreated and the Russian came silently on, exposing himself only for an instant until he found another natural feature behind which to crouch.

He was coming now and there was nothing Bravo could do to prevent it.

JENNY opened her eyes, saw sunlight filtering down through a layer cake of leaves. A swift flew by, its sharp call bringing her fully alert. Short-term amnesia gripped her and she felt a chilling wave of panic, but then she sat up and pain lanced through her side. Everything flooded back, then: the fight with the Albanian, Camille shooting him, stabbing him—the pearl-scaled switchblade, the twin of hers, that Camille used to attack her. Putting her hands on her waist, she felt the sticky warmth seeping out of her. The blade had been partially deflected by a rib; she knew the wound wasn't deep, wouldn't be fatal. Nevertheless, loss of blood could render her useless. Ripping off the bottom third of her blouse, she wrapped it around her rib cage so it covered the wound, tied it as tight as she could stand.

Where was Camille? She looked around, found herself alone in the forest, with only a corpse for company.

"Christ!"

She levered herself onto her feet with the help of a tree trunk against which she leaned. Her head swam and whatever was in the pit of her stomach threatened to disgorge itself. Her pulse pounded, and she forced herself to take a series of long, deep breaths.

Pushing away from the tree, she started her search for the Witness, but the gun was nowhere to be found. Bad news—that meant that Camille had found it and was still armed. She wished she had her cell phone so she could warn Bravo of his friend's treachery.

Still, there were weapons to be had—she could see the muzzle of a gun peeping out from under her attacker's waist—all she needed to do was roll his corpse over. There was a terrible stink rising up from him, almost unbearable as she knelt beside him. Her hands hovered above his torso as she gathered her strength to roll him.

"All right now," a voice said in German-accented English, "back away."

Reflexively, she looked over her shoulder, saw Kreist, a Knight of the Field whose face and dossier were known to her.

"I'm injured," she said, indicating the makeshift tourniquet, though which blood was already beginning to seep. "I can't move."

"You're not listening to me," Kreist barked. "I said back away. Now!"

Jenny took some rather obvious gulps of air. "Give me a moment, will you?" The hand closest to the corpse gripped the muzzle of the gun. "My head is still swimming."

Kreist took a threatening step toward her. "I will not ask you again."

Saying a silent prayer, Jenny said, "All right, all right, I'm getting up now, okay? Just don't shoot."

Kreist spat. "Little bitch, what the fuck are you doing out here?"

Jenny began to get to her feet, in doing so showing him quick a bit of her provocatively bare midsection. She saw his eyes shift. At the same time, using all her strength, she jerked the gun free of the corpse's bulk, grabbed the grips with her other hand and, turning, pulled the trigger. Kreist, not understanding, staggered back and, Jenny, remembering all too vividly what had happened with the first attacker, kept firing until she had put four shots into the German and he was lying face up on the ground, his eyes fixed and staring.

Without a backward glance, she turned and ran, ignoring as best she could the searing pain in her side, the blood seeping from her wound. Once, she fell to her knees, winded, exhausted, her head lolling, but she heard Bravo's voice in her head and she forced herself first to her knees, then to her feet, put one foot in front of the other, faster, faster.

"The cavern is a kilometer northeast," he had said.

THE cache was hidden beneath a semicircular altar to the Greek goddess Aphrodite. The stone altar was without adornment of any kind, having been looted decades ago. In fact, had not his father delivered precise instruction as to how to find it, Bravo might never have known its original use. Bravo had a flashlight, but it was not necessary here. This section of the cavern was a honeycomb of small caves, passages and chimneys, some of which rose all the way to the surface of the mountainside. As a consequence, sunlight, colored by the greenish minerals in the rock, provided eery illumination. Along with the light came sound, the wind moaning in mournful melody, as if through a gigantic panpipe.

He positioned himself in front of the dark stone altar on which, presumably, animals had been ritually slaughtered by pagan Greeks before the Virgin Mary came to these shores, perhaps even after, for the goddess of love held a special place in the hearts of Greeks. Wasn't everyone in need of her help?

He heard a sound, no more than the wind made, soughing through the chimneys, and the hair at the back of his neck stirred. He was not alone in the caverns—the Russian, and behind him, surely, Jordan. What had happened to Jenny and Camille? Who had fired the shot? Were they okay?

He heard the sound again, nearer to him this time, and he put his plan into effect, leaping to his right, arms outstretched in front of him as he hurled himself through one of the holes in the cavern.

He winced at the deafening sound of a gun being fired, the echo roaring through the passage he was in. When he turned, he saw the Russian on his hands and knees, coming after him. The Russian paused, raised his Makarov. Just before he squeezed off another shot, Bravo leapt upward into a chimney. Under cover of the noise, he scrambled into the first passage he came to. He crouched there, waiting, steeling himself for what had to be done.

The moment he saw the top of the Russian's head he attacked, slamming the heel of his hand against the Russian's ear. Launching himself forward, he kicked down, dislodging the gun from the Russian's hand. This was essential—it disarmed his adversary and evened the playing field—but it also allowed the Russian the time he needed to recover from the blow to his head.

The man reached out, butting his head into Bravo's sternum. As Bravo fell back, the Russian hauled himself out of the chimney. In the horizontal passage there was precious little room to maneuver. Within the space of three blows being delivered, Bravo had the measure of the Russian. He was ex-military, FSB or perhaps Spetsnaz. The modern battlefield being what it was, these soldiers had little use for hand-to-hand combat and so were trained only in what was known as "short and sharp," the killing blow to be delivered within thirty seconds of engagement.

Having absorbed three of the Russian's blows on bone and heavy muscle, Bravo got inside his adversary's defenses, broke the man's nose with the edge of his hand, his cheekbone with the knuckles of the other.

But he was mistaken if he thought that would finish off the Russian. It only got him going. He rushed Bravo, bulling him backward against the passage wall. Pinning him there with his superior weight, the Russian began a series of lightning-quick blows to Bravo's body and head, aimed at numbing Bravo's major upper-body muscle groups. Without them, Bravo couldn't defend himself, let alone launch a counterattack. Within moments, he'd be helpless.

He was going into shock, his vision a blur. He tried to get at Lorenzo Fornarini's dagger, but his side was pinned to the wall. He had only one hope. With his free hand, he dug in his pocket. Switching on the flashlight, he shone it directly into the Russian's eyes.

The Russian, blinded, staggered back, slammed into the opposite wall. Bravo went in beneath his raised arms, buried a knee in his groin. As the Russian doubled over, Bravo drove the same knee into the man's chin. His head snapped up and Bravo delivered a blow to his temple. The Russian slid to his knees, tears streaming down his face, but still managed to grab hold of Bravo, shake him until his teeth rattled. The man opened his mouth to bite Bravo, to rip a chunk out of him, and Bravo smashed the flashlight into his face, again and again, the blood running, the skin flayed off, until at last the Russian keeled over.

Blood was everywhere. Bravo collapsed where he stood. He put his head in his hands, but they were shaking so badly he immediately lifted it up back. The Russian wasn't breathing, he was gone.

His body aching, Bravo crawled to the edge of the chimney, shinnied slowly down it, his knees pressed to either side of the hole, until at length he dropped to the cavern floor. He saw the gun he'd kicked from the Russian's hand and, bending over, reached for it.

At that moment, pain exploded at the back of his head, and he pitched forward into unconsciousness.

32

"I HAVE TO HAND IT TO YOU, BRAVO—YOU AND YOUR FATHER—
you ran quite a race." Jordan came around into Bravo's line of vision.
"But, in the end, all your scheming, all your machinations didn't matter,
because here we are and—" He held something shiny between the first
and second fingers of his right hand. "Here *it* is—the key to the Order's
cache, the key to immortality."

He crouched down beside Bravo, who lay on the cavern floor, hands
behind his back, wrists and ankles tightly bound. "Go ahead, by the way,
try as hard as you can to work your way out. It won't do you any good."

"Why are you doing this, Jordan? What happened to you?"

Jordan laughed. "You make it sound as if I'm suffering from a blow
to the head. Poor Bravo. I never was the helpful, straight-shooting lad I
pretended to be. I did a good job lying to you, don't you think? No,
don't bother to answer. It doesn't matter what you think anymore." He
patted the top of Bravo's head, as if he were an old pet who'd sadly but
inevitably come to the end of his life.

"Happily, that phase is over, along with pretending to listen to my
mother. While she's been out here, keeping tabs on you, I've staged a
coup d'etat of sorts. The Knights tied to that disgustingly inbred cabal
at the Vatican, the Knights my mother has been desperate to take over,
the Knights of St. Clement are no more. They're my Knights now—the
Knights of Muhlmann."

"That will be enough."

Jordan's head whipped around and Bravo strained to get a look,
though he recognized the voice well enough.

Camille stood, training the Witness on her son. "Untie him."

Jordan laughed. "Mother, you can't mean it."

"But I do, darling, I very much do."

"Are you still pretending to be his friend? I've already told him you're not. You're every inch his enemy, just like me."

"Fortunately, I'm nothing like you, Jordan. I killed the Albanian, by the way, and judging by the amount of blood dripping down that shaft I'd say Bravo put away your Russian, what's his name, oh, yes, I remember, Oberov."

"Did you sleep with him, too, Mother?" Jordan said bitterly. "Have you slept with all the Knights of the Field?"

"You're not jealous, are you, darling?" Camille waggled the business end of the gun. "Now do as I say. Untie him."

"Really, Mother, it's unnecessary because, you see, I've already—"

"Now, you stupid child! And not another word!"

Blood rushed into Jordan's face in direct proportion to the amount that fled his heart. As he mechanically undid the knots he'd so painstakingly and lovingly tied, it seemed to him as if his heart had ceased to beat. He was still breathing, still moving, still thinking, but on another level whatever had been left of his heart had vanished beneath a shell as hard, as immovable as the black rock of this mountain. Cocooned within the organization of the Knights he'd always felt separate, apart from the rest of humanity—and grateful for it, too. But now, for the first time, he felt the chill of the space he occupied, as if his aloneness had taken on another, altogether baleful quality, as if he had misread it all along, hadn't realized until this moment that it was, in fact, a vacuum, greedily absorbing light, connection and emotion.

"There." He stood back. "It's done." He turned to his mother, to the woman who he despised most in the world. "But toward what end?" He held up the key for her to see. "I already took it from him. I did what you dreamed of doing."

"No, Jordan. I'm your mother, you will obey me."

"My time of servitude to you has ended. And do you know why? I'm no longer willing to be bound by your secret."

A look of horror marred Camille's beautiful face. "Jordan, no! You can't!"

"But I can, Mother, and I will." He turned to Bravo. "Here it is in a nutshell, my friend—my very good and faithful friend—the short story of the lie your entire life has been. My mother was your father's mistress. That's right, he was shacking up with her for years, while you and your siblings were growing up and, in one case, dying. Your mother never suspected and you were too young. In any event, he was so good at keeping secrets, wasn't he? And then, when you were just past your fifth birthday, she became pregnant with his child."

"Wait," Bravo said.

Jordan laughed harshly. "Oh, look at his expression, Mother, isn't that the look you've dreaded? Yes, yes, I think so! I, too, am your father's son, so that makes us, what, brothers, yes? Well, half-brothers, if you need to be technical. Not to worry, it's all relative under the skin." He laughed again.

"Wait," Bravo repeated. His head was pounding so hard, he felt as if his brain would explode at any minute. He turned to Camille, "Is this true?"

Jordan continued, relentless. "He betrayed your mother, he would have betrayed you, too, so Camille believes. She says he had agreed to leave you—leave his family—to live with her, with us. But then your brother Junior died, and he couldn't bring himself to make the break."

Bravo stared into Camille's face and for the first time saw naked emotion. It was so raw, so devastating that he had the urge to turn away, as if from a terrible injury. And so the truth burst in on him with the force of a grenade blast.

Jordan shrugged. "If it makes you feel any better, I don't believe that fairy tale. Your father never would have left his family. He didn't want my mother, he didn't want me, either. He proved that over and over when I tried to contact him."

Camille's head swung around, her eyes open wide. "You did what? I expressly forbade you to contact him."

"Did you really think I'd listen to you? Jesus Christ, he was my father. Of course I tried. But he wouldn't see me, wouldn't even talk to me. You see, Mother, if he never wanted anything to do with me, why would he leave his family for you?" He laughed. "Dexter Shaw played you just as you were playing him."

"You're insane. Dexter never knew a thing."

"You're right, Mother, I have no proof, except what was once in my heart, and now I can never reach it again. *C'est la guerre.*" He shrugged.

"It's of no matter now, is it? We planned Dexter Shaw's death and now he's dead. End of story." He pointed. "What matters is that we've succeeded. After we tortured Molko to no avail we knew Dexter wouldn't talk, no matter what we did to him, so we had to find another way to the cache. And that way was you, Bravo. We knew from our man inside the Order that Dexter had trained you to be his successor. We realized what we needed to do was take Dexter out. Difficult, almost impossible, but in the end we did it. We banked on you leading us to the cache; we knew we could control you, we'd had so much experience at it.

"And we were right. You solved every cipher your father threw at you. Because he had trained you, you knew him better than anyone. You had the knowledge he'd given you, locked away inside you. You see, Bravo, you've never stopped working for me. Don't you find that ironic?"

Bravo wanted to curl up and die, he wanted to lash out. An inchoate shrieking filled his mind so that he could not speak, could not think clearly. He could only listen to the horror that came pouring out of their mouths: the lie of his own abominable existence.

Jordan moved slightly, a twitch of long-held expectation. "Now, finally, the time has come to open the cache; everything inside will be mine."

"*Alors,* that was always what you longed for, wasn't it?" Camille fairly spat out the words. Her mind was still reeling at the possibility that Dexter had seen through her lies. No one else ever had, how could he? "You didn't care about my revenge, about the destruction of the Order. You wanted their secrets for yourself."

"Oh, yes. Especially the Quintessence. With it, I can rule the world."

"No." Jenny moved into one of the circles of sunlight, the Albanian's gun aimed at them. "You'll never get the chance now."

All at once, chaos. Everything happened simultaneously, in the blink of an eye. Camille turned, aiming the Witness at Jenny, Jordan grabbed Bravo who had managed to get to his knees. Jenny squeezed off two shots, both of which struck Camille in the chest, taking her off her feet.

She slid across the floor, fetching up against the far rock wall. Not that she felt the impact; she was already dead. But by the time Jenny swung the Albanian's gun back to Jordan, he was standing behind Bravo, Lorenzo Fornarini's dagger poised across Bravo's throat.

"You have his life in your hands, Guardian," Jordan said. "What will you do, I wonder?"

Bravo called to her, but she had already thrown the gun aside.

"There's a good girl." Jordan tossed the key at her. "Pick it up." When she did, he pointed to the altar where Bravo had begun to dig. "There. Go on. You know what to do."

Jenny began to cross to the altar.

"Not so close," Jordan ordered. "I'm not about to give you that chance."

Obediently, she altered her course. As her position changed, Jordan swiveled, keeping Bravo's body between himself and Jenny. She knelt and began to dig with her hands. Within ten minutes she had come to a hard surface. She brushed away the dirt, revealing the top of a box.

"Go on," Jordan said as he pushed closer, Bravo in front of him. "Faster."

The box, as Jenny uncovered it, was perhaps forty-five centimeters in length by about half that in width and depth.

"Now lift it out."

"But I—"

"Do it!" Jordan shouted.

Gritting her teeth against the pain, Jenny reached into the hole she had dug and with a grunt lifted it out. The effort cost her a great deal both in energy and in blood. She knew she was nearing the end of her rope, that she would have to get to a doctor sooner rather than later or the wound might turn fatal. At the very least, she was in danger of passing out from loss of blood.

"Now use the key," Jordan said, his voice as avid as his eyes. "Open the cache!"

Jenny did as she was told, sliding the key into the old-fashioned lock. She turned it to the left, heard the tumblers click. All at once, a wave of black despair inundated her. *This can't be happening,* she thought. *I was supposed to help protect the cache, not help the Knights steal it.*

With numb hands, she opened the lid. She peered inside, aware of Jordan bending over to get his first look at what he'd lusted after almost all his life.

But there was nothing inside, nothing at all.

Jenny began to laugh, Jordan cried out in rage and dismay, and that was when Bravo twisted his torso, viciously slammed his elbow into Jordan's kidney. While Jordan was still off-balance, Bravo threw him forcibly into the rock wall. Jordan slashed out blindly with the dagger and Bravo chopped down with the edge of his hand. Jordan's hand went numb and he dropped the weapon.

He struck out with his other hand, then rushed at Bravo. They hit the wall again, then, as they grappled, fell backward into an opening. Bravo punched Jordan, but it was without his full force. He kept trying to understand his new reality: Jordan was his brother. Jordan, however, was holding nothing back. He pounded Bravo, as Bravo retreated back along the passage toward a shaft of sunlight.

Jordan was on top of him, connecting repeatedly with punishing blows to his head and torso.

Bravo pushed back and they crouched, staring at each other, panting, abruptly motionless. "Why are you doing this?" Bravo gasped. "Because my father rejected you, is this what it's all about? You should have come to me."

Jordan bared his teeth, an animal scenting the kill. "And then what? You would have hated me, just like your father did. You would have taken his side."

"His side?"

"I was his little mistake, an indelible stain on his stellar reputation. I was the reminder of what he had done, of his betrayal. Why else do you think he wanted nothing to do with me?"

"I don't know," Bravo said truthfully. "But if you'd come to me, if you'd told me the truth, we could have worked it out. We were friends; we're brothers, after all."

"I'm not your friend, I'm not your brother," Jordan said. "I'm your enemy."

"It doesn't have to be that way."

"But it does. There's no other path for us than to be at each other's throats."

"Why? You said it yourself: the Knights have been reborn. The old enmity between them and the Order can be a thing of the past. Think of what we could do if we joined forces, the good we could achieve."

"Oh, yes, of course—why wouldn't I love to be your right-hand man?"

"Christ, Jordan, that isn't what I meant at all."

"Oh, but it is. You're just like your father: arrogant, judgmental, you think you're smarter, better than anyone else. No, thank you, I have my power base, I've spent years sacrificing, compromising, kowtowing to my gorgon of a mother, all in the service of consolidating it. Fuck you, I'm not going to share it with you or anyone else."

Bravo tried not to think about how he'd been just that way with Jenny—felt he knew more, condemned her, and had been proven wrong. Had he done the same with Jordan? "Listen," he said with mounting desperation, "you're making a mistake—"

Jordan smirked. "It's so like you to think that, isn't it? You see how right I am about you?"

Bravo tried to ignore what Jordan was saying, ignored the accusations that had sunk their barbed tips deep into his psyche. It would be easy to dismiss Jordan as a deluded monomaniac, but the truth was he knew Bravo too well, knew his failings just as Bravo now knew Jordan's. Still, some font of goodness inside him impelled him on what he now knew was a fruitless course. "Despite what you think, we still have a chance, if you only—"

"Listen to you? I'd rather slit my wrists."

"I'm offering you a family, Jordan. Why can't you see that?"

"Why can't you see that you're trying to lord it over me again? Not again, Bravo, never again, this I promise you. You're the one with a past, a history, a family. Offering me a family? No, you'll come to pity me, if you don't already. In fact, the process has already begun. It's pity that has motivated you to make your offer. 'Poor Jordan,' you think. 'I can help him.' But you can't help me, Bravo, you'll only want to take over, to make decisions for me, to tell me what's right and wrong. You always felt you knew the difference between good and evil, but it turned out that you knew nothing.

"You have what I want, what I never will have. Can you give me that? Would you, if you had the chance? You fucking—"

He leapt at Bravo, struck out blindly, with a rage-filled heart, with the full intent to maim, to destroy what he hated most. Bravo defended himself as best he could, but all too rapidly he was being plowed under by the ferocity of Jordan's rage. He kept retreating down the passage, further and further toward the shaft of sunlight, until at length, Jordan knocked him partway into the chimney and, with one leg hanging in space, he saw that it not only went up, but down as well.

Blocking Jordan's next blow, he tried to twist himself back from the brink, but Jordan blocked him with his body, forcing him back against the rim on the rock floor. He could feel the shaft of air at his back. His foot slipped over the edge. How far down did the chimney plummet?

Taking advantage of Bravo's momentary loss of concentration, Jordan got inside his perimeter of defense, landing a blow to his ribs. Bravo went down onto his knees. Jordan struck out with his foot, but Bravo caught it before it could land, took Jordan off his feet. Bravo fought his way on top of Jordan, swinging his balled right fist into Jordan's face. In so doing, they both moved further over the edge.

Bravo struck again, but this time Jordan was ready, blocking the blow as Bravo had blocked his kick. Twisting Bravo's arm, he reversed their positions. Now it was Jordan who was on top. Very quickly, Bravo realized his intention. Jordan was pushing and shoving, trying to tip Bravo over the edge, to push him into the rock chimney, to be rid of him forever.

Bravo's head and shoulders were already into the chimney. In a moment, he'd be too far over the edge to be able to save himself. It was now or never. He knew he had to put aside his feelings of wanting to save Jordan from himself, of forging by his will alone a new expanded family that would, somehow, expunge the bitter taste of his father's betrayal. As Jordan had said, it was pure arrogance. He couldn't do it: he would fail, and if he persisted, he would certainly die trying.

He looked up into the face of his enemy, absorbed his vicious blow, saw a vulnerable spot and, as Jordan drew his fist back to repeat the blow, used the points of his stiffened fingers to jab Jordan in the spot between his sternum and diaphragm. Bravo struck hard and true, disrupting the important nerve bundle.

Jordan reared back and Bravo rose up, shoving him hard so that his head struck the rock wall. He toppled off Bravo, fell forward, pitching over Bravo's head, down into the chimney.

Bravo flipped over, reflexively reached out in an effort to catch him, but there was no chance, there was never any chance. Jordan was gone.

JENNY grabbed him as he crawled out of the rock passage.

"Jordan?" she asked.

He shook his head. He felt light-headed, his hands cold and bloodless. He reached for her, as a drowning man reaches a line thrown overboard. She winced, bit her lip so as not to cry out, and through his own pain and misery, he realized that she, too, was hurt.

"Jenny, what happened?" Then he saw the tourniquet she'd tied around her abdomen. "You're hurt."

"A flesh wound, that's all. Nothing to worry about."

But her blood-soaked shirt told him otherwise. "We've got to get you to a hospital, or at the very least a doctor."

She nodded. "But first, there's something I have to show you." Leading him over to where Camille lay, she lowered herself gingerly until she was squatting, then she went through Camille's clothes until she found what she was looking for, which she displayed in her palm.

Bravo knelt beside her. "Your knife."

"Not quite." Jenny drew out her own small switchblade.

"They're identical." He looked at her. "She had a duplicate made. That means—"

"She found my knife."

"At the hotel in Mont St. Michele, while you were unconscious. I went to the bathroom, left her alone with you. I didn't want to leave you, but she assured me it was okay."

"Of course it was, she was poring through my things."

He looked down at Camille's face, pale, porcelain-beautiful even in death. "*She* slit Father Mosto's throat, not Cornadoro. She jumped me in the corridor outside his office."

"I wonder how much she enjoyed it," Jenny said bitterly.

"Jenny—"

"She must have enjoyed tearing us apart."

Bravo nodded sadly. "That was her plan all along, I can see it now."

With a soft groan, Jenny rose. "What a supreme bitch."

A gorgon, Jordan had called her. In this, too, he wasn't wrong, Bravo mused. But she had been even more than that. He rose at last to stand with his arm around Jenny, looking down into the face of the devil seen and recognized by Father Damaskinos.

SUNSET SHROUDED THEM IN ITS COOL EMBRACE. THE SKY was on fire, layered with tiers of pink clouds. It was a relief to be free of the cavern, of the horrors that had awaited them there.

"The cache," Jenny said. "What happened, Bravo? Did your father lead you astray?"

"On the contrary," he said. "I never read you or Camille his last cipher, because he warned me against it."

"What do you mean?" In the soft swirl of shadows in the small meadow, she turned. "Wait, he knew you wouldn't be alone, didn't he?"

"Well, it was a supposition, one that makes good sense when you think about it," Bravo said. "You see, the moment the Knight attack began, he'd taken the precaution of moving the contents of the cache out of its original container. But he was adamant that if I was with anyone—anyone at all—I go to the original burial site. This way, I could draw out whoever was against me. Over the centuries, the power of the Quintessence has had the ability of corrupting even those who thought themselves steadfast. My father was told that it was the origin of all the traitors within the Order."

Jenny looked at him with the sun in her eyes. "He was told? By whom?"

"Fra Leoni."

An early evening wind had sprung up. All around them, the wildflowers bobbed, bent their heads as if in obeisance.

"He's still alive." Jenny's voice was an awed whisper.

"Against all logic, it would seem so."

"Logic has nothing to do with it," Jenny said. "It's all about faith."

He nodded. "I understand that now."

"IT'S here," he said, kneeling by the Cauldron, the sacred spring of the Orthodox Greeks. From the reddish earth in front of him rose the cracked plinth of an ancient pillar. Jenny leaned on his shoulder as she lowered herself beside him. Bravo cleared away a layer of pine needles and leaf mold. Beetles and centipedes scuttled for safety. The smell of decay that fed new life rose up to them like the aroma of a cool morning.

"Are you all right?" Bravo asked. "You can do this?"

She smiled, and all the pain was erased from her face. "I can do this, I have to do this."

Together, they dug down, lifting handfuls of earth, piling it higher and higher until there appeared beneath the worked stone plinth a small wooden chest. Painted with primary-colored boats, fish and birds, it was wholly unlike the original container she had unearthed in the cavern.

Bravo sat back on his haunches and laughed. "It's the toy chest I had as a kid."

"Oh, Bravo." Jenny put a hand on his shoulder.

Silently, reverently, they went back to work, brushing the last of the earth off the top of the chest, digging out the sides. At last, it was revealed, and they lifted it out.

As Bravo reached out to open it, Jenny said, "I don't think—" Then her eyes rolled up and she collapsed. At once, he laid her flat, listened for her breath, took her pulse. She was alive, but his hand came away covered in blood. Quickly now, he took off his shirt, ripping it into strips. With a rising sense of urgency, he unwound the tourniquet she'd fashioned out of her own shirt. He was appalled to see the wound. He wiped away the blood seeping out of it. There was no doubt, the wound was far more serious than she'd made it out to be. He bound her again, using two of the strips he'd made of his shirt, making a double layer, tying them both tighter in an effort to cut down on the rate of blood loss. He looked around. Of course there was not a soul in sight. It was at best a kilometer to the Sumela Monastery, and from there a twenty-minute ride to the clinic at Macka. He took her pulse again and was alarmed to discover it slower than it had been before. If it became erratic . . . Even so, he might not get her back to civilization in time.

He wiped his sweating face, turned to face his toy chest. He knew what lay within. With a trembling hand, he opened the chest. Here were the secrets the Order had been amassing for centuries—documents, secret treaties, clandestine histories, suppressed memoirs, incriminating financial records. And there, among them, was the Testament of Jesus Christ. He touched it, but did not pick it up. Funny, now that he had found it, he had no time to read it. His attention was elsewhere: the small clay phial with its stone stopper.

The Quintessence.

All he had to do was open it, apply the tiniest amount to Jenny's wound. She would be healed, her life saved. How could he not do it? He picked it up, cupped it in his two palms. It was almost without weight, as if its contents were lighter than air, like angels' wings.

Open it, apply a small amount to her wound. She would live—absolutely, no question. If he didn't, there was only faith to go on, faith that he could get her to the clinic, that he could save her.

His fingers curled around the stopper.

And then what? What would happen to her afterward? Would she live to be 150 years old? two hundred? four hundred, like Fra Leoni? Would she want that? Had he the right to do it, to change the natural order? Surely, his father had had the same agonizing decision to make when Steffi grew gravely ill. . . .

And then his father appeared beside him.

"Dad, what should I do?"

"It's your decision now, Bravo."

"I love her, I don't want her to die."

"I loved Steffi, I didn't want her to die."

"But you betrayed her, you slept with Camille."

"I'm human, Bravo, just like everyone else."

"But you're not like everyone else, Dad!"

Dexter smiled. *"When you were a child, it was good for you to see me that way, it gave you comfort and security, that's the way of the world. But now you're an adult, you have to accept me as I really was, you have to provide your own comfort and security. . . ."*

Bravo, blinking away tears, found himself once again alone by the seething Cauldron, Jenny beside him. He heard her labored breathing, looked down again at the vessel that held the Quintessence.

Faith. Was his faith strong enough?

He carefully replaced the Quintessence in the chest. But it was as if the phial were alive, it was so difficult to let it go, to pull his hand away. With an extreme effort he did, closed the lid and lowered the toy chest back into the hole his father had made for it.

The buried Quintessence nevertheless beat like a telltale heart as he replaced the soil, tamped it down, replaced the bed of pine needles and forest detritus. Then, with a fervent prayer to the Virgin Mary, cradling Jenny in his arms, he began the trek back to Sumela.

EIGHT hours later, in the middle of the night, Jenny awoke in terrible pain. She cried out. Then Bravo had her hand, was bending over her. She could see his face in the soft lamplight.

"Where am I?"

"Macka," he said. "Next door is the clinic's surgery."

"The cache?"

"It was just where my father buried it," he said. "Breathe easy, Jenny, it's safe."

"I want to get out of here." She tried to rise, moaned. With a rattle of tubes that ran into her, carrying blood and saline, she sank back against the rough pillow.

"Tomorrow or the next day," Bravo said, "when your fever is completely gone, we'll move you to Trabzon."

"We?"

"I called Khalif. He's out of the hospital and is all too happy to come get us with an ambulance. I wasn't going to trust you to a car for the three-hour drive out of the mountains."

He gave her some water, waited a moment while she swallowed. "Go back to sleep now, you need your rest."

"And you don't?"

He laughed, but all she could muster was a smile. For the moment, it was enough.

"Bravo, what will happen now?"

"Now that I have control of the cache, you mean?" He watched her eyes, large and serious. The time had passed for joking, he saw. She needed answers, no less than he had, which was why he hadn't slept a wink since he'd brought her to the clinic at Macka. He'd been too busy thinking, then making a series of calls.

"I've spoken to my sister, Emma," he said. "She's the networker, in touch with all the members of the Order, at every level. They have voted. I'm the new *Magister Regens*."

Her eyes opened wide. "And what of the Haute Cour?"

"It will advise me, just as it advised the *Magister Regens* centuries ago. New members will have to be nominated, of course. The first one I'll nominate is you."

"Me?"

He laughed again, more softly.

"Then you must also nominate a Venetian nun named Arcangela."

"The Anchorite—yes, I know about her." He nodded his assent. "It's past time the valuable women of the Order were recognized, their ideas, schemes and insights brought fully into the fold."

"And where will we go from here?"

"Sleep now, Jenny. Tomorrow will be soon enough—"

"Not for me. I won't sleep until you tell me."

He sat in the semidarkness contemplating her question. It was a good one, the only one that counted, and he had pondered long and hard through the night as to what needed to be done.

"First, you and I will move the cache to a safer place. I'm going to need time to evaluate its contents, determine what our power really is. The Order needs to continue my father's work. Even as we talk here, the world is changing, and not for the better, I fear. There is a new war coming, Jenny. In fact, it's already begun. My father knew it, and now so do I. A religious war that will rock every nation unless it can be averted. The fundamentalists on each side—the Christians and the Islamics— are determined to exterminate the other, and neither cares who gets in their way. We can't let that happen, can we?"

"No," she said. "We can't."

"Then you'll help me." His excitement rushed out of him like sparks from an engine. "The first order of business is to make contact with all the elements of the Order's ancient religious network my father kept alive and running."

Jenny smiled. It was what she most wanted to hear. But she was already slipping into sleep, and she answered him only in her dreams.

KHALIF did not arrive alone. With him when he drew up in the ambulance were two paramedics, who immediately jumped out with a stretcher and went to get Jenny. When Bravo was done directing them, he came out into the narrow street to greet his friend. Khalif's shoulder was bandaged and his arm was in a cast; nevertheless the Turk seemed remarkably chipper.

"Your call was manna from heaven. It's good to be back in the game."

They embraced was if they were long-lost brothers.

Khalif's face turned sober. "How is she?"

"She'll be okay, she's tough."

It was only then that he noticed another figure standing in the shadows across the street. At first, he seemed unfamiliar. Then Bravo recognized him as the old priest he had first given the coin to at the Church of l'Angelo Nicolò in Venice. He remembered Jenny asking him if he could trust the old man. Somehow, Bravo had known that he could.

The electric blue eyes watched him as they had in the church, with a mixture of curiosity and amusement. But now there was something else in them: he no longer felt a child in the old priest's eyes.

The paramedics appeared with Jenny on the stretcher. They paused long enough for Bravo to lean over, press his lips to hers.

"I'll be right next to you," he said, "all the way home."

The paramedics put her into the rear of the ambulance, and Khalif climbed in after them. The driver sat behind the wheel, picking at his nails. A dog barked somewhere along the sun-blasted street, otherwise all was still. Not another soul in sight.

The old priest crossed the street.

"You didn't use the Quintessence, did you?"

Bravo felt the weight of the priest's solemn gaze on him. He had spoken in Trapazuntine Greek, but Bravo suspected it could just as well have been Latin, or Greek or any number of ancient languages.

"No," he replied in the same language.

"Why not?" the old priest asked. "You had cause."

"But not just cause."

The old priest's robes were black, his long, wild hair pure white. Around his neck was a short chain that held a key—a key, Bravo saw now, that was the twin to the one his father had left for him, the key that opened the original chest that had for centuries held the order's cache of secrets. It was the key held by Jon Molko, Dexter Shaw's backup. Dexter must have given it to the old priest for safekeeping.

The old priest inclined his head imperceptibly. "I've waited a long time for this moment."

Bravo took a deep breath. He knew he was looking at living history. "And if I'd opened the Quintessence?"

The old priest smiled. "It is sealed with wax, but over the centuries the seal cracked, and when your father removed the lid he found that the contents had evaporated."

Bravo waited, stunned. His heart was a trip-hammer beating in his chest. "He tried to save my mother."

"Though I counseled against it." The old priest locked his fingers together. "He wanted to be *Magister Regens*. His idea was correct, but he was not the one. Now you know why."

Bravo bowed his head for a moment, trying to gather himself. Then he said, "What is to be done with the Testament?"

The old priest's gaze held steady. He had not blinked once, not even in this bright sunlight. "That is for you to decide."

"It is not for me alone to decide. I am asking for your advice."

The old priest stroked his beard for a moment. "You already understand the extreme danger of the Quintessence, you've felt it yourself. The Testament of Christ is just as dangerous. What it contains—the words of Jesus—has the power to upend all Christianity. Is this what you want?"

"But it's the truth."

"Ah, yes, the truth." The old priest took a step toward him. "During its long history the Order has continually struggled with the truth. How the debates raged back and forth within the Haute Cour! Now I must ask you what we asked ourselves: which will better promote the natural order of things, truth or perception? When you have answered that question, Bravo, you will know what to do with the Testament."

He began to walk up the street, in the direction of Sumela.

"Wait," Bravo said. "Will I see you again?"

The old priest paused. "Oh, yes."

"What shall I call you, then. Surely not Fra—"

"That name is ancient, it has outlived its moment," the old priest said at once. "Call me, rather, by my Christian name, the name my father and mother gave me at birth.

"Call me Braventino."

THE HISTORY
BEHIND THE FICTION

Virtually all of the history in *The Testament* is real. The Franciscan Observatines are recorded in history, as are the Knights of St. John of Jerusalem, who inspired my own Knights of St. Clement of the Holy Land.

It seems inevitable that the Gnostic Observatines and the Knights would be at each other's throats. From as far back as the early 1300s, there was a deep division within the Franciscans regarding the strict vow of poverty demanded by St. Francis upon the founding of the Order in the beginning of the thirteenth century. The Observatines (also called Observantists) believed in it, the Conventuals did not. The dispute came to a head in 1322 when Pope John XXII sided with the Conventuals and their allies, the more established Dominican Order.

The pope's papal bull, *Cum inter nonmullos,* which said among other things that the rule of poverty was "erroneous and heretical," was likely a subterfuge. It seems far more plausible that the pope wanted to stamp out a faction of the Franciscans bent on roaming the world, spreading their gospel, their power and influence, rather than staying put in monasteries, as the Conventuals were bound to do. This is the real reason he ruled against the Observatines.

However, the ruling was hardly the end of the Observatines. Quite the opposite, in fact. In the latter part of the fifteenth century and the first two decades of the sixteenth century, a good number of Observatines who had accepted the papal bull were in the Middle East, especially Trebizond, ostensibly serving both as emissaries and proselytizers. It seems likely that they were also carrying on the business of the Observatines. It is here, at the place where East and West meet, that I have imagined my Gnostic Observatines discovering many of their secrets, including the fragment of the Testament of Jesus, and the Quintessence, which is also recorded in history as the fabled Fifth Element, sought after by every Alchemist on earth.

To conform to history as much as possible, I have set the official founding of the Gnostic Observatine Order more or less to this date, though certainly there were stirrings within the Observatines in the decade before 1322.

Gnosticism is, in and of itself, anathema to the Vatican and its staunchly traditionalist orders. Its name derives from the Greek word for "knowledge." Gnostics, to put it simply, believe that the physical world is corrupt, evil, that the way to salvation lies in adhering to the wholly spiritual path to goodness. Some even hold that Jesus was a purely spiritual being, so only appeared to die on the cross. Some gnostics also pursue studies in the so-called "esoteric mysteries," which the Church has judged to be magic, and so, heretical.

The Knights, champions of both Christ and the pope, would naturally be predisposed to despise and fear the Order, who took quite seriously St. Francis's edict to roam the world, spreading his gospel. It's entirely logical that the Knights would be only too happy to do the pope's bidding in dismantling the Order's power.

The Secret Gospel of Mark is recorded in history, as well. Sections of it are quoted in a letter attributed to the second century church father Clement of Alexandria to Theodore. Clement claims that after Peter's death, Mark brought his original gospel to Alexandria and wrote a "more spiritual gospel." The letter was unearthed by the biblical scholar Morton Smith in 1958 in the Mar Saba monastery just south of Jerusalem. Not surprisingly, its authenticity is disputed by many biblical scholars, who do not believe that the historical Jesus was a miracle worker.

However, that is precisely how the Secret Gospel of Mark portrays him in this passage: "And they come into Bethany. And a certain woman whose brother had died was there. And, coming, she prostrated herself before Jesus and said to him, 'Son of David, have mercy on me.' But the disciples rebuked her. And Jesus, being angered, went off with her into the garden where the tomb was, and straightaway, going in where the youth was, he stretched forth his hand and raised him, seizing his hand."

Smith's subsequent study of the gospels led him to the following contention: that Jesus "could admit his followers to the kingdom of God, and he could do it in some special way, so that they were not there merely by anticipation, nor by virtue of belief and obedience, nor by some other figure of speech."

In any event, no matter one's personal beliefs, the possibilities Smith—and, indeed, history itself—have revealed remain fascinating, the stuff of endless speculation, the basis of fiction that continues to enthrall us all.